NOTHING ～～～～～～～～～～

～～～～～～～～～ SO STRANGE

JAMES HILTON

NOTHING
SO STRANGE

AN ATLANTIC MONTHLY PRESS BOOK

LITTLE, BROWN AND COMPANY • BOSTON

ATLANTIC–LITTLE, BROWN BOOKS
ARE PUBLISHED BY
LITTLE, BROWN AND COMPANY
IN ASSOCIATION WITH
THE ATLANTIC MONTHLY PRESS

PRINTED IN THE UNITED STATES OF AMERICA

There is nothing so powerful as
truth — and often nothing so strange.
— DANIEL WEBSTER

PART ONE

PART

ONE

"YES, I knew him," I said, "but it was years ago — in England . . ."

You can make things sound very simple when you are answering questions on oath and there is a girl at a side table scribbling shorthand and giving little shrugs of appeal if the words come too fast. You don't know what the questioner is trying to get at, and you almost feel that your answers are cross-examining him; you watch for the extra flicker of interest, the sudden sharpness of the next question. And all the time, behind the facts as you truthfully state them, there's the real truth that you remember slowly, as when you stretch in bed the morning after a long walk and explore the aches. That, of course, isn't the kind of truth you've promised to tell, but it probably shows in your eyes and makes you look as if you were hiding something. Which, in a sense, you are.

"Where did you first meet him?"

"In London. At a party."

"When was that?"

"Nineteen thirty-six. I remember it because of all the Mrs. Simpson talk that was going on." (The unsolicited detail, to account for an answer that had been perhaps too prompt.)

"Were you friendly?"

"Off and on — for a time."

"What do you mean by that?"

"I mean . . . well . . . some weeks I might see him twice or

3

three times, other weeks I wouldn't see him at all. . . . I didn't
have an affair with him, if that's what *you* mean."

Shock tactics, but it failed; the man across the table referred to
his notes and said quietly: "You were seventeen."

"Eighteen," I corrected, but he had killed my line. I can't help it;
I act profusely when I'm nervous, and I'm nervous often when I've
no need to be. It's the same when I hear a motorcycle overtaking my
car along a parkway, even though I know I can't possibly be guilty
of anything; or, perhaps more subtly, because I don't know I can't
possibly be guilty of anything.

Not that the man across the table looked like anyone to be afraid
of. He had sandy hair, blue eyes, a nose that looked small because the
chin and the mouth were set so squarely, a pink healthy complexion,
rather pudgy hands. I would not have noticed him in the street or
a crowd, but if I had had to sit in a dentist's waiting room and stare
at somebody, it might have been at him for choice. He wore a bow
tie, dark blue pin-stripe suit, white shirt, and I couldn't see what
kind of shoes under the table. His name (from the letter he had
written me, fixing the appointment to see him) was Henry W.
Small. It didn't particularly suit him, except that it was a good name
to go unnoticed by.

"Bradley was then twenty-four," he continued, referring again to
his notes. Then he looked up. "What was he doing?"

"Studying at London University. So was I. That's how we met."

"You said it was at a party."

"Yes, a dinner party given by a professor. We were fellow guests."

"Did you get to know him well at that party?"

"I didn't speak to him till afterwards and then only a few words.
When I met him again at the college I knew him just about enough
to say hello to. Then gradually a bit more than that, but not *much*
more. He wasn't the kind of person you get to know *well*."

"Did he have other friends?"

4

"Very few, I should say."

"Did you meet any of them?"

"Not often."

"Did you ever meet anyone called Sanstrom?"

"Sanstrom? . . . No, I don't think I remember the name."

"But you're not certain?"

"Well, it's nine years ago. I can't remember the names of everyone who might have been at some college party."

"You lived a rather social life?"

"Fairly."

"More of a social life than Bradley, anyhow?"

"Yes."

"In other words, you knew everybody and he didn't?"

"Oh no. He knew them, but they were more acquaintances than friends. He wasn't easy to be friendly with."

"Would you call him *un*friendly then?"

"No, no . . . not that at all. He was just . . . well, shy. There was a sort of barrier you had to break down."

"Ah, a barrier. And you broke it down?"

"Perhaps partly."

"So that you became his only real friend?"

"No, I wouldn't say that either. . . . The fact was, he worked so hard he hadn't much time for personal contacts of any kind."

"Where was he living?"

"In furnished rooms."

"Did you ever visit him there?"

"Once — but only for a few minutes."

"Would you say — from that one visit — that his style of life fitted with the job he had?"

"Oh sure. He didn't earn much money and everything about him looked like it."

"Where were you living then?"

"With my parents. They had a house in Hampstead. They usually went over for the summer."

"Were Bradley's rooms also in Hampstead?"

"No. In Belsize Park. Or Chalk Farm. Just a few miles away."

"What do you mean — Belsize Park or Chalk Farm? Don't you know which?"

"Belsize Park if you wanted a good address, Chalk Farm if you didn't care. He didn't care."

He looked puzzled, but he made a note of Belsize Park or Chalk Farm. "Now on these occasions when you met him, Miss Waring, what did you usually talk about?"

"Everyday things. Sometimes my work."

"Did you ever discuss his work?"

"I couldn't have — it was far out of my range. I was taking history. His stuff was mathematics, physics, and that sort of thing."

"So he could discuss history although it wasn't his subject?"

"Anybody can discuss history whether it's their subject or not. But try talking about mathematics with an expert when you've never got beyond quadratic equations."

"All right. . . . Did you ever discuss America?"

"Sometimes he spoke of his boyhood on a farm. Dakota, I think. Early struggles . . . all that."

"Politics?"

"Not much. Just news in the paper. The Wally Simpson business, if you call that politics. We didn't agree about it — I was against the marriage, he was all for it."

"Did he like living in London?"

"I think so. Most Americans do."

"You mean you did yourself?"

"Oh yes."

"Did he ever say whether he preferred England or America . . . or perhaps some other country?"

"Goodness, no. It wasn't what he preferred, it was where he could work. London University gave him a research fellowship."

"And American universities wouldn't?"

"I don't know. Maybe they hadn't any — of the kind he wanted."

"So he might have had a grudge against them — or perhaps against American life in general?"

"A *grudge?* That man never had a grudge even when he ought to have had."

As soon as I said it I regretted the emphasis; I knew it would lead to questions I wouldn't answer at all. They came.

"What makes you say that?"

"Just that he wasn't the type for harboring grudges. He lived for his work and nothing else mattered."

"You don't think he could ever be actuated by a motive to get even with somebody?"

"I wouldn't think so."

"You can't recall any incident of such a kind?"

"No. Never."

"In fact you never saw anything wrong with him at all, did you, Miss Waring?"

I caught a faint smile on his face and answered it with a big one of my own. "Of course I did — he was far too tied to his work for any girl to think him faultless."

"So he didn't take you out enough?"

I laughed. "No, not nearly enough." I felt we were establishing the right mood and it would all be plain sailing if I stuck to it.

"Did he have other girl-friends?"

"I don't know. I don't know anything about his love life. I never asked him questions about it. And incidentally, Mr. Small, why are *you* asking all this about him now? How did you find out I ever knew him?"

"Just let me put the questions, Miss Waring." There was nothing brusque or unkindly in that, just a carefully measured firmness.

"But I don't see why you shouldn't tell me. If he's in any trouble I'd want to help him."

"Why?" The question shot out at me like the fang of a non-poisonous snake.

"Because — well, because I like him."

"Still?"

"In a sense. I don't forget people I've once liked, and I did like him. Is that extraordinary of me? Well, as I said, I'd want to help him if . . . if I could, that is. Maybe I couldn't. I suppose it depends on the kind of trouble he's in. . . ."

I stopped, realizing he was just letting me talk. When he could see I didn't intend to go on, he said: "Why should you expect him to be in any trouble?"

"I didn't say I expected it. I said *if* he is."

"What put such a possibility in your mind?"

"Because you're questioning me about him as if he'd done something wrong. Or aren't you? Isn't this a branch of the F.B.I. or something?"

He took out a cigarette case and pushed it across the table towards me. "Smoke?"

I said no thanks, because I thought my hand might tremble while I held a cigarette for him to light.

He went on: "How long since you had any communication with Bradley?"

"Oh years. Not since before the war. The English war — 1939."

"Nineteen thirty-six being the year you knew him in London?"

"That's right." I thought: Now it's coming; and was inspired to add quickly: "My parents and I returned to America the following year."

"Did *he* return to America?"

"Not that I know of."

"At any rate you didn't see him in America?"

"No, never."

"Didn't he write you any letters?"

"Only a few — for a while. Then we lost touch. I wish you'd give me his present address if you have it."

"So that you could renew your friendship?"

"Perhaps not that, but I'd write to him — for old time's sake."

"And offer your help?"

"Yes — if he needed any."

He nodded slowly. Then he lit a cigarette for himself and leaned back in the swivel chair. "Tell me, Miss Waring — and please remember I'm not trying to trap you into anything you don't want to say — all I'd like is a personal opinion, just between ourselves . . ." He made a finger gesture to the girl taking shorthand. "Miss Sutton, don't put this down — it's off the record. . . ."

My father always said that when anyone ever tells you something is off the record you should be doubly on your guard; so I was, instantly, and concentrated on trying not to show it. I smiled, pretending to relax. He went on: "You're a very loyal person — I can see that. Loyal to friends, just as you'd be loyal to your country. When you first got to know Bradley and found yourself beginning to like him, naturally you'd hope to find in him the same kind of loyalties. Did you? . . . Or were you ever a little disappointed in some ways?"

"No, I don't think so. I liked him. When you like people you don't weigh them up like that. At least I don't."

"You never felt there might be things he was keeping from you?"

"We weren't close enough friends for me even to think about it. He wasn't a very talkative person, anyway."

"You mean that if he'd had any secrets he'd probably not have shared them with you?"

"Maybe not. And I might not have shared mine with him. We were neither of us the tell-everything type."

He looked at me till I thought I was going to blush, so of course

I did blush. As if satisfied, he pressed down the clasp of his brief-case and stood up. I saw then that he wore black shoes.

"Well, Miss Waring, I guess that's about all. Thank you for com-ing over. . . . And if by any chance we should need to bother you again . . ."

"It's no bother at all to *me,* but I have an idea something must be bothering *you.* Can't you let me in on it?"

"No," he said, smiling completely for the first time. He had good strong teeth and the smile made rather babyish dimples. I took off ten years from my first guess of his age; perhaps he was thirty-five.

"A secret?" I said.

"Yes."

"Top secret?" (They like you to use their jargon.)

"Just a secret." (Perhaps it wasn't their jargon.)

"I see."

I smiled back and walked towards the door. He overtook me, yet somehow without hurry, before I reached it; turning the handle, he put himself with me in the doorway. "Nice of you to come so promptly. I hope you didn't make a special trip — any time within a few days would have been all right."

"Oh, I go downtown quite a lot."

"Your father's office?"

"Oftener the Village. More in my line than Wall Street."

"Ah yes, of course. Writers and artists." He cupped my elbow with his hand. "I'll have to think over your request for Brad's ad-dress. Might be able to oblige you, though of course we're not a bureau of missing persons. . . . Well, thanks again. . . . Good-by."

"But he isn't exactly missing if you know his address, is he? . . . Good-by, Mr. Small."

In the elevator going down I thought I had done rather well. Or had I? . . . Suddenly I realized that he had called him *Brad.* Was that to test me? But of course I would have admitted readily enough that I used to call him Brad. Nothing significant about that. It was probably their technique — to leave you with a feeling that they know more than you think they know, so that you can chew it all over and work up a fine state of nerves afterwards.

* * *

I took a taxi uptown and had early dinner alone at the house. There were plenty of friends I could have called up, but I didn't feel like making a date with anyone, or even going to a movie later on by myself. The weather was probably the last cold spell of the winter; a bitter wind swept in from the north, and ice crackled where there had been any water in the gutters. Even after a couple of cocktails the dining room looked so big and dreary I was glad to have coffee upstairs and turn on all the lights in my personal rooms. It's a cheerful suite on the fifth floor — bedroom, bathroom, dressing room, and den; I was allotted them as a child, and have never wanted anything bigger, even when the rest of the house was free for me to choose from. The furniture is good solid stuff from either New or Old England; my mother probably bought it at the auctions she liked to frequent. And the heating vents are built in the window sills, so that you lean on them and burn your elbows if you want to look down and see what's going on in the street. Nothing much, as a rule; those middle sixties between Park and Fifth keep pretty quiet. That evening, as I looked down, I saw the familiar steam curling out of the manholes, and from the look of it as it scurried I knew the temperature had dropped a good deal since I left the downtown office. The low sky held captive the glow of the city; anglewise across Park Avenue I could see the Rockefeller buildings lost in clouds about the thirtieth floor. John came in to pull the blinds; I told him not to bother, I would do it myself later.

"There's still supposed to be some rule about lights," he said.

"All right, then, pull them down." At that stage of the war New

York didn't bother much about the partial blackout, but John's a stickler about such things. We've been real friends from my childhood. My father enticed him from a duke about twenty years ago, since when he's become naturalized, but he still calls himself English except when English visitors ask him if he is, then he says he's American or, if further pressed, a Scot.

"Are you going out again, Miss Jane?"

"Not me, I'm off to bed soon with a good book."

"Not *Forever Amber,* I hope?" He has a corny humor, unchanged from the time I was young enough to appreciate nothing else.

"No. I take my history straight. Always did, ever since I studied it in London."

I don't know what made me bring that up, but I realized it was the second time that day I had mentioned something that I often go months without even thinking about.

He said, as he pulled the blinds and then the curtains: "I'd like to see London again sometime."

"You probably could, when the war's over."

"They say it's considerably changed."

"I'll bet our part hasn't. Hampstead Heath and round about there."

"Several bombs fell near the house, I've been told," he said thoughtfully. It was still "the house" to us both. "Can I get you anything?"

"No thanks — I'll be asleep very soon, I'm terribly tired. Good night, John."

After he had gone I stood at the window, pulling aside the blinds just enough to see that it had begun to snow. The two great cities, each with its own flavor, hold you like rival suitors, perversely when you are with the other; and that night, as I watched the pavement whitening, I thought of those other pavements that were called roadways, and the subways tubes, and the whole long list of equivalents

Brad and I once compiled as we tramped across Hampstead Heath on a day when other things were in our minds.

*　　*　　*

I first met him at Professor Byfleet's house in Chelsea, but I didn't catch his name when we were introduced, or perhaps we weren't — the English are apt to be slack about that sort of thing, they are civil but not solicitous to strangers, and when you visit one of their houses for the first time it's hard not to feel you are among a family of initiates, or else a dues-paying but nonvoting member of a very closed-shop union.

This dinner at the Byfleets' wasn't anything important, at least by comparison with many we went to; Byfleet was an anthropologist who wanted my father to finance an expedition to New Guinea, so he doubtless thought he'd have us meet his friends. I suppose they'd all been told we were rich Americans, with the blow softened by adding that my mother was English. My father never did finance the expedition, anyhow.

As I said, I don't remember actually meeting Brad, but when we got to the table I noticed him some way further down on the other side, next to my mother. Now and again I glanced at him, and with a rather odd feeling that I had seen him somewhere before, though I couldn't be sure; he was good-looking in a restrained way, with dark, deep-sunken eyes, a long straight nose, and a chin that was firm without being aggressive. There was also a mood of gravity over him, tempered by a sort of intermittent nervousness as if he were waiting for a chance to say something, not because he wanted to, or had anything to say, but because he thought everyone must be wondering why up to halfway through dinner he hadn't spoken a word. I hoped my mother would soon take pity on him, but his other partner moved first, and I could see that the more she tried to draw him out the more he drew himself in. She was one of those voluble unkempt Englishwomen who invade a conversation rather than take part in it, and have a conspiratorial smile for the maid or butler, just to show they've been to the house before.

I missed what was happening across the table for a while, for my own neighbor engaged me, a hearty professor of biology who mentioned, apropos of the veal cutlets, that man had only scratched the surface of his possible gastronomic repertoire, that practically the entire insect world was an untapped storehouse of taste novelties, that dried locusts made an excellent sandwich, that there were many edible caterpillars fancied by the Chinese, and that native tribes in the Andean foothills pick lice from each other's heads and eat them with gusto. He seemed surprised when I wasn't upset, and after I had accepted another cutlet he confessed that he often opened up like that to *jeunes filles* whom he found himself next to at dinners, because in the event that they were bores their distress at least made them momentarily entertaining; but he could see I was not a bore, so perhaps I would now talk about something serious. I said I could never talk seriously to any man with one of those bristly little toothbrush mustaches, and was it true that in certain crack regiments of the British Army men were compelled to have them? He answered, Good God, how should *he* know, better ask our host, who was a recognized authority on totem and taboo. After that we got along fairly well, and presently he paid me what many Englishmen think is the supreme compliment; he said he wouldn't have guessed I was American.

Suddenly I was relieved to see that my mother, across the table, was talking to her nervous neighbor. I knew then that everything would be all right. She was adept at putting young men, indeed men of any age, at their ease; she didn't mind if they talked politics or business or art or sport — even if they were intellectual she never tried to match them at it, and if they weren't she would make them

feel a freemasonry existing between her and them in a world, or at
a table, of highbrows. Actually she was cleverer than she pretended
— not that she was especially modest, but in her bones she felt that
men do not like clever women, and what she felt in her bones
counted more than anything she could think out with her intelligence. She had had an upper-crust education composed of governess,
boarding school, then finishing school abroad, and probably she had
forgotten 95 per cent of everything she had ever learned from text-
books; but she had done nothing but travel and meet some of the
world's most interesting people for almost twenty years, and the
result was a quick-minded knowledgeableness unspoiled by knowledge. It made her understand politicians rather than politics and
diplomats rather than diplomacy. She talked plenty of nonsense, and
it was easy to trap her, though not always to prove that she was
trapped; and she would go on discussing a book she said she had
read but manifestly hadn't, or she would break up a dull conversation with some fantastic irrelevance for which everyone was secretly
grateful.

After dinner I wasn't anywhere near the nervous man, but when
the party broke up it appeared we were scheduled to drop him
where he lived, which was in our direction, and because we were
also taking two other guests on their way, he sat in front with
Henry. We dropped these others first and then he moved inside, but
there was hardly time for talk before he began urging us not to
drive out of our way, his place was only a short walk from the main
road, anywhere near there would do. But my father insisted: "No,
no, we'll take you right up to your door"; so Brad had to direct
Henry through a succession of side streets, and eventually gave the
stop signal in the middle of a long block of four-story houses with
basements. He said good-night and thanked us, bumping his head
against the top of the car as he got out.

"North Dakota," my father said, as we drove away.

"Yes, he told me too," said my mother. "I'd have known it was somewhere in the Middle West from his accent."

"Thank goodness for that," I said, and mentioned the Englishman's compliment to me.

My father smiled and seemed in an unusually good humor. He wasn't always, after parties at other people's houses. He said: "I find my own Kentucky drawl a great help with the English. It makes them think me tough and guileless, whereas in reality I'm neither."

"And in reality you haven't even got a Kentucky drawl," said my mother.

"Haven't I? How would you know? . . . Well, coming back to Dakota. I had some talk with him after the ladies left the table. Seems he's a research lecturer at your college, Jane."

"Then that's where I must have seen him before. I had an idea I had."

"A young man of promise, from all accounts," my father went on. "Byfleet spoke highly of him."

My mother commented: "If we'd had any sense we'd have dropped him at the corner as he asked us. He probably didn't want us to know the sort of place he lives in."

"Oh nonsense. A boy like that, making ends meet on a few fees and scholarships — nobody expects him to stay at the Ritz. Probably has to count every penny, same as I did when I was his age in New York. It's good for him, anyway, till he gets on his feet. . . . Brains, good looks, and a tuxedo — what more does he need?"

"He's very shy," my mother said.

"That'll wear off."

"So will the tuxedo. It was frayed at the cuffs already."

My father looked interested. "You noticed that, Christine? I'll tell you what *I* noticed — he doesn't drink, he doesn't smoke, and he was hoping you'd rescue him from that Hathersage woman he was next to, but you didn't till nearly the coffee stage. . . . Must read her new novel, though. They say it's good."

That was typical of my father; he respects achievement and is always prepared to weigh it against not liking you, so that in practice he likes you if you are successful enough. Julian said that once, and he was successful enough; doubtless therefore in those days my father thought Brad was going to be successful enough. I remember arguing it out with myself as we drove home.

*   *   *

I saw Brad the morning after the Byfleet dinner; we ran into each other at the College entrance in Gower Street. I suppose this was really our first meeting; he would have passed me with a nod, but I made him stop. "So you're here too?" I said.

"Hi, there. Sure I am."

"That was a good party last night."

"Er . . . yes. . . ." Then suddenly, with an odd kind of vehemence: "Though I don't like big parties."

"It wasn't so big. Were you bored?"

"Oh no, not a bit. I'm just no good at them. I don't know what to say to people."

"Neither do I. I just chatter when I'm chattered to."

"I wish I could do that. . . . Or no, perhaps I don't. It's a terrible waste of time."

"For those who have anything better to do. Do *you* think you have?"

He looked as if he thought that impertinent. I think now it was.

"Yes," he answered, smiling.

"That sounds rather arrogant."

But now he looked upset. He didn't like being called arrogant.

"No, no, please don't misunderstand me. . . . I guess I just tell myself it's a waste of time because I can't do it. Especially amongst all the big shots — like last night. I don't know why I was asked."

"Why did you go?"

"Professor Byfleet has helped me a lot, I didn't like to refuse."

"He probably asked you on account of my father, who's an American too."

"I know. He told me. He asked me what my work was, but I was a bit tongue-tied. I'm afraid I made a fool of myself."

"I don't think you did. It's by talking too *much* that most people do that."

"Personally I agree with you." There was no inferiority complex about him, thank goodness. The truculence and the humility were just edges of something else.

"Anyhow," I said, "he liked you."

"*Did* he?" Because he looked so embarrassed I couldn't think of anything else to say. He fidgeted a moment, then glanced at his wrist watch. "Well, I must be off to my lecture. . . ." His second smile outweighed the abruptness with which he left me standing there.

When I got home that night I told my mother I had seen him again. She said, with a flicker of interest: "Really? I think Harvey had better ask him here sometime — some evening we're just ourselves. . . ."

*   *   *

But of course there wasn't often such an evening. My parents both liked company; my mother preferred musicians, artists, society people, and my father balanced this with businessmen, lawyers, politicians. Without much snobbery, he had a very shrewd idea of who was who and who really mattered; and in England he felt that he still mattered himself, not merely because he was rich, but because few English people appreciated the changes in America that had

put him out of favor. So also English and foreign politicians listened
to his advice, not with any idea of taking it, but as an act of educat-
ing themselves in some mythical American viewpoint which they
believed he represented, and they were doubtless relieved to find him
a generous host and a reliable keeper of secrets. I didn't have a feeling that I was ever completely close to him, or that, inside his own
private world, he had ever got over the death of his only son by a
former wife during the First World War.

As I said, he wasn't much of a snob, and though he had a connoisseur's appreciation of titles and liked to say "Your Excellency"
once or twice and then call the man Bill, he wouldn't have me presented at Court or "come out" in any accepted social sense. It just
happened that when I was sixteen I began having a place at table if
there were a dinner party, though at first I would go up to bed soon
afterwards; then when I enrolled at the College that seemed to
make me adult enough to stay up as long as I liked. Most people,
no doubt, took me for older than my age, just as they took my
mother for younger if they met her without knowing who she was.

Ever since I was a child we had come over to England for the
summer; once we took a house in Grosvenor Street, with real flunk-
eys, but my mother thought that was a bit too grand, so next time
my father chose Hampstead, at the top of the hill as you climb from
the tube station, and that suited them both so much that they never
looked anywhere else. For many years it had even been the same
house, which my father would have bought if the portrait painter
who owned it had been willing to sell. There was a studio attic
overlooking the Heath, with a huge north window, and from the
other upstairs rooms you could see the London lights at night and
as far as the Crystal Palace on a clear day.

I used to have a favorite walk — it was along the Spaniards' Road
to Highgate Village, then back downhill and up again through
Parliament Hill Fields. I loved it when it was crisp and sunny and

windy enough for the little ponds to have waves and for the roads to look like bones picked clean. There's no place in New York as high as Hampstead Heath and as near to the center of things, except of course the roofs of high buildings, where you look deep down; but from the Heath you look far over, which is different. My father once said you couldn't climb a mere four hundred feet anywhere else in the world and feel higher.

We had good times at that hilltop house, and when Christmas was over in New York and we were packing for Florida (where my father got out of the land boom in time to keep a fortune), already I was looking forward to April and the ocean crossing. Sometimes we spent Easter in Paris, which was exciting, but I never wanted to stay there long. Then when I was twelve my father thought it was time I gave up governesses and started a proper education, so we tossed up whether it should be over here or over there. Out of compliment to my mother he asked her to flip the coin, intending (so he told me afterwards) to give way if the result disappointed her too much. But it didn't, and I went to a boarding school in Delaware for three years, spending only a few weeks in London during the summer vacation. After that my father told me to choose a college myself, anywhere I liked.

I suppose to have been born in England means something, even the way it happened to me. It was in April 1918, when the Germans looked quite likely to win *that* war. My father had been shuttling back and forth across the Atlantic a good deal in those days; I have never been able to find out quite what he did, except that it was connected with the war and was apt to be so important that he traveled under another name with secret service people watching him. Anyhow, during one of these hush-hush visits he met my mother and during another he married her. He took her to New York, soon after which my grandmother fell ill; my mother then went back to England to stay only a few months, but she postponed returning as she postponed so many things, with the result that she was actually driving to Waterloo Station to catch the boat train for Southampton when she realized she was too late. Thus I became a Cockney, one might say, accidentally; and also, if it meant anything, I had done a good deal of traveling even before I was born.

*   *   *

I saw nothing of Brad for some time after the Byfleet dinner; his tracks didn't cross mine at the College and I didn't particularly look for him or them. I did, however, meet a man named Mathews who had a laboratory next to his in the Physics Building and shared with him certain amenities. Mathews was amused when I asked if they were friends. He laughed and said: "What's that word you used? *Friends?* The fellow doesn't have time for such nonsense. Works his head off, goes nowhere, cares for nothing but crystals under a microscope or whatever it is. Sometimes I take him in a cup of tea. He says thanks very much, but I don't do it too often because it makes him feel obligated. Once, by way of returning the favor, he insisted on buying me a lunch at an A.B.C. And I don't like A.B.C.'s."

"Does he talk to you?"

"Only about work. I sometimes think he tries out his lectures on me. You might not think it, but he's a good lecturer. He also writes a few things for the scientific magazines. . . ."

"Doesn't he have any hobbies . . . fun?"

"Oh yes. Once a week, on Sundays, he finds some hill to climb. . . . Very invigorating."

"You mean Hampstead and Highgate?"

"He wouldn't call *them* hills. Nothing less than Dorking to Guildford with a final run up the Hog's Back. I went with him once. Never again. Eighteen miles at four miles an hour. Not my idea of fun. But then, perhaps it isn't his either. Perhaps he does it

21

for self-discipline or mortifying the flesh or something. He told me
he never let rain stop him."

I wasn't surprised at that because I like walking in rain myself.
A few days later (and it *was* raining, by the way) I saw him coming
out of the A.B.C. after lunch. He wore no hat or mackintosh and
after standing a moment in the shop doorway to put up his coat
collar he suddenly sprinted across the road towards the College
entrance. Then he saw me and changed course, still at a sprint. He
went out of his way to greet me. "Oh, Miss Waring. . . . I'd been
wondering if I should meet you before . . . before we meet again."

That didn't seem to make too much sense, so I just smiled till
he went on: "I'm coming to your house next Thursday. Your father
invited me — he says there'll be nobody else there. That shows he
did notice what a fool I was at the party."

"It also shows he doesn't think any less of you for it."

"I hope so . . . but I also hope he doesn't think I really *mind*
other people. What I mean is, I wouldn't like him to put himself
out for me."

There wasn't much I could say. It didn't seem at all likely that
my father would put himself out for such an unimportant person;
on the other hand, it was rather rarely that we were ever at home
without a crowd. Afterwards I found that it was my mother who
had arranged it.

That Thursday evening began rather well, despite the fact that
our landlord dropped in to dinner uninvited. Or perhaps partly
because of it, for the talk got on the subject of painting, and that led
to music and then my mother went to the piano and played Chopin.
She was a fairly good amateur pianist and liked to play if there
were no notable musicians present; she also sang, the *diseuse* style
— you called her an English Yvette Guilbert if nobody else said it
first. That evening I thought she sang rather better than usual and
I told her so.

"And what does Mr. Bradley think?" she asked from the piano stool.

It was a silly question because it invited flattery and she might have known he wasn't the type to have it ready. He just looked uncomfortable and walked over to the piano. "I can sing too," he said.

My mother jumped up laughing. "Why, of course — that's wonderful. Take over."

"No, no — I don't play the piano. Can you accompany for me?"

"Depends what the song is."

"I expect you know 'John Brown's Body' or 'Annie Laurie.' . . ."

I then felt a bit uncomfortable myself, chiefly because of the painter, who was ultrasophisticated about art and might consider songs like that very naïve; also I thought he'd think Brad had bad manners in putting a stop to my mother's singing. I don't really mind if people have bad manners, but I don't like an American to have them in front of an Englishman, or vice versa for that matter. My mother, of course, carried it off gaily, starting at once into "Annie Laurie," and somewhat to everyone's surprise Brad turned out to have a rather good baritone. Halfway through my mother joined with him and made it a duet. They went on after that, singing other songs together, after which Brad asked her to sing some more on her own, so everything was all right. He said good-night about eleven, leaving the rest of us to conduct the post-mortem.

"Well, well," said my father. "We haven't had so much music since Cortot came here." Maybe he meant that to be ironic.

"He wasn't so shy this time," said my mother.

The painter asked who Brad was and what he did. My father answered: "A young scientist from one of our prairie states; he's working at University College where he got a Ph.D. last year."

I hadn't known that before.

"Nice voice," said the painter.

My father smiled. "It's remarkable for one thing at least, it sings more readily than it talks."

"On the other hand, Waring, when it does talk it talks sense. While we were visiting your gent's room after dinner I asked him what he thought of the landscape in the hall — of course he didn't know it was mine. He said he didn't understand why a modern painter would ignore the rules of perspective without any of the excuses that Botticelli had, and I thoroughly agreed with him. I'm fed up with that pseudoprimitive stuff I went in for years ago."

My father said: "I wouldn't have thought he knew anything about Botticelli."

"He knows how to sing too," said my mother. "I mean *how* to sing — though I don't suppose he's ever been taught. His breathing's exceptionally good."

"He takes long walks," I said. "Maybe that helps."

Anyhow, the whole evening was a success, after all my fears that it wouldn't be.

*　　*　　*

From then on I'd see him fairly often, but not to say more than a few words to. I sometimes went to the A.B.C. shop where he had his regular lunch of a roll and butter and a glass of milk, we smiled across the crowded room, or he'd stop to say hello if my table was on his way to the cash desk. Twice, I think, I joined him because there was no place elsewhere, but he was just about to leave, so there wasn't much conversation. And another time the waitress said when she came to take my order: "Dr. Bradley isn't here yet. It's only seven past twelve and he never comes in till ten past. We tell the time by him." She must have thought I was looking for him.

One lunchtime he threaded his way deliberately amongst the tables towards mine. "I've been wanting to ask you something," he began, sitting down. "I've been thinking I ought to return your

24

parents' hospitality. Of course I don't have a house where I could very well ask them to dinner . . ."

"Oh, they know that — they wouldn't expect it — "

"But perhaps a hotel — I wondered if you could tell me any particular place they like."

My father liked Claridge's and my mother the Berkeley, either of which would have cost him at least a week's pay. So I said: "They really don't care much for dining at hotels at all. . . . Why don't you ask them to tea? I know they'd love that."

"Tea? . . . That's an idea. Just afternoon tea — like the English?"

"My mother *is* English."

"Tea and crumpets, then."

"Not crumpets in the middle of June. Just tea."

"And what hotel?"

"Does it have to be any hotel? Why don't you make tea in your lab? Mathews does."

"Mathews? You know him? We might invite him too." I didn't know what he meant by "we" till he added: "Would you help?"

"With the tea? Why yes, of course."

It was fun making preparations. I had never been inside his laboratory before, or even seen what "Dr. Mark Bradley" looked like on his letter box. It was an ugly room on the top story of the Physics Building, with less scientific equipment in it than I had expected and a rather pervasive smell that I didn't comment on because there was nothing to be said in its favor and doubtless nothing that could be done about it. I tidied the place up a bit, dusted the chairs, and soon had the kettle boiling on a tripod over a Bunsen burner. Mathews came, talked, drank tea, and had to leave for a lecture. My parents had promised to be there by four, and I was a little peeved by their lateness, not because it really mattered but because I could see it was making Brad nervous. He kept pacing up and down and looking out of the window. Suddenly he cried "They're

here!" and rushed out and down the stairs. But when he came back there was only my mother with him. She was full of apologies; she had been shopping and hadn't noticed the time; and also my father couldn't come owing to a meeting in the City that had lasted longer than usual. "Of course you shouldn't have waited for me." Then she looked appraisingly round the room, sniffing just as I had. "What a jolly little place! How secluded you must be here — almost on the roof! And all those wonderful-looking instruments — you simply *must* tell me about them."

There were only a couple of microscopes, a chemical balance, and a Liebig condenser, but he went round with her, exhibiting and explaining, answering in patient detail even the most trivial of her questions, and all without the slightest trace of nervousness or reticence. It looked to me like a miracle, till I remembered that Mathews had said he was a good lecturer.

Then we had tea, and I knew that it *was* a miracle, because all at once he was actually *chatting*. She asked him most of the questions I had wanted to ask him, and he answered them all. About his early life in North Dakota, the farm near the Canadian border, droughts, blizzards, hard times, bankruptcy, the death of both his parents before he was out of grade school, and his own career since. She asked him such personal things — had he left a girl in America, did he have enough money? He said there was no girl and he had enough money to live on.

"But not enough to marry on?"

"I don't want to marry."

"You might — someday."

"No."

"How can you be certain?"

"Because of my work. It takes up so much of my time that it wouldn't be fair to any woman to marry her."

"She mightn't let it take up so much of your time."

26

"Then it wouldn't be fair to my work."

"Isn't that rather . . . inhuman?"

"Not when you feel about your work as I do."

"You mean as a sort of priesthood — with a vow of celibacy attached?"

He thought a moment. "I don't know. I hadn't figured it out quite like that."

But the oddest thing was yet to come. About six o'clock a boy put his head in at the doorway, grinned cheerfully, and asked if he could go home. "I've fed the cats and mice and fixed all the cages, sir."

Brad said: "You'd better let me take a look first." He excused himself to us and was gone a few minutes; when he came back my mother was all ready for him. "What's this about cats and mice and cages? Is that what the smell is?"

He smiled. "I hope it doesn't bother you. I'm so used to it myself I hardly notice it."

"But what do you have them for?"

"I don't have them at all — they belong to the man next door. I keep an eye on them when he's out. He uses them for his experimental work."

"You mean — " She flushed a little. "But of course, that's very interesting. I'd like to see your menagerie. Could I?"

I hoped he would have more sense and I tried to signal danger to both of them, but without effect. I didn't know him well enough, anyway, to convey signals, and somehow at that moment I didn't even feel I knew my mother well enough. She had a spellbound look, as if she were eager for disaster. Brad just said: "Sure, if you like, but I warn you, the smell's worse when you get close."

We walked down a stone corridor and into another room. It was full of cages, numbered and tagged and placed methodically on platforms round the walls. The cats had had their milk and were sleepily washing themselves; they purred in anticipation and rubbed their heads against the wire when he went near them. My mother looked hypnotized as she followed him from cage to cage. She asked him how the cats were obtained. "I suppose the University buys them from somebody," he answered. "Most of them are strays — they're often half-starved when they first come here. We feed them well, of course — they have to be healthy before they're any use."

Without reply she suddenly opened the door of one of the cages. A black and white cat squirmed eagerly into her arms and tried to reach up to her chin. She fondled it for a moment, then put it back in the cage. "What a pity I have to," she whispered.

"You like cats?" he asked.

"I adore them. Do you?"

"Yes. Dogs too."

It wasn't a very intelligent end to the conversation but I could see it *was* the end. My mother was already putting on that glassy look she has when she is saying charming things and thinking of something else at the same time. I've often seen it at the tail end of a party. "I think perhaps I ought to be going. . . . So nice of you to ask me here and tell me everything. We must have you to the house again soon."

He saw us down to the street, where Henry was waiting. In the car my mother was silent for a while, then she said: "It was my fault. I shouldn't have poked my nose in."

When I didn't answer she added: "I suppose they have to do it."

"*He* doesn't. They weren't his."

She was silent again for some time, then asked suddenly: "Do you think you understand him?"

"Not after the way he talked to you today."

"Why, what was wrong about that?"

"Nothing, only I'd always thought he was reserved and shy."

"He is."

"Not with you. He told you more in five minutes than he'd tell me in five years."

"Wait till you've known him five years. You'll be a better age."

"So you think that's why he doesn't talk to me as he does to you? Because I'm too young?"

"Perhaps. Darling, don't be annoyed. And I might be wrong too. I've never met scientists before. They must be queer people. The way they can *do* such things . . . and yet have ideals. The distant goal — he's got his eyes fixed on it and he can't see anything nearer. . . . And all his hard life and early struggles haven't taught him anything. He doesn't realize that even in the scientific world you've got to get about and make friends if you want to be a success. He lives like a hermit — anyone can see that. It would do him good to fall in love."

I laughed. "Mathews says he's scared of women altogether."

"Mathews?"

"The man next door to him."

"Oh yes . . . the one who . . . yes, I remember. . . ."

"All the same, though, he wasn't scared of *you*."

She cuddled my arm and answered: "No, darling, it was I who was scared. He's a *peculiar* man."

*   *   *

Ever since schooldays I have kept a diary of sorts, mostly the jotting down of engagements, never anything literary or confessional. Brad makes his appearance the first day I saw him; there's the record: "Dinner Chelsea Professor Byfleet. Gave a lift home to American boy researching at Coll. Shy." The entry for the day on which my mother came to tea is similarly brief. Just: "Tea in Brad's lab. Mother. Cat." And about a week later comes this: "End of College Term. Cat."

What happened was that I got home from an afternoon walk to

find my mother and Brad in the drawing room. They were talking together and my mother was nursing a black and white cat which immediately she thrust into my arms. "Look, Jane! It's the same one! Brad just brought it — he's given it to me!"

"It's lovely," I said, and I noticed she had called him Brad. So I said: "Hello, Brad."

"Hello," he answered.

She went on breathlessly: "And it wasn't what we thought at all. . . . Tell her, Brad, unless . . ." She began to smile. "Unless you think she's too young to know."

My mother and I adored each other, but ever since I was about fourteen she had talked *to* me as if I were her own age, but *of* me as if I were still about twelve; and when this happened before my face I often got confused and said just what a twelve-year-old would say.

I did then. I said: "I'm not too young to know anything."

.Brad took it seriously. "I should say not. There's nothing indecent about it."

"Oh, don't be silly — I was only joking," my mother interrupted. "Tell her."

"It's nothing much. Apparently you both thought those animals in the room next to my lab were kept for vivisection. Anything but. All they have to do is to reproduce, reproduce, and keep on reproducing. Probably quite pleasant for them. Mathews is doing some new research in Genetics — he breeds a succession of generations to find out how certain characteristics crop up."

Now that I had the explanation the fact that even jokingly I had been considered too young to know it made me almost feel I was. I said, in a rather asinine way: "Wouldn't Mathews mind you taking away his cat?"

"He hadn't begun any records of this animal, so any other would do just as well. He said so. Technically, of course, I've stolen the property of the University of London. How about calling the police?"

We all laughed and I handed the cat back to my mother.

"Mind you," he went on, "don't think I'm a sentimentalist. There's a lot of nonsense talked about cruel scientists — I've never met any myself. Certainly at the College the men who have to do vivisections occasionally — "

My mother broke in: "You mean that it *does* go on there? I thought you said — just for breeding — "

"You must have misunderstood me — all I said was that the animals *you* saw, the ones Mathews keeps — "

"All right, all right, let's not talk about it any more."

"But you do believe me when I say that scientists aren't cruel?"

Brad was like that, as I found so many times afterwards; he could never let well enough alone.

My mother said: "Many people are cruel. Wouldn't you expect *some* of them to be scientists?"

"Statistically, yes. . . ."

"Then I've won my argument. Have some tea."

I said good-by to him long before he went because I had to go upstairs and pack; I was leaving for a holiday in Ireland the next morning. I think he stayed till my father came home just before dinner.

*   *   *

My mother wrote while I was away, just her usual gossipy letters; one of them mentioned Brad and said he had been up to the house for dinner. "We had more music and sat up talking till late. He's really beginning to be quite human. . . ."

I was in Ireland over a month and returned to London for the beginning of the autumn term. It was September, and in a few weeks, if they followed their usual plan, my parents would return to America. I wondered what it would feel like to be on my own in London; I was halfway thrilled at the prospect.

I didn't see Brad for a few days; then suddenly he met me as I was leaving a lecture. We shook hands and he asked about Ireland. "Did you climb any mountains?"

"Not exactly mountains. We hiked about, though. There were plenty of hills."

"Did you visit Donegal?"

"No. Should I?"

"Someone told me that in the mountains there you get quartzite with a capping of sandstone — obviously the result of denudation. . . ." He went on, when I didn't answer: "Geology's one of the things I wish I knew more about. Do you enjoy walking?"

"Yes, very much."

"Would you care to take a walk with me next Sunday?"

I said I would and he looked me up and down as if for the first time he were reckoning me physically. "Good legs and good boots are all you need."

"Shoes," I corrected. "And I don't know *anything* about geology, but I'd like to."

I thought he might be relieved to feel there was always a topic in reserve.

*   *   *

We went to Cambridge by an early train because he had to call at the Cavendish Laboratory there to leave some papers. It was the first time I had been to the university town and I wouldn't have minded sight-seeing, but apparently this was not part of his program; we ignored the colleges and began a brisk walk along the riverbank. After what Mathews had said, I was quite prepared to cover the miles without comment or complaint, but as a great concession, doubtless, we picked up a bus at some outlying village and the bus happened to be going to Ely. The way I'm telling this sounds as if I were having fun at his expense all the time; and so, in a quiet way, I was, because people who are too serious always make me feel ribald inside. Not that he was as serious as I had expected. We didn't discuss geology once — perhaps because there isn't much geology between Cambridge and Ely. There were just large expanses of mud everywhere, and especially by the river, for heavy rain had fallen and the sky was full of clouds threatening more. Ely was like a steel engraving, but inside the Cathedral the octagon window had the look of stored-up sunshine from a summer day. I said it would be strange if some of the medieval stained-glass experts had actually discovered how to do this, and he assured me gravely that they couldn't have, it was scientifically impossible. I then gave him a short lecture on English Perpendicular, to which he listened as if he thought me clever though what I was saying relatively unimportant. "But of course you're only interested in scientific things," I ended up.

"No, that's not true. Your mother played some Mozart to me the other evening — it was the first time I really liked classical music."

"She loves Mozart."

"Of course when she was younger she had time and opportunity to cultivate a sense of beauty — that's hard for the average American."

"Oh, I don't know. I think it's Americans who do cultivate things, as a rule."

"Then she just *has* them — was born with them, perhaps. Generations of aristocratic background."

"My mother's people wouldn't like you to call them aristocrats. They're a fairly well-known Yorkshire family — commoners, but we can trace ourselves back for a few centuries without much trouble."

"She happened to mention a sister — Lady Somebody, I forget the name."

"That's nothing. Titles don't mean aristocracy. All my aunt did

33

was to marry a man who got knighted — that can happen to anyone."

"You sound rather cynical about it."

"I'm not. But it's amusing, sometimes, the way Americans make mistakes. My aunt and uncle were once visiting us in Florida and the local paper called them English blue bloods. They're no more blue-blooded than you are."

"Speaking scientifically?"

"No, speaking snobbishly. If you want the snob angle, at least get it right. Of course I don't mean you, I mean the Florida paper. Personally I don't think much of titles."

"Because you come of a family that's proud of its age rather than rank?"

"I guess you're right. It's probably an inverted snobbery. We certainly think we're superior to a lot of these businessmen baronets."

"You say 'we.' Does that mean you feel yourself more English than American?"

"When I'm talking to you I do. When I'm talking to an Englishman I feel I want to chew gum. It's the perverse streak in me."

"Does that mean you feel American when you're with your mother?"

"Sometimes. . . . Though she's not so terribly English. I've met Russians and Irish that are more like her. She's more true to herself than to any nationality. Not that I mean she doesn't act, sometimes. But when she does, she doesn't really mind if you see through it. And you can act back. She doesn't mind that either."

"I'm afraid I'm not much good at acting."

"I wasn't meaning you personally."

"I'm sorry. I thought — perhaps — well — "

"I was just talking generally. I'm sorry if you — "

"How did we get onto this argument, anyway?"

34

"I forget."

He thought for a moment, then said: "We were discussing beauty — the sense of beauty — "

"Were we?"

"Mozart, it started with. . . ."

"Oh yes, you said you were beginning to like classical music."

"I think I *could* like it, if I heard more. It's strange how — if you're in a certain mood — the awareness of beauty comes over you — "

"It comes over me in *any* mood. I mean, it can *put* me in the mood. When we were in the Cathedral just now, for instance . . ."

"Yes — but it didn't get me as much as Mozart."

"Maybe we should have asked the organist to play some Mozart."

"I'll ask your mother when I'm next up at the house."

"Yes, do. . . . You come up quite often now, don't you? While I've been away . . . I'm so glad."

We returned to Cambridge by bus and he called at the Cavendish again to pick up something — "results," he said, that he had left there in the morning for a check. When he glanced over them later in the train I tried to tell from his face whether everything had been satisfactory, but he looked neither pleased nor displeased — only preoccupied. Presently, as he put the papers away, he said: "Well, that's that."

"What is?"

"A month's work and it turns out to be wrong."

"Oh, I'm sorry."

"Nothing to be sorry about. It's not an emotional matter."

"But a whole month! Couldn't you have found out you were wrong sooner?"

"Perhaps not — though the Cavendish does have better facilities. Might save time in the future if I had access to them more often."

"Couldn't you work there?"

He smiled. "You don't know how lucky I am to be able to work anywhere. You should have known me the last time I went inside a cathedral."

"Where was that?"

"St. Patrick's, New York."

"Are you a Catholic?"

"No. I used to go in for warmth and rest when I was looking for a job. That was in 1931."

"You've come a long way in five years."

"It's not how far you come that counts — it's the direction you take and whether you ever find the right track."

"Do you think you've found it?"

"I think I know where to look for it. And a few wrong answers won't put me off."

There was a sort of grittiness in his voice that made me think he was fighting down disappointment over his wasted month. He added almost ferociously: "The trouble is, I don't *know* enough. I'm trying to build too high without scaffolding. . . ."

*   *   *

After that day at Cambridge I thought I was bound *to* have crossed some sort of barrier, and that henceforth I could count on seeing him fairly regularly, either at the College or at the house; but in fact a rather long interval elapsed, so that I stopped Mathews once and asked how Brad was. He said he was wearing himself out as usual, or rather more than usual — indeed, he'd given up one of his teaching classes in order to devote more time to his own work.

"Can he afford that?"

"Evidently. Or else he's making himself afford it."

"Do you know what work it is?"

"Vaguely. Some sort of mathematics. But you can't know much about other people's work nowadays, not when they get past the elementary stage. Even genetics has its mysteries. Why don't you come and see my mice? I don't have cats any more — they're not quick enough on the job. And besides, they're apt to attract visitors." He always joked about my mother's acquisition.

I went up with him. "I wouldn't disturb him while he's busy," he said, as we passed Brad's door. I hadn't had any such intention, but the warning made me ask what special reason there was for all the high pressure.

He said he thought something had "happened" at Cambridge. "He goes to the Cavendish there fairly often. He told me after one trip that a physicist was no damned good unless he was also a mathematician, so that's what he's doing now, I suppose — in what he calls his spare time. . . . Come and see these creatures again when you feel like it. Perhaps he won't be so busy."

He was, and I didn't bother him. But one afternoon, inside the College near the Physics Building, I met my mother walking along as if she had far more right to look surprised than I had. She asked if I were going up to see Brad. I replied: "Certainly not. Have *you* just been to see him?"

"Darling, why 'certainly not'?"

"Because he hates to be interrupted when he's at work. It's a thing I'd never dream of doing. . . . But I suppose you *have* seen him?"

"Yes, but not in the way you think. I've been to one of his lectures."

"*What?*"

"I don't see any reason against it. He has a beginners' class — anybody can join who enrolls. I've enrolled. It's interesting. And he explains things so wonderfully. One ought to have something serious in life, oughtn't one?"

"What does Brad say about it?"

"Brad? . . . yes . . . it suits him, doesn't it? . . . Or perhaps it's just that I never did like Mark and I couldn't go on calling him Mr.

37

Bradley — Dr. Bradley, I mean. . . . Anyhow, I think the less formal we all are the better. That's what the trouble is with him — he's
too formal — he doesn't seem to believe in any pleasure, amusement,
relaxation. . . . But I have an idea I'm beginning to convert him —
gradually."

She looked so adorable as she said it that I laughed. "And he's
managing to convert you a little at the same time, eh?"

No, she answered, he was not converting her — not really. He was
only showing her something she had already been aware of in life,
or had guessed existed. Physics was a symbol rather than the thing
itself. "I've often thought I have a rather empty existence — just dinner parties and social engagements and treading the same old beaten
path — London, New York, Florida. I've never been completely satisfied with it. Even when I was a girl I wanted to be a nurse." (This
was news to me, and it may have been true, but my mother was always capable of reinforcing an argument with some happy impro-
visation.) "Darling, you at least ought to understand, because you've
chosen to do something worth while instead of wasting your time as
so many girls in your position would. Surely it's the happy medium
we must all strive for. For instance, he *ought* to waste a little bit of
his time, and I've quite an ambition to make him do it — I'd *love*
to make him break a rule — just one little rule. . . ."

"Did he break any at the lecture when he saw you?"

"Not him. He's so different when he's lecturing. Not a bit nervous — and yet still shy."

"Did he know you were going to be there?"

"Of course. I *enrolled* — didn't I say that? I asked him if he
thought it would all be above my head and he said no, it was as
elementary as he could make it — he's not exactly the flatterer, is
he? . . . But never a smile or a look during the lecture — I was just
one of his students. And when he finished he picked up his papers
and dashed away as if he was afraid of someone chasing him."

"Perhaps he was."

"Now darling, are you trying to make fun of me?"

I wondered if I were; it wouldn't have been surprising, for my mother and I got a good deal of amusement out of each other. But I had a curious feeling that we were both more serious than we sounded, and that the badinage was a familiar dress to cover something rather new in our relationship.

She said, as if it finally clinched the matter: "Well, he's coming to dinner on October tenth. I *did* chase him to ask him that. He said he couldn't make it earlier because he's working for some examination that finishes on the ninth."

"But will you still be here? I thought the end of September was when you and Father — "

"We're staying a few extra weeks this year. We thought it would be nice not to leave you too soon."

I said I was glad, which was true enough, though of course I knew I'd be perfectly all right on my own.

* * *

It wasn't a party on the tenth, but that rare "just ourselves," with not even a chance visitor after dinner except Julian Spee. Julian was a rising English lawyer; still in his middle forties, he had already taken silk and found a seat in Parliament; there seemed nothing to stop him from whatever he aimed at, which was probably high. He was handsome in a saturnine way, a brilliant talker, unmarried, and an accomplished flirt. He lived in a house not far from ours, facing the Heath, and had formed a habit of dropping by whenever he felt like it, whether we had a party or not. He was sure of his welcome and one knew he was sure. I think he liked my mother more than most women, and she in turn was flattered by his attentions and always willing to give advice about his love affairs. A pleasantly romantic relationship can develop in this way, and it had done, over a period of years. I wasn't at ease with Julian myself, because I never felt he was quite real, but on the few occasions when he hadn't treated me as a precocious child I had been aware of his attractiveness. My father, who collected him as he collected all celebrities, once said that in any other country but England you would have taken him for a homosexual, to which my mother replied mischievously: "And in any other country he would have been." As often it wasn't very clear what she meant.

My father had got back from Germany that day, tired from the trip and gloomy about affairs over there. He didn't any longer attend to ordinary business matters, but if something cropped up of a kind in which his personal acquaintance with politicians and diplomats might help, the job was usually passed on to him. I think the Nazis were interfering with some of his "interests"; the State Department hadn't been able to do much, and because he had once met Hitler during the twenties he'd been called in like a rainmaker after a prolonged drought. But big shots were always apt to disappoint him after a while — Lenin had, and Lloyd George, and Mussolini, and Ramsay MacDonald, and now it was Hitler's turn. Roosevelt hadn't yet, but one felt sure he would. My father was too rich to care for money for its own sake (despite the Marazon disclosures that did him so much harm); he knew, as moderately rich men didn't, how little you could bribe those whose real currency was power, and this in turn made him flatter poor men who became powerful. But of course, because they were powerful, sooner or later they let him know that he had only money. I think now (though I knew nothing much about it then) he must have been having this kind of experience in Germany, and it hadn't been pleasant.

Fortunately Brad's mood that night was at the other extreme. With his examination over even he couldn't help relaxing, the more so under the influence of good food and my mother's gaiety. Then, somehow or other, when we were in the drawing room afterwards and Julian had joined us, the conversation grew personal and the atmosphere changed. Julian had met Brad before, and they had seemed to like each other well enough, in spite or perhaps because of their obvious oppositeness. But now I sensed a hostility between them which my father was quietly fanning; it was as if he were holding his own unhappy thoughts at bay by encouraging both my mother and Julian to put Brad on the spot. Soon they were in the thick of a discussion of Brad's ambitions, what he wanted to do in life, his ideal of science as something to be lived for, and so on. All ideals sound naïve when brought out under cross-examination, but my mother had a special knack of creating naïveté in others — something in the way she used wits rather than brains for an argument, certainly not knowledge, which she didn't have much of about most things. But she was always fluent, and couldn't endure to wait while others hesitated or pondered, so she would tell them what she thought they were going to reply, and it was often so deceptively simple that the other person would agree in a bemused way and presently find himself defending some vast proposition more suitable for a school debating society than anything between adults. I think this must have happened to Brad that night, for he got to telling us eventually that scientists were actuated by a desire to "save" humanity, and that science, in due course, would do this in spite of other people whose chief concern was worldly success. (Which was probably a dig at Julian.)

"Meaning," said Julian, "that scientists don't go for that sort of thing?"

Brad answered that no true scientist could, or if he did, it proved he wasn't a true scientist. As neat as that!

"But my dear boy — " (Julian always called people "dear," which sounded more affected than affectionate till you got used to it, and then you realized it was neither, but just a habit) — "my dear boy, if you ignore all worldly success, how do you suppose you're going to get a chance to prove *anything?* You can't sit in a corner all on your own and just *be* a scientist — it's not like writing an epic poem or contemplating your navel — you need money for food, equipment that you couldn't afford, a room to work in that your house doesn't have, and a job to make it worth somebody's while to pay you a regular salary!"

"Well, a job's all right. There's nothing worldly in that."

"But unless it's a good job you'll wear yourself out marking papers and teaching teen-agers to blow glass! I know, because I remember my own schooldays."

"There *are* good jobs."

"And how do you suppose they are got? College heads aren't supermen, they don't know much about science themselves, and because they can only judge a reputation by the look of it, they're human enough to favor a man who knows how to draw attention to himself. So if he's smart, that's exactly what he does. Politics is one way — though dangerous. Social success is safer. And doing stuff on the side that attracts publicity — you Americans know the kind of thing — pseudoscientific articles in your Sunday supplements that aren't *too* phony, just phony enough." (Julian liked to use American slang, which he said was enriching the English language at a period when otherwise a natural impoverishment would have set in. We had another big argument about that once.)

"So you don't think real distinction counts, Mr. Spee?"

"I didn't say that. Of course it counts — but it counts a good deal more if you add salesmanship and what your Hollywood people call glamour."

"*Glamour?*"

"Certainly. . . . An interesting new theory, developed by Professor So-and-So in Vienna . . . it's like your sparkling new comedy, straight from its phenomenal success on Broadway . . . even if it only ran three nights. . . . Vienna is the Broadway of the scientific show business. . . . I'd strongly recommend a year or two there for you."

Brad had the same trouble that I had in deciding whether Julian was serious or not, and I could see him wondering about it now.

My father said quietly: "Might not be a bad idea at that."

Brad was still puzzling over Julian's epigram. "Show business, eh?" he echoed, in a rather shocked tone. "I hope it isn't quite so bad."

"It's not bad at all, my dear boy, it's human. We live in an age of headlines, not of hermits."

"Someday," said my mother, in her random way, "the hermits may make the headlines."

"Vienna's a good place," said my father. "A very good place indeed."

It seemed to me that everyone was talking at cross-purposes. "I can't believe that the true scientist cares much about headlines," Brad said.

"No?" Julian gave his rather high-pitched feminine laugh. "I could mention the names of at least a dozen who care about them passionately. And they're big men, not charlatans, don't make any mistake. They'll give you some competition if you go after the plums."

"But I don't want the plums. I'm not a bit ambitious for things like that — I wouldn't enjoy the kind of thing some people call success. All I ask is the chance to work usefully at something that seems to me worth while." He added, as if he had listened to his own words: "And if that sounds priggish I can't help it — it's the only way I can express what I mean."

"Oh, no — not priggish at all," Julian assured him. "Just an honest mistake you're making about yourself. Do you mean to tell me you really *wouldn't* like to head a research department of your own somewhere, to have no more drudgery, to get yourself recognized as an equal by those whose names in the scientific world you know and

43

respect? . . . Of course you would. . . . And as for scientists being worth-whilers and world-savers, let me prick that bubble for you too. I've known a good many of them, and in my experience, though some may fool themselves about it, they have one simple and over-riding motive above all others . . . *Curiosity.*"

"Brad's motive isn't that," my mother interrupted.

"Then by Christ, if you'll pardon the expression, it had better be, unless he's a mere moralist hiding behind a rampart of test tubes!" He turned to Brad with his easy confident smile. "Perhaps you are — perhaps you'd really be more at home in a pulpit than a labora-tory."

"No, no, Julian," my mother interrupted again. "That's absurd — he's not a moralist, and why should he hide anywhere? He's a real scientist — he even defends vivisection!"

It was part of my mother's charm that her mind flew off at tan-gents usually capable of changing a subject. This time, however, both Brad and Julian ignored her and the argument went on. "Of course, my dear boy, I'm neither defending nor attacking — I'm just diagnosing what I've always felt to be the real germ of the scientific spirit. You probably know much more about it yourself, but my own opinion is, it's Pandora's box that lures, not the Holy Grail. And I haven't yet met a scientist who wouldn't take a chance of busting up the whole works rather than not find out something. Maybe civilizations have been destroyed like that before. History covers too small a fragment of life on earth for anyone to say it's un-thinkable. After all, we know the Greeks excelled us in several of the arts and perhaps in one of the sciences, that of human govern-ment — why not some earlier civilization in engineering or medi-cine? Anyhow, it's a beguiling thought — that all the great discov-eries have been made and remade over and over again throughout the ages. What do you say, Jane? You're the historian."

I said it all sounded very pessimistic and somewhat Spenglerian.

44

"Personally I find it more agreeable than what the last century called progress."

"It's worse than pessimism," Brad said. "It's a sort of nihilism."

"Coo . . . listen to 'im! Sech lengwidge!" Julian mimicked banteringly.

My father, who had taken little part in the argument and had seemed to be listening in a detached way, now intervened almost irritably. "Nihilism . . . *nihilism* . . . just a word. At various times in my life I've been called an economic royalist, a communist, a fascist, and a merchant of death . . . so don't let nihilist floor you, Julian."

"I won't," Julian retorted, though he looked as if my father's sudden support had rather startled him.

Brad was hanging on to the argument. "But at least, Mr. Spee, the peak of each civilization could be higher than the one before?"

"Why *should* it? We don't know. Perhaps there've been vast cycles of civilizations — some upward in trend, others downward — and these cycles, in turn, may have belonged to even vaster movements. All pure speculation, of course. You can argue about it endlessly, just as — " and he turned deferentially to my father — "just as your Dow-Jones theorists do when stocks drop and they try to figure out whether it's a real bear market or just a dip in a boom. Wait and see's the only solution, but if the waiting means a few million years, what can you do? Even Spengler won't go that far."

Julian laughed, but as if he had become already uneasy about the argument. He was extremely sensitive to timing and atmosphere, and soon afterwards he made rather abrupt excuses and left us. Brad stayed, and my father rallied himself into an appearance of affability. But I was still at odds with his mood; I couldn't quite understand it, and his totally unnecessary mention of having once been called a merchant of death was especially strange. It was true, he had been called that, but it wasn't true that he had been unconcerned about it; on the contrary he had been much hurt at the time and would have prosecuted somebody for libel if his lawyers had let him.

I also noticed that he was refilling his glass rather oftener than usual. "Well, Brad," he said, switching over to his side. "We certainly had him on a soapbox, didn't we? I hope you weren't too impressed."

Brad laughed. "So long as I don't have to agree, that's the main thing. I'd like to think over what he said in terms of the Second Law of Thermodynamics. Might be interesting."

"What beats me," my father said, "is the way that fellow knows other people's business. . . . Yours . . . and mine . . . the Dow-Jones theory . . . how does he get that way?"

"Probably most of what he knows is on the surface," Brad answered, entirely without malice.

It was late and he looked at his watch. I think we were all a little tired. Just before he left my father called me to the library. "Henry can drive him back," he said. "Why don't you go with him for the ride?"

I was surprised at the suggestion and wondered if he thought there was anything emotional between Brad and me—that would have been too ridiculous.

"He'd probably rather take the tube," I said.

"No, let Henry bring the car round."

"He'd hate to think he'd been keeping Henry up. He's fussy about those things."

"Then get a taxi and you can come back in it."

"He doesn't have taxis—he can't afford them and he wouldn't like me to pay."

My father's irritation showed through again. "Well, for once he can—because I want you to tell him something. Tell him I wasn't joking, even if Julian was, about the idea of him going abroad. I've been thinking for some time it might not be a bad thing. Tell him that."

"Why don't *you* tell him?"

"I did, but I don't think he heard me. I'm sorry Julian talked of it so flippantly — it's really what Brad ought to do. He's probably got all he can out of this London job by now. . . . So tell him, will you? There's a bunch of physicists in Vienna, if he could get fixed up with the right connections. I might be able to help him in that."

"*You* might?"

"Yes. I have — er — contacts there."

"In Vienna?"

"Yes."

"But what about the Cavendish at Cambridge? Isn't that as good?"

"Cambridge isn't the only place where they're doing interesting things in his line. The Continent would give him a different angle . . ."

"You mean the glamour?"

"No, no . . . or anyhow, that's not the word for it. I wish Julian hadn't butted in with his witticisms. . . . Well, you talk things over with Brad. Ask him how he'd like to spend some time working with Hugo Framm."

"*Hugo Framm?*"

"He'll know who Framm is. Ask him. Ask him."

The telephone then rang; I took it, as I often did; it was New York. Those business calls were generally very dull as well as private, so I handed him the receiver and edged away towards the hall doorway across the room.

And then I saw Brad. His back was towards me, and in front of him, almost hidden, was my mother. The lights in the hall were subdued, and all I could see of her distinctly was the knuckle of her right hand as she held his sleeve. She had been talking to him ear-

47

nestly and I caught what was evidently a final remark: ". . . and you mustn't take any notice, Brad. . . . I'd *hate* you to be influenced at all. . . ." Only that, whispered very eagerly.

He said nothing in reply, then suddenly, glancing round his shoulder with a little side movement of her head, she saw me, I think, though she pretended not to. I stepped back into the room. Presently my father finished his call.

"Well, as I was saying, Jane, see how he feels about it."

I answered: "Yes, but not tonight. I'll talk to him at the College tomorrow. I *know* he'd rather go home by tube."

*   *   *

I could have met him at lunch the next day and been sure of not interrupting his work, but I went straight to the lab about eleven-thirty, committing the unforgivable sin, if it were one, with a certain gusto. After all, he couldn't already be working for another examination — or could he? Anyhow, I caught him (so far as I could judge) doing that rare thing, nothing. But he looked preoccupied and not really surprised enough; he asked me to sit down, but I said it wouldn't take me long to deliver a message. Then I told him what my father had said about Vienna and Hugo Framm. His whole manner changed. He seemed bewildered at first, then slowly and increasingly pleased. He went to a shelf of books and showed me everything he could find that had anything to do with Framm, who was apparently a scientific star of magnitude. There was a paragraph about him in a recent issue of *Discovery,* and an article by him in a German magazine. Altogether I began to think it rather wonderful that Brad should have a chance to work with such a man. "But I don't see why he should even consider me," he kept saying. "There's nothing I've done yet that could possibly impress him."

"But my father knows him, Brad."

48

"Of course I realize your father has influence, but in a question of pure science . . ."

"Perhaps it isn't a question of pure science. Perhaps Framm's a bit human. Perhaps he takes notice of what his friends say about people. My father's opinion of you might be high enough for someone to *want* to have you."

"But is he such a close friend of your father?"

"I never heard his name mentioned before, but that doesn't mean anything. My father knows so many people everywhere. He meets them once and then they're on his list of — well, I suppose you could call them *distant* friends."

"Very remarkable."

"My father *is* remarkable."

"So's your mother — in a different way."

"Oh, she's a darling."

"I'd guess she's a good bit younger."

"Than my father? . . . Twenty years."

"As much as that?"

"Your surprise doesn't flatter her. Or perhaps it flatters him."

He thought that out. I added: "I don't think years matter much, anyway — especially as you grow older."

"That's true. It's when you're younger that the difference counts."

I wondered if he was thinking of the difference between his age and mine. Then he went on: "Not that I *feel* she's any older than I am."

"She is, though. Nearly twice as old."

"Oh no, that can't be. I'm twenty-four."

"And she's thirty-eight."

"Well, that's not twice. . . ."

"I said *nearly* twice."

"You also said years don't matter much."

"And *you* said they *did,* when people are younger."

"I think we're getting tied up in this argument. Let's have some lunch."

That was a novelty, and a further one when we didn't go to an A.B.C., but to an Italian place near the Tottenham Court Road. We had minestrone and chicken *cacciatora,* meanwhile talking about Framm; or rather, he did most of the talking — I could see him building up a vision and I hoped he wouldn't expect too much. After all, my father's influence had its limits. But apparently it was only an already existing vision in a new form — a sort of frozen white-hot passion for whatever it was that couldn't be satisfactorily explained to a first-year history student. I let him rhapsodize all the way back to the College.

There was grand opera at Covent Garden that evening and someone had lent my parents a box. We went to dine at Boulestin's first. I don't care for opera and all afternoon as I thought of it I grew more and more out of humor. Then when I got home I found my mother still lingering over tea. "I asked Brad to come," she greeted me, "but I don't suppose he will." She overdid the casualness and as soon as I looked at her she began to look at me in what I think she thought was the same way.

"I shouldn't imagine so," I answered. "He was here only last night and it's quite a trip for a cup of tea."

"You like him, don't you, Jane?"

"Yes. He'd be rather hard to dislike."

"I shall miss the lectures when he goes to Vienna."

"*If* he goes. Or is it settled yet?"

"I think your father's written to somebody. I hope it works out all right. . . . I can't help wondering if he really wants to go there. He always talked to me about the Cavendish."

"To me too, but at present I think he's quite set on Vienna — on account of this man Framm."

"I wish I'd had a chance to help him more — not as Framm can, of course, but that's not all the help he needs. I'd like to have made him — well, a bit more at home with life. More . . . sophisticated . . . easy-mannered . . ."

"Worldly?"

"Oh no, no, Jane, not that. He's naïve, but I love it and I hated the way Julian talked the other night. I don't know what possessed him — he seemed to be trying to break down every ideal the boy had. . . . No, let him keep his ideals — he doesn't even have to be a worldly success if he doesn't want — but he ought to learn to get some fun out of life, that's my point. Worldly success has nothing to do with having fun."

"It has just a bit, Mother."

"Oh, just a *little* bit, perhaps — one must have *some* money. But not too much. I could be perfectly happy on a thousand a year. Pounds, I mean."

"So could a great many English people who have to live on a fraction of that."

"Well, say five hundred . . . provided of course I had other things to make life worth living."

"What other things?"

"Darling, don't cross-examine me. . . . All I know is that Brad needs to learn what happiness there *can* be in life, and he ought to stop being such a hermit. But I'm all against him giving up his ideals, whatever Julian says."

"It seems to me I'm the only person who's satisfied with him as he is."

"Are you, darling? *Entirely* satisfied?"

She gazed at me measuredly, as if the question needed a careful answer. But there wasn't time, for at that moment Brad arrived. He looked nervous, and almost as shy as when I had first seen him. He said he hadn't thought he'd be able to come, but at the very last he'd managed it. He was sorry he was so late and hoped he hadn't kept her waiting.

"Did you come up by tube?" I asked.

"No. I took a taxi."

"I'll send for some fresh tea," my mother said, and rang the bell, but nobody came; the servants were preparing for their evening out and hadn't expected to serve any more. I said I'd go to the kitchen and see about it, which I did, and then went upstairs to change.

* * *

Looking back now, I can see so much more than then. Even when you are supposed to be adult for your age, it's hard to think of grownups as in the same world; you only want to feel you can be in theirs, and you just hope any mistake won't be noticed. And yet you are aware of things often more acutely than ever afterwards, your mind has antennae roaming into the unknown; you can even walk into it with eyes peering, but the step that isn't there always brings you up with a shock and a jolt.

I had that shock about Brad, though I couldn't put any sufficient reason for it into words. When a man, after working three times harder than he should, slows down to twice as hard, there doesn't seem much for any of his friends to worry about. Nor when the same man spends a wet Sunday afternoon listening to a charming woman play Chopin, instead of drenching himself to the skin on Box Hill.

Brad gave notice to the College authorities and they were very reasonable about it. They waived the full term they could have held him for, and said he could leave whenever he wanted. And my parents postponed again their return to New York — still presumably on my account.

Meanwhile my mother kept on attending his lectures, at which he never (she said) gave her a look or a smile; but he did break a few of his other rules, whether it was she who tempted him or not. He began going to piano recitals, theaters, movies, and private views — sometimes alone with her, sometimes with my father or me also. There was nothing to stir gossip, much less scandal, in our fairly sophisticated circle; Julian Spee had escorted her similarly when he was less busy. She had often been in the throes of some fad or other, and perhaps my father figured that Brad was just an unusually masculine successor to Dalcroze Eurhythmics, Japanese flower arrangement, or the English Speaking Union. And it was sometimes my father himself who would make the date; he would say — "Oh, by the way, Christine, I've got a card for Marincourt's new exhibition — it's next Tuesday at the Wigmore Galleries. I shan't have time to go myself, but you might take Brad and show him what passes for art nowadays. . . ." But when he had issued these invitations he had an odd look of only half pleasure whether they were accepted or not.

That diary of mine jots down all the times Brad came to the house to dine. On Wednesdays it was, most often, and as the weeks passed it came to be every Wednesday, and always quite informally, without special invitation, with few or no other guests, and with plenty of music afterwards. He learned to sing "Schlafe Mein Prinzchen, Schlaf Ein," which suited his voice very well.

Then all at once he let go his work. With anyone else I wouldn't have been surprised, since he was leaving the College so soon and there couldn't have been much to finish up before the end of term. But he did it with such abandon, and idleness didn't fit in with his personality. I used to see him wandering up and down Gower Street as if he had nowhere else to go; even Mathews made a comment. Probably the waitress at the A.B.C. did also, for he took to dropping in for coffee at unexpected times, and often lunched at better places. All of which adds up to nothing at all except an idea that grew in my mind and was never put into words.

One morning towards the end of November my father announced

that the great Hugo Framm was on his way to London to receive some degree or deliver some lecture, I forget which. "We'd better give a dinner for him. Good idea for Brad to meet him first at our house."

My mother agreed it would be a good idea, but she lacked her usual enthusiasm for party planning. "Give me a list of people to ask," was all she said.

"Brad can help you. He'll know a few professors and you can mix them up with anyone else you like." And he added, thoughtfully: "I don't think it has to be champagne."

"Oh God," exclaimed my mother, "let's have champagne even if it *is* only professors."

They tiffed about it in front of me in a way which was not only new in my experience, but out of character for both of them — my father being the last man to act the parsimonious host, and my mother not normally caring what wines were drunk.

*   *   *

I didn't see Brad again till the party. If my mother saw him she didn't tell me, not that it would have been a secret, but somehow we didn't talk about Brad much, and perhaps for that reason we talked a great deal about Hugo Framm. My mother was no respecter of celebrities, and we shared the same sense of humor, ribald and vagrant and often rather rude. Between us we built up a huge joke about Professor Framm that made us both afraid we might laugh indecently when the man actually took shape before our eyes. We first said he would be fat and pompous, with a thick German accent and a mustache that would get in the way of the soup; then we changed the picture because it seemed too much the conventional *Punch*-cartoon-type of German professor; we finally decided on a tall thin man more like Sherlock Holmes, with the most exquisite manner and an Oxford accent. He would kiss my mother's hand

and look up at her at the same time, which made her say she wouldn't shoot till she saw the whites of his eyes. I said he'd probably engage in some scientific argument and shoot somebody else, or at least demand a duel on Hampstead Heath. "Now that's enough," she laughed. "We'll never dare to meet him if we keep on. . . ." We didn't bother to ask my father what the man was really like, and I suppose I could have found a photograph of him somewhere if I'd wanted.

It snowed a little the day of the party, just a white film over roofs and lawns; the traffic soon scoured it from the streets. There were about twenty people, and I wondered how Brad would like that, or if he cared any more. He had suggested only a very few of the names. But my mother, or else experience, had certainly done something to him socially; he was still shy, but not awkwardly so, rather now as if he didn't care whether he were shy or not. On the whole it was a dull crowd, far too many people who were only distinguished enough to be unsure whether others knew they were distinguished at all. The man next to me had explored some buried cities in Honduras, and my other neighbor was shortsighted and thought I was Lady Muriel Spencer, whom he had been talking to over cocktails. Brad was between my mother and the real Muriel; Framm was opposite him between my mother and Baroness Regensburg, who threw a little German at him occasionally. But there was no need; he spoke good English, though with an accent; while as for his appearance, it was nowhere near either my mother's foolery or mine; and that, perhaps, introduces him best, for he was the kind of man it would have been hard to imagine in advance. I had certainly never met anyone who so obviously looked important; you would have stared at him anywhere, if only on account of his large frame and massive, wide-browed head. In age he might have been anything between forty and sixty; the bushy hair was iron-gray, the eyes were blue and keen, the lips sensitive and also sensual. He gave an impression of physical and mental vigor that dominated without effort, and therefore without offense; and his voice had a matching quality that lured the listener from whomever else he was listening to, yet it wasn't loud — there were times when you wondered how you had managed to hear it. I think I was not the only person at that dinner party who was fascinated, but I wished there had been something in him to catch my mother's eye about and smile.

Looking back on that first and only time I ever met Hugo Framm it is tempting to overload the diagnosis; but I do recollect, during dinner, wondering what faults a man like that would have, and deciding they must include vanity (since he had clearly so much to be vain about), and a kind of arrogance, since the continual experience of other people's admiration would give him either that or shyness, and he certainly wasn't shy. Yet these were deductions, not observations; and I cannot say that at any time he was either boastful or overbearing. Whether he was talking to my mother, or to the Baroness, or to Brad, or to the whole table, there was a constant radiation of what, for want of any other word, must be called charm; and in the end it was the constancy of this that seemed to me its only possible drawback. If only one could have caught a glimpse of something beneath the charm; one knew it was there, so there was no taint of superficiality, but one was teased, after a time, by the withholding.

After dinner we sat in the drawing room in changing groups. It was not the sort of party for music, but there was a billiard room across the hall where card tables were set up. A bridge four detached themselves from the main party; they weren't missed and I wasn't aware of it when they returned. It must have been an unsatisfactory game. My father kept moving from group to group, the considerate host, and during one of these movements he found a chance to whisper in my ear that Brad had decided to accept Framm's offer.

"You mean he's only just decided? I thought it was all settled weeks ago."

"Well, no. Apparently he wasn't sure till they talked just now."

"I didn't see them talking much."

"It was after you left the table. They had quite a private chat. Framm has to go back to Vienna tomorrow night and if Brad can make arrangements in time they'll go together."

"*Tomorrow night?*" That came as a shock.

"Yes."

"Isn't that quick work?"

"He won't have much to pack — Brad, I mean. Lives in furnished rooms, doesn't he?"

"I don't know — I've never been there."

"Well, your mother must have — or else he once told me."

"Father, do you really think it's the best thing he can do to go with Professor Framm?"

"Why, don't you like Framm?"

"I think he's very charming, but it does seem rather sudden if Brad only made up his mind tonight and he leaves tomorrow. I hope it's the right thing."

"It's a great chance — if he uses it. Of course if he doesn't use his chances, nothing at all will do him much good. . . . We shall miss him when he's gone — your mother will, I know. . . . By the way, where is she?"

"In the billiard room, I think. There's some bridge going on."

But later I noticed that the bridge players were back in the drawing room, and I also couldn't see Brad anywhere. I was sure people had begun to notice my mother's absence and I ran upstairs to see if she were feeling ill, but there was no trace of her. I could see my father a little preoccupied behind his façade of suavity, and every now and then Hugo Framm's voice would somehow make a silence and then quietly fill it. About eleven o'clock John served more

champagne and I hoped this was not a sign that the party would
continue late, for I was beginning to feel a tension in the atmosphere
— or perhaps it was only in my own mind. About a quarter past
eleven my mother walked into the room with flushed cheeks and
clenched hands. Few actually saw her, but she seemed to look for an
audience from the doorway before speaking out as if to gain one.
"I hope you'll forgive me for being terribly discourteous, but I've
been at the radio — we've got one that picks up New York — it's
the only way you can get the latest about the Simpson case over
here. . . ."

It was a few days before the story broke officially in England,
though the American tabloids and radio were agog with it, and London's informed society was already gossiping. There had been talk
of it at the dinner table, and nobody seemed unwilling to discuss it
again. While this was going on I saw Brad enter the room behind
her. He edged into the crowd and stood by the bookshelves in an
alcove, listening in a detached way and not taking sides in the argument, though I knew he was pro-Simpson. So was my mother — and
never more emphatically, or perhaps I should say more naïvely, than
then. Others differed and there was a lively exchange of views. Suddenly, amidst the chatter, I heard Framm's voice again and saw him
towering above my mother with his large expansive smile, the charm
turned on full.

"I entirely agree with you, Mrs. Waring. There is no reason at all
why your King should not marry whomever he wishes. There are
many precedents for such marriages. Your Queen Mary's own
grandmother was a mere Hungarian countess — Claudine Rhédey,
I think her name was, who married a Duke of Württemberg who
was nephew to the Emperor. And there is, of course, the well-known
example of Mrs. Fitzherbert's marriage to the Prince of Wales who
later became your George IV. Two other direct descendants of
George III were also married morganatically — Prince George to

Louisa Fairbrother, an actress, and the Duke of Sussex to a lady called Cecilia Buggin . . . *Buggin* . . . which is not, I have been told, a very nice-sounding name in English. . . ."

We all gaped at this display of erudition, and I couldn't myself decide whether it proved how thoroughly Framm made himself master of subjects outside his own field, or that he was just a snob. Anyhow, he sounded so authoritative that nobody tackled him from the other side, if there was any other side.

The party broke up soon after that, and Brad left with the rest. I thought it was strange he didn't stay for a more personal good-by when the others had gone, but my father said he was probably hoping to get a lift into town with Framm. "He hasn't much time to spare if he's to catch the evening train tomorrow. It leaves at eight."

I said: "He might have given me the chance to wish him well."

"I'm sure he knows you do. Anyhow, you can telephone tomorrow."

"He's not on the telephone. It's another of the things he can't afford . . . like taxis."

*   *   *

Rain fell during the night, but the next morning there was blue sky and sunlight. I had breakfast before anyone else, then went out for a walk on the Heath. It was more than sunshine there, it was pure radiance. I followed my usual trail, along the Spaniards' Road to Highgate and then down the hill. I kept thinking of Brad and Framm and how odd, in several ways, the previous evening had been.

Suddenly, as I was crossing Parliament Hill Fields, I remembered my father's remark about Brad's furnished rooms and that my mother "must have" been there; if that were so, or even if it weren't, the conclusion leaped at me that there was no reason against my calling on him myself. I also remembered the address from that night of the Byfleets' party when we drove him home and he gave directions to Henry; it was 25 Renshaw Street, off the Camden Road. I found a tram that took me near by. In daylight the street seemed what it mainly was, a slum; but in London appearances can be deceptive; some of those identical houses have declined to different levels, so that they are not always either as bad or as passable as they look. The one Brad lived in had the remains of quality; it was dingy but not dirty; one could have lived in it if one had to. There was a rack of names in the hallway, and the stale smell of cabbage and floor polish that seems to pervade so many London houses whether slums or not. Brad was on the second floor; I climbed to it and tapped on his door. He called "Come in," as if he had left it ready for someone to open.

It wasn't such a bad room, especially in the morning sunshine. The windows were tall and there was a marble mantelpiece surmounting a small gas fire. The furniture was shabby and the whole place littered as one might expect when anyone has a day's notice to pack for abroad. I took in the surroundings first because Brad was in some inner room; he came out fixing his tie. "Well . . ." he exclaimed. "This *is* a surprise. . . ."

I said yes, I imagined it was, and I hoped he didn't mind my having called on him without warning. "I was just taking a walk, it's such a lovely day, I thought I'd drop in to say good-by properly . . . there wasn't a chance last night."

He laughed. "So many things were happening."

I laughed also. "I see you're packing and I know you must be terribly busy . . . but I did want to wish you plenty of fun and success."

"That's nice of you — very nice of you."

I decided I wouldn't stay more than ten minutes, but in the meantime I might as well sit down. When I did so he moved over to the mantelpiece, leaning his back against it and looking as if he didn't know what to say next.

I said: "I'm glad I've seen where you live. These old houses do have big rooms, that's one thing."

"I changed from the set upstairs a few months ago. These are bigger and there's a kitchenette. I couldn't exactly afford the change, but I decided to spend more on luxury. I'm not such an austere devil at heart as some people imagine."

"I wouldn't call it *luxury*."

"Well, of course, *you* wouldn't."

There was a silence then which both of us, I think, kept up deliberately till it was broken by some rather noisy plumbing in another part of the house. He laughed again. "Do you wonder I didn't give any dinner parties here? Impossible place, isn't it?"

"No, I don't think so. You once said all you wanted was to do useful work. Plenty of useful work has been done in rooms like this."

"And you think I've changed since I said that?"

"I don't know. Maybe it's just the mood you're in at the thought of leaving."

He said suddenly: "Let's take a walk."

"*Now?* A walk? But . . . can you . . ." I looked round at the unfinished packing.

"You said it was a lovely day."

"On the Heath, yes, but — "

"Then let's go there."

"Are you sure you've enough time?"

"Yes."

"All right then."

We took a bus up the Hampstead Road, and during the ride he went on talking of his rooms and their amenities so ironically that I began to see less and less point in it. Was he trying to hate the place just to help him over the wrench of departure? I hinted at that, and he answered: "Wait till we start walking and I'll let you into a secret."

We got out at Jack Straw's Castle, then took to the open Heath. "Well?" I asked.

"I'm not going away."

I had a curious instant of relief that surprised me more than he had; then I was shocked.

"You mean you're not leaving for Vienna tonight?"

"I'm not leaving for Vienna . . . at all."

I asked if that meant that the whole arrangement with Framm was canceled.

"Yes . . . or will be when he gets to hear of it."

"You haven't told him yet?"

"I called him at his hotel and they said he wasn't to be disturbed until noon. The prima donna."

"You don't like him?"

"Oh yes — he's great. A genius, if ever there was one."

"But you were packing?"

"Yes . . . until I changed my mind."

"When was that?"

"I didn't look at the clock."

"You just *suddenly* changed your mind?"

"I'd been thinking it over most of the night. I didn't sleep."

"Oh, Brad, I'm so sorry."

"Sorry that I'm not going? That doesn't sound as if I were very popular."

"You know I don't mean that . . . I'm just sorry you've had all this worry. You must have been worried if it kept you awake all night."

"And you're also sorry I've decided to stay here . . . aren't you?"

"Brad, it's no good asking me for an opinion till I know what

62

made you change your mind. Maybe you have a perfectly good reason."

"And what if I haven't? Supposing I just don't want to go? Dammit, I've a right to please myself, haven't I?"

"Of course."

"And to change my mind as many times as I like?"

"Of course."

We walked some way without speaking; then I said: "You should know best. Whatever the reason is, I hope you're right. My father will be disappointed, but that doesn't matter."

"It does, though. He's been very kind to me. You've all been kind." I caught the tremor in his voice and thought how foolish it would be if we both broke down and wept in the middle of Hampstead Heath for no reason that either of us would mention.

"Oh, don't keep on saying that, Brad. My father often helps promising young men — he gets a kick out of it. I don't mean he doesn't genuinely like you, but I wouldn't want you to feel so terribly grateful . . . he enjoys it, just as he enjoyed it while Julian was baiting you the other night."

"Baiting me? . . . *Julian* . . . ?"

"That argument you had — about science and civilization, all that. Julian was trying to break down something you believed in."

"That's what your mother seemed to think."

"Of course a good deal of what he said may be true. It doesn't pay to be too idealistic. You said just now you weren't as austere as some people imagined, and that's a good thing — you used to be *too* austere. But you needn't go to the other extreme."

"Have you any idea what you're talking about?"

"I think I have. Only you don't help me to understand you. Perhaps you don't want me to."

"It isn't that. I'm not sure that I properly understand myself." We walked a few hundred yards, then he took my arm (the first time he had ever done so); he said quietly: "Let's chuck the argument. Do you mind? I told you the secret — nobody knows yet that I'm not going . . . till I can wake the professor. I don't think it'll bother him much, that's one thing."

"The real secret is why you changed your mind."

"You're a persistent child."

"I'm not a child at all, but that would make another argument."

"Yes, let's not have one. Not even a small one, from now on. Change the subject — talk of something else — anything else. . . . It *is* beautiful here, as you said. I didn't somehow expect this sort of weather. Everyone in Dakota knows about London fogs, but this bright cold air. . . . Look at those boys — they're optimists — they've brought sleds . . . or sledges, isn't it?"

"Sledges over here. Sleds in America."

He picked up the topic with grateful artificial enthusiasm. "Lots of words like that, aren't there? Sidewalk, pavement — but in England pavement's called roadway. And of course subway and tube. Though that's not quite right, because there aren't any real tubes in New York. . . . But the oddest of all, I think, is thumbtack and drawing pin. . . . *Drawing pin.* . . . Can you beat that?"

I tried to, and we kept it up till we reached the pond at the top of Heath Street. Then, as we were so near, I felt I wanted to go home. There was nothing else I could say, and nothing at all I could do. I asked him not to see me to the house and we separated at the tube station. "Oh, Brad," I said, as he put coins into the ticket machine, "you don't have to tell me anything you don't want, but I hope you aren't going to make a hash of things."

He gave me an empty look and my arm a final squeeze, then dashed for the elevator . . . lift, my mind checked, just as emptily, as I walked away.

My father had left for the City, John told me; also that my mother was out shopping and would not be in to lunch. So I lunched alone, then went to the library, listened to the radio (wireless), played phonograph (gramophone) records, then got out my history notes and tried to concentrate on Stubbs's Select Charters. It wasn't particularly easy.

My mother came home in time for tea, and I couldn't help thinking how beautiful she looked, with her face flushed from the cold and her hair a little wind-blown. And there was a quality in her eyes, too elusive to describe, but "trancelike" occurred to me even though I had never seen anyone in a trance; a sort of serene observance which, if there is any difference between the words, must be a less active and more ritual thing than observation. She pulled off her gloves with long slow movements, gossiping meanwhile about her shopping and the special shortcakes she had been able to get at Fortnum and Mason's, and the trouble Henry had had to avoid skidding on the slippery roads. "It wasn't really a day for driving — more for taking a walk."

That was my cue, if I had wanted one, to tell her about my own walk on the Heath with Brad and his change of mind about Vienna. But I wondered also if she had deliberately given me the cue, and that made me decide to say nothing. I just watched her, as she poured tea, and thought how close you can be to someone you love, so close that you dare not go closer lest you break that final shell of separateness that is your own as well as the other's precious possession. Dusk came into the room; she went over to the fire to poke it into a blaze, and as she did so, carrying the poker and chattering all the time, she looked like a gay sleepwalker, if there ever has been such a person.

Presently she asked me what I thought of Framm.

I said: "He wasn't a bit funny, as we thought, was he?"

"Darling, nobody is ever funny like that."

"Did Brad listen to the radio with you?"

"Brad? Why?"

"I saw him come in from the hall just after you."

"Perhaps he was in the billiard room." She began to laugh. "I'll ask him if you like."

Ask him? I saw the flush on her face deepen as she caught my eye. She added: "I mean — when I see him — or write to him. Or don't you think I'll ever see him again?"

I said: "It was all settled he should leave London this evening."

"I know, but things sometimes happen at the last minute. A most absurd rush, if you ask me. Why couldn't he have more time? And so close to Christmas. . . . Maybe he just won't go — I wouldn't blame him."

"Framm's leaving tonight too, so it seemed a good idea for them to go together."

"It seemed, *it* seemed. All so impersonal. People are human . . . or don't scientists think so?" She lit a cigarette and offered me her case. Her hand was trembling. "Your father would worry about that."

"You mean your hand trembling?"

"Darling, we really are in two different worlds today. I was cold in the car, I'm still a bit shivery. . . . No, I meant he'd say I oughtn't to encourage you to smoke."

"He lets me have drinks at parties."

"But you don't drink much, I've noticed. I'm very glad."

"I don't smoke much either."

"I know. You don't do anything to excess. And you're truthful and decent and growing up charmingly. Really, I'm very happy about you, Jane."

"I don't always tell *all* the truth."

"Who does?"

"I'd like to be able to, though."

66

"One of these days you'll fall in love, then we'll see."

"See what?"

"Whether you do *that* to excess . . . and also if you tell all the truth about it."

"I wouldn't want to fall *half* in love."

"Wouldn't you? It's pleasanter sometimes."

"Not if you're in love with someone who's in love with you."

"Oh, don't be too sure. That doesn't always make it plain sailing. Or plain telling, either."

John came in with the week-old *New York Times* that had just arrived. It reminded me to ask if there were any definite plans for her return to America with my father.

"We'll spend Christmas here anyway. After that I don't know. New York's impossible in January and February, it simply means going straight to Florida. Harvey likes Florida, of course." Calling my father Harvey was a sure sign she was thinking of something else.

She went on: "Oh Jane, darling, don't bother me for plans. How can one make them so far ahead? Things are all going to pieces, anyhow . . . in Europe . . . everywhere. . . . They're building up for another war."

I said, deliberately: "I wonder how that would affect Brad in Vienna."

"He's an American, he'd be neutral. Of course I know that wouldn't stop him from getting into trouble. You might not think it from the shy manner he has, but he's very impulsive."

"I know that."

"Such a one-idea'd creature. All or nothing. No compromise . . . and sometimes so impractical."

"I know that too."

"But a very delightful person." The cat had followed John into the room and was now curling about our legs. "To give somebody a cat, for instance. I'll never forget John's face when Brad brought it that afternoon. It broke the ice, though. After that we got to be friends quite fast."

"The cat and you?"

"No, darling. Are you still in that other world of yours? The cat and I were friends instantly. Some men take a little longer."

"I was in Ireland."

"So you were. . . . I saw quite a lot of him while you were away. . . . More than when you came back. . . . I don't know why. It's a pity he's so poor . . . poor and proud . . . it's a frightening combination. . . ." The cat purred loudly into the silence that followed. Then John re-entered and some kind of spell was broken. "Mr. Waring just telephoned to say he wouldn't be in to dinner, madame, and he might be late, so please not to wait up for him."

"I certainly shan't — in fact I'll have a snack in my room and go to bed early. I need some rest after last night. . . . What about you, Jane?"

"I'll be all right. I've got work to do, or else I'll find someone to go to a movie with."

"You're not thinking of going to the station to see Brad off?"

"No, of course not — he wouldn't want me."

"It isn't exactly that, but . . ." She didn't know how to finish the sentence, and then I sensed, almost with certainty, that she knew of Brad's change of plan, or at any rate suspected it; and that out of simple affection for me she didn't want me to hang about Victoria Station in the cold, looking for someone who wouldn't turn up. At least I think that was her motive. As I said, you get so close, but the very closeness brings you up against the barrier.

*   *   *

The mail always came to the house early; John used to sort it and bring it to the bedrooms. There was a letter for me the next morning with a London postmark and addressed in a writing I didn't recognize, yet as I tore it open the thought came to me, clairvoyantly if you like, that I had never seen Brad's writing before.

It said: "My dear Jane — " (and he had never called me that before, either — in fact I don't think he had ever called me anything after the first few Miss Warings at the beginning) — "Thank you for coming to see me, and the walk and talk on the Heath. I'm just leaving for the boat train at Victoria to join Hugo Framm — we shall be in Vienna the day after tomorrow. After all, I've a right to change my mind as often as I like, and he needn't know how narrowly I missed the chance of working with him. When I say work, by the way, that's just what I mean, *work*. So don't expect me to write too often, but there's a warm welcome if ever you come to Vienna, as perhaps you might some day — who knows? — In great haste — Brad."

I took the letter downstairs but didn't mention it; not that they would have dreamed of asking to see it, but it might have seemed peculiar if I hadn't offered to let them.

We never talked much at breakfast; my father would read the papers and sometimes make comments on the news; if he didn't, or if we had nothing much to say in reply, nobody thought anybody else was surly.

However, this morning he folded the paper at last and put it by his plate with a gesture I knew meant he was going to read something from it; first of all, though, he spread marmalade on a piece of toast and crunched off a big corner. "Well, well," he said, still crunching, "our friend will be halfway across France by now. . . ."

I looked at my mother.

He went on: "It says here 'Professor Hugo Framm left for the Continent last night accompanied by his young protégé, Dr. Mark Bradley, who will spend some time in the professor's Viennese laboratories. . . .'"

69

My mother put her hand to her face for a moment and when she took it away she had on that glassy smile, as if she were about to say hello to a maharajah.

"I shouldn't have thought it was important enough to put in the paper," she said.

"It wouldn't have been," replied my father, "but for Framm's instinct for publicity. This is how it goes on . . . 'Asked what would be the subject of their work together, Professor Framm replied: "I don't know yet, but Dr. Bradley is an excellent chess player, so I shall certainly put him on to something difficult" ' — Newspapers go for things like that. Incidentally, I didn't know he was a chess player."

I said: "Neither did I."

"Nor I," said my mother.

Then she rang the bell for more coffee.

*   *   *

I have tried to tell all this as it looked to me then; which is perhaps the best way when nothing happened afterwards to make completely certain any of the things that were conjectural at the time. Of course, as I grew older, I balanced the probabilities more maturely; for instance, it seems to me now far less unthinkable that my mother was capable of a love affair. When you are young you tend to feel that things like that can only happen in newspaper cases, and that your own family has some special exemption from frailty; then as you live on, you learn, and what you principally learn is a frailty in yourself that makes you include others for sheer companionship. I know now, looking back on it all, that it was the first major "situation" in which I felt myself involved, and that I was so anxious not to blunder that I tiptoed all around it, deliciously thrilled as well as troubled, whereas nowadays I would probably cut in with a few straight questions to somebody.

And yet I am rather sure that the affair, in any downright sense, never came to anything. Perhaps only because Brad left in time. I think they were both in love, but after the first shyness he may have been more breakneck about it than she, partly from inexperience, but chiefly because my mother had a very realistic valuation of what life could offer; she loved comforts and gaiety and society; I don't believe she would ever have been happy with a poor man in spite of what she said.

I think it possible that after Brad had met Framm at the party and had definitely decided to go to Vienna, she saw him alone and persuaded him against going; that he then asked for some rash showdown, perhaps even suggested her running away with him. Of course she wouldn't consent to that; what she really wanted was for things to go on as they had been, agreeably and perhaps dangerously, with Brad taking her about everywhere and my father an appeased if not entirely deceived spectator. It wouldn't have been heroic, but it was the sort of thing my mother could have carried off with virtuosity, if only Brad had been willing. I would guess that he was not. Yet after the argument between them she probably thought he would change his mind (as he actually did, before he changed it back again), and this gave her that trancelike happiness the next day, that confidence that somehow or other she could always hold him where she wanted and on her own terms. I know she was dumbfounded when he left, and for a time quite shattered.

Had I been a little responsible for his second change of plan? Perhaps. I have often thought that the walk and the talk we had on the Heath may have just tipped the scale.

Neither of them ever discussed it with me afterwards, but three years ago, when my mother was dying from the effects of a motor smash in Texas, my father said something under stress of great emotion. It seemed she had been driving too fast, alone and at night, and the police sergeant who had reached the scene of the accident met us at the airport and told us she had given as an excuse that she was hurrying for a doctor to attend her son who was ill. Of course she may have been half out of her mind when she said this, but I also think it possible that she didn't know how badly she was hurt and was just trying to talk herself out of a traffic summons. It would have been like her.

As we left the hospital when it was all over, my father mumbled: "It was like that with the radio that time. Did you ever try to get America on the set we had in London? . . . You couldn't." I didn't tell him I had known that all along.

*　　*　　*

PART TWO

AGAIN I was in the little room on the twenty-fifth floor with Mr. Small. I was much more aware of my surroundings than on the first occasion; I noticed how the desk between me and him had kick marks on the front and cigarette burns on the top, how dirty the windows were, and how last month (and it was already the eighth of July) had not yet been torn off the pictorial calendar.

"Ah, good morning, Miss Waring." He half rose and bowed; I smiled and sat down as before. He opened his briefcase, riffled through its contents, then found some papers which he laid on the desk. "I was hoping I wouldn't have to bother you again, but something cropped up."

I said it was all right to me, no bother at all. But as a matter of fact it had been; I was leaving New York that night and had many last-minute things to do. I suppose I could have ignored the letter and pretended afterwards that it didn't reach me in time, but I had a curiosity to know what Mr. Small still wanted — indeed, it was more than curiosity, there was a touch of apprehension that had grown since my earlier visit.

Perhaps it was imagination that Mr. Small's manner seemed a little brisker than before, if not actually brusque.

"Miss Waring, according to your statement on March fourteenth, you didn't see Bradley after the year 1936, when you were both in London?"

"I . . . I don't remember saying that."

75

"You don't?"

"Not exactly."

He picked up a sheaf of papers. "Here it is . . . verbatim . . . Question: 'How long since you had any communication with Bradley?' — Answer: 'Oh years. Not since before the war. The English war — 1939.' Question: '1936 being the year you knew him in London?' — Answer: 'That's right. My parents and I returned to America the following year.' Question: 'Did he return to America?' — Answer: 'Not that I know of.' Question: 'At any rate you didn't see him in America?' — Answer: 'No. Never.' . . . Would you like to verify this?" He slid the typewritten sheets across the desk.

"I'm sure it's all right," I said, taking them.

Mr. Small lit a cigarette for himself but did not offer me one this time. "Perhaps it would be a good idea for you to read through the entire transcript. Then you can tell me if there are any answers you wish to withdraw or qualify. And if everything's correct, sign it. You really ought to have done that when you were here before."

I read it, pretending to do so slowly so that I would have more time to think. It was curious and not at all reassuring to note how some of the questions now seemed far more challenging and my own answers far more evasive than I had thought at the time. But I said cheerfully in the end: "Okay. Where do I sign?"

"At the bottom of each page." He handed me a pen.

After that was over he thrust his hands into his trouser pockets and tilted back in the swivel chair. "And now, Miss Waring, what about the time you saw Bradley *after* 1936?"

I had myself under control.

"You did, didn't you?"

"Yes, I did."

"When was it?"

"The next year — 1937."

"The year you said you and your parents returned to America?"

"Yes, but . . ."

"Yes?"

"Nothing."

"Please tell me what you were going to say."

"All right. I was going to say that all the statements I made were actually and literally correct. I *did* return with my parents to America in 1937, but later in the year I went back. And I didn't see Bradley again *in London*. You didn't ask me if I saw him again *anywhere*."

"Wouldn't it have been natural for you to tell me? Unless of course you weren't anxious for me to find out."

"If you'd been anxious to find out you'd have asked me."

"Maybe I was more anxious to find out whether you were being altogether frank."

"I'm not on oath to be frank. I'm on oath to tell the truth — "

" — the whole truth and nothing but the truth," he finished for me. "Have you had a legal training?"

"No."

"Then you probably aren't aware of the narrow difference between *suggestio falsi* and *suppressio veri*."

I was but I chose not to say so. Either he didn't think writers knew much or else he didn't know I was a writer; the first might have been less personally unflattering, yet I hoped it was the latter because I could excuse him more easily.

He went on: "Well, no need to argue. Perhaps I can save time by referring to a few notes I have." He consulted them. "I see you were in Vienna in 1937. Bradley was also in Vienna then. . . . Now let's begin from there, shall we?"

I tried to absorb the shock and perhaps succeeded. "Certainly. There's no secret about any of it. But I still don't like your saying it would have been natural for me to volunteer information. It isn't as if we'd both been having a friendly chat."

That was a mistake. He said: "If you'd rather chat than answer questions, do so by all means. Chat about the time you met Bradley in Vienna."

But of course it was next to impossible with that shorthand girl at my elbow; the words fizzled out like a car stalling; I had to press the starter again and again. Finally came the full stop, then silence. I think all I said was: "My father was in Europe on business — I was with him — he had to pass through Vienna, and while I was there I naturally took the opportunity to look up an old friend. He was working in some laboratory. We only met for an hour or so."

"What work was he doing in this laboratory?"

"I don't know exactly. Probably the same sort of thing he did in London . . . physics . . . mathematics . . . whatever it was."

The second full stop. Presently: "Did you meet any of his friends in Vienna?"

"No."

"Do you think he liked working there?"

"He seemed to."

"Did he speak German?"

"Not very well."

"How do you think he got on with the people he was working with?"

"I don't know. I expect if you work in a laboratory you have to get on with the others or else quit."

"He didn't take you to visit the laboratory?"

"No."

"Or suggest it?"

"No. There wasn't time, anyway."

"Where was he living?"

"In rooms. Somewhere near the East Station, I believe. I didn't go there."

"Was he very busy?"

"I imagine so."

"And so far as you could judge he was satisfied with his position?"

"Oh yes."

"Would you say it was a better job than the one he had had in London?"

"He said it gave him more time for research, which was what he wanted to do."

"I understand the London University people were sorry to let him go. Did you know that?"

"No, but it doesn't surprise me."

"Did he ever complain that he didn't get enough time for research in London?"

"He never complained of anything. Not to me."

"So you can't think of any particular reason why he might have preferred the Vienna job?"

"Perhaps he wanted a change of scene, but that's only a guess."

"I'd rather you tell me what you *know.*"

"But I *don't* know. It's so many years ago, for one thing."

He looked me over in a way I didn't quite like. "*Eight* years ago. So that trip to Vienna doesn't stand out very importantly in your life?"

"Hardly. My father and I were only there a couple of days."

"But what about the *next* visit . . . in 1938?"

I don't think I succeeded in disguising much of the shock then. I said, when I was ready: "So you know about that too?"

He made a grimace that was almost a smirk. "You bet. But you'd have gotten around to chatting about it sooner or later, I'm sure."

I decided to be brazen. "No, perhaps I wouldn't. I can't see the reason for all this questioning. I'm the sort of person you'd get far more out of if you'd tell me what it's all for. And also where Bradley is now."

79

He began doodling on a scratch pad. "I don't think you quite appreciate your position, Miss Waring. . . . However, we might as well call a halt for this afternoon." He signaled to the shorthand girl, who thereupon closed her book and crossed the room to a typing table. "Have Miss Waring sign that before she leaves."

He got up, concentrated his glance on my left thigh, and said: "Going away, then?"

I looked down and saw that the airline envelope containing my ticket was sticking halfway out of my coat pocket. Perhaps he thought it proved how honest I was, for when I merely said "Yes" he didn't ask me where I was going or seem particularly interested. He shook hands with me before he went out.

That girl took half an hour to do the job. She was so slow I was tempted to offer to do it myself except that I knew she wouldn't let me. I smoked and chafed at the delay and read the only literature lying loose in the office — a 1945 *World Almanac* and a book called *This Man Truman* which was all about that man Truman.

*   *   *

It's partly a wartime neurosis, maybe, the feeling that Uncle Sam is always stern and monitory, and that any of his official inquiries can only be directed towards somebody's undoing. But it's also an American (and for that matter a British) tradition that you do not have to be afraid of your own government if you have done no wrong. Thus, as I left Mr. Small's office for the second time, I realized how unco-operative I had been again, but I was not in the least scared on my own account — though that may partly have been due to a family background of wealth and security. When I was a child it really mattered to be a Waring, and I was fortunately grown-up before I realized it could also be a handicap.

I was, however, a little bit scared on account of Brad. That he had got himself in a jam of some sort seemed obvious, and I wanted to help him, whatever it was, but without exactly perjuring myself. Of course if he turned out to be guilty of something serious my attitude might have to change, but so far I hadn't been allowed to discover anything. This gave me a sort of alibi; even if Brad *were* guilty of anything serious I could give him every benefit of every doubt so long as I was myself kept in these doubts.

Throughout the plane journey to California that night I kept turning over question and answer in my mind. I wondered if I had been merely cautious, or so *over*cautious that I had actually made things worse. How much did Mr. Small already know about Brad in Vienna? . . . I tried to sleep, and between Chicago and Kansas City succeeded; but after that the climb to high altitude wakened me and I stared for miles out of the window. We were flying through cloud, and all I could see was a part of the wing, shimmering like a silk dress with silver buttons; there must have been a moon, but the effect was of pale air, infinite, shadowless. Gradually I dozed off again, and then Vienna came back to me, eager to be remembered, over the wastelands of New Mexico.

*   *   *

I went there with my father in the summer of '37. Earlier in the year I had returned to London after a short trip to America, and had failed to pass the examination that was the first step to a history degree. I don't know quite why, beyond the obvious reason that I didn't get enough marks; I had studied fairly hard, and am not exactly stupid, but perhaps I am also not a good examinee — if a question interests me, I spend too much time on it, so that I have to rush through some of the others. The only relevance my failure has here is the effect it had on my father; it made him just slightly aloof, as if I had told him a risqué story he had heard before. My mother's attitude (by letter) was to ignore the whole thing completely. She had lost her interest in educational attainments since

Brad's departure, and I never heard that she ever attended a physics lecture again.

My father's business would take him to several European countries, so he picked me up in London when term ended and we made a tour that included Paris, Berlin, and Rome. We flew most of the way, were given parties and receptions, and met various people of political and financial importance. Being the first time I had traveled alone with him as a social equal, it proved an exciting experience for a nineteen-year-old. In Rome he learned he would have to go to Budapest, and only this chance put Vienna on our itinerary. We stayed a night at the Bristol, and after some trouble the next morning I managed to telephone Brad at his laboratory and ask him over to lunch. His voice was calmer than mine and he told me he couldn't ever lunch so far from his work, because it would take up more than the hour he permitted himself, but if we cared to sample a local restaurant he would be pleased to entertain both of us.

This sounded chilly, and when in due course I saw the place I was glad my father had excused himself at the last moment. It was a pavement café on the Mariahilfer Strasse, crowded and rather dingy, the outside tables occupied by unshaven furtive men who looked as if they were plotting revolution but were probably only watching for some girl. Brad waved from an inner table as I entered; he seemed well enough at home there. He was cordial, rather detached, and said he was sorry my father couldn't come, sorry also our stay was so short (I had told him on the telephone we were leaving for Budapest that afternoon), and sorry especially about the hour limit for lunch. It was some scientific equipment that had to be constantly tended, otherwise of course he could and would have got away for longer. The explanation took the sting out of his behavior, and I gave him a look that told myself that I still liked him. Then the proprietor came up with a greasy typewritten menu, everything very cheap, and I realized how far Brad had developed from the shy boy who had timidly asked me to suggest some expensive London hotel where he could wine and dine my parents in the style to which they were accustomed. Obviously now he took the view that what was good enough for him was good enough for anybody, and on the whole I approved the change, though it would doubtless show itself truculently till he got used to it. He seemed much more than six months older to me, but that again was likable; it gave the impression of an adult process, a maturing of personality, nothing to cause worry about what had "happened" to him. I commented that he did not drink or smoke, but he said he did sometimes, an occasional cigarette or glass of beer. "And it's uncommonly good beer in Vienna," he assured me, as if he had been a connoisseur of beer in many other cities; it was almost reassuring to find that his naïveté, though disappearing, was still there in patches.

The food was not bad for its price, and I noticed that he got special attention from the waitress who served us and who talked to him familiarly in German. His own replies were halting, and he said he made a point of practicing on her as much as possible, because textbook German, which he could read quite well, was so heavy and uncolloquial.

All in all, he looked settled and by no means unhappy, and after what had been in my mind as a possibility I was much relieved. He also said, when I asked, that his work was making progress, though of course it had so far hardly more than begun.

"And how do you like Framm?"

"He's remarkable. His sort of mathematics is beyond anything I could have dreamed of."

"So he's teaching you?"

"He's giving me time to learn. He has to, before I can be of any use to him. It's like a new language — in fact, that's what it really is."

"And what about him being of use to you?"

"Naturally that goes with it. I can't ever be grateful enough to your father for giving me such a chance."

"You still haven't told me how you like him, though. Framm, I mean."

"He can be very charming."

"But do you *like* him?"

"Well enough. And it wouldn't matter if I didn't. He's the sort of man you don't have to like."

I said I didn't know what kind of man that was.

He laughed and said: "All women like him, anyhow."

"That's still not an answer."

"All right . . . let's change the subject. How's Hampstead?"

"Fine. . . . Do you still manage to get your long Sunday walks?"

"I've been to the Semmering several times. That's not far away. Very beautiful country."

"And altogether you're quite happy in Vienna?"

"Oh yes."

"Well, that's fine too." We sat over coffee and I told him about my failure to pass the examination. He sympathized. "But you'll try again next year?"

"If I'm still in London. I don't have any exact plans. I'm beginning to think I'd like to earn a living."

"How?"

"That's the trouble. Journalism maybe. I'd like to get on a paper but the fact that my father controls one inhibits me. I've a feeling I'd either be favored or else never be given credit even if I deserved any. Perhaps I could change my name."

"The easiest way to do that would be to get married." It was the sort of remark he couldn't possibly have made a year before, but there was still naïveté in it — a small boy's approach to intimacy.

I said: "Yes, if there were anyone I *wanted* to marry."

"Isn't there?"

"Not at present. . . . What about you? Any nice *Fräuleins?*"

"Plenty, if I had time for them." But he said it now with a smile, and felt the need to add: "I'm serious — I *don't* have the time. I work ten hours a day as a rule."

"And then go home and dream mathematics?"

"Often."

He looked at his watch, paid the check, and signaled a taxi for me on the pavement outside. "Where do you live?" I asked, detaining him.

"Near the East Station. About the same kind of place I had in London, but the plumbing makes a different kind of noise. A Viennese noise."

"That ought to be quite musical."

He laughed. "You could come and hear it if you were staying longer, but since you're leaving today — "

"Yes, it's too bad. I wish I weren't, but this is just a flying visit — literally. I must try to manage another trip."

"And your mother — she's not with you?"

"No, she's in Maine. I don't think she'll get across this year — she probably thinks she owes America a summer."

"Well, remember me to your father."

"Of course. And you remember me to the charming Professor."

"I will. . . . And have a good time in Budapest. I've not been there, but they say it's well worth seeing."

"I'll let you know," I cried, out of the taxi window. "Good-by. . . ."

* * *

I did let him know, in a chatty letter, which rather to my surprise he answered, and for the next six months we corresponded fairly regularly, though at longer intervals. They weren't interesting letters, except one. He usually mentioned the weather, any particular walk he had taken, the fact that he was still very busy, and his progress with German. No reference ever to theaters or concerts or operas. He might have been living in a village instead of one of the world's gayest capitals. Actually he had reverted to the sort of life he had had before meeting my mother, except that the background was different and he himself stood bigger in the foreground. But once he wrote, quite exceptionally and rather astonishingly:

Scientists in movies and magazine ads are always shown examining test tubes as if on the brink of some great discovery, but I guess the outside world doesn't know how rarely one ever discovers anything, the road to the frontier is already so long and difficult, and when you get there you feel rather lonely and undramatic like someone who finds himself off the trail on a mountain at night, with just a small flashlight and an average amount of nerve. I can't push the metaphor any further because the mountaineer only wants to find the trail again, whereas the scientist wants—well, what *does* he want? (You remember that argument with Julian Spee?) Anyhow, if he gets it, even the smallest fragment of it, then there comes a moment of sheer exhilaration comparable, I suppose, to what an artist feels when he knows he's done something good. Next comes the doubting period, the check and countercheck, and—as often as not—the disappointment. It wasn't new after all. Or else it wasn't true. And the reason I'm writing all this is that today, I think for the first time, I've had that exhilaration without, so far, the disappointment. Of course that may come tomorrow. It's just a few lines of equations—a trifle, most people would think, to get so excited about. But if it stands up after all the tests it will get, especially from Framm, then I'm an inch or so into the unknown. That's all. I didn't feel like celebrating at first, but I went into the streets for a breath of fresh air, and the sight of all the people concerned with other things—chiefly politics, these days—made me feel aloof and rather pitying, until I realized how they'd pity me if they knew the hours I work and what sort of a life I have. So I turned into that little restaurant we had lunch at and drank a couple of beers. There happened to be a man there who likes chess, and we played till two A.M., which was about an hour ago, and that's the full extent of my celebration. Not very thrilling, perhaps?

. . . Perhaps not, but I still think those beers had something to do with his sending me such a letter. He never wrote like that again, and incidentally, it was the only time he ever mentioned Framm.

*   *   *

Later that year, 1937, our correspondence seemed to peter out, probably my fault as much as his. I didn't try for my examination a second time, because I hankered more and more after a journalist's life; what I really wanted was to travel and write about what I saw, especially the political and economic side of things; but here again I was up against the curious obstacle of my name. As this is not my family's story, or even primarily my own, I can pass over the matter briefly. My father has acquired that basic unpopularity in public life which comes of personifying the wrong kind of myth for his age. A century ago he might have been held as a model for American boyhood; a century hence historians may give him his due, which won't be overwhelming, but may well be adjusted to the realization that he was no worse than others whose reputations now stand higher. I think he knows all this, and it makes him grateful for chance encounters on trains and park benches where people listen to what he says because they don't know who he is. He once called himself the Forgotten Man whom everybody remembers, and another time he said he hadn't only backed the wrong horse, he *was* the wrong horse. Anyhow, it's ironical that I got my first job from people who were anxious to please him, and was fired because the stuff I wrote didn't show any similar anxiety on my own part. Then I tried the people who weren't anxious to please him, but mostly they weren't anxious to please me either, because I was his daughter.

However, I had money, so I traveled on my own, writing what I liked, sometimes getting it into print, mostly not. I suppose I was too young even to expect to free-lance successfully, but I didn't feel I was; one never does, at the time, though since then I have thought there was a certain impertinence in a girl barely twenty bombarding editors with articles about the state of the world. I did, however, discover by experience that my reporting was preferred to my opinions, so I wisely concentrated on the former, and tried to be where reportable events were happening. This was the main reason I arrived in Vienna in the early part of 1938. The political kettle there was coming to the boil, and all the signs were that Hitler would make *Anschluss* with Austria the first big test of his rising power.

I wrote to Brad ahead of my arrival, announcing it and giving details. Because the weather was unsuitable for flying I traveled from Paris by train through the Arlberg. I thought it just barely possible he might be on the platform at the West Station to meet me, and when I couldn't see him I had a cup of coffee at the station restaurant in case he came late and would look for me. While I was there, with my small suitcase and a portable typewriter on the floor near by, I noticed that a young woman was eying them, as I thought, suspiciously. Then she came over and asked me, in quite good English, if I were Miss Waring.

That name has so often heralded me badly into fresh company and new places, I've almost developed a suppression complex about it.

I answered rather rudely: "What do you want to know for?"

She said: "I'm Mrs. Bradley. He sent me here to meet you."

I pulled the luggage aside and made her sit down and ordered more coffee, all to gain time while I came to terms with any emotion in me that would follow the shock. It didn't prove to be too much, or at any rate whatever it was surrendered to discipline. But the shock lingered; I kept looking at her, trying to make my glance less scrutinizing; in the end I decided to be frank. I said: "You must excuse me for staring — I've known Brad off and on for several years — I always hoped he'd marry someone nice, and already I'm thinking he has."

She smiled a quiet, composed smile, as if she liked the compliment, but was not going to be overwhelmed by it. No doubt she was just as curious about me, as any wife is about her husband's premarital girl-friends, but I was slightly piqued that she was able to conceal it so well; I envied her the achievement, knowing how incapable I was of matching it. She was attractive, and the more so after you decided she was; you could then evaluate her good features, dark timid-looking eyes, clear complexion, and exceptionally small and beautiful hands.

I reached for one of them and pressed it. She kept on smiling. Then, because I felt my emotion again needed disciplining, I flagged the waiter. "Let's go . . . and while we're in the cab, tell me about him. How *is* he? I suppose he was too busy to come himself, so he sent you. . . . I'm glad — it was a lovely surprise. . . . I'm so happy about it . . . but *tell* me about him. . . ."

"He's ill," she said, as we left the table. "That's why he sent me."

"*Ill?*"

"Oh, nothing serious — just a high temperature. I thought he ought not to go out."

"Of course. Quite right. And you mustn't let me bother him, if you think I oughtn't. . . . Perhaps it would be better if I saw him in the morning?"

"No. He sent me. He expects you."

There was something both dutiful and inexorable in that.

During the taxi journey we discussed Vienna and general affairs, and probably I began talking as freely as I might have done in London or New York, for she interrupted: "It is best not to talk politics outside."

89

"*Outside?*" There was no one who could have heard except possibly the taxi driver.

"It is better to be careful," she answered. "Especially when you mention names."

We drove along the boulevards and even though I had seen so little of the city on my first visit I had an impression of deterioration. People looked tired, peevish, strained; there were many signs of poverty and unemployment. Soon I became aware that the taxi driver *was* listening, so I talked trivialities for the rest of the journey. When he pulled up at the address he carried my luggage across the pavement with almost excessive cordiality and gave a sketchy version of the Nazi salute.

"Evidently he didn't understand English," I said when he had driven off.

She answered judicially: "One cannot be sure. He may have."

"Then why would he be so polite after what I said about Hitler?"

"He would know you are foreign and that might make him wish to be polite so that you could go back to your country and say the Nazis are all right in Austria because the taximen are so polite. Like the trains in Italy that run on time. So many foreigners are impressed by things like that. But of course I know you are too sensible. You will soon get underneath the surface of things, and then you will realize how careful one has to be."

I think I did realize that, fairly soon, but it led me into a misunderstanding about Pauli that wasn't cleared up until she, being careful herself, trusted me sufficiently.

*　　*　　*

No doubt he was bound to look a little different. He was sitting in an armchair under a reading lamp, and that gave him a look of thinness and pallor that wasn't real. He seemed quite genuinely pleased to see me — much more than when we had met a year earlier at that restaurant. But the brightness of his eyes was probably due to temperature, I told myself cautiously. I rallied him about being ill — I said I had always thought he enjoyed the sort of health that is called rude. He said yes, that was true in the main, and he had been perfectly well till a couple of days ago, when he had caught a chill. His temperature had been at one time as high as a hundred and three, but was now down to ninety-nine point five, which showed that he was almost better.

While we talked, just chatting about this and that, Pauli moved about the small apartment with the quiet efficiency I was beginning to expect in all that she did. Presently there was a meal on the table, nicely served and well cooked. Yet it didn't give an impression of being specially achieved for my benefit. I noticed too that everything was neat and homelike and spotlessly clean, though there were no elegancies and nothing that showed any sign of money to spare. It was not a place one would have chosen to live in, however austerely, if one could have afforded something a bit better. Every city has its prevalent smell, and this apartment had the Vienna smell at full strength — a mixture of coffee, bread baking, paprika, and drains. There was nothing anyone could do except to learn to tolerate it.

"Well?" Brad said, when Pauli was in the kitchen.

"She's lovely," I answered. "I think you're very fortunate."

"You bet I am. . . . She's quite a scientist, too — used to work in the laboratory with me — that's how we met. She also taught me German. I taught her English. We have a rule that we speak nothing but English and German every other day, but today we broke it — in your honor."

"You shouldn't have. I can speak German fairly well too."

"How fortunate," said Pauli, coming into the room with a plate of pastries. "It will enable you to study the political situation, which is what I understand you have come here for." (I suppose Brad had shown her my letter.)

Brad yawned. "That's a signal for me to go to bed. *Politics.* Vienna's leading industry nowadays. Where I come from they have a big dose every four years, but here it keeps on all the time. . . . Good night, Jane. You'll get all the politics you want from Pauli."

He called me Jane so easily now. And he had also said "where I come from" as if I weren't American also.

Pauli said she thought it best for him to go to bed early, because of his temperature. I said I wouldn't stay long myself, but she begged me not to leave immediately. "All right," I agreed, "provided we skip politics. I'd much rather talk about you . . . and Brad."

"So would I," she answered, smiling that same composed smile. "So you call him Brad? . . . *I* call him Mark."

"Sounds reasonable. His name *is* Mark." And then, for no reason I could think of, I added: "It was my mother who started calling him Brad."

"Oh yes? . . . He was once in love with her, wasn't he?"

"*Was* he?"

"He told me so. I think it is lucky when the first woman a young man falls in love with is someone very charming and much older than himself whom he knows he cannot marry because she is already quite happily married."

Well, I thought, if that's what he told you, or how you look at it, fine.

She went on, still smiling: "So you see I am not a bit jealous. Mark and I are very happy."

"I'm sure you are."

It seemed to me she was laying a foundation on which we could be friendly, and that the only difference in our attitudes was that I was prepared to be friendly without any foundation at all.

I said: "Brad told me you worked with him in the laboratory."

"Oh yes, but *for* him, not *with* him." A sort of proud humility in that. "He is going to be a very great scientist, did you know?"

"Scientist or mathematician, which is it?"

"The one includes the other, in his case. Of course the work he does is far beyond me now, but it is still possible for me to save some of his time. I type out all his notes."

"That must be a help. And incidentally, you speak excellent English, and you cook so beautifully. . . ."

"I am glad you think so. You must come here as much as you can during your stay."

"If Brad doesn't mind. He might. I was just a friend, that's all."

"I know. He doesn't have any *close* friends. But you were the nearest to it."

Had I been? It would have been more thrilling to learn it less retrospectively.

She went on: "He used to take walks with you, he said. If you have time, when his chill is better, I wish you would do that with him here . . . some Sunday. That is one of the things I cannot do, owing to a lack of strength." A slight accent and an occasional phrase like that were the only signs that her English was studied. Brad had done his job well.

I told her I'd be very glad to, if Brad asked me.

"I will suggest it," she answered, with that same touch of inexorableness matching the humility. "He needs the recreation. He works too hard. Far too hard."

"Professor Framm must be a bit of a slave driver," I commented.

"I would not say he is to blame," she replied, in a curiously guarded way. "It is Mark's own desire to work that drives him."

"Of course," I agreed. "He always was like that."

"But now he is more like that than ever. And if it goes on, I am afraid there will be a disaster." She then told me that since he had come to Vienna two years before he had had no time off except

Sundays, and often even then he worked at home. "It is true of course that we could not afford a holiday," she added, as if anxious to be fair.

"Doesn't Framm pay enough?"

But she wouldn't admit that either. "In Austria, unfortunately, there is very little money."

"Nor is there anywhere — for anything educational. Even in America, which is supposed to be rich, teachers are the worst paid of all the professions."

"Ah, but in America . . ." I have so often heard those words spoken by Europeans, and nearly always with the sentence unfinished. It is as if the words stopped short at the beginning of the dream.

I left soon after that, telling her I'd use my influence, which wasn't much, and my walking capacity, which was considerable, to make Brad give himself a day in the fresh air. She took me to a corner where I could find a cab. There was a parade passing the end of the street, with banners, uniforms, and scattered raucous shouting. "This is a district where there is sometimes trouble," she said — not nervously, but with a certain watchfulness.

*   *   *

He said he was too busy to take a full day off, but I had him and Pauli to dinner at my hotel several times, and one Sunday, after I had called at his apartment after lunch, he and I took a tram to the center of the city and walked in the Burggarten. There seemed little reason why Pauli should not have come with us, but she said she had his notes to type and that was that. She was the sort of person who makes up her mind, and I wondered whether she had at some exact moment made up her mind to marry Brad. That she loved him and would devote herself to him was obvious, but whether in all things he liked to be managed quite so efficiently I also wondered.

There had been rioting in the streets that morning, with many casualties and arrests, yet the open-air orchestra in the Burggarten was playing the overture to *Egmont* according to advertised schedule, and a throng of all ages and classes listened intently. The music seemed to make a little island of truce in the ocean of political turbulence; one did not feel that listeners were indifferent to the political issue, but — much more wonderfully — that for an hour or so they were putting it aside. I was impressed by students who followed the score from large folios, and by the shocked glances turned on someone who struck a match. All this could not have happened in Hyde Park or in Central Park, I thought, but neither could the marchings and countermarchings in which many of these listeners would take part when the truce was over. There was something both frantic and pitiable about the whole Viennese situation, and as we moved away from the crowd when the overture ended I gave Brad a cue to talk about it.

But he had little to say. Politics was not in his line. He had a typical American phobia for foreign issues; his view of Europe as a group of squabbling states with no Washington (the city, not the man) had that large simplicity that was, at root, pure Dakota — a rationalization of the farmer's exasperation with distant city-bred troubles. But in addition to that, he had taken refuge in the scientist's ivory tower, much higher and less accessible than artists had ever had. He said he did not like the Nazis any more than I did, but he thought the basic idea of *Anschluss* was sound economically, except that it was far too fragmentary — there should really be an *Anschluss* of all western Europe, though not under German dictatorship. Such a large concept was doubtless impractical, but that, after all, was the fault of the politicians who made it so and of the peoples who elected the politicians. As far as Vienna was concerned, he hoped that the Nazis would not come into power, but if they did, he hoped they would stop the disorders in the city; that at least would confer a benefit. "Anyhow," he ended, "I'm not a politician. I don't pretend to know much about the various methods of hoodwinking the electorate."

"And to you it's all nothing more than that?"

He smiled as if my seriousness required a concession. "Perhaps it's a bit in my bones to feel that way. I had an uncle I was very fond of as a child because he was a bit of an amateur geologist and I used to think he knew everything. As I was at the age when I wanted to know everything too, I asked him once what had formed North Dakota — I meant geologically. He answered 'The Republican Party, because they wanted two extra seats in the Senate.' I puzzled a lot over that answer then, and politics still puzzles me. Whenever I hear a hot political argument I feel I'm eavesdropping in somebody else's world."

"You once said the aim of science was to save the world. You can't do that if you don't know what to save it from."

"From politics, maybe — or from itself." He laughed, then looked embarrassed. "Did I really say that about saving the world?"

"You did. One night at the Hampstead house when Julian Spee came in after dinner."

" 'M, I remember. No wonder he asked me if I wouldn't feel better in a pulpit than a laboratory. But even he didn't go so far as to suggest a political career. . . . By the way, what happened to Julian?"

"He's still doing quite well . . . but I'd rather talk about what's happened to you. So you don't think any more that science could save the world?"

"I don't know what you mean exactly."

"Whatever *you* meant that night."

96

"Probably I was thinking of mere technics."

"What's that?"

"Oh . . . crop management, reforestation, sanitation, health and welfare . . . that sort of thing."

"Nothing very mere about it."

"True — and I expect there *are* a hundred men in the world today — most of them names one hasn't heard of — who could blueprint a paradise on earth and organize it into existence . . . provided everyone else would take orders from them for a few generations. But what chance is there of that?"

"Sounds like a good idea."

"It would be, until the politicians got hold of it. Then you'd see some changes made. Where would *they* be without the vested interests that make and duplicate their own jobs?"

"So you'd require science to stage a world-wide revolution as a first step?"

"That's a big order too. There's supposed to be a science of revolution, but I never heard of any scientist who was interested in it — only the politicians, for their own ends. Where are we, then, after all this argument? We agree that the world needs saving, and that's as far as we get."

"We also agree that the world could save itself by letting scientists save it if they *would* save it."

"Maybe the world doesn't want to save itself. It often behaves as if it didn't. Anyhow, until it makes up its mind, science has enough to do to follow its own natural aim — which is to discover truth simply because it *is* truth."

"Curiosity, Julian called it."

"Yes — to an outsider it might look like that."

"And I love that word 'outsider.' It fits in perfectly with the ivory tower."

"If you knew us better you wouldn't think so badly of us."

"You put yourselves on a pedestal."

"If we do, it only makes us a better target. The politicians all hate us. They're also a bit afraid of what we might do someday — so they label as well as libel us whenever they can. Bolshevik science, Germanic science, Jewish science — you hear plenty of that sort of nonsense nowadays in Vienna."

"Tell me about your work."

"You mean my own work — at Framm's laboratory?"

"Yes. Or is it private?"

"Of course not — nothing's private. But I think you'd find it a bit dull if I went into details. To put it vaguely, we're trying to find what the world's really made of — what makes it go. . . ."

"And where it's going?"

"Yes, that's all included."

"I suppose it's silly to ask if you've had any luck yet."

He smiled. "We've got a few ideas, but they can't be expressed outside the language of mathematics."

"I see. Not much good to the man in the street."

"None at all. I know that sounds superior, but I can't help it. From an everyday standpoint it certainly isn't of any immediate practical importance."

"You say 'we.' Do you mean yourself and Framm?"

"Well no, that would be flattering myself — *yet*. I should have said *they* — meaning a few investigators scattered about the world who don't think a century or so's too far to look ahead. They keep in touch. They exchange results through articles in scientific journals. They don't bother about frontiers or nationalities. Even wars don't interrupt them. During the last war, for instance, Einstein put out his general theory, and certain proofs of it required astronomical observations that could only be made on a certain date from a certain place in the Atlantic Ocean. British scientists wanted to make these observations, and I've been told that the German Navy was contacted and agreed not to torpedo the ship. As it happened, the war was over before the specified date, but the idea of pure science as something above and beyond ordinary affairs had survived a pretty good test. . . . Of course the whole thing had to be kept dark. Neither the British nor the German public in wartime could have endured the thought of anything international quietly going about its business as if all the nonsense weren't happening."

"Do you and Framm work together?"

"We have our separate angles of research, but they overlap somewhat the further one gets."

"And your own angle . . . is it coming along well?"

His voice became slightly excited. "Yes, I'd say it is. That's why I've been working my head off lately. I'm beginning to feel I'm *near* something. . . . Remember that letter I once wrote you? Well, it's like that again, only the whole thing's bigger. Perhaps soon I'll be ready to publish something. Of course it won't make any headlines."

"I'm sure it will make one person very happy."

"Who — me?"

"Actually it was Pauli I was thinking of."

"Oh, sure — and she'll deserve it after the way I've been neglecting her lately. We could take a holiday somewhere — go on a real spree. You might not think it, but she can be very gay at times."

"Thanks for telling me she's human."

"And I'm not — is that what you mean?"

"No, I think you're *very* human, but you sometimes don't like people to know it. . . . Why didn't you write to me about your marriage?"

He thought a moment, then said: "I'm wondering why myself. Maybe it was because of a talk your mother and I once had — that time she came to tea at my lab. I was so emphatic in saying I'd never marry, so I suppose I thought it would make me out a fool when I did . . . though she's probably forgotten the whole thing long ago. . . . Where is she, by the way?"

"In New York."

"She doesn't come to England for the summers any more?"

"She didn't last year and she probably won't this year."

"What's happened to the house at Hampstead?"

"The painter died and the place was sold. My father didn't know till too late, or he'd have bought it."

"Is he in New York too?"

"I think he's in Paris at present. We don't keep exact track of each other's movements."

We walked on, through the park to the boulevards. One could feel the rise of tension like a physical change in the atmosphere, and on the tram there was some sort of row in progress that we couldn't exactly diagnose — at one moment it sounded political, then it turned domestic and seemed to be concerned with the rival relationships of two women and a man. It went on, intermittently, till we got out, by which time it was political again; and I suppose many rows were like that, personal animosities fanned by and fanning a rising flame.

Pauli had finished typing when we reached the apartment. Brad seemed anxious to go over what she had done; he gathered up the script and went into the bedroom to be alone. Pauli then made coffee and talked. She was genuinely pleased that I had been able to persuade Brad to take even a few hours' recreation, and I felt she had at last decided I was really a friend and to be trusted. We discussed the crowds in the park and the incident on the tram. Till then I had assumed, doubtless because she was always urging me to be "careful," that she was nothing but that herself — and especially careful to avoid taking sides. I did not blame her, though I had made no secret of my own feelings. But now she told me how warmly and bitterly she shared them. It surprised me; I had not suspected such partisanship, and I was even more surprised at the effort she must have made to avoid disclosing it before. "One has to be careful," she said again. "It was not that I did not think you were sincere. But you are American — you are so used to saying anything you like — anywhere — as you did in the taxi when we first met. I have waited till you learned a little."

"I'm glad you think I have, but really, I was always able to keep a secret — even in America."

"In America surely there can be no secrets like ours."

"Not quite like yours. But we have our own."

"At least there can be no work for the *agent provocateur*." She looked all at once conspiratorial, with a darting glance to the doorway as if to confirm that the handle wasn't being slowly turned; and I reflected then, as I have often done, how in moments of complete sincerity yet of rather unusual tension, so many people adopt the attitudes and gestures they have seen on the stage. The phrase *agent provocateur* seemed to have touched off a series of them; presently she became once more her normal undemonstrative self. "We live in peculiar times," she said, with apologetic triteness.

"Yes, indeed."

"How is your study of the situation progressing?"

"It's not exactly a study. I'm just looking round and sizing things up."

"And writing articles for American newspapers?"

"Yes, a few. They don't always take them."

"I read one. I thought it very good."

This startled me because she couldn't possibly have seen any in print; she added, perhaps interpreting my look: "It was one evening we dined at your hotel and I went up to your room afterwards. There was a piece of typing in your machine and I could not help seeing it was an article for a newspaper."

True, and I could imagine myself doing the same thing in somebody else's room, only I doubt if I would have admitted it afterwards. Perhaps this also she read in my face, for she went on: "I wanted to tell you . . . I wanted to tell you how much I liked it . . . and also to warn you not to leave things like that where anyone going into your room can read them. . . . But I did not know you well enough then."

"Well, you do now, thank goodness — and as for leaving papers about, I'm careful not to do it any more."

"You are wise. Though of course it will be known what you have written. The Nazis soon learn who their friends are."

"But we don't always learn who the Nazis are."

She gave me a shrewd glance. "I think you understand things very well. It is a state of mind, to begin with. Even in the educational and scientific world you meet with it." She waited a moment, then said: "Professor Framm, for instance."

"Oh? Is he one of them? Secretly, I suppose?"

"I think today he does not mind so much if people suspect it."

"Does Brad know?"

"Of course. But he says they never discuss politics."

"So they get along?"

"I would not say they are friends. But doubtless they respect each other — as scientists."

"I'm not sure that would be enough for me. Or for you either."

"That is so. . . . And I am worried about the position Mark is in. It becomes more difficult every day. There have already been riots in the university. The students are divided, so are the professors. It is a grave problem."

"What do you think he should do?"

"That is hard to say. I am so much against the Nazis myself — I have reasons that Mark does not have. If there were some other job, in another country . . . but that, I know, is not easy to find."

"You worked for Framm yourself, didn't you?"

"Formerly." I waited for her to say more, and presently it came in a little rush of words through tightened lips. "He does not like me. He showed that when Mark and I were married."

"Oh?"

"We had been hoping I might keep the job, so that with the two salaries there might have been more comfort."

"I see."

Though sympathetic, I could not help discounting a little after this confession, with its mixture of frankness and inconsistency, and its reminder of what I had seen on the tram — the personal and the political intermixed, each one inflaming the other. She added, clinchingly: "Well, it is good that you should know all this, then I do not have to mention him again."

The more I saw of Pauli the more I liked her, though the more she told me about herself the less I felt she gave me her complete confidence. It was a curious progress into intimacy — she letting me see into her life a little, I realizing with each new view how much more there was than I had previously suspected.

* * *

The following week I went to Prague. It was the first time I had been in Czechoslovakia, and after Austria it was a nerve tonic. The Czechs were prosperous and cheerful; Hitler was unpopular among them, but it was still possible to believe in the Czech Army and the Czech Maginot Line and to have confidence in the future. Events, however, provided a fascinating though ominous drama across the border, for at such a distance the Austrian dilemma was in sharpest focus — less huge and blurred than in Vienna itself, yet arresting and of spectacular importance. There could not have been a better grandstand for an objective view of the European crisis, and as I was staying at the house of politically-minded people the days passed in a flurry of discussion, newspaper snatching, and radio dialing.

Something would happen soon; rumors started that the Luftwaffe was already poised at Munich, waiting for the word; some said that if Austria resisted she would have the support of both France and Italy. I wrote a few articles for American papers, and for the first time in my life an editor cabled his acceptance and asked for more.

One afternoon, at a pavement café, I picked up a paper that some-one had left on the table. Every journalist has a technical interest in newspapers, even in a language he doesn't read; he likes to see the format, to judge how modern or antiquated the plant must be, and so on. My own Czech was limited to a few phrases; I could just make out the general sense of the headlines, which told of nothing particularly new that day. But on an inside page I caught a word that leapt to the eye as if it had been printed in red ink — the word *Framm,* embedded in a half-column of small type date-lined Berlin. I could not make anything else of it, so I took the paper to my friends and had them translate. Even for them it was not easy, for it appeared to be the report of a lecture delivered by Framm to some scientific group in Berlin — highly abstruse, but apparently of news value. Framm, I gathered, had done something to correlate a theory of electromagnetism with some other theory — an achievement which his Berlin audience had received with all the greater acclaim because of its Viennese origin. It demonstrated, one was asked to believe, the essential and triumphant unity of pan-Germanic science.

My friends were cynical enough to suggest that Framm was giv-ing himself a sweet piece of publicity. They were unqualified to assess the value of his discovery, but of its timeliness there could be no doubt; for if Hitler should take over Austria there would be scientific plums as well as other kinds to be distributed among the faithful. My Czech friends, like Pauli and Julian, were clearly of the opinion that scientists did not live for science alone.

That evening I had a wire from Pauli. It asked me to return to Vienna, if I could possibly manage it, and she would meet me at the station. I felt a sudden aversion to mysteries, suspense, speculation of all kinds, so I wired back "Will come if necessary but what is wrong? Is anyone ill?" — which may not have been too courteous, but expressed some of the irritation I felt. I didn't want to leave Prague; I only realized then how refreshing it was as an antidote. Back after a few hours came the answer: "No illness but please come it is very important." So I left the next day, fully prepared for a small tiff with her if the reason for summoning me were not adequate. I couldn't think of anything but illness that would be.

*   *   *

She was a little distraught when we met. She rushed up to me amongst the crowd leaving the train and dragged me aside to assure me that Brad wasn't ill.

I said: "Of course not — you told me in your wire that nobody was ill."

"But I thought you might think I had said that just to reassure you."

That was too subtle for me. I said: "No, I believed you. Illness isn't a thing to fool people about — one way or the other."

She said: "I am sorry. You are yourself so direct. It is much worse than his being ill, anyhow. Unless he were *seriously* ill."

"Just tell me what's the matter." I took her arm as we crossed the concourse; she did not make for the cab rank, but turned into a small restaurant. It was fairly empty and there was a table in an alcove that offered privacy. I ordered coffee, and put my hand across the table as I had done once before to touch hers. It was cold but quite steady; the distraughtness was in her eyes. They roved over the restaurant as if apprehensive of who might be within seeing or hearing distance; then they searched the coffee cups for specks of dirt. She wiped them with a paper napkin before pouring. "I did not do this when we first met," she said, "because I thought you would consider it not good manners. But it is a fact that they are not very careful in these places."

I said: "Now, please, what *is* the matter?"

She watched the waiter back to his counter, then produced a folded newspaper from her handbag. It was a Vienna paper of the previous day; she passed it to me with her finger marking one of the pages. After a few seconds I could see that it was just the Framm news over again, in German instead of Czech and dressed up with a local personality angle.

I said: "Yes, I happened to see this in Prague."

"There also?"

"Well, it's news, I suppose. I don't know how important it is, but Framm certainly seems to have done himself no harm by bringing it out just now."

Her lips tightened. "So you think it is just . . . a *stunt*?" She often used words like that, with great deliberation and as if they were bound to effect some miraculous conveyance of ideas between an Austrian and an American.

"Perhaps hardly that. There doesn't seem anything catchpenny about it . . . like a cancer cure or a new rejuvenation technique — that's the sort of stuff to make the headlines. Electromagnetism is for scientists. . . . What does Brad say about it?"

"That is just the point." She tried hard to be calm. "Because . . . because . . . it is his own discovery . . . *Mark's* . . . and Hugo Framm has stolen it." This took a little time to take in, and meanwhile she had to go on saying the hated word. "Do you not understand? Hugo Framm has *stolen* it. It is Mark's work, not Framm's at all."

"That's a pretty serious accusation," I said at length. "How would you prove it?"

"I have hundreds of proofs. Pages and pages of Mark's notes. I have been copying them out for him every night when he came home from the laboratory — every night for months. And I know his work enough to recognize that all the conclusions are the same . . . Mark was only waiting for some final tests before assembling the whole material into a thesis." She tried to give me technical details, but they weren't comprehensible; she could only assure me that the theft was flagrant, and one thing I was convinced of, her sincerity. My silence made her exclaim: "You do not think I speak the truth? You think it is impossible?"

"Of course not. It just takes my breath away — the idea of Brad doing all the work and Framm getting all the credit — "

"Oh no. . . . Because I am not going to let that happen. Something must be done to upset this. Something *will* be done. Do you think I would stand by and see my husband cheated?"

Her face then, lit by passion, seemed almost that of another person. She was even speaking loudly enough to be overheard, if anyone else in the café were acutely listening. The "carefulness" had been like a mask, suddenly dropped, or perhaps like a habit, momentarily forgotten.

"You didn't tell me what Brad said. You can't do much on your own."

"I know. That is why I sent for you. Because you are of his nationality and would understand perhaps better how to talk to him."

"You mean he doesn't even know about it yet? You haven't told him?"

"He knows. He saw it in the paper himself. But he refuses to do anything. . . . That is the trouble. That is what you have to talk to him about. . . . I shall go back now — alone. You visit us later, then I can tell you all this again, in front of him, and you can say how much it shocks you." She stared at me hard. "But perhaps you are not so shocked?"

"Of course I am. It's a scandalous thing that a man's work should be — "

"But it does not surprise you that he refuses to do anything? Perhaps you understand him better than I?"

"Don't be silly."

"You have known him longer."

"But not so intimately . . . ever. . . . And I *am* surprised, except that I'm not surprised to be surprised, if you know what I mean . . ."

"Intimately?" she repeated. I could see she was thinking of a specific meaning of the word. But that was equally true, and what I had partly meant, and it certainly gave her the edge, if she needed one. There was a deep, friendly, and highly intelligent jealousy between us, something both of us recognized, concealed, and refused to waste time in worrying about. It had its own queer limits too; she did not, for instance, in the least object to my walking with Brad in the Burggarten while she stayed at home to do his typing. But once, when she had seen me using my own portable, she had said, almost cattishly: "Only two fingers? That would not do for me. It is necessary for me to be quite expert when I work for Mark."

*   *   *

It was towards ten o'clock when I reached the apartment, and what happened was much simpler than Pauli had planned. I told Brad I had seen in the Prague paper a report of Framm's lecture, and this was to have been Pauli's cue, but Brad picked it up quicker. "You've touched on a tender spot," he said, suddenly reaching for his hat and overcoat. "Pauli and I have just had our first quarrel about it. . . . Tell her if you want, Pauli — I'm going round the corner for a glass of beer."

And he stalked out, leaving us to a conversation that was not part of our program.

"It is unlike him to do that," Pauli said anxiously.

I said a few drinks might not be a bad thing, they might loosen him up and we could then hammer the whole thing out with fewer inhibitions. I asked if there had really been a quarrel and she replied: "Of course not. I told him what he must do and he said he could not do it, that was all." But that, I reflected, might well be his idea of a quarrel, even if not hers.

He came back about midnight, looking relaxed, good-humored, almost jaunty. Perhaps the beer had done this, though there was certainly no sign that he had drunk too much. He said he had found someone to play chess with, and had won the game. I asked if it was the same man he had played with that night he wrote me the long letter about science, and he answered: "No. I don't know his name and he didn't ask mine. That's the good thing about chess. You just play it with anyone who can."

I had suggested to Pauli that she leave us alone to talk things over, and this she now did, though rather reluctantly. As soon as I heard her busying herself in the kitchen I said: "Well now, Brad, what's it all about?"

"Our little quarrel? Didn't she tell you?"

"Yes . . . and is she right, that's what I want to know. Did Framm steal your stuff?"

He smiled, as to a child who has asked something uncomfortably naïve. "I like simple words, Jane, but when they're too simple they don't always help. . . . You talk about somebody stealing my stuff. *What* stuff? A few pages of algebra — how can such a thing be *my* stuff — or anybody's stuff? So what do you mean by *stealing?* Mathematicians don't take out patents. We don't have copyrights, trademarks, Good Housekeeping seals of approval. . . . And besides, Pauli's prejudiced — she hates Framm. Well, that's all right — I don't blame her. But it's no reason why I should accept her viewpoint in everything. She has a great sense of possession — most women have. To her the whole thing's just as if I'd left an umbrella on the tram and someone had run off with it."

All of which impressed me only until I realized how completely it evaded the issue. I answered: "Brad . . . will you answer me this question . . . honestly . . . how much of Framm's discovery covers the same ground as your own work?"

"Oh, a great deal. It actually confirms my work. That's fine. To have a scientist of Framm's eminence state with confidence something which you yourself have postulated only tentatively — it's a great encouragement if you look at it the right way."

"Are you being sarcastic?"

"I thought you understood me better than that."

"I don't. Or rather, I don't know whether I do or not. But I think I understand Framm a little, even though I've only met him once. He's ambitious and unscrupulous and I'd say he's quite capable of grabbing anybody else's work to bolster his reputation — to cut a dash in Berlin so that if events move the Nazi way he'll get a big job."

"Might be. As a politician he's probably the worst shyster in the world — it's only as a scientist that I can guarantee him."

"How about him as a man — a man of honor?"

"I haven't any idea. We don't cover that territory."

"You mean you're indifferent? Don't you really *mind* what he's done? You don't think any less of him for it? It's what you were willing to have happen? You feel you can go on working with him —"

"One question at a time," he interrupted, "or I won't remember them. To begin with, you're making all this far too personal. It isn't a question of whether I like Framm less or more or even at all. As I told you once he's the kind of man you don't have to like — not when you work with him professionally. And if you ask me whether I'm willing for him to use my work, then that's an easy one — of course I am. Any scientist can use my work. And I can use his. We take that for granted. . . . Don't look so indignant. Your slant's a bit better than Pauli's, but it still makes everything too simple. From pinching an umbrella we've progressed to quoting from a copy-righted author without proper permission . . . am I right?"

"Brad, if you were in this mood with Pauli I don't wonder she quarreled with you. What I'm trying to get at, and what you've evaded so far, is whether Framm did anything which in your own world, amongst scientists who knew all the facts, would be considered unethical. I can't answer that question — maybe Pauli can't — but you can. And so far you haven't. Why not?"

"Suppose I said because it's nobody else's damned business."

"All right. That's a straight answer and it leaves me nothing else to say. I'll go now . . . let me know when you're next free for a walk."

He answered with sudden cordiality: "Any time — tomorrow if you like, provided we don't get onto arguments like this."

I went to the kitchen and whispered to Pauli that I hadn't had any luck in influencing him, maybe it would be better to try again some other time when we'd both had a chance to think things over. "I've a feeling if I stay I shall mess things up. It's late, anyhow, and I'm tired."

So I said good-night. Brad came downstairs and accompanied me along the street to the corner where I usually found a taxi. There were still crowds everywhere; a Nazi rally had just broken up and the participants, inflamed with oratory, were drifting belligerently home. As we passed a café that was open late, Brad suggested going in for a drink.

We found a table. The place was very hot, smoky, and noisy. "Is this where you played chess?" I asked, for something to say.

"No, I've never been here before. It's pretty bad, isn't it? Do you mind?"

"Not a bit, if you don't. But I'm not exactly in sympathy with these roisterers."

"Neither am I. They're getting bolder — they're not afraid of being arrested nowadays. . . . We'll find somewhere else if you like."

"No, there's not time. I'll have to go soon."

We drank beer. A mechanical piano struck up to add to the racket. A girl began to sing shrilly.

Brad said, contemplatively: "So you don't like my mood."

"I don't, but as it isn't normal, I guess I can stand it. In some ways it's an improvement. You wouldn't normally ask me to drink beer with you at one in the morning, and never before have you said 'any time' when I've asked when you were free for a walk." He called for another beer. "And it's the first time, to my knowledge, that you've drunk so much."

"Do you mean *so* much or *too* much?"

"So much. You're not an alcoholic yet."

"Five beers."

"Good. You ought to do this oftener."

"Then you ought to be here oftener with me."

"That clinches it. You're *not* normal. I've never known you gallant before."

He laughed. The surface badinage was working us both into a feeling of intimacy. "To tell you the truth, Jane, I got tired of arguing when I knew Pauli was listening from the kitchen all the time."

"It's a small apartment."

"I know. But she does have several attributes of the successful female spy. Among them a great loyalty to whoever or whatever it is that she serves."

"*You,*" I said.

"I know. And I'm not really worth the kind of devotion she gives me."

"I don't think she's wise to give it, anyway. She might come a cropper sometime."

"She doesn't get as much out of me as she'd like. That's my fault.

I don't think any woman would. I guess the truth is, my work comes first. But she knew that when she married me — she'd seen the way I work at the lab — she knew how it — *consumes* me."

"She probably fancied herself as a reformer. Women do. And there are women who *could* reform you, I daresay."

He stared at the table, and suddenly I knew he was thinking of my mother, and that he knew I was also. It made us both somehow uncomfortable, so that I went on with forced lightness: "Well, we were talking about your apartment. I still think it's small enough for her to have heard without listening."

"And this place is noisy enough to listen without hearing. Wouldn't you really like to try somewhere else?"

"No — the noise is all right — especially if we're going to argue again."

"But we're not. *I* won't, anyway. I don't like the feeling you're against me."

"I'm not against you, Brad. But I'm against other people pushing you down and you pretending you accidentally fell. . . . Did Framm behave unscrupulously or not? It's a simple question if you choose to answer it."

"Better not mention names here."

"I'm sorry. Let's call him *he*. *Did* he?"

"Did he what?"

"Did he do what you would have done in his place?"

He looked at me quizzically for a moment, then said: "God, I wouldn't be in his place for anything."

"That's evading the point again."

"No, it isn't. It's the real point. . . ." He leaned forward across the table so that our faces were close; it was the only way he could drop his voice and still be heard. "You know what Pauli wants? She'd have me raise a stink, hire lawyers, start a fight about it. I won't do that. I wouldn't even if it were actionable, which I doubt."

"I could get an opinion. I know a very good lawyer here."

"Don't waste your time. I wouldn't fight. And I don't mind a bit if you call me a coward. Too many people have wasted time fighting just to be thought not a coward. Because in my own mind I've nothing to fight about. I was quite sincere when I said his lecture encouraged me."

"*Encouraged* you?"

"Yes. I'd had just a slight doubt about a certain item in my chain of reasoning — it was beginning to keep me awake nights. His — his announcement cleared the matter up, because he wouldn't have made it if he hadn't been sure there wasn't a flaw."

"You have that much faith in him?"

"Yes."

"Why?"

"Because . . . because he's a much better scientist than I am — or ever will be. Sorry to keep on using that word — scientist, *scientist*. Most people think of them as romantic pioneers, or else plodders trying one thing after another till the miracle simply has to happen — like the Curies with radium. . . . Actually it's mostly plodding without the miracles and pioneering without the romance. Yet there *are* moments — moments that none of those words suit — moments when what's needed is the guess of sheer genius — the bull's-eye of a first-class mind operating with a flair. It's hard to explain, but there's almost poetry in it as well as logic and luck. I've seen *him* at such moments. He may be other things too, but he's a — here's that word again, I can't help it — he's a *scientist*."

There wasn't much I could say to that. The beer had made him a little expansive. He went on: "Besides, the truth is, I'm not really ambitious in *his* way. All the fuss that was made over him in — in the place where he lectured — all that would just bore and bother me to distraction if I ever had to put up with it. And I certainly don't hanker after some big administrative job where I'd have to play politics. So everything he can possibly have deprived me of, he's welcome to."

"Wouldn't you even have liked the slightest acknowledgment from him?"

"That's another ambition of his I don't share — to sit pretty with the — those — " He checked himself in time. "Let's call them *them*. You know what I mean."

I nodded and glanced round the café. "There seem to be plenty here."

"Sure. It's too bad that science has to be interfered with by such arrogant nitwits. They've even closed down the laboratory."

"Yes, Pauli told me."

"Why are you smiling?"

"Because you called them arrogant. They are, but you are too, whenever you use the word 'science.'"

"Am I? I can only say that my own work makes me feel very humble."

"That's only another form of arrogance. Mystics have it. Makes them pretty hard to get along with."

"Then I can't be one . . . and I don't think I'm a mystic anyhow. A bit monkish, if you like — perhaps scientists *are* the modern monks. They shut themselves up in their cells and let the nonsense go on outside — and they have a distant goal that makes them myopic about the foreground. . . . I remember your mother once asked me if I felt my work as a sort of priesthood — it startled me at the time, but now I think she might have been partly right."

"She also mentioned a vow of celibacy."

He laughed. "Oh, count me out of that. . . ."

"Good."

"You too, I should think?"

"*Should* you?"

He laughed again. "Well, I've sometimes wondered. You're attractive, intelligent, on your own, and you travel about the world meeting all kinds of interesting men. . . . What *can* I think?"

"Exactly." We both laughed.

He began to assemble the saucers that would show the amount of his bill. "This conversation's getting too personal. Shall we go?"

"Yes, after one more question. Mind?"

"I might. But go ahead."

"Just this. You once told me that scientists are in constant touch through scientific journals — a sort of international freemasonry, quite small, but very elite. Now if *he* hadn't jumped the gun, wouldn't you have liked to see your work in one of these journals, with your own name on it?"

He said quietly: "Yes, it would have given me pleasure. But honestly, not as much as to know that for the last two years I've been on the right track, not the wrong one."

"But you'd have had that too."

"I have it now, that's the main thing. That's why I'm celebrating — like this."

"Brad, I don't believe you. I think you're quite a bit hurt by what's happened. Only you're tied to an ideal — you feel you oughtn't to care about credit, therefore you try to make yourself not care."

"And if I succeed, then it's true that I don't care."

"But that could make you a bundle of complexes and inhibitions."

"Freudian stuff, eh?"

"I don't know why so many scientists sneer at Freud."

"We don't. All we have against him is that the field he opened up became an immediate playground for amateurs. I'm glad my own field doesn't offer the same attractions."

"There's something chilly about your mind, Brad."

That made him laugh again. "Only about my mind, though.

Tonight I can almost understand why people like to shout and get drunk and beat their wives."

"But to understand why people do things isn't the same as wanting to do them yourself."

"Let's hope not. Would you like me to beat Pauli?"

"Quarreling with her might be worse."

"Listen . . . get this straight about me and Pauli. She's a wonderful wife, I'm in love with her, and she has her own way nine times out of ten."

"But this is the tenth?"

"Yes."

"And more important than all the others?"

"To me — naturally. Otherwise I'd have been delighted to give in as usual."

"You'd rather fight Pauli than *him*."

"That's an unfair way of putting it and you're quite smart enough to know it is. I wouldn't mind fighting him at all if it were on ground where a fight would be in order. If he'd announced something I thought wrong, for instance — though I'd have been a bit hesitant to set my mind against his — still, I'd have done it, no matter how impolitic it might have been. I'm not that sort of coward."

"But his discoveries don't happen to be wrong. They don't even happen to be his."

"I told you before that in the sense I look at it, they're neither his nor mine, but the common property of anyone who can use them."

"Holy ground, eh? Only strictly scientific fights permitted. If you want a private one, run home to your wife. You must be pretty hard to live with, Brad."

"No, I'm easy. I have few vices and my virtues are decently hidden. Furthermore, I'm a very affectionate animal. So is Pauli. We get on pretty well. You don't have to worry about us."

"I know. She's very happy with you — personally. . . . And by the way, I'm neutral."

"In what?"

"In anything you have arguments about with her."

He had paid the bill and we were walking out of the café. He summoned a taxi that was already curving towards us. "I can see *your* side, Brad, and it's wonderful and superb, like the Matterhorn, but if I were Pauli I'd probably see her side better."

"Oh no, you wouldn't. You'd still see mine," he said, timing it for the last word as he waved good-night.

*   *   *

I didn't meet or hear from him again for several days, despite his expressed readiness to take a walk; but I did mention the matter to my lawyer friend, a brilliant young Austrian named Bauer, strongly anti-Nazi, whom I had met at a party and liked exceedingly.

It was the political angle that interested him most, and he confirmed the likelihood that Framm was boosting himself in Berlin with an eye to a big job if and when the Nazis moved into Austria. "It's a smart thing to do, the way things look, and they certainly look worse every hour."

I asked him what chance he thought Brad would have, supposing he were willing to begin any legal action.

"Probably not much. To begin with, those documentary proofs you say exist — the notes and so on — they're all abstrusely scientific, I suppose? — you couldn't explain their meaning to a court — you'd need expert evidence from other scientists even to interpret them. Well, where would you get such witnesses? Why should anyone back an unknown person against an influential big shot? And furthermore, even if you *could* show that Bradley's notes were more or less in line with the Berlin lecture, who's to say that your friend worked independently?"

"Pauli could testify to that."

"She wouldn't count — she's his wife. She was also, I understand, a former employee of Hugo Framm till she was dismissed by him. . . . Not good, not good."

"But it could be proved that Bradley left his notes lying around in a desk at the laboratory, where Framm could have had access to them."

"Perhaps Framm did the same and Bradley could have had similar access. What if Framm were to say that Bradley copied *his* notes?"

"You mean he copied them with a view to bringing an action later? Isn't that farfetched?"

"A jury might think it looked like blackmail."

"*Blackmail*. . . . That's fantastic."

"You understand, Miss Waring, the idea's purely hypothetical. I'm only trying to imagine what I might say if I were Framm or his counsel."

"Of course. But it's still fantastic."

"No more than the whole issue. That's the trouble. If it were plagiarism in a book or a play you could get the hang of it, but all this scientific stuff . . . What's Bradley's salary, by the way?"

"I don't know exactly, but far less than it ought to be — which is another thing that might show a jury the kind of man Framm is."

"It might also be used to show them the kind of man Bradley is. Framm could say: 'These are good wages for a mere laboratory assistant working under my supervision all the time.' . . . And there's another thing . . . The legal issue would narrow down to whether Bradley had any ownership claim on work done while he was a salaried worker for Framm, even if you could prove that Bradley did do everything on his own."

"So you think it's all rather hopeless?"

"Nothing's *quite* hopeless in a court of law. Sometimes a decision goes against all logic as well as evidence. Framm's a charmer — I've seen him in action — he has that kind of brilliant ruthlessness that makes him nearly irresistible — and yet, you never know — some people might side with David against Goliath. What's his type?"

"He hasn't got a type exactly. He's shy in manner and quite good-looking. Of course he hasn't the slightest intention of bringing an action. I told you I was merely asking out of curiosity."

He said, just before I left his office: "The real dynamite in a thing like this would be political. Nobody cares about electromagnetism. . . . But if the case were even to be started it would do Framm harm, and that might be worth while from a number of angles. . . . Look, I'll take it on. I don't think we'll win, and unless we do win and get damages, it's understood there'll be no fee."

I said I was positive Brad wouldn't bring any case.

"Ask him again." Bauer's enthusiasm seemed to be rising as he contemplated the matter. "After all, what can he lose? Tell him my offer."

I promised, and when I did tell Brad, the result was emphatically what I had expected. Brad said: "So I'm to provide a nice little *cause célèbre* for the politicians to smack their lips over? Tell your lawyer friend I've *everything* to lose — everything that I care about — my time, my work, and my peace of mind. The only thing I haven't to lose is doubtless what he was thinking of . . . *money*."

"All right, but don't be sarcastic. He's not as different from you as you'd think. Why don't you let me arrange a meeting? You might even like him. You could use a few more friends in this town."

"No, Jane, please keep him out of my affairs. And for heaven's sake don't tell Pauli you've found a free lawyer. It's the cost of the case I've been stressing to her."

"Why?"

"Because it's easier to explain than the other reasons I have."

The international sky darkened, with Vienna as its storm center. The city throbbed with rumors and counter rumors, ranging from the dangerously plausible to the sheerly impossible, but behind the smoke screen one thing was clear: events were now too presaging to be gainsaid, either by wishful thinkers or by those whose adherences tied them long after the expiry of either wishing or thoughtfulness. I have been a witness of several upsets that could be called revolutions, and one thing that strikes me as an almost clinical sign of approaching crisis is the way it is smelled ahead by those who have never been extreme enough to make a change of views difficult, or important enough to have such a change suspected. Perhaps the bulk of people go this way and that, not so much aiming to be with the tide as to avoid any feeling that it exists.

There was a curious vacuum in the Viennese atmosphere during that pre-crisis week, a definite break in tension; the crowds in the streets diminished, or perhaps one thought so because they went about more quietly; a few misread the signs and wondered if everything would now "blow over." But from across the frontier accurate reports came more alarmingly than before, so that the seeming lull was ominous rather than satisfying. To me it was as if curtains were being drawn over big store windows, while behind them dressers were at work, changing the display for some moment of sudden unveiling in a now predictable future. Few people, probably, are consciously hypocritical when, to suit their convenience, they swap sides. Even to themselves the move must be rationalized, must be given that appearance of sincerity which it partly has; and this requires a little time, a few days at least, a small tribute of delay paid by human apathy to the freedom which it surrenders.

I wrote articles during those strange days, and once I called at Brad's apartment but did not stay long. I was distressed to see that the issue between him and Pauli had already caused a rift, and I knew that especially now I must avoid making Pauli resent my own friendship with him. There had been no sign of this so far, but it could doubtless thrive on any backing I gave him in his attitude. For Pauli, however, mere neutrality was not enough; I soon saw that to keep her warm to me I would have to be on her side against Brad, and this was even less possible.

Meanwhile it was in the papers that Framm had returned from Berlin, a considerably more eminent personage than when he went. The laboratories were still closed, owing to the likelihood of further political rioting, but Framm contrived to get himself into a steady limelight of statements and interviews. He was clever enough not to seem boastful about his Berlin success, but to allow the common knowledge of it to support his political attitude, which now became openly pro-Nazi.

During this interval I also heard a curious story from Bauer to the effect that Pauli had approached another lawyer, denouncing Framm and inquiring about the possibilities of a lawsuit; to which this lawyer had replied that since action could only be started by Bradley himself, there was no point in discussing it except with him. However, the story got around. I thought this a pity, since it made Brad's attitude look somewhat unheroic; but again there was nothing I could do either by argument or by advice.

Then came a memorable afternoon when I walked in the Prater, watching children play their games as if nothing were amiss in the world — as perhaps, for children who can romp, nothing is. The first hint of spring warmed the air and touched the trees; workmen were taking down barricades from the sideshows in the amusement park, and there was something both comforting and sad in all this — comfort in the thought that fun would still be bought and sold, whatever happened, sadness when one reckoned how many of the quiet unpurchasable pleasures of life were at stake.

I came out of the park to the Lasalle Strasse about four o'clock and waited for a tram to take me to the center of the city. The usual knot of newsboys stood at the corner, selling their rival editions. They did not look particularly excited, nor did those who bought from them. Then suddenly another boy jumped off a passing truck with a sheaf of papers under his arm and began shouting something I could not catch above the traffic noise; but its effect was to magnetize a crowd, so that the next minute nothing happened but people edging out of it, taking a few slow paces while they read, then scampering across streets or onto passing trams. By the time I reached the corner all the papers had been sold, but a passer-by told me what had happened: Schuschnigg had surrendered to Hitler at Berchtesgaden. It was the first step to *Anschluss*.

In the Opern-Ring when I got there by tram special editions of all the papers were out; I then learned the details. Seyss-Inquart was to have a post in the Austrian government, all Austrian Nazis under arrest were to be amnestied. I read and reread the meager reports of what had happened at Berchtesgaden; it was several minutes before I caught sight of another news item on an inside page. This reported that Professor Hugo Framm had been attacked and wounded by a woman not yet identified.

Of course I thought immediately of Pauli and then forced myself into statistical argument; surely there could be *other* women who hated Framm . . . yet when, shortly afterwards, I read her name in print in a later edition the absence of further shock proved how one's mind jumps all hurdles at such a time; the real surprise would have come if it had not been Pauli.

The details were that she had telephoned for an interview with Framm that afternoon, had been told he was busy and could not see her, but had later seized a chance to force her way into his private office adjoining the laboratories. These were still closed to students, so that no one had seen her enter. Sometime later a janitor, passing along the corridor, heard angry voices, and as one of them was a woman's, he thought it more tactful not to intervene. A few minutes after that came shouts and screams. The janitor then rushed to the scene; the woman was held and the Professor taken to the hospital with a stab wound in the chest. The woman, it was said, "made a statement."

I went to Brad's apartment, hoping he already had the news. It does not always help to have a friend break things gently; sometimes it is easier to take the first shock alone, without an audience and without that compulsion to act before one that afflicts all of us at such times, especially those who reckon to be best controlled. But I was too early; Brad was working and had heard nothing; aware of political excitement mounting both in the press and on the radio, he had deliberately avoided contact with them all day. So I told him what had happened, not only in Austria's life but in his own; I showed him the paper. Then I left him for a moment while I went in the kitchen and pretended to tidy a few things.

He took it quietly, as I had expected he would; after the first moment of incredulity a slow stricken glare in his eyes became the only outward sign. Of course his first thought was that he must see her.

"I'll go with you, Brad. Where do you suppose they took her?"

"There's a police station almost across the street from the laboratory."

We drove there in a cab. On the way I asked what had happened during the day.

"Nothing out of the ordinary. I was working at home. We had a meal together about noon, then she went out. She didn't say where she was going or when she'd be back, but that's not unusual either. I was working pretty hard, I didn't notice the time passing."

"Had she talked of going to see Framm?"

"Never a hint. She hated him."

"I wouldn't tell them that at the police station."

"No, of course not. What *would* you tell them?"

"As little as possible. . . . But you might as well be frank with me. Did you have a quarrel with her before she went out?"

"No. Just the regular argument about the lawsuit, she was still urging me to start one; but it's hardly an argument any more, it's a sort of wall between us and we push our heads against it now and again just to see if it's still there. . . . But for her to do a thing like this . . . I can't *imagine* it. She's not the type."

"The crime isn't a typed one either."

He rocked his head in his hands. "I still can't imagine it. She was so quiet, so . . . so discreet. Never lost her temper. Of course she liked to get her own way — who doesn't? But violence . . . it's *unthinkable*. . . ."

"But it's happened," I said, "and you must pull yourself together."

"I've got to help her," he kept saying.

At the police station they wouldn't even let him see her, but they took particulars about both of us and forbade us to leave the city. The police attitude seemed confused as well as worried — as if they expected blame to attach to them for what had happened and must therefore make haste to blame others equally guiltless. I think most of their hostile manner was due to that; it showed itself in a trifling fuss because we had broken the rule that whenever an alien visits a police station for any purpose whatsoever he must bring along a passport for identification. Behind this nonsense one could sense the political winds rising; everyone seemed preoccupied with more than the thing itself.

After the police let us go I intended to take Brad to see Bauer (which I already felt I should have done first of all), but he said immediately: "Now let's go to the hospital."

I suppose I must have been concentrating on one thing all the time, because I answered blankly: "Hospital? *What* hospital?"

"The Margareten — that's where the papers say they took him."

Then I realized what he was talking about. Beyond any surprise

I felt, I had the fear that we should miss Bauer at his office if we didn't get there soon.

"They probably won't let you see him," I said.

"But I'd like to find out how he is."

"They may not know yet. Perhaps he's unconscious."

"Then I could leave a message — "

"A *message*?"

He said irritably: "Dammit, what else can I do? Your wife flies into a temper and stabs a man you've been working with for over a year — surely you ought to say *something* . . . or don't you think so?"

I hadn't thought out the problem at all till he mentioned it, which establishes, perhaps, a gulf between his mind and mine. But I could see the minutes slipping by; if Bauer left his office we might not be able to see him till the morning, and the loss of a day might be important. "Let's go to the lawyer first," I said. "We can call at the hospital later. There'll be all evening for it."

He then consented, we took a cab across the city, and were lucky to catch Bauer just in time. He had seen the newspapers and looked very grave. He asked immediately if Brad wanted Pauli's case to be handled by him, and when Brad eagerly agreed, he replied: "All right — but it's only fair to tell you that my known views might not help her at the trial. What's happened now is vastly different from the civil action I wanted you to bring. I'll be glad to do everything I can provided you realize that with events hastening the way they are I might not be your best choice. On the other hand, I can't recommend anyone else. A lawyer of opposite political opinions probably wouldn't handle the case at all. Or if he did, he might handle it badly — *deliberately* badly. It's just a question of which risk you'd rather take."

Brad said he would engage Bauer whatever the risk, and I think there was already an awareness between them of some kind of basic division of humanity in which they would generally find themselves on the same side. Bauer then said he would try to get an immediate interview with Pauli; he did not know whether he could at such an hour, but he arranged to meet us again at eleven o'clock at the Erzherzog Karl Hotel, where I was staying. Brad turned to me and said this would give us plenty of time to call at the hospital during the interval. But then Bauer questioned him, and when Brad disclosed his intention to send Framm a message Bauer said: "I can see you're the kind of client a lawyer has to watch. Take my advice and don't go near the hospital. . . ."

"But surely . . . after all . . ."

"Very well — write what you want and let me read it when I get back. Then we'll have the argument if it's necessary. . . ."

I took Brad to my hotel for dinner, but we neither ate nor talked much. He came up to my room afterwards and I mixed him a stiff whisky. He said he had never tasted whisky before and couldn't think why anyone should drink it for pleasure. We made a joke of that. I said I would write to my father in Paris and see if he could pull any strings through the Embassy. The Austrians, of course, would not concede that Pauli had become even halfway an American citizen, but it was possible, nevertheless, that some degree of influence might be exerted.

Brad then wrote his note to Framm and asked my opinion of it. As it simply and briefly expressed regrets and good wishes for a quick recovery, I said I thought it couldn't be improved on.

Before the arranged time Bauer rejoined us, helped himself to a drink, and read the note which was still lying open on the writing desk. Without commenting on it then he gave us the news. He had managed to see Pauli, though not alone. He thought she was a little out of her mind; she kept denouncing her victim and defending her action. And she had evidently told the whole story about Brad and Framm and the electromagnetism issue; the papers had got hold of it; there would be headlines in the morning. "Oddly enough," Bauer said, "she's so emphatic and unrepentant that the thing almost carries a bit of conviction. Of course it's her only possible defense."

I looked at Brad, who said after a pause: "You mean I'll have to back her up in all that?"

"If you didn't, you'd be signing her death warrant," Bauer answered.

"*Death* warrant?"

"Yes . . . because Framm's not expected to live. She punctured one of his lungs."

"Good God," Brad muttered.

"In a struggle," I intervened. "Didn't it say there was screaming and shouting? How do we know what really happened? Framm's a big powerful man. . . . Suppose she picked up whatever it was on the spur of the moment . . ."

"Unfortunately she didn't. She stabbed him with a kitchen knife she took with her when she left home. It was premeditated. She admits that, anyhow. . . . So all she can rest a defense on is the reality of her grievance. That won't be a strong defense, but if her husband confirms it . . ."

I looked at Brad again and for a fraction of a moment I was unsure of him. Then when he spoke I knew it was my fault, not his. He said quietly: "I'll do that. Tell her she can count on me."

Bauer put his hand on Brad's arm. "Good. . . . Then in that case, if you don't mind . . ." He went over to the writing desk and crumpled the letter. "Not that there's anything bad in it, but you can't quite tell how it might be interpreted by the other side. . . . Now tell me more about this mathematical stuff. Where's all your material about it?"

"At my apartment."

"We'd better get it now before the police make a search. Might occur to them to do that, once they gather their wits."

"All right."

We got to the apartment about midnight and in an hour or so had everything sorted and packed into a suitcase. Then I said good-night to Brad and promised to see him again in the morning. Bauer took the suitcase and we returned to my hotel. "Dr. Bradley had better come here tomorrow and start work," he said. "I can't do it for him, and neither can you, I imagine. . . . In a way, though, all this has made things easier to prove. People will say there must be *something* in it if a woman would try to kill for it. . . . Proof by murder — rather appropriate to our day and age. . . . By the way, you call him Brad — do you think he would mind if I did? . . . I like him very much. . . ."

* * *

The next few days passed with something of the unarguable quality of a dream; one did strange things for strange reasons, as if events had twisted motive and behavior alike. Brad set himself to the task of building up a case against Framm — the very last thing he had ever wanted to do; but now, because Framm's life was in danger and Pauli was in jail, it was what he had to do. Even the pages of algebra seemed to take on meaning under this added stress of circumstance, and as I watched him riffling through his notes I had a curious impression of existence on different levels — the personal melodrama of danger and rescue, the larger battleground of nationalism and conquest, and above them both, dim save to a few, the icy eternal truths expressible only in symbols such as the square root of minus one.

The authorities still would not allow Brad to see his wife, and Bauer could give us little news except that Pauli's truculent attitude

remained unaltered. Meanwhile the affair grew larger in the newspapers as its political angles were further explored; it was now revealed that Framm had been high in the confidence of the Berlin
government, and the rumor even spread that the crime was entirely
political and that Pauli had improvised her story to conceal it. Brad
then wanted to announce publicly that he was prepared to testify to
its entire truth, but Bauer advised against this, thinking it better tactics to spring the thing as a surprise when the actual trial came on.
By this time we had got hold of a Berlin scientific journal that contained a presumably verbatim report of the lecture, so there was a
good deal to work on, though most of it was meaningless to Bauer
and me. Nevertheless, after Bauer had given it a careful reading he
commented: "You know, Brad, there's one thing strikes me — assuming that Framm did use your stuff, he wasn't too smart. All he
had to do was to mention your name just once — to say at the end
of the lecture — 'I want to express thanks to my assistant, Dr. Mark
Bradley, for helping me in this work. . . .' Supposing he'd said
something like that, he could still have kept 99 per cent of the credit,
and you wouldn't have had even a talking point against him. . . .
I wonder why he didn't say it. Sheer hoggishness, I suppose. . . ."

Brad went on with the quiet preparation of his case, needing no
spur to effort, yet at the outset (he told me) despising unutterably
the task of reducing a complicated and beautiful mathematical concept to the terms of a legal brief. (He used the word "beautiful"
without embarrassment.) Presently, however, this touch of intellectual fastidiousness left him, or was submerged in sheer anxiety
about Pauli; and though I had all along guessed that Brad loved her
very deeply, I had not been prepared for the emotion, quite frantic,
that he began to show. I found a task for myself in calming him into
a mood in which he could sit up till midnight, working against
time, and then, with the help of a drug, get a few hours of heavy
sleep. Several times he stayed in my room all night, and once Bauer

arrived in the morning to find him asleep on my bed. I neither knew nor cared what anyone thought, till Bauer hinted that hotel gossip might be an adversely complicating factor that we should do well to avoid. So we did, after that.

When at last the notes were finished I typed them out, performing Pauli's job with only two fingers. Then I took the script to Bauer's apartment. He gave it cautious approval, but seemed distraught by the return of tension in the streets; all of any lull was over. We talked for a while; then I went back to my hotel and found Brad prudently gone. I took several sleeping pills myself and did not wake till nearly noon the next day, March the twelfth.

That was the day on which Hitler's troops crossed the frontiers into Austria.

*　　*　　*

The marching, the swastikas, the tanks and armored cars, the hysteria of a city applauding the pageant of its own extinction, all were described at the time by eyewitnesses; it is history now, not ten years old, but already in a former world. I wrote articles that sought to convey what I thought I should have felt had not my mind been obsessed with a personal projection of the issue; but perhaps the obsession was really a prism through which I saw the thing more and not less clearly. And I was wryly amused to note that my waiter at the hotel, a decent timid fellow, became stanchly Nazi overnight — the pluperfect type, Bauer called him — one of those who knew now they *had* been Nazi all along.

Brad watched the crowds from my hotel window, saw them progress from ecstasy through intoxication to hang-over, though his own private nightmare was so intense that I doubt if he realized fully what was happening. We were not far from the head office of the German Tourist organization, where a huge portrait of Hitler stimulated the crowds to especial fervor; day and night this did not cease, but grew more malevolent in its outcome; soon began the attacks on Jews, and those also progressed from roughhouse bullying to acts of quieter but more sinister sadism. Bauer had now little hope, either for Pauli or for himself. He had heard that Framm's death was expected momentarily, and he thought the new regime might well feel that a disciplinary example must be made. He even wondered whether, for her sake, he ought to turn the case over to some lawyer in better standing, but he had no success in finding one, and was too loyal to quit for personal reasons of his own. The sole chance lay now in some possible international angle; the Nazis might conceivably wish to placate American opinion. Were there not strings to be pulled through Washington or the Embassy? Was not my father an American of wealth and influence?

I said I had already written to him in Paris, but so far had had no reply.

"Maybe your letter didn't reach him. I happened to hear the other day that he's in Linz."

"*Linz?* What would he be doing there?"

Bauer shrugged, and I don't know any certain answer to this day. Nor have I much idea how Bauer knew he was in Linz. I found out later that the lawyer was a member of an anti-Nazi group which, after the *Anschluss,* went underground; I imagine that the movements of a man like my father could have been the subject of secret information. There are those who say that my father backed Hitler, but I don't believe he did with any consistency, certainly not with any conviction after his trip to Germany in 1935; I would think it more probable that he fumbled around, as he had done with Lenin during the N.E.P. period, and as he did with Roosevelt during the early days of the New Deal, hoping that by some sleight-of-brain he could make himself a power behind any sort of throne. He never could. He had a shrewd sense that the world had passed into different hands, and he wished to touch them with his own, the old dead

Midas touch of an earlier age. Somebody once said that in the twilight of capitalism my father stalked around like a frustrated ghost, wondering whom he should haunt.

"Why don't you go to see him?" Bauer urged. "Take Brad with you and see if you can get him to do anything."

*   *   *

So happened the curious visit to Linz. We left Vienna by a slow train that traveled all night and should have reached our destination in the early morning. But frequently we were held up in sidings while a procession of troop trains passed; half sleeping in the compartment we heard shouts and cheers that still celebrated the bloodless conquest. We reached Linz several hours late in pouring rain. Bauer had said that the likeliest hotel for my father to be staying at would be one called the Kaiserhof, facing the Danube near the quays where the river boats put in. We went there, clattering over the cobbled streets in an old droshky, since all motor vehicles had been commandeered. The town looked dreary in the rain, and even the newly arrived German soldiers had dropped their spirits to match the gray skies. There was a general feeling of anticlimax.

We found the hotel in a state of utter disorganization; a line of German officers waited at the desk, making demands for meals, beds, and other accommodations which the staff met with a head-on courtesy that had already become mere nervous obsequiousness. While Brad was trying to push his way through and make inquiries, I had wandered across the hall to the dining-room entrance; and across that room, at a table next to the windows overlooking the rain-swept river, my father was having breakfast with a woman.

I went back for Brad, and we then entered together. My father gave us a courteous greeting, but he was naturally surprised, not having known I was even in Austria. He introduced his companion, a Madame Larousse, who spoke fairly good English with a French accent and was rather charming. Then he asked us to breakfast with him, but as they had almost finished their meal I said no, only coffee. We chatted about the weather and everyday topics (not politics, of course) for a while, and Madame Larousse joined in with an evident desire to be pleasant to my father's daughter and to a man whom she doubtless took to be my father's daughter's future husband; then she tactfully said she had letters to write and left us.

The waiter brought more coffee and when he too had gone I told my father briefly all that had happened. He had seen in the papers about the attempted assassination (that was what he called it, and I suppose it was that, though somehow the description startled me), but he had missed the name of the arrested woman, and the rest of our story was news indeed. "Well?" he said unhappily, when I paused.

I murmured something about his using influence, pulling strings, and so on.

"Where do you think I have influence any more? They don't listen to me in Washington. Might even do the woman more harm than good if I put in a word. . . . It's a political crime, the way they'd see it. You couldn't get them to believe all that stuff about mathematics. And if they did, where's the angle? She's not an American citizen."

"But married to one."

"I don't think that would mean a thing."

Brad said heavily: "We just thought it was worth making the trip to see you about it, sir." I had never heard him call my father "sir" before, and it sounded less a sign of respect than of antagonism. "Since apparently it wasn't, we'd better be getting back to Vienna — there's perhaps something we can do there on our own."

My father bowed slightly. "I hope so. I do indeed."

"Brad," I said, "go out and wait for me in the lobby. I'll join you in a minute."

"Okay." He nodded to my father and walked away. Then I said: "Excuse him for being brusque. He's going through a terrible strain."

"Naturally. I understand that. . . . He's grown into quite a fellow. . . . A sort of you-be-damned look in his eyes . . . different from the way he was in London. . . ."

My father's detached appreciation of an attitude that had been slightly insulting was typical of him; but at that particular moment it irritated me. I said: "He has that look now, maybe, but it's not normal in him."

"But he's acquired poise . . . he's more sure of himself. . . . I think he's developing very well."

And at any other time this too might have pleased me, but not now. "Isn't there anything at all you can do for his wife?"

"Not a thing, I'm afraid."

"Of course you can't *promise* . . . but won't you give it a try? There might be other places besides Washington where you could put in a word."

He checked me over with his glance, then replied: "I can't think of any, at the moment."

"Father . . . I hate to put the matter to you personally . . . but you know, in a sort of way, you were in this business at the beginning—I mean you recommended Brad to go to Vienna and you had him meet Framm at our house. . . . I know that doesn't make you in any way responsible, but surely it gives you an interest . . . an extra interest . . ."

"I don't have to have an extra interest. I'd help him willingly if I could. You ought to know that."

"Then you will if you can—is *that* a promise?"

"Certainly, but I don't see how . . . at present. If anything should occur to me . . ."

"And it might! You'll try to think of something?"

"Yes, yes, of course." I kissed him and he went on, a little patheti-
cally: "You and I don't see as much of each other as we used. You
go roaming all over the Continent looking for trouble . . ." He
pinched my ear in the almost standardized mood of a father pretending to have all the standardized fatherly virtues.

"So do you," I said.

"No, not *looking* for it . . . just *finding* it." He dropped the pose
and his voice also; when he spoke again it was in an almost petu-
lant undertone. "I don't really *like* these people. Even when they do
the right thing they do it the wrong way. And they won't *listen*. . . ."

Whether he had any special reason for saying so on that rainy
March morning in the city of Linz I have often wondered but have
never been able to determine exactly.

I rejoined Brad and we took the next train back to Vienna. I told
him my father had promised to think the matter over, and that with
even such a limited result the trip could not be called a waste of
time. But he was too dejected to respond much, and most of the
journey we dozed against the cushions. It continued to rain and at
Vienna was still raining. We went to my hotel and telephoned
Bauer's office and home, but he was away from both. It was almost
dinnertime by then, and we had had no food all day, but neither of
us was hungry. We were served a rather bad meal in the hotel dining room, which was crowded with German officers. Then Brad said
he would go back to his apartment and get some sleep. I walked
with him to the corner of the Opern-Ring, where he usually took
a tram. On the way he said suddenly: "Who was that woman your
father was having breakfast with?"

"I got the name as Larousse — Madame Larousse. French, from
her accent. I never heard of her before."

"Do you think your father's living with her?"

I was startled by his asking the question rather than by the question itself; after a second or so I answered: "I shouldn't wonder. She looked nice."

I noticed that a tram passed by which he could easily have caught. He said: "Not, of course, that it's any of my business."

"It isn't really, is it? Or mine either. . . . To tell you the truth, I know very little of his private affairs. He and my mother haven't seemed to be getting along lately. . . ."

"They haven't?"

"Oh well, how do I know? Perhaps they have, when they've been together. But they've been so often separated."

"They didn't have to be. She used to go with him everywhere."

"She got tired of gadding about, I suppose. Or else she likes a different kind of gadding about . . . maybe that's it. . . . I've often thought they weren't very well suited."

"I used to think that too, in London."

We waited for the next tram in silence, but I could see that his mood was changed, and it struck me as odd that such a matter should be capable of lifting him out of dejection into something like a controlled excitement. The tram came up and I said "There you are — run for it!" — because I didn't want him to continue the conversation.

* * *

Towards the end of March Bauer had news that the date of the trial was postponed and that in the meantime Pauli had been removed to a prison outside Vienna. He had no idea where, and could not find out; nor did he think they would allow him to visit her again. Brad was still unable to obtain permission to visit her at all. The new regime was getting into its stride and Bauer was utterly downcast; he no longer hoped for a fair trial, or that he would be given a free hand as counsel for the defense — many of the normal rights of lawyers in dealing with clients had already been suspended. He wasn't even certain he might not be arrested himself.

Then one morning the telephone rang and I heard my father's voice. He was at the Bristol, he said, and could Brad and I see him as soon as convenient?

We were in his sitting room within an hour. The baroque furnishings, so typical of the age in which these luxury hotels were built, seemed strangely inappropriate to the heaviness in our minds; and I never see a Buhl writing desk now without remembering one on which, at the end of the interview, Brad wrote his signature.

He and my father shook hands as we entered, then my father glanced along the corridor before closing and bolting the door. "The chambermaid comes in at such odd moments," he said, playing down his precautions. "She's quite dumb, but it would be a nuisance."

He settled himself in an easy chair. "Tell me, Brad," he began abruptly, "what's the real thing you're after?"

I suppose the question seemed so general that Brad hesitated — perhaps he even wondered if it had anything at all to do with what was uppermost in his mind.

My father went on: "What I mean is, does your wife come first in all this?"

"Of course!" The reply was decisive enough now.

"All right. So you have one aim only — to get her out of trouble and resume your life with her?"

"Absolutely."

"And you'd do anything possible for such a thing to happen?"

"Look here, Mr. Waring, you don't have to waste time asking me questions like that . . ."

"Please . . . let me deal with this my own way. I want to be quite sure that in bringing these accusations against Framm you're actuated solely by a desire to come to your wife's defense."

"That's right."

"You're sure you've no *personal* interest in substantiating them? You're not thinking of your professional standing — anything of that sort?"

"Not a bit."

"As a matter of fact, you never had, prior to the . . . er . . . the attempt on Framm's life . . . any idea of bringing a civil suit against him?"

"Never."

I intervened. "Pauli urged him to, but he refused. It wasn't the kind of thing he could be bothered with. That's not to say that Framm wasn't guilty. There's plenty of evidence — "

"Please, Jane. . . . This is between Brad and me. I just want to be certain of his position."

"He's told you. He wants to save Pauli, that's the only thing that matters now."

Brad nodded emphatically.

"All right. Then I can put forward a proposition . . . and one which, if he accepts it, will enable Pauli to join him in some other country within a few months."

As the full meaning of this came to him, Brad's face was illumined. He made as if to get up and seize my father's hand but I tugged at his sleeve.

"I'll do *anything,*" he muttered. He had no voice for more.

"First of all, this is what will happen if you agree to the proposition. Your wife will be brought to trial and found guilty, but there'll be medical evidence that she's insane. She'll then be sent to some place of detention for a time. However, after a reasonable interval she'll be allowed to leave, provided she doesn't stay in Austria. . . . You understand?"

Brad still could not reply. I had never seen him so moved.

I said: "He understands. Now what is it he has to do?"

"I'm coming to that. It's quite simple and if he feels as he says, he can have no possible objection. What the . . . er . . . the authorities will require is a statement from him . . . as a matter of fact, I have it here with me now — all he has to do is to sign it . . . a simple statement to the effect that there's no truth whatever in his wife's accusations against Framm. That's all."

Brad looked up, but I could not read what was in his mind.

I said bitterly: "I see. They want to whitewash Framm's reputation."

"Put it that way if you like. The main thing is that they're prepared to pay for it by giving Brad what he says *he* most wants."

"So he has to go into court and swear his wife's a liar?"

"I doubt if there'll be any need for that. She may not even have to testify. I expect Brad will just read his statement and that will be all that's necessary."

"Let me see it. You said you have it here."

"Certainly." My father went to his briefcase, took out a large Manila envelope and passed it over. I read for a moment, then exclaimed: "Why, this is the biggest swindle I ever heard of! Brad has to give his whole case away and gets nothing in exchange! There's not a mention of any promise to release Pauli."

"There couldn't be. That sort of thing never gets into a document. . . . However, I understand on quite high authority that what I have said will be done."

"What high authority?"

"I don't see that it matters, but one source is Professor Framm himself."

"I thought he was dying."

"They say now he has a slight chance of recovery."

"But what guarantee has Brad?"

"None at all. He just has to take somebody's word."

"For what it's worth."

"Yes."

"And how much is that?"

"You can judge as well as I can."

"Did you see Framm?"

"I saw his representative."

"But supposing they break their word? Brad's got no redress. He's giving away everything . . . everything that could possibly help her at the trial!"

My father said grimly: "What you must remember is that *nothing* can help her at the trial — except this signed paper. If he doesn't sign, she'll be found guilty after a short hearing and the sentence will be carried out. Assuming that Framm doesn't die, the penalty for attempted murder is, I believe, from ten to fifteen years."

"You think they'd do that?"

"I can't see anything to stop them. Framm's an important man — and going to be more so if he lives."

All this time Brad had said nothing. He had listened in a half-bewildered way, sometimes nodding or shaking his head. Now, however, he reached over and snatched the paper from me. He went over to the Buhl desk and I followed him, grabbing the paper back. "Don't do anything yet, Brad — we've got to think this out — we need at least a day to decide in — we'll take this with us and come back tomorrow — "

My father snapped: "That won't do. You have to decide now. I promised an answer this morning."

"Then let me call Bauer. He's the lawyer. Brad oughtn't to sign anything without consulting him first."

"We can't do that either. If anyone else moves in you might as well tear it up right away, signed or unsigned. This isn't a matter for lawyers. . . . It's what you might call . . . well . . . well . . ." There was a saving irony in his voice as he added: "A gentlemen's agreement?"

"With the only gentleman in the case offering everything in exchange for nothing."

"I don't think we can gain much by going over the whole ground again. For one thing, there isn't time."

"Why is there such a hurry?"

"People who can conquer a country in two days get the habit of being in a hurry."

There was silence after that, during which my father fidgeted impatiently. If it were true that he was being pressed for an answer, I could well understand his mood, for it was the kind of situation he would find humiliating as well as irksome.

At length Brad muttered almost inaudibly: "How long was it you said . . . till they release her? . . . A few months?"

My father nodded.

"She's going to have a baby in September."

I turned to Brad, wanting to say something quick and warm, but the words would not come at such a moment; I could only smile at him in case he looked my way.

My father said quickly: "I think you can count on it she'll be with you before then."

"Then I'll sign."

So he did so, at the Buhl desk, with the scratchy hotel pen. My father verified and witnessed the signature, then put the document back in his briefcase and grabbed his hat and coat. We all went out together. As we stepped from the elevator on the ground floor he said: "Good-by, Jane . . . Brad . . . I think we probably go in different directions. . . ."

We let him walk ahead through the lobby on his own, while we pretended to study the list of entertainments on the hotel notice board. *The Great Ziegfeld, Romeo and Juliet,* and *Scarface* were among the movie attractions. *The Magic Flute* was at the Opera

House. But the little cinema round the corner where I had seen some of the best French and pre-Hitler German films was now, it appeared, closed until further notice.

I was due to leave the next morning for Rome, where I had people to interview for a magazine. As I should be away about a week Brad took me to an appropriate farewell dinner at a small Italian restaurant near the Stephans-Dom; we drank a bottle of Chianti and he grew cheerful towards the end of the evening, as one who has taken the only possible course and might as well hope for the best from it. I agreed with him it had been the only possible course. After the strain of recent weeks, it was perhaps natural to react excessively, though even while he was doing so the more sober part of himself made the necessary corrective. "I'd better not let myself go," he said, midway through the second bottle. "It would be too bad if I caught myself feeling grateful to these sons of bitches. . . ."

It was near midnight when we separated outside my hotel. "Anyhow," he said, having talked all round the compass and back again, "I'm glad Framm's got an outside chance. Not that he deserves it, but he'd be a loss to science. . . ."

Those were practically the last words Brad spoke to me for years, though I was far from guessing it then. He was a little drunk and would have kissed me good night, perhaps, but for knowing he was a little drunk.

From my room a few minutes later I telephoned the Bristol, thinking that my father deserved at least the few words of thanks I had till then had no time to convey. But a voice told me in unctuous German that he had left a few hours before by the Orient Express for Paris. I waited a few more minutes, then telephoned again and asked for Madame Larousse. The same voice told me she had left a few hours before by the Orient Express for Paris.

I remembered also for years those parting words of my father's: "Good-by, Jane . . . I think we probably go in different directions. . . ."

I think we always have.

* * *

High authority, as he had tactfully called it, kept its word at the trial, which came up a few weeks afterwards. Pauli did not testify, and Brad gave his stipulated evidence — legally irrelevant, the judge observed, but desirable in order to refute certain mischievous rumors that had been widely circulated by enemies of the Gross-Deutschland. Pauli was then declared guilty but insane, and the whole thing was over within a matter of hours. The newspapers gave great prominence to the high character of Professor Framm, so strikingly vindicated by his American colleague and assistant, and the total impression was that the two of them had been bosom friends, that the young man had unfortunately married a homicidal lunatic, and that thanks to the large-hearted wisdom of the new regime such a distressing matter was being wound up both equitably and expeditiously — in contrast, doubtless, to what would have happened earlier or elsewhere. I think also that anyone unacquainted with the inside story (which meant nearly everyone) could easily have concluded that this young American was a warm sympathizer with the Gross-Deutschland, its policies, personalities, and plans for the future. The court proceedings were stage-managed with extreme skill, and Brad's statement, read by him in English, sounded much more emphatic in the German translation that immediately followed.

I heard all this from Bauer, because when I tried to return to Vienna from Rome, the German consulate refused to renew my visa. Certain articles of mine in the American press had, it appeared, made me *persona non grata* with the Nazis. So I went to Switzerland and there waited for Brad, if he should care to join me for a time; but he wrote that he would rather save his money for a long holiday with Pauli as soon as she was released. That made me insist on lending him a thousand dollars, which he returned, and when I sent it again even more insistently he returned it with a note in which he laïd bare the entire state of his finances. He had about five hundred and thirty dollars, he said, which he reckoned ample for all expenses until he found another job; and for any emergency he owned twenty shares of A.T. and T. Common which his uncle in North Dakota (the amateur geologist) had willed him before he died. I thought it was a good stage in our relationship, if not a romantic one, that he should give me details of this sort.

I did not hear from him again, and several of my letters were returned as undeliverable. I wrote to Bauer for news, but also without answer.

Then one evening at a London cocktail party I met a half-tipsy Englishman lately in Austria who said he had a vague idea he had heard somewhere that Pauli was dead. I didn't tell him that my interest in her was in any way personal. It was a noisy party and I had to yell the next question in his ear. "And her husband? Did you hear anything about *him?*"

He yelled back: "Well, he practically ditched her, didn't he, at the trial? . . . American chap . . . Don't know what's happened to him since." He flicked an olive stone into an ashtray and ventured: "Maybe he went back to America. . . ."

* * *

145

PART THREE

PART

THREE

I WOKE to see the hostess nudging me. "Sorry to trouble you, but we're coming down at Palmdale. There'll be a bus to take you into Burbank. . . . It's on account of fog."
She moved to the passenger in front and delivered the same message. The plane was already noticeably descending and instruction to fasten seat belts came on while I was blinking myself awake. I felt a little irritated at the thought of a long bus journey and wondered whether the studio would have sent a car to meet me at Burbank.

My trip to California was mainly because I had recently published a book called *Great Circle,* in which I gave an account of my world wanderings to date. It had sold quite well, and a Hollywood studio bought the movie rights. Presently someone discovered, as should have been apparent from the outset, that there was no "story" in it, but so far from discouraging them, this merely whetted their desire for the authoress herself to construct one. I told them I had no talent for that sort of thing, but I suppose such frankness convinced them far more than if I had jumped at the idea; anyhow, in the end we compromised on my spending a few weeks in Hollywood for "consultation." Everything about the arrangement sounded reasonable except the fee, which was absurd.

I had been to California before, several times, and had liked it fairly well, and the fact that my father was now living there would give me a chance to pay him the visit which I felt was due, after a somewhat longer interval than usual.

149

There was a full moon and a clear sky at Palmdale, but no sign of a bus. The disembarked passengers converged towards a make-shift army hut in that peculiar mood of strandedness inflicted nowadays only on those who travel the modern way. The bus, we were told, was "coming" — had been delayed by a flat tire. I was just about to doze off again in a chair when a loudspeaker yelled my name and the information that a car was waiting for me outside. Everybody stared, waiting for a person called Waring to move, and something of my chronic phobia surged up and almost made me decide to remain anonymous, but I knew I should be found out after succeeding yells, so I pushed rather ill-humoredly through the small crowd and was doubtless the object of comment and envy.

A large black Cadillac stood at the curb, attended by a uniformed chauffeur who saluted in style. As he fixed me inside with a rug he remarked how fortunate it was that he'd been able to arrive before I got on the bus. I thought so too. Warmth and comfort began to pacify me even before we left the airport precincts, and soon I was musing on the hospitality of Hollywood studios and whether it would change when they found out I hadn't fooled them. Or would they think I had?

I must have slept, because the next thing I remember was the crunch of gravel as the car slewed through big gates into an upward curving driveway. I thought this could hardly be where a hotel room had been booked for me, and I was rousing myself to lean forward and question the chauffeur when we pulled up in front of a rather immense Spanish-type portico.

"But where *is* this?" I asked, when he held open the door.

"Vista Grande, miss."

"*What?*"

"Mr. Waring's house, miss. Vista Grande. . . ."

"Mr. Waring's? . . . My . . . but . . . but I'm supposed to go to a hotel in Beverly Hills. . . . I thought this was a studio car. . . ."

"Mr. Waring's car, miss. He telephoned the airline and found you were coming down at Palmdale."

"There must be some mistake, though. Mr. Waring didn't expect me here . . . or maybe he didn't know about the hotel. Better keep my bags in the car — I'll be going on there later. . . . Is Mr. Waring in?"

By this time several servants from the house had joined in the proceedings, and it was all adding up to the kind of fuss I dislike.

"Mr. Waring is in the library," somebody said.

As I climbed the steps the chauffeur called after me, in a friendly way: "I shouldn't think you'd want to go to Beverly Hills tonight, miss. It's about a hundred and fifty miles from here. . . ."

*   *   *

Entering Vista Grande through the large vaulted hall, with a servant leading the way like a stage servant, I couldn't help thinking how my father's life must have changed since losing my mother, first by divorce, then by her death. She would never have been happy in a place like this. I could almost hear her voice protesting: "But Harvey, this is *impossible*. . . ." She had always liked a gay, cheerful, offhand sort of house, and though she had a flair for furnishing, she mixed styles and periods "for Pete's sake," as I used to think as a child. For when my father came back to our house, wherever it was, to find some new carpet or curtains or a reorganization of the furniture, he would say: "Christine, for Pete's sake, what's been happening?" But now it had stopped happening for some years, and the result was all opulence, impeccability, and loneliness. The place looked like a cathedral that wasn't sure there was a god. Even the name was typical — the second word, anyhow. It lacked the touch of humanly bastard Spanish that enlivens so many of the homes of Southern California; it was the real thing, for those who sought their realities in wood and stone. I admit that after I had got used to Vista Grande I liked it better, but I never quite overcame that first chilling impression.

The library was a long room, walled with books in alcoves between heavily curtained windows; the lamps were dim, but a log fire sent spears of light to show the carved ceiling and the leather bindings on the shelves. This was not so alarming as the hall; indeed, in a somber way it was rather fine, though personally I would have expected to write with more comfort in a motel.

As I entered, my father rose slowly from an easy chair by the fire, and he looked so much older that I was immediately touched. We had drifted apart after the divorce; it wasn't that I had sided with my mother so much as the plain fact that I liked her better, and since it was she who had taken over the New York house (and John), I saw her oftener during the scattered intervals when I wasn't traveling. After she died I acquired the house myself, though it was far too big and unnecessarily expensive; I wasn't, however, in a mood to find somewhere else. I saw my father occasionally and in various places till he began to change in slight but noticeable ways that set him further from me. As this had to do with politics, and largely out-of-date politics now, there is no point in going into detail. We corresponded from time to time; he told me his health wasn't so good, and I learned (long after he had mostly recovered from it) that he had had a slight stroke. The next I heard was that he was compelled to rest a good deal and had bought a place in California which was quite isolated and fabulous.

And now he was welcoming me to it. "Jane . . . How *are* you? . . . Good to see you after all this time. . . ."

He kissed me, and the servant (a young Italian-looking boy with a beautiful face) helped him back into his chair.

My father went on: "It's just lucky your plane came down at Palmdale — much nearer here than Burbank. You've saved at least an hour."

After that I could see I should have to spend the night there, but already I didn't mind so much. The Italian-looking boy, still hovering around, seemed to read my acceptance of the situation, for when I went to bed later my bags had been taken up and unpacked without further instructions.

"So you're quite a famous person now, Jane! *Hollywood*. . . . I saw it in the papers. Well, you can make this your headquarters as long as you want — it's only a couple of hours' drive."

More than that, I reflected, if it were a hundred and fifty miles; but in any case, I was certain that Vista Grande would not suit me at all. There was no point, however, in arguing the matter then. I said: "I'm glad to find you settled down like this, Father. It all looks rather stupendous, but of course I haven't seen it yet in daylight."

"You'll like it when you do. There's a fine view over the mountains."

I hadn't realized it was in mountain country, which I prefer to any other kind. My father went on: "Now tell me about yourself. Not married yet, I know. But not even engaged — or interested in anybody?"

"Interested in a great many people, but not engaged."

"Twenty-six, my dear. Getting time. Or is it twenty-seven?"

You put up with that sort of thing all the more easily when you have received and rejected quite a number of proposals. Also it occurred to me that he was matching his behavior, as he matched his furniture, to an approved style — perhaps Lewis Stone or Lionel Barrymore or some other popular father-myth.

"Twenty-seven," I answered, "and I know it makes me very old, but I started everything early — you remember I began dining out at sixteen. . . ."

I said that lightly, not expecting it to echo along the corridors of his memory and finally wake something.

"Yes . . . yes . . . I remember. . . . That painter fellow at

153

Hampstead let me down over the house. I told him if he ever wanted to sell I'd buy."

"Oh well, never mind. You wouldn't be living there now, anyway."

"Not now, of course . . . but when the war's finally over everywhere—"

"England won't be the same, though. Europe won't be the same. Only America will pretend to be the same."

"That's what you said in your book. . . . But how are they going to put that sort of thing on the screen?"

"They aren't. I can't think why they bought it unless they just want to use the title."

"H'm. . . . I didn't think it was such a wonderful title."

"Neither did I."

We talked on, as inconsequently as that, and presently I telephoned the hotel that I wouldn't be arriving that night. Then we climbed the stairs and he showed me to my room. I took his arm with more meaning because I knew he needed it. The bedroom and adjacent bathroom and dressing rooms were so sumptuous that I couldn't restrain a whistle, whereupon he remarked, as if making a confession: "I know—it wasn't cheap."

I said jokingly: "Even income tax doesn't get you down?"

"I have so much in tax-exempts," he answered seriously.

He led me to the open window and pulled a curtain. Very dimly, in the clear moonlit sky, could be seen the horizon of a mountain range. "There's a little snow on some of them—it stays all the year sometimes. You'll like the look of things in the morning, Jane."

"I'm sure I shall. And such utter silence—that's strange after New York. How far are you from your nearest neighbor?"

"About four miles. It doesn't bother me."

"Why should it? Only a few minutes' drive."

154

"But I don't even *know* them. I care for company less and less."
He added, with frail gallantry: "Except *present* company."

"Thanks," I said, a little touched.

"Good night, then. . . ." But he paused on his way to the door.
"You know, Jane . . . this is what I ought to have done after the
Marazon inquiry. I should have settled down in a place like this
instead of spending so much time abroad. . . ."

God, I reflected — how my mother would have hated it. But I was
also surprised because this was the first time I had ever heard him
refer to that unhappy incident directly. Of course I had been too
young when it happened to know much about it, but I had read of
it since, and the fact that it doubtless still cropped up in many people's minds when his name was mentioned (or mine either, for
that matter) had become a quite unspeakable thing between us.
For this reason his broaching of it now and so casually seemed to
me a pathetic sign of age and weakening.

"Oh, why bring that up?" I said. "Good night, Father."

He fumbled his way out and I was surprised to find myself sor-
rier for him than I had felt even at my mother's graveside. He *had*
been rather unlucky in that Marazon business. Maintaining a representative to watch your business interests at an international peace
conference must always require a good deal of tact. My father's
representative on that occasion was not tactful, and as he was also
the son of a Senator the whole thing became a political football.
That was the time when my father was publicly attacked as a merchant of death, and I think he would have done better to ignore the
attacks than to argue, as he did, that cement was not a war material
and that he had no idea that the sale of it in huge quantities to a
European government could have had anything to do with the
construction of fortifications. But cement was not the worst of the
things my father had interests in, nor was it revealed that he had

been selling to one side only; indeed, the thorough investigation that ensued was the last thing he should ever have courted.

*   *   *

The next morning I woke early, drew the curtains, and saw the breath-taking view across the Santa Modena Valley. The range that had been palely visible in the moonlight was now a deep green meeting the blue of the sky, and beyond it, at some far distance, were higher ranges tipped with snow. I came to know and love that view during the weeks that followed; it was the kind that had a different enchantment for every time of day and variation of weather.

My father did not get up till noon, the Italian-looking boy told me (and also that his own name was Dan). He added that all arrangements had been made to drive me into Hollywood whenever I wished. I took a solitary breakfast on an outdoor terrace overlooking the view, then said I would leave at ten o'clock. That gave me time to wander about the house and grounds. It was a large property and, considering the wartime labor shortage, excellently kept up. In strong sunlight the house itself did not look so somberly impressive, which was all to the good; and I could admit the value of dark interiors as a contrast to the vividness outside. The air was already so warm that I suspected the place might get uncomfortably hot at times, and I commented on this, but Dan said it was too high up — about four thousand feet — to be ever unbearable, and that in any case the house itself was air-conditioned.

I drove into Hollywood with no clear decision in my mind about returning. I felt I ought to have explained that the distance was much too great for driving often, and that a hotel room on the spot would really suit me better. But my father hadn't come down to breakfast and I didn't want to hurt his feelings; perhaps another night would do no harm, and I could tell him after dinner.

We drove for miles over a succession of ridges, passing hardly any traffic, till we joined the main Bakersfield–Los Angeles highway. Arrived at the studio I found everyone at lunch and no apparent sign that I had been missed or was wanted; but about three o'clock I was welcomed with great courtesy by the head of the organization. He chatted for a while without supplying any evidence that he had read my book, and apologized for the absence of a Mr. Chandos, who was visiting the dentist. Mr. Chandos was expected back at the studio about four — would I perhaps care to wait, or would it suit me better to meet Mr. Chandos some other day? I said I would wait, and somehow would have minded less if everyone hadn't apologized so much. It was almost as if I were being told that waiting was humiliating and that therefore it was too much to ask me to do it. Perhaps for this reason I grew rather bored as four o'clock came, then half past, and still no Mr. Chandos. Every few minutes his secretary put her head in at the door and said she was sure he wouldn't be gone much longer, but if I preferred, she knew he would understand if I chose not to wait. That made me wait more exasperatedly than ever, though it was really not hard to pass the time in Mr. Chandos's office, equipped as it was with radio, phonograph, armchairs, and all the latest magazines. These Hollywood magnates do themselves well, I reflected; and that set me wondering what sort of man Mr. Chandos was, as my mother and I had once wondered what sort of man Hugo Framm was. But it wasn't much of a game to play solo, and my expectations of Mr. Chandos were hardly amusing and not very cheerful. I suppose subconsciously I thought of the Hollywood one reads about, because when finally Mr. Chandos did appear he surprised me very much.

To begin with, he was young — not more than thirty-odd, quite good-looking, and exceedingly literate. He apologized briefly for his lateness, but obviously considered a sudden tooth extraction reason enough (which it was); he also said a few polite but not extravagant things about my book. Then we began talking about various parts of the world we had both visited; and by five o'clock I knew a few of the facts of his life, such as that he was unmarried, had been rejected by the army for medical reasons, and had come to Hollywood originally from Harvard Law School by way of journalism in Chicago and a doctor's recommendation of the California climate.

"So you like it here," I said.

"It's good for my lungs," he answered.

"Not for anything else?"

"Well . . . for my pocket, if you count that."

"Let's be realistic and count everything."

He laughed. "All right. But I warn you — I'm an idealist. I'd like to make a picture that would cost a couple of millions and lose at least one of them. Hollywood won't let me. It's all I have against the place. Or nearly all."

"So what do you do in the meantime?"

"I compromise."

"Why do you suppose your ideal picture would fail commercially?"

"Why do you suppose so many pictures that are not ideal succeed commercially?"

"That's not answering my question. I want to know whether you believe it's Hollywood's fault or the people's."

"Both . . . and also neither's. Think of the task of making fifty-two pictures a year for a public that expects to see a new one every week. How can fifty-two per year of anything in the creative field be more than averagely competent? Are there fifty-two good books every year? Or good canvases or good musical compositions? . . . You can't expect Hollywood to be an exception. It's a machine for the production of financially profitable entertainment, and it does that pretty well — so well that if it produces a miracle now and again it really *is* a miracle. It's almost as if one car on the Ford assembly line should suddenly turn out to be a Hispano–Suiza."

"So to work miracles you should get out of Hollywood."

"Yes, but the even greater miracle of getting a miracle out of Hollywood always tempts me. It's such a wonderful place for sheer technical competence. . . . Look, why don't we celebrate this first meeting?" He turned to a cabinet which proved to be a miniature bar and began setting out glasses.

I said I would have a very dry Martini, not too large, because I had a drive ahead of me. He made it with some of the sheer technical competence he had been talking about, and this challenged me to say: "Since you've been frank, I might as well be also. I can't imagine why your studio bought my book for filming. There's no story in it, and its real value, if it has any, couldn't be got on the screen."

"That's what *you* think," he answered, quite rudely. "And see here . . . in my office there's one taboo — one only. Never say that a certain thing can't be got on the screen. What would you have said to anyone who set limits to music or painting only half a century after their first beginnings?"

"All right," I said. "But I've heard that before in another form. The difficult we do immediately, the impossible takes a little longer. It's the sort of gag you see framed on the office wall of a toilet-paper manufacturer. Art isn't half so arrogant. It accepts limits — in fact, the limits are part of it. . . ."

We went on talking and arguing till past six, and set a date for another meeting the following Wednesday. I wasn't quite clear what the purpose of these meetings was to be (so far we hadn't discussed the picture or the book at all in any specific terms), but I was being well paid for whatever Mr. Chandos wanted from me, and if it was only general conversation I could not complain. I drove back to Vista Grande with a growing conviction that I rather liked him.

My father had held up dinner and his patience in doing so seemed
to me quite pathetic. He asked many questions about my visit to
the studio, and then I suddenly got the angle of his interest, which
was also pathetic — he had heard some of the classic stories of Hollywood dilatoriness and hoped I would be one of those people who
come originally for a few weeks and stay on endlessly. As this was
precisely what I intended should not happen, it was hard for me
to give him the kind of replies he wanted. He reiterated how pleased
he was to have me staying at Vista Grande — that it was what
he had hoped for ever since he bought it. He also told me something about the house, which had apparently been modernized from
the shell of an old ranch house dating back to Spanish–Mexican
times. He had chosen it, he said, because he thought it a pleasant
place to end his days in; and when I protested (aware that we were
both conforming to a certain pattern of behavior), he said that of
course he didn't mean to die yet, his doctor had said it might be
years — many years, if he took care of himself. So he was doing
that, and the climate suited him; he took drives and found the
mountain air invigorating; he also went to Santa Barbara or Palm
Springs occasionally and just pottered about the streets, well content
that nobody ever recognized him. Which reminded him: it happened that he had been fortunate in getting a private supply of gaso-
line — quite unofficially, of course — so that my trips to the studio
were all right, so far as he was concerned, though perhaps I had
better not tell anyone I was driving so far.

I thought it again pathetic that he should so easily switch from
talk of death to a confession of black marketeering; for both were
further signs of the change in him — perhaps also of a change in the
world around him. The truth was, I figured, that though his career
had doubtless contained many incidents of a dubious character, they
had all been large matters, like that of Marazon Cement; in the
small things, until the war, his right to priority and privilege had

never been questioned; indeed, an army of underlings had always been at call to ensure that he got the best seat, the fastest plane, the promptest service, the ringside table, the choicest cut. But now this was changed also, and though he could still get most of what he wanted, he had to chisel like any small-time grafter.

I told him I certainly wouldn't wish to use gas for frequent trips, but that in any case I hadn't to visit the studio again for a week; which meant that tacitly I was agreeing to stay at Vista Grande. (And I later telephoned the hotel canceling my room.) We sat by the fire in the library after dinner listening to the radio — just the news and a commentator. I had never known him bother much with the radio in years gone by, for the reason that he never wanted to listen except when he was tired, and then he would certainly have been too tired to listen to a commentator. But now he was only too tired to comment on the commentator. Some kind of declining equilibrium seemed to have been reached, offering perhaps a tranquility that offset even the loneliness. He went up to bed about ten, kissing me good night as he had kissed me when I used to go up to bed as a girl. It was all more like a home than I had had for years, although (or else because) there was something in it that dragged at the heart.

I stayed up myself till nearly midnight, examining the books and generally pottering about. They were a sound collection of mainly modern authors, quite unnecessarily rebound in full calf, and with a few good first editions, among them a boxed copy of the 1847 Currer Bell *Jane Eyre,* which I remembered my father had once bought in London. I took it down to reread that immortal opening sentence — "There was no possibility of taking a walk that day" — with its hint of English rain and Victorian servitude. I was still at the books when Dan entered. He had forgotten to tell me, he said, that someone had telephoned during the day . . . a Mr. Small.

"Small?"

"Yes, miss. He said he'd like to see you tomorrow morning."

"To *see* me? But he's — he's in New York!"

"He said he'd be here, miss. Shouldn't I have told him you'd be in?"

"No, no . . . it's all right. I'll see him, of course."

*   *   *

The thought of Mr. Small kept me restless till almost dawn, after which I slept a few hours and woke up wondering what part of my life I was in. Then I saw the sun through the curtains and felt the silence that was, of all things after New York, least familiar. It was past nine. I bathed and dressed hurriedly, having told Dan to take Mr. Small to the terrace and offer him breakfast if he came. But when I got down I found there was another man, whom Mr. Small introduced as a Dr. Newby. They had declined anything to eat, but were sipping coffee, sniffing the air, and taking in the view with a good deal of quizzical admiration. Mr. Small had made concessions to California in the shape of two-color shoes, sunglasses, and a Panama; he seemed quite cheerful and asked if I were surprised to see him again so soon.

"Nothing surprises me any more," I answered, deciding on a line. "You must have taken practically the next plane. How did you know where I'd gone?"

He smiled. "You didn't make it very difficult for me."

"I didn't try."

He nodded. "That's so." Then he looked around. "Nice. Good place to settle down and write another book. . . . Is that the idea?"

"No. I'm in California on a short business trip. But I'm still puzzled how you found I was here, because I'd originally intended to stay at a hotel."

"That's what the hotel people said."

"How did you know which hotel it was, or did you try them all?"

"I knew where the picture company had booked you a room."

"For heaven's sake how did you know there *was* a picture company?"

"It was in *Variety* that they'd bought your book to make a film.
. . So you see none of it was really difficult."

I suppose it was a very elementary example of sleuthing, and it probably impressed me more than it should have. I smiled ruefully. "All right. So you know everything."

"No. There's a lot that you still haven't told."

I thought I might as well force an issue then as later, so I retorted: "And I'm not going to — unless I'm given at least a ghost of a reason for all this grilling. No doubt it's very important, or you wouldn't have followed me out here, but that doesn't alter my attitude — I'm just not going to answer any more."

"Of course you know you could be legally compelled to."

"Sure — by subpoena. And then you'd be surprised how little I could tell you. I'm apt to have a bad memory about things that happened so many years ago."

"That would certainly put us in a spot."

"Not you. Bradley's the one who's in a spot, and you won't tell me why."

He thought that over for a moment, then said: "You'll notice, Miss Waring, I haven't brought a shorthand writer with me. You're not even on oath."

"As I don't intend to lie, that doesn't make much difference."

"I thought it might make you feel more inclined to co-operate."

I didn't answer. He went on: "At any rate, it ought to set the key for a friendlier talk than we had last time."

"What's happened in the interval to make *you* feel friendlier?"

He smiled. "I don't see why I shouldn't tell you. I read your book." He stared at me through his sunglasses. They gave him a moonfaced appearance that belied certain of his qualities that were

known to me. He might be kind, but I couldn't see him ever as be-
nign. "My wife read it too. She said it gave a very fine picture of
Americanism."

I hadn't ever thought of it that way, but when you have written
a book you get so used to unusual compliments that you blink at
them no more than at unusual insults.

"My wife's a very good judge of a book — and of a writer. She
said you looked at things without prejudice and you had a passion-
ate devotion to freedom, so that what you wrote was what you felt
as well as what you saw."

This somewhat took my breath away, because it was so nearly the
epitaph I would choose, if any, to have inscribed on my tombstone.
I was making up my mind to remember it when he added: "That's
why she called it a picture of Americanism. And I must say I agree
with her. It seems to me as American as — as — "

"Apple pie?" I suggested.

"Well yes, if you like."

"Or cornbread . . . chewing gum . . . clam chowder . . ."

By that time he realized I was trying to be funny. And I don't
know why I was, except in relief at the vision of Mr. Small at home
with his intellectual wife and their solemn discussions of books.
Perhaps they discussed them from one twin bed to another.

"Well, well," he summed up, "your book certainly made a hit
with her. She also said it could only have been written by one who
knew from deep experience what it means to be born in this
country."

"Except that I wasn't."

"Oh?"

He must have known; it would be the first and easiest thing to
discover about me. Was it just another test to see if I were being
frank? I went on with a sort of nervous facetiousness that I don't
like but sometimes can't help: "The great event happened in Lon-

don, England, and if my mother had been taken ill a few hours later it would have been on the *Olympic*. What would that have made me — an Olympian?"

He blinked. "I must tell her that. . . . An Olympian, eh? . . . One thing, anyhow, it convinced *me* of . . . the book, I mean."

"What?"

He took off his glasses and became suddenly an alarmingly different person. "That you're somewhat your own worst enemy, Miss Waring. You're not always wise in what you say, or how you behave. I should think you've got into a good many scrapes, one way and another . . . haven't you?"

"Yes," I said. It was the simplest and truest answer.

"But your heart's in the right place. And you're loyal. You've been careful all along not to say anything against a man who was once your friend. You've been equally careful not to lie — even if you've concealed a good deal of the truth. As it happens, the problem ought not to arise for you again. At least we hope not."

"Who's we?"

"The authority I represent."

"And a nice frank answer, I must say."

"You couldn't expect much better in wartime."

"Something to do with the war — I guessed that. So what do you do if I lose my memory? Send me to jail?"

"Perhaps I should first tell you some of the things we already know. We know all about Bradley's activities before the war, we know of his friendships with Nazi professors, we know how he defended one of them — "

"But that's not true!" I interrupted. "I daresay it may have looked like that, but — "

"We're not questioning you about it — that isn't what I've come for. I'm fairly satisfied that your friendship with this man must have been just personal — "

"Yes, but — "

" — which is fine — no blame attaches to you at all."

"But you think it does to *him?* . . . I see. So he's under suspicion. . . . I can only tell you how utterly wrong you are."

"Possibly. There may be perfectly good reasons for everything he did, even for the fact that he worked in Germany up to the very day war broke out in 1939 — "

"*What?* He worked in *Germany?*"

"Oh, so you didn't know that? . . . Well, let's not worry too much about it. The main thing for you to realize — as his friend — is that being under suspicion means exactly what the word means — no more and no less. He may be completely innocent — "

"But of *what?*"

"Of anything we could possibly suspect. . . . We certainly *hope* he's innocent, if only because of his army record."

"Army?"

"Does that startle you too?"

"No . . . no . . . but I hadn't heard from him for so long — I didn't even know he'd come back to be drafted. Where is he now?"

"In this country. In a hospital."

"*Wounded?*"

"Well, injured. A flying accident. He pulled a pilot out of a burning plane. . . . At some risk to himself."

"But what happened to him? You said he was injured."

"Not very seriously, though he probably won't be any more use in the Air Force."

"Where's the hospital he's at?"

"In Arizona."

"Can I . . . could I . . . go to see him?"

"You'd like to, wouldn't you?"

"Yes — and since it's only the next state . . . *Could* I?"

"I don't think there'd be any objection." He smiled. "That's what you get for writing a good book."

If he hadn't mentioned the book again I might not have had the misgiving that suddenly came to me. I stared over the Santa Modena Valley and wondered vagrantly if those snow-tipped summits in the distance were reachable, and if the quest for truth would somehow be easier alone at that level than across a breakfast table between two persons sparring for position in what was still a conflict of minds. For already I sensed that it was not quite permission to see Brad that I had been granted, but rather that Mr. Small was quite anxious now that I should see him.

I said: "Well, thanks." And then, jumping the gun as usual: "Of course I don't suppose for a moment you're doing all this to please me. It's all part of some plan or other."

"Sure, what do you take me for? I've a job for you if you'll do it. You'd probably be doing it anyway — you're that kind of person."

"I don't understand."

"Keep your eyes and ears open — that's all."

"Why? . . . When?"

"When you meet your friend. Same as you did when you were traveling all over Europe to get material for your book. If you saw anything then that struck you as odd or significant you made a mental note of it — I'll bet you did. You certainly didn't miss much, and I'm inclined to think it took someone pretty smart to fool you."

"Maybe you're smart and you're fooling me now."

"No." He added quietly: "I think you'll know what I mean when you see Bradley."

"Why? What's the matter with him? You said it wasn't serious?"

"Physically, no. . . . He's almost recovered. Now don't get alarmed. He's not a raving lunatic either."

I said as calmly as I could: "Please — since you've said so much about him — tell me the whole truth. What's wrong with him?"

"That's part of our problem. Dr. Newby here can talk about it — he's a psychiatrist. He's studied the case. He thinks Bradley has something on his mind."

I looked then at the other man, who hadn't spoken a word so far, but who now seemed to emerge into a private limelight of his own. He was middle-aged, pale, and soulful-eyed, with a somewhat fussy manner and an air of reaching out for sympathy but hardly expecting it. Of the few psychiatrists I have known personally, all have seemed in need of a psychiatrist themselves, and my snap judgment was that Dr. Newby was no exception. He said in a rather dulcet voice: "Yes, that would be my opinion. Something on his mind."

"Why? What makes you think so?"

"We — ell, his behavior — to the trained observer — has been sending out certain warning signals."

"Such as what?"

"I don't know whether you are at all familiar with the field of psychiatry, Miss Waring?"

"Fairly." I don't think I am, but I wanted an answer.

"We — ell, then you will know what is meant by a complex. Persecution complex, guilt complex . . ."

"Is that what he has?"

"To some extent."

"*Both* of them?"

"Ye-es, I would say so. Plus some queer ideas that are just a little bit on the psychopathic borderline. . . . And a neurosis about flying — which, of course, isn't uncommon after a plane crash."

"But he'll get better — normal again?"

"No reason at all why he shouldn't — when the cause is removed."

"Is what you're doing for him helping?"

"I hope so. . . . But he doesn't co-operate very well. He *resists*. If only he'd talk about himself more."

"I should have thought that proved how thoroughly sane he is."

"We — ell, that could be true, in some cases. But in his case I think it merely shows he has something to hide."

"I don't follow that at all."

Mr. Small interposed. "Let's stick to the original phrase — that he has something on his mind. If he has, we all know it would do him good to talk — but he *won't* talk — so far — to anybody. That's his problem as well as ours."

"Then why should you think he'd talk to *me?*"

"Because he wrote to you, Miss Waring. He's been several months in hospital and you were the only person he wrote to the whole time. That's what brought you into the picture. We figured that if you meant that much to him and nobody else did . . ."

"So you intercepted his letter. May I have it?"

"Certainly. But it wasn't a letter."

Mr. Small took something from his wallet and handed it to me. It was a highly colored picture postcard of a desert scene, dated the previous March, and addressed to me care of my publishers in New York. Scribbled in pencil was the hospital address and the message: "Good book, especially page 117, last paragraph. — Yrs. Brad."

"So this is why you got in touch with me in the first place?"

"Yes. And why I got your book. But I really ought to have read it through instead of just page 117. It would have helped me to understand *you* better."

"He must have been wondering why I didn't reply."

"Maybe."

"I don't remember what was on page 117."

Mr. Small opened his briefcase. "You see I carry it around." He passed it to me. It opened at the page where the corner was turned down. The last paragraph read:

One day I walked with a very good friend of mine into the Burggarten where the open-air orchestra was playing the Overture to *Egmont*. We watched as well as listened, because the spectacle of so many music-lovers following the score, which at some trouble they must have brought with them, seemed the strangest possible contrast to the rioting in the streets, and perhaps a reassurance that when all the nonsense of the modern world has exhausted itself, Beethoven will remain, together with (my friend insisted) the Binomial Theorem and a few other intangibles. . . .

"Was Bradley the very good friend of yours?" Mr. Small asked.
"Yes."

He had been keeping his eyes on me with a sort of lie-detector intensity, but that didn't bother me, because I usually tell the truth, as I did then, and I only lie when I can justify it to myself enough to be able to stare anyone in the face. There was, however, a core of puzzlement in me about the whole business that I thought might soon make me look confused, so I was glad when Dr. Newby created a diversion by asking: "What exactly do you mean by a very good friend, Miss Waring?"

I stared at the doctor and thought how dreadful it would be to have that melancholy raffishness around all the time, which presumably was Brad's fate. He looked as if his experiences, whatever they were, had converted a slight original eagerness about life into mere inquisitiveness. I couldn't resist the temptation to shock him.

"I mean that I'd have gone to bed with him if he'd ever asked me."

"Even though he was married?" Mr. Small put in quickly.

"Oh, so you know that too? . . . No, I didn't really mean it. I was just joking."

"Did you know his wife?"

"Slightly."

"What happened to her?"

"I heard she died."

"How?"

"I don't know. . . . You said I could visit him at the hospital. When?"

Before he could answer Dan came from the house to say that Mr. Chandos was on the phone. I was glad of the chance to excuse myself. All Mr. Chandos wanted was to convert the following Wednesday's appointment into a lunch date; he sounded very cordial and chatted so desultorily that, thinking of Mr. Small waiting for me all the time, I was probably rather abrupt in my replies. When I did return to the terrace, however, there was already a changed atmosphere. I guessed they had been discussing me during my absence, and that some kind of clinching conclusion had been reached. It was not long in disclosing itself, for Mr. Small opened up briskly: "We've had an idea, Miss Waring. Perhaps a good idea, if you think it is too. How would you like Bradley to visit you here instead of you going to Arizona to see him?"

I was a bit amazed by the proposition. "Well yes," I answered, perhaps seeming doubtful. "Yes, that sounds all right."

"Only all right?"

"All right is all right, isn't it?"

"So you agree to it?"

"Sure . . . why not?"

"Would it be convenient for him to stay perhaps a week or ten days?"

I hadn't envisaged that even as a possibility, but it came as an increasingly welcome one. "I think so. It's my father's house, as you know, but I'm pretty sure he wouldn't object. And it's big enough — nobody need get in anyone else's way."

"Exactly. An excellent place from every standpoint. . . . Why don't you write today, asking him here for a visit if he can get leave? Dr. Newby will arrange the rest."

"Very well. I'll do that."

"In fact you might write now and we can air-mail it from town — that'll be quicker."

I went back to the library and wrote a brief note, as in answer to the postcard, which I said had been unaccountably delayed through reforwardings. I sealed the envelope and stuck some of those charity stamps over the flap; when I handed it to Mr. Small I saw him notice them; perhaps he thought they would make it harder to open the envelope and reseal it. I was fairly certain he intended to read what I had written.

They left soon after that, and I took them to the car in the driveway. "Maybe he won't resist *you* so much," said Dr. Newby, pumping my hand up and down.

"I shan't mind if he does. He's not the type for all this confession business — you ought to have seen that for yourself. You'd probably rather confess to him, but he wouldn't like that either."

Mr. Small smiled as he took my hand after Dr. Newby had let go of it. I think he enjoyed the way I tore into the poor little doctor.

* * *

A week passed, probably the laziest of my life, and doubtless it did me good. I had been leading a rackety sort of existence in recent years, all work and travel, full of interest and sometimes excitement, but a bit hard on the nerves. I began to realize what I had missed when I woke up on those bright summer mornings, stared at the mountains, and remembered I had nothing to do all day. I pottered about the gardens and sun-bathed by the pool, enjoying myself with all the greater abandonment because I knew how this *dolce far niente* routine would begin to bore me within measurable time. And I took long naps in the afternoon and chatted to my father during and after dinner. He had been perfectly agreeable to having Brad as a house guest, but he wondered how Brad would like it; and then he told me something I had not known before — that in the summer of 1938 Brad had written him a rather bitter letter, blaming him for everything.

"What do you mean — *everything?*"

My father looked uncomfortable. "Oh, the whole business. It was a wild letter — the kind I could forgive because the boy was so obviously not himself when he wrote it. You see his wife died before they could release her."

"You mean she died in the Nazi prison?"

"Or wherever it was they were keeping her. . . . I could understand how he felt, so when he blamed me I didn't hold it against him."

It was like my father to cling to any edge of circumstance in which he could be an injured party.

He continued: "I answered his letter but there wasn't much I could say. He didn't write again . . . so you see how it is . . . if he comes here . . ."

"I guess he won't then. But you didn't mind my asking him?"

"Oh, not at all. And if it's still on his conscience that he blamed me unjustly — "

"I should hardly think it would be."

My father shook his head wearily; I could see he had already chalked up Pauli's death as his own tragedy more than Brad's — one further proof of some vast unluckiness clinging to everything he touched. Which was absurd, if one appraised the opulence of Vista Grande. But it was also true that the possession of money had never outweighed his own personal failure to attain some ideal — and what exactly that was I have often wondered — maybe some impossible combination of Maecenas and Napoleon. Something impossible for these days, anyhow.

"Did he give you any details about Pauli's death?" I asked.

He shook his head again, not so much negatively as helplessly. "It wasn't a sensible letter. Accusations . . . reproaches . . . not like him at all."

Yes, that was true; it was unlike him. I remembered I had told Mr. Small during our first interview that Brad never had a grudge even when he ought to have had one. My father evidently thought that in 1938 he ought not to have had one.

"You didn't keep the letter?"

"No. . . . I think your mother took it — and you know what happened to letters when *she* got hold of them. . . ." The flicker of a smile.

"You were with her when the letter came?"

"Yes — we were staying with Princess Franzani at Cannes. A whole batch of forwarded mail arrived there — matter of fact, I think she opened it first."

I had heard about that visit to Princess Franzani. It was the last time my father and mother appeared socially together before the breach. They had agreed to patch things up for a last try, but perhaps a house party at Cannes was not the happiest background; and since it was presumably my father's choice (the Franzanis being *his* friends) it was like him to have made that final blunder. Anyhow, the patching didn't work and the divorce was started soon afterwards.

I could see that these memories were distressing him, but I had to ask one last question. "What did my mother think of the letter?"

"She didn't say much. She talked of writing to him herself, but I don't know whether she ever did. As you know, she often said she was going to do things and then forgot about them. . . ."

It was curious how my mother's faults — numerous enough, especially the small ones — were all neatly assembled in his memory, ready to be smiled over sadly, or indulgently excused. But her virtues, of which she had some big ones, gave him no task at all. Not that he denied their existence — merely that they did not fit the mood in which he could keep himself, a weather-worn Hamlet, always in the center of the stage.

When I looked at him across the dark expanse of oak dining table, with the silver gleaming in candlelight and the paneled walls carrying the eye into sepia shadows, I saw why it was my mother had finally tired of him. She wanted *life;* he wanted something else. I believe that of all the treasures of Vista Grande the only one she would have keenly appreciated was Dan's face. She loved beauty — physical beauty — and in people more than in views and things.

*   *   *

Wednesday I lunched with Mr. Chandos. I had a special qualm about gas after my father's assurance that I could use all I wanted, so I refused the Cadillac and chauffeur and compromised on borrowing Dan's midget car to drive myself; which doubtless sizes up my patriotism well enough, for with only small extra trouble I could have taken the bus from the main road. Mr. Chandos was very affable and decided on lunch at the Brown Derby. We made the short distance from the studio in his rather rakish sports car; he drove with a certain abandon that fitted his conversation but made me feel I should not be happy on a long trip with him. We were already in the midst of an argument by the time we left the parking lot; he was saying that his early training as a maker of B pictures, mostly comedies, had given his mind a kind of contamination he did not think it could ever quite shake off. "For instance," he said, as we passed a gas station, "if I notice a thing like that —" and he pointed — "I immediately think of how you could get a laugh out of it. Fade-in the drawing room of an apartment high above the street — there's a woman singing opera at a grand piano — exaggerated tremolo and considerably off key. Camera then moves out of the window down to the sidewalk where a young man can hear the voice — he has a quizzical look, as if he too isn't sure whether he likes it or not. Then he walks on and sees *that,* and you get your laugh." The "that" was a notice in the gas station that said "We Fix Flats." "Isn't it terrible? And done with practically no mental effort at all — that's the danger of it."

"I've seen worse gags on the screen," I said, smiling.

"But to go through life with an eye for them — it's the worst kind of occupational disease."

"Journalists have it too. Anything to catch the reader's attention — nothing much to catch his mind. And yet if you catch his mind by even a little, it's worth it, and sometimes only a gag can do it. A few good gags about the world's future might help to ensure that it has one."

"Don't let them hear you talk like that in any studio."

"Why not?"

"They might offer you a writing job at four figures a week."

"It wouldn't tempt me."

"I'm glad of that, but also curious. Aren't you interested in money?"

"Of course I am, but I earn enough the way I like without doing something I don't think I should like."

"And you haven't any uncles and aunts in Scranton whom it would be nice to send help to, and your father isn't still struggling along at a job he can't properly afford to retire from?"

"No. My father's well enough off to support himself whatever happened to me."

"Oh?" he said; and then suddenly the idea dawned on him, later than it does to most people. "Why . . . he's not by any chance . . .

or *is* he? . . . Are you the daughter of . . . *the* Waring . . . *Harvey* Waring?"

I nodded.

"That's odd. Somehow I didn't connect you with him at all."

"There's no reason why you should."

"Now what exactly do you mean by that?"

It was as good a way as any other into the kind of talk we had during lunch. We dawdled over coffee till nearly three, then he drove me back to the studio where my car was, having made another lunch date for the following Wednesday. Again we had discussed almost everything except the book and the picture, and I still thought I liked him — perhaps more than after the first meeting.

When I reached Vista Grande towards dusk I found two notes awaiting me, one from Brad to say he would be glad to come and would arrive at San Bernardino the following day at 5:20 P.M.; the other was from Dr. Newby to say he happened to be traveling to Los Angeles on business and so could accompany Brad and hand him over to me if I were to meet the train; of course in that case I would be careful not to disclose any previous acquaintance we had had.

I wired back to Brad that I would meet the train.

*   *   *

I took Dan's midget car again and was at the station by five. It was very hot, at the low level, and the great wartime trains kept pulsing through in both directions, like part of some tremendous heartbeat in a creature too large for comprehension. The soldiers leaned out of the windows, bronzed and sweating, ready to whistle at a girl because doing so, in this war, appeased some of the loneliness that was also too large to be comprehended.

Presently the train came in, and I thought at first he wasn't on it; the windows I ran alongside were full of other faces. Then I caught sight of Dr. Newby, half hidden behind a Pullman porter. He let Brad get down and approach me, and when that happened I forgot all about the doctor till he came up to us a moment later.

We stared at each other, Brad and I; then we shook hands rather solemnly and I said: "Hello, Brad."

"Hello," he answered.

We went on staring and the moment stretched itself into impossibility. At length I asked if he had any luggage.

"Yes, a suitcase. They'll put it out."

"Did you have a nice trip?"

He said slowly, still staring down at me: "Not very. It was crowded. And the cooling system didn't work."

Then Newby came up, and I was glad in one sense, because it gave Brad the necessary job of introducing us. But Newby seemed to enjoy overdoing the show of never having met me before. "Well, well . . ." he beamed, pumping my hand up and down. "So *this* is the young lady? . . . Lucky fellow. . . . Take good care of him, Miss Waring."

"You bet I will."

"And no night clubs. Plenty of sleep . . . fresh air . . . and your own charming companionship. I envy him the cure!"

The porters were shouting "All aboard"; Newby remained waggish to the last.

Then we walked along the platform to the piled-up luggage. Brad found his suitcase and carried it to the car in the station yard. "The fool," he muttered. "He's the doctor who's supposed to have been looking after me."

I said nothing, because already I had forgotten Newby again and it was Brad I was thinking of, trying to decide what he was like, as if a first impression might tell me something clairvoyantly. I couldn't see anything wrong with him at all. Of course he looked older, much older; but then he *was* much older, so was I; seven years make a difference, even without a war. I said: "It's hot here, but cooler up in the mountains where we're going. You know California? It was hot in Arizona too, I expect. Why do they put hospitals there? Good for lungs, I suppose. . . ."

As we entered the car he told me I looked very well.

"Yes, I'm all right. I'm fine. You look all right too."

"I enjoyed your book. It was in the hospital library."

"Was it? . . . By the way, I looked up what you said on the card — page 117. The *Egmont* Overture in the Burggarten. . . . Yes, I remember that so well."

We threaded through the town traffic, then took the road to the mountains. At two thousand feet the air was noticeably fresher; at four thousand a cool breeze held the warmth of the sun in pockets. The nameless mountains clothed in chaparral rose all round us. I wondered aloud if he were nervous of mountain roads, but he said no.

"Only of flying, then?"

"How did you know that?" he asked sharply.

And of course I couldn't have known it without being told; it was a slip. I covered it as best I could. "Elementary, my dear Watson. You're a flyer out of hospital. Injured flyers often have nerves afterwards — about flying. The ones I've met did, anyhow."

"I wasn't a flyer, as you call it; I was a navigator. I could fly, and damn well, but I was too old to be an Air Force pilot . . . too old at thirty-one, that's a nice thing."

I seemed to have touched a sore spot, but at least it tided over the slip I had made; he had evidently accepted my explanation. He went on: "You don't fly yourself, do you?"

I do, all the time; I love it, and I'm taking lessons; I've done seven or eight hours solo already. I said: "Sometimes."

"I wish you wouldn't."

"I won't if you'd rather I didn't."

179

The strain lifted from his face; he smiled and said that was sweet of me. But I was not too happy over his swift change of mood. There was something odd and rather frightening in the casual way he accepted the idea that I would change a habit just to please him. It was either arrogance of a kind I had never seen in him before, or else he knew I had made the promise without intending to keep it, and he was yet able to find satisfaction in the promise alone.

He asked me again about my book, how successful it had been, the Hollywood sale which he had read of, and so on. I told him about Mr. Chandos and my studio visit. He said then he was glad I hadn't visited him at the hospital because we shouldn't have been able to talk like that.

"Why not?"

"Newby would have listened all the time."

"Well, it wouldn't have mattered — there's nothing confidential about it. . . . Not that I'd choose to have him around, though."

He didn't speak for a while and I asked him why Newby did so much listening.

"It's his job. Psychiatrists aren't supposed to have any manners or decencies — one doesn't expect them to, but Newby has embarrassments, which makes everything rather worse." He laughed. "You know, if an ordinary person hears you yelling in your sleep he wakes you, but a psychiatrist comes rushing into the room with a notebook and pencil to take it all down."

"Does Newby do that?"

"Practically. But I don't think he's got much out of it so far. Matter of fact, I fool him a good bit. Whenever he comes in with trick questions I give him trick answers."

"He probably knows you're only joking."

"He never knows anybody's only joking. The man has no sense of humor at all. That's why it's such a holiday to be away from him."

"I'm glad you feel it is. It's wonderful to see you in such good spirits."

"I'm not really in good spirits. I'm damned low."

"I'm sorry then. I hope you're going to enjoy staying at the house. Nobody will bother you there. And if you yell in the night I'll probably hear and I'll rush in to wake you, but I won't listen to anything, I promise that."

We drove on through the gathering dusk, and at the level of the pines the mountain air had a touch of ice in it. Then the sun dipped, and the last few miles were in darkness.

Vista Grande was dim and cool, sheltered a little in its high valley. We had rum cocktails on the terrace, where there were patches of warm air lingering from the day; I introduced him to Dan, and he said afterwards: "I like the look of Dan. Where did you get him from?"

"I haven't an idea. For all I know my father took him with the house."

"How is your father, by the way?"

"Fairly well . . . or rather, not very well. You'll notice a difference."

"So will he, I expect."

I wondered if this meant that he regretted the angry letter but I thought it better not to let him know I knew anything about it.

Then my father joined us, Dan helping him. He and Brad shook hands and the ticklish moment passed without awkwardness. But I soon noticed that my father's presence seemed to put a damper on the conversation, so I filled in most of the gaps with chatter of my own. As the dinner progressed I noticed also a peculiar waywardness in the remarks Brad occasionally made — not the flashing, puckish waywardness that my mother used to have, but something sharper, acider — as if, out of a tired distillation of his day's events, the last drops were bitter. I did not think he would enjoy the usual after-dinner hour in the library listening to the radio, and when my father suggested it I was not surprised that he excused himself and said he would go to bed early. I took him upstairs to his room. He said: "Tell him I'm sleepy. I've had enough of the radio. At the hospital it was on day in, day out. I used to count the number of times the announcers said 'And now' and 'But first.' And now, but first. But first, and now."

I left him muttering that, before and after he said good-night.

*   *   *

The next morning I found him already on the terrace when I came down; he was admiring the view and talking to Dan. He said he had slept well and I said I hadn't heard any yells from his room, but maybe that was because I had slept well too. He answered seriously: "It doesn't often happen. The yells, I mean. Only when I dream of flying — or people watching me."

"*Watching* you?"

"Yes — I'm supposed to have what Newby calls a persecution complex. Everybody watching, listening, waiting, setting traps. And they do, too. That's what I tell him when he says I have hallucinations about being spied on all the time — how can it be a hallucination when *he* spies on me all the time?"

"A nice question for a psychiatrist."

"And he couldn't answer it, naturally. He's not much good. I told you I fool him. He keeps on asking if I'm getting over my fear of flying. Once I said yes, I'd like to go up again, because I wanted to be a skywriter, I wanted to write an obscene word in the sky. I spelled it out for him. He was fascinated. I could imagine him telling his fellow psychiatrists about a most remarkable case he had, a patient with a unique exhibitionist symptom. . . . I got a lot of fun out of it."

"But it wasn't quite fair," I said, "even to Newby. After all, what science would ever get anywhere if people fed it with deliberately wrong information?"

"Ah," he said, with sudden harsh intensity that made me feel I had touched a wrong note somehow or other. "But who's talking about science? Psychiatry isn't a science. It's a conspiracy."

He glared, as if waiting for me to say something, and I was anxious now not to blunder again. "Well?" he continued. "Are you going to tell me that science is a conspiracy too?"

"Of course not. Why should I?"

"Because it would be a damned good answer — for this day and age."

His face was clouded over and I devoutly wished I hadn't begun the argument. Dan brought breakfast and we ate for a while in silence. Then he said moodily: "What does one do in a place like this all the time?"

"Anything one likes. I haven't been here long enough yet to establish a routine."

"Ever take walks nowadays?"

"Like the one we had once from Cambridge that day? Not often. I don't believe I've ever walked so far since. . . . Do *you* still keep it up?" I realized the absurdity of the question and added: "I mean, *did* you, before — before you were in the hospital?"

"Before I was in the hospital I was in the army and they walk you plenty during training. . . . In Alabama, that was. Too flat. I prefer mountains."

"Cambridge to where we walked was flat."

That proved another conversational blind alley. I broke the silence this time. I said: "Have you done any mountain climbing?"

"Yes."

Then the dark mood spread over him like some final curtain, and I knew there *was* something wrong with him, something on his mind — perhaps even, as Newby had said, something he was trying

183

to hide. I wondered how I could approach the barrier, but then I decided the best thing was probably not to approach it at all, but to let it stay till he liked it between us as little as I did, if that feeling should ever come to him.

I said cheerfully: "Well, you can swim or sun-bathe or read or play some game or just do nothing."

"And what about you?"

"I'll do whatever you do, unless you'd rather be left alone."

"No, no, of course not." He put his hand on mine across the table — a gesture instead of an answering look. "But I'm afraid I won't always be very good company."

"Oh, Brad, don't talk like that. Good company is being with people you like. I like you, that's enough."

"Do you play chess?"

"Not very well."

We played most of the morning, and of course he beat me so easily it must have been as boring to him as it certainly was to me; not that I was bored by being bored, which is the main thing. Then Dan came by and watched our game, and Brad asked him if *he* played. It seemed he did, and I was glad to resign in his favor; moreover he played so well that I knew I shouldn't be asked again. I sat around, reading the papers and wondering what kind of film would eventually be made out of my book. Then we had lunch, and in the afternoon Brad took a nap; my father joined us for cocktails and dinner, after which Brad went to bed early again. It wasn't exactly an exciting day, but doubtless the kind that would do him good — more good, anyhow, than being psychoanalyzed all the time.

It was several days before he suggested any variant of chess. Then one morning, when the sky was unusually clear, he pointed to the snow peaks in the distance and asked what they were, how far and how high. I told him and fetched maps. "We could drive as far as here," he said, pointing, "and then climb this way if there's a trail. . . ."

"And Dan will lend us his car and we can take a picnic basket. . . ."

"Rucksacks," he said.

"I'll see if there are any."

"Have you enough gas?"

"Oh yes," I said, with no qualms at all.

Dan managed to find rucksacks and by ten o'clock we were on the road. We drove the length of the Modena Valley and then through winding foothills to a ridge whence the mountains heaved up in a huge panorama. I asked him if he would like to drive, but he said no, he felt sleepy; and for half an hour he did sleep. I think there is a peculiar happiness in seeing people asleep when you like them and they are in your charge; there aren't many ways it can happen, but a car provides one even when the other person snores and you can only give a half-glance now and again because the road is narrow and winding and has precipices on one side. He woke when we were almost at the place on the map. "You've been asleep," I said.

"Yes, but I didn't dream."

I said nothing, and he went on: "I'm so used to that question — what did you dream? I invent dreams too, just to give Newby something to think about."

"Is it worth it?"

"Is what worth what?"

"The effort of inventing dreams just to give Newby something to think about."

He laughed. "I didn't dream just now, anyway. I'd have told you if I had."

"I don't see why you would. I wouldn't want to tell all the dreams *I* have."

We parked the car where the paved road ended in a dirt track that led steeply upward. There was no other car, or any sign of habitation. We hitched up the rucksacks and began to climb. The sun was hot through the cool air, giving every breath a chance of being warm or cold. After a mile or so the dirt track narrowed to a trail that zigzagged through the chaparral; presently came the first manzanita with its reddish trunk and olive-drab leaves. He said that was a sign we were above a certain height, I forget how much, because I was thinking of an even happier sign — that he had a trace left of his old lecture urge. I asked him a few leading questions and he talked on about trees, but soon the trail grew too steep for conversation. We came to a gap where a valley opened out. The snowpeaks were now so near that we knew how far they were, and that we couldn't possibly reach any of them and get back that day. I said we should have started earlier.

"Next time," he answered indifferently, but I liked the indifference because he had assumed there would be a next time.

We sat on a patch of grass, ate sandwiches, and drank coffee out of a thermos. Then we smoked, and he went to immense trouble to stamp out the stubs. I am just as careful as anyone about brush fires, but I do it with less commotion. However, it was good to see him fidgeting. Presently he lay on his back and closed his eyes till a plane flew over, too high to see but loud enough to look for. I wondered if he had any fear of planes, as such, or as a symbol of something, or if it were only a matter of flying in them; and I wanted to be frank with him about my own flying. I was just about to be when he said suddenly: "I suppose you knew that Pauli died."

I lay down also looking up to the sky. "Yes, I heard so. I was terribly sorry."

He said nothing for several moments; then I said: "Is that what's been on your mind, Brad?"

He shook his head, irritably rather than in denial; then he exclaimed: "What's the matter with me? Do I look as if there's something on my mind? There ought to be something on everybody's mind, anyhow."

I didn't know what to say to that. He went on: "They follow me around expecting me to spill the beans. *What* beans? They're going to spill their own beans soon . . . human beans." He laughed. "That must be a joke. Newby would get out his notebook."

I still didn't speak. He continued: "You're a good listener. Yet you don't look like Newby when you're listening—ears pricked up, memory all at attention. . . . I guess you're just casually interested in me."

"Not so casual."

"Casual enough. I like it."

There was yet another silence and presently he raised himself on one elbow to look at me. "I'd say there was something on *your* mind too."

"Well, I'd like to smoke again, but if you're going to worry about setting fire to the mountains I won't bother."

"I'll trust you."

"I think you can." So I lit a cigarette. "And I mean that, too, Brad. If there *is* anything you want to tell me . . . about anything."

"Is there anything you'd like to know . . . about anything?"

"Oh, plenty. I haven't an idea what happened to you after we said good-by in Vienna seven years ago. I was barred, you know, from going back."

"Yes, I heard. You were against them and they thought I was for them. Where were you when the war started?"

"Which war? Nineteen thirty-nine or nineteen forty-one?"

"Nineteen thirty-nine."

"I was in Brazil."

"Writing?"

"More or less."

"You've been around, haven't you?"

"I've been around, but I don't know exactly where it's got me. . . . Perhaps back to where I started. Living in my father's house amidst all the luxuries . . . and taking walks with you. . . . That's how it did start."

"But it's so damned different now."

"Of course. I was only joking."

"*Joking?*"

"Well, your joke was worse — about human beans."

I had noticed before that there were certain things that made his face cloud over, as if some hidden nerve had been touched. I said hastily: "Let's not talk about my life, anyway. Most of it's in my book — which, by the way, I thought you'd read."

"Parts of it. I find I can't concentrate on reading nowadays."

"You find chess easier?"

"Not easier — but less troubling."

"What *really* troubles you, Brad?"

"Still the casual interest?"

"Yes — if that's all you want."

"I'll let you know someday. I can't now. But I'll tell you what happened after Pauli died."

He leaned over and took a cigarette out of my pack. "I went a little bit out of my mind," he said, lighting it. "That's what happened — chiefly. I was waiting for her to join me in Switzerland. The authorities hadn't let me see her or even write a letter. I don't know that she ever knew why it was I defended Framm at the trial — I don't suppose they ever told her it was a bargain to get her released. I expect she died thinking I'd deserted her at the crucial moment. Probably others thought that too. It must have seemed strange. . . . How did it look to you?"

"Well, of course, I knew the reason, so I didn't think it strange."

"But others did?"

"Maybe."

He fidgeted, then added: "Did people talk about it — to you?"

"Sometimes."

"And you had to tell them they'd got it all wrong."

"I didn't tell them anything at first. I didn't want to queer anything till Pauli was actually released."

"But afterwards — when you heard she'd died?"

"Then it was too late for people to be interested. Things are so quickly forgotten — every journalist finds that out. Even a newspaper sensation like Pauli's trial doesn't leave more than a few scattered recollections. . . . And besides, there's another thing. Suppose I'd tried to convince people you were really *against* Framm and the Nazis, how could I have explained why you went to work for him in Germany afterwards?"

"So you know that too?"

"I didn't then, but what if they'd told me?"

He gave me a wry smile. "You'd have been considerably puzzled?"

"I still am."

"Yet you — you don't think badly of me?"

"Brad, that's another thing I've learned as a journalist. The world's so full of strange actions and strange motives — don't condemn people just because they do what you can't immediately understand. Or even always because they do what seems to you not good. Wait till they've had a chance to explain."

"So that's my chance now?"

"Only if you want it. I'm quite willing to go on taking you on trust."

"If I told you I worked for Framm in Germany because I planned to kill him, would you believe me?"

"Yes . . . but did you?"

"Did I work for him?"

189

"No. Did you kill him?"

He grimaced. "You're so damned matter-of-fact, that's what gets me. You can take plenty in your stride. I like you for that. . . ."

Tempting though this was as a side issue, what I really wanted was his story, and soon he began. It came in fragments at first, but not reluctantly. And he urged that if he wasn't clear about anything I was to interrupt as he went along and ask for any further details I wanted. I think my remark about not condemning people for an absence of apparent motive made him specially anxious for me to understand his, and sometimes he would pause as if to invite questions. The whole thing built up to something I can put more connectedly at this stage into the third person; so here it is.

*　　*　　*

PART FOUR

WHEN the time came near for him to expect Pauli's release, Brad went to Switzerland to await her. He had been told he would not be permitted to meet her in Austria; she would be put on a train under escort to the Austrian border town of Feldkirch; the train would then take her, unescorted, across the international bridge to the Swiss border town of Buchs. The Teutonic exactitude of all this irritated him, yet seemed also a perverse guarantee of authenticity. At any rate, he would be at Buchs when the day came.

Meanwhile he found an inexpensive but comfortable pension at Interlaken and began to plan the quiet holiday they would both have together before the birth of their child. He chose Interlaken mainly because he knew a doctor there, but it was also a good climbing center, and during the time of waiting he built up his own physique after many years of overwork.

The porter brought the letter to his bedroom along with coffee and brioches. When he saw the postmark "Wien" and the official seal on the envelope he thought it was what he had been waiting for. A minute later he knew he must do something drastic with himself or he would go totally mad. It was the morning of a perfect September day, and out of the window he could see the mountains. He stared at them for a long time. Then he dressed, packed a rucksack, put on heavy boots, and told the proprietress downstairs that he was off for a few days' climbing. She smiled and wished him a good time.

He walked through the town and took the train to Lauterbrunnen. By evening he had reached the high ground. He was a good climber, though not quite an expert. After a night at the Roththal Hut he crossed the rock and ice *arête* to the main peak of the Jungfrau, climbed it, and made a descent towards the Jungfraujoch. By that time he was at a point of uttermost physical exhaustion, and the last hours across the glacier were endured amidst a peculiar vacuum of sensation that left his mind swinging clear like a compass needle. It was then that he reached a decision.

He took the cog railway down from the Joch through Scheidegg and Wengen; by midnight of that second day he was in his bedroom at the pension. There he slept off his tiredness, packed his bags, and told the proprietress that he had to leave for good. She was a friendly woman, who had grown to like him during his weeks with her; he had never talked much about himself, but perhaps she sensed there was something wrong and wondered if it were money trouble — so many people nowadays couldn't get their funds out of other countries. If that were so with him, they could come to an arrangement; she told him this, but he said it wasn't money, he had to leave for another reason.

He then made the long roundabout train journey through Lucerne, Zurich, and Sargans, to the frontier at Buchs. He wondered if he would have trouble there, but his former Austrian visa was apparently still good, and at Feldkirch the uniformed official stamped it without comment.

A day later he reached Vienna. He found a room at a cheap hotel, slept, and was up early.

Bauer's office was occupied by another firm; they very pointedly could not tell him where Bauer was. He then tried Bauer's apartment, with the same result. But there had been a tired elderly secretary named Sylvie; he had once had to leave some of Bauer's papers at her home, so he remembered where it was. He now went there again. She was very nervous on seeing him, admitting him reluctantly into the small shabby apartment. She said she didn't know anything, couldn't remember anything — all Bauer's papers had been impounded; she herself was Aryan and had been promised a job in the Deutsche Bank — it must be understood that she retained absolutely no connection at all with her former employer's business affairs.

"I'm not asking you about them. I just thought you might be able to tell me where Bauer is."

He placed money on the table with a gesture he disliked all the more in such surroundings; at least, if one bribed, one ought to do so handsomely and without the indecent help of another's obvious poverty. But the small sum was all he could afford. He said: "I'm not mixed up in politics — never have been. I just want a talk with him, that's all."

"Unfortunately, sir . . ." She began to slide the money back across the table.

"That's too bad."

"I am very sorry, sir."

He got up briskly and left the money where it was. "All right. I don't blame you. . . . I'm staying at the Kaiserling Hotel on the Laudongasse if you change your mind. . . . Good day."

*   *   *

Next he went to the American Embassy. The young man who listened to him there was polite but not very helpful.

"But Mr. — Dr. Bradley — what is it you expect us to do?"

"I want to find out some details about my wife's death."

"But on the evidence of this letter . . ."

"I'm not satisfied with this letter."

"Have you made any personal inquiries of your own?"

"That's what I want to do. They didn't send for me in time. Not even for the funeral. I thought you might be able to help me. I'm an American citizen."

"But your wife, I understand, was Austrian. . . ."

"Does that matter?"

"Unfortunately, so far as we are concerned, it leaves us without much *locus standi*. And this private arrangement you claim to have had with the authorities could hardly be made a basis for any . . ."

"Sure, I know all that. I don't expect you to declare war or send a gunboat up the Danube."

He knew that from then on the young man's only aim was to get rid of him.

"Frankly, Dr. Bradley, I don't know how we can help you. If you were contemplating a return to America, you might try to interest someone in Washington . . ."

"Meaning that you're not interested here?"

"It isn't that at all. But for certain things it is almost a disadvantage to be on the spot. Of course if your request were for something definite, practical . . ."

"It is. An autopsy."

"*Autopsy?*"

"That's what you have when you want to find out how somebody died, isn't it?" No point now in lengthening the argument.

But the young man was still polite. "A formal request for additional information can be lodged with the authorities, but even then . . ."

"They'll take no notice of it — is that what you mean?"

"I was about to say that without supporting evidence you could hardly expect . . ."

He went away with growing awareness that he had been rather stupid and probably unfair.

When he returned to his hotel he found a message that someone had telephoned in his absence but would call again later. The second call came during the afternoon; it was a woman's voice that sounded as if it might be Sylvie's with an attempt at disguise. The voice told him that if he still wished to meet the person he had asked for, he would find him at a certain street corner in the Leopoldstadt district at ten-thirty that night.

He kept the appointment, and after a few minutes of waiting a man touched him whom he did not at first recognize. Then he saw that it was Bauer dressed in rough clothes with a beard grown stubbly; he would have passed for an out-of work laborer. He took Brad along a side street and presently down some steps to a slum basement. Noisy voices could be heard from the next room. "Speak quietly in German," Bauer said. "Would you like some beer?"

"No, thanks. Why are you like this?"

"I am on my way out of this country. The police are looking for me, but I hope to be in Bratislava within a few days. I have friends there. You must forgive me for making you wait at the corner. I had first to make sure that it was you."

"I understand."

"Now tell me why you are here again. It is an unfortunate country to return to."

"I want to find out about Pauli."

"I am sorry to say she is dead."

"I know that. I was waiting in Switzerland for her to join me — that was the arrangement. Then they sent me a letter. It said she died in a hospital at Wiener-Neustadt."

"Have you got the letter?"

"Yes." He passed it to Bauer, who read it and gave it back without immediate comment.

"Well?" Brad said at length.

"What is there to say, my friend?"

"Ought I to believe it?"

After another pause Bauer answered: "Perhaps yes — for your own peace of mind."

"What do you mean by that?"

Bauer gave a shrug which Brad had already begun to adopt for his own use; it was a gesture of not knowing where to begin in the enumeration of losses, problems, tragedies, injustices; the Masonic sign between those who accept despair but refuse defeat. Ever since those moments on the glacier Brad's mind had been building a framework within which he could come to similar terms with events; but this framework was so strange at first that nothing seemed strange inside it, neither Bauer with dirty nails and patched clothes, nor a basement cellar in which one lit a solitary candle on a table and saw the cockroaches scurrying into their holes.

He repeated: "What do you mean?"

Bauer replied in a whisper: "I know she did not die in Wiener-Neustadt. She died at Graz. She was sent there about a month ago."

"How do you know that?"

"We have ways of finding out these things."

"What else have you found out?"

Again the shrug.

"Who is responsible?"

Bauer gave him a long look and answered: "Who do *you* think, my friend?"

"Framm?"

"He was in Berlin when she died."

"Does that answer the question?"

Bauer said after another pause: "I wonder whether you are wise in asking it. The thing is done and cannot be undone. You are an American — you can go back to your own country where things like this do not happen. And if I were you — "

Brad interrupted: "I *must* know. Framm had motives — she knew a great deal about him — *against* him — and if he could not silence her — "

"Please do not speak so loudly. And I do not want you to stay long here. . . . Yes, he had motives. . . . And when you leave you had better go alone."

"One more question . . . Was it pneumonia?"

"It may have been. But that would not affect the issue."

"Because it was due to something else — something that led to — "

"In one way or another it should not have happened, my friend. I would rather leave it at that . . . for your sake."

"Bauer, I want information, not sympathy. You have evidence against Framm?"

"We have enough — of the kind of thing one gets. Much of it would be inadmissible in a court of law — if there were any left that deserve the name."

"Doesn't interest me — I've had enough experience of courts. I want to know for my own . . . for reasons of my own. *Was Framm responsible?* Yes or no? Or can't one get that sort of answer out of a lawyer?"

Both men's nerves were risingly on edge. Bauer stood up, leaned across the table, and seized Brad with both arms. "For God's sake, man, talk softer! . . . What do you want from me? I have told you enough. Do you want me to say there is a hundred per cent proof when there is only . . . perhaps . . . ninety-five?"

Brad subsided. "I am sorry. Thank you. I now understand."

"Then you had better go."

Brad proffered his hand, which Bauer took. "Again I am sorry. Your legal mind and my scientific mind do not condemn easily. . . . It is good of you to have arranged this meeting. I hope it has involved no risk to you."

"Perhaps not much, since there are many of our friends in Leopoldstadt. It is unfortunate, however, that the wrong impression was given at the trial. . . . Most of them would not trust you now."

"Perhaps the other side does, and that will not be so unfortunate."

"I see your point. But do not look for certainties — only probabilities."

"That's beginning to be good advice even in mathematics."

Bauer smiled then, the first time, and Brad shook his hand again, wished him luck, and climbed to the street.

*   *   *

He spent several days after that in a solitude of thought. Aware that he would never tackle a scientific problem before minutely scrutinizing all the elements in it, he realized that his own problem required no less, perhaps more. It appalled him now to recollect his naïve approach to Sylvie and the man at the Embassy — truculent as well as naïve, which was a bad mixture. There must be no more such improvisations, he decided, but a clear blueprint in his mind for every possible behavior; he must be attitude-perfect, not merely word-perfect, when the moment came.

He knew already that Framm was back at the laboratory, having made a remarkable recovery. There were frequent references to him in the newspapers — gossip that he might shortly organize an Austrian branch of the Reichsforschungsrat, a report from Berlin that he was in line for an appointment there. It was this latter, with its likelihood of an early departure from Vienna, that made Brad speed up his intention.

He called at the laboratory one morning in August. It was like stepping back into his own past to climb the familiar steps to the portico, push open the swing doors, and walk the length of the corridor. But there was an iron gateway now to intercept a visitor to the main building, and a tough-looking trooper of the new regime eyed him up and down when he gave his name and said he wanted to see Dr. Framm. "You'll have to wait," the man muttered, and began some complicated telephoning. Presently he said: "Dr. Framm will see you in an hour's time. Will you wait here or come back again?"

"I'll come back again," Brad said.

He walked about the hot streets, rehearsing any number of parts. When he returned to the gate the man was ready for him, unlocked it, and led the way to the room Brad knew so well. It was large, with an enormous littered desk, high bookshelves, various tables of instruments, and a few worn and nondescript chairs. Along one entire wall was a blackboard scribbled over with mathematical oddments; Framm liked to work out his thoughts in chalk rather than pencil; it made for easier erasure, and also saved his eyes from overstrain. Another wall contained a huge and evidently recent map of the combined Germany and Austria. Except for this, there was not much change in the appearance of things; but in any event the change in the professor himself would have demanded first attention.

Reports of Framm's recovery had led Brad to assume that he would look much the same. Actually, in some ways, he looked better now; he had lost surplus weight, and the slight physical excess of every feature-quality had been fined down to a spiritual extreme. The large strong nose seemed longer because it was thinner, the eyes were more sunken and gleamed brighter, so that their ranging glance had a mystical aspect superimposed on the merely magisterial. And all this because of a punctured lung, Brad reflected; it was almost as if the man's personality had put suffering itself to work to make himself more remarkable.

When he saw Brad he got out of his chair, and the whole effect was then concentrated; he looked fabulously aquiline as he held out a bony hand. But he had not changed in another way; charm came out of him as before, an instant distillation. "Well . . . well

. . . *Bradley!* . . . How . . . how *generous* of you to come. . . ."

"I hope you're better," Brad said.

"Yes, I'm pretty well. Not so fat, as you can see, but that's all to the good. . . . Now tell me how *you* are." Brad hesitated, a little dazed by the reception, not because he had expected anything different, but because (he now realized) he had been quite incapable of expecting anything at all; but he held to his resolve to talk little about himself and nothing at all if in doubt about his answers. Then Framm went on: "Come, come . . . there are things we have to say and it is well to get them over. . . . First, I was distressed indeed to hear of your wife's death. There are words that would put that more fulsomely, but I know you would not care for them. . . . Second, your publicly expressed loyalty gave me the keenest gratification, and I only regret you had the ordeal of displaying it in such sordid and tragic circumstances. . . . And third . . . I was — and of course you must have realized it — deeply grateful for your help in those electromagnetic researches that have lately attracted some notice. . . ."

He reached to a shelf and took down a volume, opened it and found a page. "Here . . . you see?" Brad saw it was an official collection of the lectures delivered to a Berlin scientific society; one of them was Framm's lecture, and at the conclusion of it there was a sentence expressing "sincere gratitude to my American assistant and co-worker, Dr. Mark Bradley, for his aid in the preparation and assembly of these results." Brad remembered Bauer's remark that if such an acknowledgment had been made there would have been no case at all, either legal or ethical, and that if Framm had been really smart he would therefore have made it. So now it appeared that Framm *had* made it, at any rate in time for the issue of an official text; probably he had done so deliberately when there seemed to be a chance of the matter being raised as part of Pauli's defense.

Brad smiled and handed back the volume. He wondered if it

would be possible to find out definitely that the acknowledgment had not been made in the original spoken lecture. Not that he cared at all, except to the extent that it revealed Framm's behavior.

Framm went on: "I'm sorry you haven't been with me lately — you'd have been interested in one little matter . . . Perhaps you remember this equation . . ."

He swung round to the blackboard, grabbing a piece of chalk and a duster. The blackboard had hardly any room on it, and it had always been his habit to begin at the top, writing with one hand, while he rubbed away space with the other. From the back, with both arms thus outstretched, he looked like a scarecrow, and that would have been the time to kill him, except that as soon as this occurred to Brad, the hands stopped moving, and an image in his mind changed from a scarecrow to a crucifixion. Then came an equally odd idea — that it was taboo to kill a professor while he was writing on a blackboard; it would be like killing a priest while he was at his prayers.

Framm swung round. "Now, Bradley, this is the point . . ."

He swung back to the board and resumed rapid movement with both hands. When he next turned round there were lines of equations. "Look that over," he said suddenly, throwing down the chalk and duster. "I'll be back in a moment."

He went out and Brad had a feeling that the absence was deliberately timed, though for what purpose he could not decide. He stared at the equations, unable to summon enough concentration to give them meaning; it was months since he had done anything more mathematical than check his change; his mind for this sort of thing was tired, clogged, out of gear. But all at once something turned over like a rusty key in a rusty lock; he reached for paper and pencil on the desk and began copying the top line. He could work only on paper himself.

Presently Framm came back. "Well, how goes it?"

Brad said: "Extraordinary—that's the one thing that bothered me all the time—I wasn't sure of it till I read your lecture. Then I knew I'd been right."

"But you hadn't been. Neither had I. Because look . . ." And he went to the blackboard and wrote again for several minutes; then he explained and they argued for several more minutes. It had to do with contravariant tensor densities. Finally he said: "I shall issue the correction in time for any reprint. Will you set it out?"

Brad stared at him incredulously. "You mean I should work . . . here . . . *again* . . . ?"

"If you want to. I thought that's why you came to see me. There are very few people qualified for this sort of thing—it would seem a pity for you to be doing anything else. . . . And by the way, I might be taking a post in Berlin soon—if you liked you could come along with me."

Brad said: "I'll . . . I'll have to think it over."

"Yes, of course. Let me know in a week or so."

As he left the building Brad realized that going to Berlin would give him ample opportunity for what he intended, and perhaps the only possible opportunity.

*   *   *

He stopped talking and lit another cigarette. The sun had moved round, so that we were now in shade, and that made the air instantly cold. "Perhaps we should move," I said, meaning move a few yards into the sun.

He said: "Yes, let's go down. We don't want to be back too late. And I've talked enough."

"We can come here again."

"Oh yes. Tomorrow if you like. But let's start earlier and climb higher."

"Yes."

We gathered up the picnic things. "These are good rucksacks," he said. "Norwegian style. They fit squarely down the back. Where on earth did you get them?"

"I haven't an idea. Maybe they came with the house."

"Like Dan and everything else?"

"Maybe."

"What made your father want to live in a place like that?"

"He says it suits his health."

"I thought he preferred Florida."

"Perhaps it had too many memories after my mother's death."

"I read about that. I was terribly shocked. I wanted to write to you but I didn't know any address. . . . Were you with her?"

"I was in Canada. There was just time to join my father and fly to where it had happened. She died soon after we got there."

"Texas, wasn't it?"

"Yes."

"What was she doing?"

"Driving too fast at night."

"Why?"

"God knows. Why do people do things?"

He nodded. "That's the same question, isn't it? The one we were talking about."

We followed the rest of the trail to the car in silence. Dusk falls quickly in the mountains and before we were many miles along the road it was almost pitch-black, with just the feel of high earth or empty air out of the window. Despite the climb and the long conversation he didn't seem so tired as during the outward drive; at any rate, he didn't sleep. Once the headlights focused on a coyote in the middle of the road ahead; I slowed down and eventually stopped, for the animal did not move, but seemed hypnotized by the glare. Finally I switched off the lights and heard it scampering away. The darkness was alarming then; it invaded the car like something unleashed on us. Suddenly he leaned over and kissed me, not passionately, but rather experimentally.

I said after a while: "I hate to put on the lights but if we're going to stay here in the middle of the road . . ."

He laughed. "Put them on."

I did so and then drove a little ahead, parking at a safe place.

"Well?" he said.

"Well?"

"I guess you didn't like that."

"I did, but I'd hate to be run into. After all, you were fussy about fires."

"I know. They scare me. Maybe one reason is the way I was injured. The plane caught fire. I thought I was going to be roasted alive."

"And I understand you pulled the pilot out?"

"Who told you that?"

"Never mind."

He said sharply: "Don't figure me a hero, that's all. I never got within a thousand miles of the enemy. *I* smashed up in Texas too."

"I don't see that it makes much difference where you happen to be when you risk your life for other people."

"You're being far too romantic about it."

"You're being much more romantic in belittling yourself. All the storybook heroes do that. They say — Oh, it was nothing. But I know it wasn't nothing, or you wouldn't have been in a hospital for the past six months."

"I wasn't badly hurt. I was damned lucky."

"But you keep on thinking about it — as you showed just now."

"Not *thinking* of it exactly."

"It might do you good to fly again sometime."

"Maybe. It isn't important, anyway."

"What do you mean — not important?"

"I mean, compared with other things." He paused, then said: "Shall we move on, or . . ."

I switched out the lights. He was still nervous and rather sweetly afraid that being kissed in a car was not quite the sort of thing I cared for. He said "cared for," but I expect he meant "used to." I said: "I'm not used to it, but it's not the first time it's happened."

He answered: "Nor with me, either. But in Europe one doesn't have a car so much."

"Yes, it's a great convenience, a car."

He said: "I always used to wonder what affairs you had, traveling about everywhere and meeting so many people. . . . I thought perhaps there'd be some hints in your book."

"No . . . I can keep secrets."

"Thank God for that."

And the cloud again, the hidden nerve touched. It was so obvious, even while I was keeping one eye on the road, that I said: "Oh, Brad, what comes over you at times when you suddenly look like that?"

"Nothing that I can tell you about."

"All right. I don't mind."

"If that's true, it's wonderful."

"It *is* true, Brad. Please get it into your head that you don't have to say a thing. You've explained why you went to Germany, that's what I was really curious about."

"And now you understand?"

"Well, you said you went there to kill Framm."

"But you don't really believe me?"

"Of course I believe you if you say so."

"But it doesn't even startle you?"

"No more than so many other things. The world's been a bit full of queer happenings these last few years. I've seen a lot that weren't pretty. I've seen people beaten up, starved, terrorized, bombed — I've seen them under stress of all the crude emotions that you could only make credible to Park Avenue if you got Lillian Hellman to write a play about them — and then the audience wouldn't believe in *them,* they'd only believe in the play. . . . When you tell me you decided to kill somebody it doesn't seem too remarkable in a world that nowadays seems to have decided to kill everybody."

"By God, you're more right than you know. But you take it so calmly."

"How else can I take it? You were calm when you visited Framm in his office that day. You must have been, or else he'd have suspected you."

"I used to wonder whether he did. He certainly must have puzzled over my motive in coming back to work for him. And *his* motive too — because after all, *he invited me* . . . but why? It was an odd situation. He'd grabbed all the credit for my work, and he must have known I knew that; he knew too that my public defense of him was only for Pauli's sake. And he must have doubted whether I really accepted what had happened to her as a natural death. Of course he may have thought I was just a sucker about everything — except mathematics. Perhaps that fascinated him, to have someone like that around all the time . . . I don't know. I've often tried to think it out. He was a strange man. There were different layers of his mind all revolving oppositely in concentric circles. And then, mixed up with everything else, was the work we did. I don't mean that it brought us together in any sentimental sense, but it kept us apart from all other issues, while we were both at it. It was a sort of world in which being either a murderer or a sucker was irrelevant . . . if you can understand that."

"I think I can. But it makes me wish I knew that world myself."

"Too bad I can't explain much — if I tried to make it simple you wouldn't get the right idea. It wasn't anything dramatic or romantic. Those discoveries you read about in the papers — everything twisted out of its context to make the whole business seem like a treasure hunt—science isn't really like that at all. But people think it is—it's the kind of science they want to believe in, so they choose it, just as in an earlier age they chose the kind of religion that suited them. I remember once Framm got hold of an American comic strip—Buck Rogers, I think—he'd never seen anything like it before, and it amused him enormously—he passed it to me with a roar of laughter and said—'Look—*Science!*—the opiate of the people!' That's why it's hard to discuss science with nonscientists. It isn't that they don't know what you're talking about—I wouldn't know what a biochemist or a biologist was talking about, but as a member of the same general trade, so to speak, I should know the language of his thought even if I didn't have the jargon. And it's the jargon that people get a smattering of so easily these days. Framm once said that in medieval times the really popular argument was how many angels could dance on the end of a needle, whereas nowadays, judging from the magazine ads, people prefer to worry about how many microbes can dance on the end of a toothbrush. . . . And he wasn't sure that was progress."

"I believe you rather liked Framm," I said.

"*Liked* him? Good God, no. But when you've made up your mind to kill somebody and you're not sure when or how the chance will come, it's surprising what a tie that makes between you."

I wondered if he were serious till I saw his face. It was under the cloud again, and we were at Vista Grande having drinks before it lifted.

*   *   *

We didn't climb the next day, for a number of reasons; Brad was tired and got up late, and Dan's car showed a flat that had to be repaired in the nearest village several miles away. It wasn't perfect weather, either—rather moist and misty, but towards evening the sky cleared and Brad said he reckoned we should start at five in the morning if we wanted to reach the snow line. He didn't promise the summit.

We drove as before and by ten o'clock were at the place where we had picnicked. We stopped for coffee, then pushed on with the added zest of covering new territory. We hadn't talked much, during either the drive or the climb, and I realized, as the trail steepened and became more overgrown, that we were on ground that might not have been trodden for weeks or even months by any other human being. Not that this was a feat, merely that so few people cared for uncelebrated mountains, or in wartime had the time or the gas for them. The whole enterprise, I said to Brad, was thoroughly unpatriotic whichever way you looked at it.

"Suits me," he said, refilling the thermos with water. Then he walked on ahead, and as I guessed he was in a mood to be alone, I followed a few hundred yards behind. We must have climbed for an hour like that. Suddenly we came to a point where we could see the ridge above us flattening out into a kind of meadow meeting patches of snow. "That's where we'll stop," he said, pointing, and though I thought we should do better after another rest I kept on without making the suggestion.

The trail grew sketchy, then lost itself in a wilderness of boulders, and with that curious change of perspective that mountain scenery offers, the ridge itself looked more distant as we climbed. There came a moment when I knew we were off the trail and that the rocks were hazardous if one of us should slip. He was still ahead of me, often out of sight, and I began to wonder how much more of it I could stand. Then, having scrambled up a chimney with knees and elbows, I found myself against a huge slab, steep and smooth, with only a crack for a foothold and a hundred-foot drop if one missed it. There was no other way of continuing, and I didn't think

I could keep my nerve. I shouted and heard nothing but an echo. I called his name again and again. Then I saw him. He had crossed the slab and was a stage higher, but at a place that led to a sheerly perpendicular rock face that hadn't even a toehold. He was staring up and down as if bewildered. It seemed impossible that he had not heard my calls. "We can't do it," I shouted. "At least I can't. Let's go back."

He waved to me, but did not speak. The way he was standing hid his eyes and expression. But suddenly, as if a message had come directly between us, I knew he was scared. I called out: "Stay there, I'm coming up. It's all right."

That made him yell back: "No, don't. You stay where you are. It's no use."

"I know it's no use, but you're in a bad spot. I'll help you down."

"For Christ's sake, don't try it. I'm all right. Give me time."

I waited, perhaps for several minutes, then began to inch my way across the slab. I don't know if he even saw me doing it. The crack was crumbly in places, and when a fragment fell the interval before it hit anything gave me an extra qualm. I don't know how I got across, but at last I could relax and steady myself for a moment, gasping with a kind of fear that was new to me. I once stood in a doorway in a Paraguayan town with bullets crisscrossing the street and smashing windows all round, but I wasn't quite so terrified.

"You're crazy," Brad said, when I reached him. His face was gray and his hands still trembled.

"You're crazy too."

"Why the hell didn't you stay where you were?"

"Because I could see you weren't very happy up here."

"You're damn right I'm not. I'm stuck. I've no nerve to go up or down. That's no reason why you should have come, though."

"You'll get your nerve back soon."

"I don't think I shall. I'm stuck, I tell you."

"That's nonsense. You don't suppose you're going to be left here to starve, do you?"

"Very funny, very funny."

"Now look here. Pull yourself together. Let's sit down for a while and rest. Then if you're still scared I'll go down myself and bring men with ropes or something."

"Men with ropes? What the hell are you talking about?"

"Got to be done, if it's the only way. There must be people in the valley — forest rangers, maybe. They could climb up higher and drop a rope. Of course you might have to spend the night here first."

"Too damn cold."

From the way he said that I knew he was already calmer. I made him sit and there was so little room that we practically clung to each other for equilibrium. It was far too uncomfortable to be in any way romantic. We had left both rucksacks below, but we had a few cigarettes. We smoked, and all at once he began to laugh. "It *is* funny," he cried. "I've climbed all those mountains in Switzerland —the Jungfrau, the Matterhorn, even the Finsteraarhorn — and now I get stuck in a place like this that hasn't even got a name!"

"You're not stuck. You'll be all right in a minute."

"I'm a nervous wreck, that's what's the matter with me."

"No, you're not. I was nervous too. Most people would be. I'd like to see how Newby would shape up here."

"Oh God, Newby! Think of it!" He thought of it and it set him laughing again. That way it effected a cure — perhaps the only time Newby really did him any good.

"Well, what do we do?" he asked at length. "Is it to be up or down?"

I liked the question even if it were partly bravado. "Down," I said, "unless you want to get us into some real trouble."

"All right, but I'd like to try this again someday. I had my eye on that snow."

"Yes, we can come here again."

But I didn't think we should; it was about *my* limit, anyhow. We finished the cigarettes and began the descent. It wasn't as hard as I had expected and we both kept our nerve. Half an hour later we were eating sandwiches and drinking the ice-cold spring water. I suppose the small adventure gave us sensations of special ecstasy now that it was all over and no harm done. The snow still beckoned, but our eyes were much more drawn to the rock slab that had perhaps (though perhaps not) come near to finishing us off. I told Brad I felt I could gloat over it.

He answered: "Perhaps that's how Framm felt about me, if he could really read my mind, but I don't think he could."

He stared at the rock for a long moment, then went on: "Perhaps I was gloating too, in a different way. Over Framm, I mean. The motive of personal revenge isn't an adult one for a civilized person, so, if it comes, he has to do something to it, or else let it do something to him — or more likely, both things meet in a compromise. You said I liked Framm — no, I didn't — I *loathed* him, but there were times when I'd have been sorry if I'd heard he'd died in his bed. Once he had a bad cough — his chest was always weak after the injury — and I insisted on taking his temperature and making him go home. . . . And once the screen of the X-ray machine wasn't fixed properly and he nearly got electrocuted — fifteen hundred volts — that would have finished him off, but I wasn't thinking — I dragged him away in time. It gave me an idea, though. Meanwhile our show of getting on well and being on friendly terms would doubtless provide a good psychological alibi. The thing began to appeal to me as a problem as well as an act of retribution. I don't know whether you'd call me mad for having such thoughts. And, as I said before, there were *his* motives too — they gave me another problem. I could never be certain how he felt about me, apart from knowing I was damned useful to him. Because I was, by this time. I did all the routine stuff that cropped up in his computations. I had begun to be a real mathematician, and he knew that, and I knew that he knew it, and there was that unspoken awareness between us that always exists when two people can share a tough job without wasting each other's time."

"He seems to have worked much more closely with you in Berlin than he did in Vienna."

"Oh yes. In Vienna we only met when he came around every few days to check the galvanometer or glance at the graphs — he'd say 'Getting along all right?' — and I'd answer 'Oh yes' — and that would be all for perhaps another week. He probably thought I wasn't much good, so why should he bother."

"He didn't think your work was much good until he found it worth appropriating."

"In a sort of way, that's exactly true, and from him it was the perfect tribute. . . . He'd used other people's work before — I found that out. . . . On the other hand, I can see now there was a special reason why he didn't think I was much good when I first started with him in Vienna."

"Why?"

"Because . . . well, it concerns your father."

"How?"

"I don't know whether you knew it, but he paid Framm to take me as his assistant."

"He *paid* Framm?"

"I didn't find out till I was in Berlin, and then, of course, I understood why Framm hadn't taken me very seriously at first. He just thought I was a rich man's protégé, so he set me to work on what he thought wouldn't come to anything and left me to it. He had a few rich students he treated the same way. He'd take anybody's money, but you couldn't exactly buy him with it — he'd let you think you could and then secretly go back on the bargain."

I couldn't help smiling. "My poor father! If he knew that he'd have to add Framm to the list of all the other people who disappointed him. . . . Just for curiosity, have you any idea what my father *did* pay?"

"My whole salary."

"Good God! So all the time — "

"Yes, all the time I was in Vienna I was costing Framm nothing."

"That's one way of looking at it. But I was thinking also that if the arrangement was for my father to pay your salary, then my father was a bit responsible for you being underpaid."

"Or else generous for offering to pay for me at all."

"Perhaps. . . . It's odd, though, how much easier it is to forgive Framm for exploiting you totally than to excuse my father for not putting up a few extra dollars. Particularly as . . ."

I stopped in time. It had been on my tongue to say: "Particularly as he had a reason to get you out of the way."

"Go on," Brad said.

"Particularly as he's so rich," I answered. But perhaps it sounded as improvised as it was.

"Shall we start going down?" he asked, and we tramped a mile or more before he spoke again.

We had cached a thermos of coffee at the old picnic place and it made a pleasant excuse for another halt. But we were tired now, exhausted in nerves and bones; the feeling came on suddenly while we were lying on the grass. We smoked cigarette after cigarette and, as the afternoon progressed, rolled over in deep lassitude to stay in the sun.

"What exactly did you do in Berlin?" I asked, lazily. "Routine work for Framm, you said. But wasn't there anything you did on your own?"

"Not so much. Now he knew I was good and he was paying me himself he kept me busy most of the time. But of course his work and mine weren't so far apart. Electromagnetism links up with the entire field of quantum mathematics."

"But didn't you have any personal life? Any fun? Didn't you go anywhere?"

"Berlin wasn't a gay city in those days."

"But there must have been a few places — theaters, movies . . ."

"Yes, I went to a few."

"Didn't you visit anybody's home? Of course I remember what you were like in London. . . ."

"That was different. I was shy then. I wasn't shy in Berlin. But I didn't go anywhere — except once to a party Framm gave."

"Oh? At his house?"

"Yes. I wanted to see what it was like. He had a big villa in Charlottenburg. His wife was all right — quite pleasant — the gracious hostess — probably what we should call in America a socialite. But domestic also. The place was swarming with little Framms. Kids of all ages from two to twelve. It was a big party — professors and professors' wives, and the kind of half-professors they call *Privatdozenten*. All very Nazi, of course. And nobody packed the kids off to bed, as they should have, and the more they romped and misbehaved the more Framm seemed to enjoy it."

"Just one happy family."

"Maybe . . . if you can work that in with the fact that Framm was notorious for his affairs with other women. I'd known that in Vienna, but I didn't meet his family there, so it hadn't looked like such a paradox. To see him playing silly games with those kids, who obviously adored him, when all the time one knew what a swine he was . . ."

"Did you ever visit his house again?"

"No, I'd had enough. Perhaps he'd had enough too — I wasn't

asked. But he'd introduced me very charmingly to everybody. Of course they knew what had happened in Vienna — who I was, and about Pauli. I was his American specialty — the young mathematician for whom the privilege of working with Hugo Framm outweighed all personal and private complications. . . . Or no — perhaps that's going too far. I don't know what was in his mind about me. He had an air of showing me off as a novelty, but then I *was* a novelty. Not many Americans studied in Germany after the Nazis came to power."

"Of course they must have thought you were sympathetic."

"Sure. I wanted them to think so. It was part of my plan. . . . You'd better let me tell you the whole story consecutively. . . ."

*　　*　　*

The Technische Institut was outside Berlin, a functional edifice, deliberately unacademic in style; different branches of science were housed floor above floor, and as in London, Physics was at the top, not from any symbolic recognition of its importance but for the opposite reason that more favored sciences chose the more accessible space. Brad, however, did not mind that. To ascend by the slow elevator through the sounds and smells of so much practical experimentation in other fields, most of it geared for war, and to reach finally the quietude of his own room under the roof gave him a feeling that he was in, but not of, the hive.

He soon realized that it was a political as well as a scientific hive. Within the aggressively Nazi framework of staff and student bodies there were continual interdepartmental struggles — for government appropriations, extra personnel, and that continuance of political favor on which very existence depended. Framm spent at least half his time and energies on these exhausting battles, and usually he won them. He was utterly unscrupulous, a wily tactician, a dangerous enemy and a false friend; but Brad had to admit that, so far as dealing with the higher authorities was concerned, these attributes were necessities of survival. It was when they showed in his treatment of subordinates that Brad hated him with a pure intensity that nourished his own personal decision.

He had wondered at first how his co-workers would accept him into their midst, but he found he had so little contact with them, professional or personal, that problems of behavior rarely arose on either side. He had been at the Technische Institut for weeks before he exchanged more than a good-morning with anyone except Framm and Framm's secretary.

Then for some reason this girl gave up her job and another arrived one morning in her place. She was friendly, and since Framm happened to be away most of her first day, she used her conversation on Brad, who would not have encouraged her but for a curious circumstance which he soon discovered — that the girl knew what had happened in Vienna, but did not yet connect Brad with it. And she was most anxious to chat about her new employer, for whom she had already conceived the ardent admiration that women so readily felt for Framm. Wasn't he wonderful? Such a brilliant mind . . . and his eyes — they seemed to bore through you. And so pale — perhaps he didn't have good health. She had heard he nearly died after that madwoman attacked him in Vienna.

Brad thought this as good a method of exploration as he was likely to find. He said "yes" in answer, and added a few details to whet her eagerness both to give and to take. Presently she said: "Of course you know what was really behind it all?"

So the accusations Pauli had made against Framm were common gossip, Brad reflected; he wondered how that would help or hinder the accomplishment of his purpose. He said: "No? What was it?"

Then she said something that so utterly shocked and amazed him that even the girl, who had expected to create a small sensation, was surprised at the larger size of it.

What she said was this: that Pauli had been Framm's mistress and that when the Nazi movement in Austria began to flourish, Framm got rid of her because she was a quarter Jew.

Brad had known this latter fact, which had meant nothing to him, but the suggestion of her relationship with Framm was shattering, even though he was aware that the girl might only be repeating untrue gossip. Nor did he know quite what it shattered. Not his faith in Pauli; nor his hatred of Framm, which in many ways it accentuated. Eventually he decided it must be something inside himself that had nothing to do with either.

Later in the same day the girl came to him, full of apologies and embarrassments; doubtless during the interval somebody had told her who Framm's assistant was. He patted her arm and said it didn't matter, it hadn't been her fault; but they talked no more on any subsequent occasion, and soon Framm's temper and temperament made her quit as had her predecessor.

Brad found that coming to terms with the new idea, true or not, put Framm in perspective, made the focus of his own observation almost fascinatingly sharper, so that he accumulated data with less impatience. When he saw Framm's ruthlessness in trampling opposition he felt more certain than ever that the man had been responsible for Pauli's death, yet he was also willing to wait longer till he discovered some final clinching evidence. For this reason he welcomed and even relished every fresh display of Framm's malice; each instance added a fragment to the mosaic of indictment. There was a clever young biologist who had criticized some administrative scheme that Framm was trying to put over — sound criticism, since afterwards Framm changed his scheme accordingly. But he could not forgive the instigator, and had him hounded from a minor university post on a racial count. Not that he believed in the prevalent nonsense about Aryanism, but he found the nonsense useful. If one of his subordinates were part Jewish, a good scientist, and also subservient to him personally, he would protect him, but if he weren't good or showed any sign of independence, then the racial angle provided a weapon. The way he used it against the biologist was typically improvised; he spread the story that the man was a Jew when actually he wasn't. In all such maneuvers Framm had no conscience, no hesitation, and no pity. He despised the mob and the Nazi mob as much as any other, but he was willing to pay it all the necessary kinds of lip service.

Sometimes, overhearing in Framm's office half of a telephone talk that revealed either the lip service or the ruthlessness, Brad would be unable to keep back a look that told plainly enough what he thought; and Framm would catch the look, interpret it correctly, yet seem by no means displeased. Gradually Brad came to realize that these interpretations did not put to hazard a relationship which, on the surface, he still wished others to take for one of close friendship; on the contrary, Framm at times seemed to derive perverse enjoyment from the situation. And perhaps because of this, and also because Brad was an American, Framm was less guarded in what he said in front of him. He agreed that the division of science into good Germanic and bad Jewish was sheerly idiotic; he had admitted this, freely and cynically, when Brad had argued the cause of the biologist. And when he saw the look in Brad's eyes, he said: "You'll probably kill me one of these days, Bradley, but I know you won't peach on me."

In this fantastic way he trusted Brad, and no less when Brad's hostility became outspoken. He too became then more outspoken; he began to make Brad an audience whenever he had trouble with the authorities or with his rival department heads. He would rehearse an argument, or conduct a post-mortem on one; he would unleash his wits in dangerous territory after carefully making sure that the doors were closed and that his secretary was at lunch. He was capable of referring to Hitler as "that inspired *Quatschkopf* into whose hands God has entrusted the destiny of the world." He confided in Brad all the details of his continuous and frustrating feuds with the Nazi higher-ups, he would read over his briefs in defense of theoretical work; and then, less tactfully, he would let loose a devastating blast against the intelligence of certain persons in authority. Nor could anyone be much more devastating than Framm when he was in vitriolic form. His voice and gestures were of such excellent acting quality that Brad once asked why he wasted them on a single hearer. Framm replied: "They are not wasted — they are indulged in."

As for the work, that too progressed so well that it reached many an abstract discussion point. Framm would enter Brad's laboratory after some tigerish outside struggle in which he had bested an opponent, placated a superior, or sacrificed an underling; and for very relief he would launch into an expounding of his own scientific philosophy — a synthesis of the practical and theoretical in which, at the higher levels, there was no necessary basis of deduction from observed facts, but the mere waving of theory, like antennae, to set a course for later experimentation and possible discovery. The mathematician, he was fond of saying, could construct a field theory for the unknowable as well as the unknown; and he was also fond of a quotation from (of all persons) G. K. Chesterton to the effect that "the difference between the poet and the mathematician is that the poet tries to get his head into the heavens while the mathematician tries to get the heavens into his head." Good, Framm commented, except that there was no fundamental difference between the two behaviors, and he would scribble some half-impish equation on the blackboard to illustrate.

Brad's habit was to do his own experimental work mostly in the mornings; but later in the day, when he had his graphs and computations to assemble, he would move into a world of pure symbol-expression; and sometimes then a curious trancelike ecstasy would take possession of him, an ecstasy that Framm's hand on his shoulder did not disturb.

What *was* disturbing, whenever he was outside his own workroom, was the whole bludgeoning atmosphere of Nazi domination during that last year before the outbreak of war. He was in Berlin during the period after Munich, and on a March day in 1939 he heard Chamberlain's Birmingham speech over Framm's special radio. When the storm troopers marched into Prague and Memel, Framm's exultation had been unbounded. Brad realized that beneath the skin of derision which was no more than a privately intellectual arrogance, Framm was a perfect Nazi. That *Quatschkopf,* as he put it, had been inspired again. Presently there would be moves on Danzig, then Poland. The European democracies would not fight, because they had no fight left in them. And as for America, Framm added contemptuously . . .

It was years since Brad had been in his own country, yet Framm's scorn took him back in mind immediately. While he saw the towers of Manhattan and the wheatfields of the Dakotas, he looked at Framm with the cold answering thought: I must do what I have to do and then get going. . . .

*　　*　　*

I said I was glad he had felt like that about America. "I'd been afraid you were getting to be the kind of American that Julian once said was like some kinds of wine — they don't travel well. . . ."

He answered moodily: "I don't know whether I travel well or not, but I sometimes wish I hadn't traveled at all. It would have been better fun to stay where I was born."

"And know no more mathematics than I do?"

"Sure. Plus no more politics and history than I do. Then **we** might both have been happy."

"Together?"

He laughed. "There comes the flaw. I wouldn't even have met you if I hadn't traveled."

"You'd have met somebody else and I'd have met somebody else."

"But that's exactly what we did. I met Pauli and you met — oh, everybody."

"Not quite that. But even if I had, I don't know what we can do about it now. We're so old."

"Now you're kidding. . . ."

"Yes, but you're not. You really feel we're aged in the wood and the wood's a bit rotten. I don't blame you. I just managed to miss one world war — you've had two. But I had a head start on you by being a precocious brat even when I was eighteen."

"You certainly were. And I was a bit of a prig until . . ."

He hesitated and I said laughing: "This sort of confession ought to be good for the soul, if a scientist believes in one."

"And even if he doesn't."

"I wish I was sure about souls. I wish I knew as little as my mother did and understood as much."

"What made you think of her?" he asked sharply.

"I often think of her. I miss her more than I ever thought I would. She was a darling. You knew her — you remember what a darling she was."

"Yes, I remember." He looked uneasy.

"But get on with your story. Tell me about Framm — if you still want to."

I lay back and waited. When he resumed, it was abruptly and faster, as if he had got to a part that had to be carried in stride. "Framm often worked at night and so did I. We'd have the whole floor practically to ourselves when the others had gone home. That of course would provide the opportunity. And yet, you know, I

wasn't *eager* in any sense of time — I mean, it didn't have to be today or tomorrow or the next day, provided I knew it was going to
happen someday. And meanwhile inside our own private world I
was able to admire and envy his sheer brain stuff more than that of
anyone else I have ever known, before or since. That's a plain fact
and I'll never deny it. It hadn't anything to do with *liking* the man.
But at odd moments, when a certain quality in his mind revealed
itself, I had a feeling that I can only call a religious one . . . of worship, if you like . . . not worship of *him,* for Christ's sake, but of
something quite distant, impersonal . . . the soul, if you like the
word, that a scientist believes in. You were talking about that just
now."

There was no comment I ventured to make. At length he said
roughly: "Do you get me?"

"Partly."

"Wouldn't be surprising if you didn't. Perhaps you think they
were right to put me in a psychiatric ward. They had their reasons,
maybe. If only they hadn't kept on watching me all the time, as if I
carried the secret of the universe in my pocket. Perhaps somebody
thought I did and gave them orders — Follow that man, he knows
too much, he worked with Framm. . . . He has the magic formula,
economy size, made like a doctor's prescription, not one ingredient,
but several. . . ."

I could see him becoming excited in a peculiar way, and I thought
it bad for him. "It's getting late," I said. "Don't you think we ought
to start back?"

"Yes, yes, let's go."

I hated to do that, but above all things I wanted the wild look out
of his eye. We hoisted our rucksacks and began to trudge down the
trail, tiredness now in every limb and muscle, so that when we
reached the car he slumped inside and slept all the way to Vista
Grande, while I kept myself awake by thinking about him.

That evening his behavior had that raw edge that made me realize he was still in trouble. I don't think my father noticed it, but for me there were danger signals in the way he fidgeted and talked. His face, too, carried a flush that wasn't sunburn, and when afterwards he quite docilely submitted to having his temperature taken I found it was two degrees above normal. It was possible, I judged, that the nervous strain of our rock adventure had caused this, and I was not especially worried, though I began to wonder what we should do if some physical ailment required a doctor. There was my father's doctor, who paid a semisocial call every few weeks, but it would be awkward to bring him onto the scene. However, in the morning Brad was sleeping hard and did not look worse, so I left instructions that he wasn't to be disturbed, and then made my own departure to see Mr. Chandos again.

During the night I had been wakeful for hours. I knew by now that I wanted to help Brad far beyond the casual desire I had had at first; I knew also that this intention was fixed, unless events or revelations should take some quite appalling turn. But most of all I knew I had a quest of my own, separate from anything Small might have, because it occurred to me at this stage that the killing of Framm might be what was really on Brad's mind; or perhaps, I even thought, he had come to a point in his story beyond which he didn't know definitely what had happened, since the final act might have taken place in one of those trancelike moods he had talked about. Amateur psychology, perhaps; but whatever had happened, or how, it seemed to me there was one simple step to be taken immediately. So that morning I called at the central library in Los Angeles and looked for Framm's name in various reference books. I could find no recent information about him; the war years had left gaps in the biographies of enemies. But then it occurred to me to try a newspaper office; they would have files there, possibly, or some way of checking on whether a fairly well-known scientist was or was not still alive. I was lucky enough to find a man who had read my book and could think of a number of reasons (but not the real one) why I was interested in the matter; he was very obliging and assiduous, and in due course brought me the news that Hugo Framm was undoubtedly dead, because in one of the books he had consulted there was the phrase "after Hugo Framm was killed."

I'm afraid my face showed shock, so that he added waggishly: "Not a pal of yours, by any chance?"

"I should say not. Did it happen to say *how* he was killed?"

"No, but perhaps I could find out. Is it urgent?"

"Not exactly *urgent,* but — well, I could call back in the afternoon or perhaps telephone if you think you'd have the information by then."

"Sure, I might. Give me a ring. . . . How's the picture coming along?"

Like most Los Angeles journalists he read the *Reporter* and *Variety* and liked to feel that movie affairs were within a home-town gambit; and as I was anxious to undo the effect of the shocked look I gossiped a bit and told him I was just about to lunch with Mr. Chandos at the Brown Derby to discuss matters. He said he knew Mr. Chandos, who had once visited the office in search of background material for a newspaper story — a very fine producer, full of ideas; I was certainly fortunate in having him do my picture. (He too called it *my* picture.)

Half an hour later, still holding myself casual though with some effort, I found myself in a booth at the Brown Derby with Mr. Chandos, who had called me Jane as soon as we met at the studio and whom I was trying to think of as Paul without immediately being reminded of Pauli. He probably noticed my look of preoccupation, for he asked: "What's on your mind?" in a way that wasn't quite the conventional opening.

"Oh, things in general."

"The war looks like being over pretty soon."

"I know. And what then?"

"Ah, that's the problem. And all the answers you get are gags —
a plastic helicopter for every back yard — soldiers coming home to
find everything just the same, including Mom's mince pies . . . ever
read the ads in the magazines?"

"I've even written some of them. But not any more."

"You with your ad-writing and me with my B pictures. We're a
fair match. . . . What are you going to do next? Another book?"

"Probably — sometime. At present it's in the air — like the two-
million-dollar picture they won't let you make. What would that be
about, by the way?"

He laughed. "What *wouldn't* it be about? I keep on getting new
ideas. I got another one last night, while I was driving home. I live
in the Valley — not far out of town, but there's a mile or so of fairly
dark road before you come to my house. Of course I know every
inch of that road — even the holes in the pavement — but last night,
as I was driving, I suddenly thought — What if I *don't* come to my
house? Suppose I just drive on, without thinking at first, and then
of course the thought would soon come to me — What's happened?
Where *are* you? You must have passed your house . . . so I stare
out of the window, expecting to recognize something, but I can't —
it's just a road with trees and hedges — not a house in sight. So —
quite a bit puzzled — I make the turn and drive back. Presently I
must come to my house. But I still don't. I drive four or five miles
— and the road's still just trees and hedges. Now this is beginning
to be really queer. Four or five miles from my house in any direction would take me to other houses, shops, schools, and so on. . . .
Well, there's nothing to do but just go on driving. Maybe I'm on a
road which, for some quite extraordinary reason, I never knew
about before. But after ten miles a queer sort of tingling sensation
gets into my spine — because there hasn't been a side turning . . .

and no car has either passed or overtaken me, and I know that within a score miles of Los Angeles such a thing simply isn't possible! However, I still drive on and on — there *must* be something soon . . . but there isn't — there's nothing but the road — paved — white line in the middle — fairly straight and level — *but it doesn't go anywhere!* And there isn't a light, or a sign, or a mailbox, and in a few more miles I shall run out of gas! . . . So what do I do?"

"You turn on the car radio," I said.

"By God, I never thought of that!" He grew suddenly excited. "Yes, I turn it on. . . . But what do I get? . . . Why, just nothing . . . all round the dial. Everything's dead. Maybe it's an air-raid warning — the Hundred and Nineteenth Interceptor Command has ordered all stations off the air . . ."

"Or else," I said, "you *do* get something. You get the same thing from every station."

"But *what,* Jane? Tell me *what?*"

"Gabriel Heatter reading the Hundred and Nineteenth Psalm. . . . 'Teach me, O Lord, the way of thy statutes; and I shall keep it unto the end. Give me understanding, and I shall keep thy law; yea, I shall observe it with my whole heart. Make me to go in the path of thy commandments; for therein do I delight. Incline my heart unto thy testimonies, and not to covetousness. Turn away mine eyes from beholding vanity; and quicken thou me in thy way . . .'"

I don't know quite how or why, but as I spoke the words, which I remembered from having learned them at school, the thing that had begun as a gag became somehow serious, so that my own voice trembled and I saw tears come into Paul's eyes. He reached for my hand across the table and presently muttered: "Well, I guess there's not much for either of us to say after that. . . ."

We were silent for quite a while and the hubbub of the restaurant rose around us into a roar; the place was filling up; flash bulbs were popping at personalities; the cartooned faces of famous patrons stared down from the four walls.

I said at length: "I'd like you to meet a friend of mine sometime. He reminds me a bit of you."

"Sure. I'd be glad to."

"He's not in your line, though. A scientist."

"That's all right. I've nothing against scientists. Bring him along the next time."

"I don't know that I can. He's ill at present. He was in the Air Force and crashed. . . . But I'd like you to meet him sometime."

"Sure."

The waiter appeared, carrying a telephone which he plugged in to a near-by socket. "For you, Mr. Chandos. . . ."

He took it, listened a moment, then said: "No, it's for you, Jane."

"For *me?* But it can't be. Nobody knows I'm here."

"Probably someone saw you coming in and thought of a good way to bother you — they do that, you know, in this town. . . . Shall I handle it for you? If it's autographs or interviews I'll stall. . . ." He spoke back into the instrument: "Yes? . . . No, Miss Waring isn't here, but I'll take a message — what is it? . . . Yes . . . yes . . . *What?* . . . Say that name again . . . Spell it . . . Spell the other name too . . . Well, I don't know what it's all about, but I'll tell her when I see her. . . . Okay. . . . G'by. . . ."

Thus it came about that Paul Chandos gave me the details about Hugo Framm's death, and though he was obviously curious, he was tactful enough not to ask a single question. I liked him more than ever for that.

*   *   *

I got back to Vista Grande during the late afternoon and found Brad sitting by the pool. He looked tired, which wasn't remarkable after our previous day's exploit; and there was still the look in his eyes which I didn't like. I thought I had best get to the point quickly. "Brad," I said. "I found out what happened to Hugo Framm. He was killed in a British air raid on Peenemünde in 1944."

He didn't look surprised. He said: "I knew that. At least we were told so at Oak . . ." He stopped. "Oakland. . . . I was there when I heard about it. Peenemünde's the place on the Baltic where the Germans had their experimental station for V-2s. That wasn't much in his line. God, what fools they were, not to give him a free hand. Drop all the theoretical stuff — that was the cry at the beginning. Then afterwards it was too late to catch up. He probably fought them as long as he could, but I guess he didn't win. He made too many enemies."

"And you didn't kill him."

"No, I left that for the R.A.F. I told him a lie instead, which certainly killed him in one sense if it sent him to Peenemünde. But perhaps it didn't — so much could have happened in the interval. But I do know Peenemünde wasn't where he should have been. It was some other place — in Norway — where they were making heavy water."

"Heavy water?"

He nodded. "That was his idea all along if they'd given him a free hand." He added, changing the subject with marked abruptness: "By the way, Newby called this afternoon."

"What did he want?"

"To look me over. To see how I was getting on. To hear if I'd had any more dreams. Perhaps to see you if you'd been in. I told him I still dreamed of being a skywriter but I'd changed the word I wanted to write. I spelled it out for him. It was a German word that Framm used a lot — not a nice word at all. Newby didn't know that, but when he gets back he's going to ask someone who under-

stands German and that'll fix him for a while. I think of the darned-
est ways to keep that man interested, don't I?"

"You shouldn't," I said. "It isn't worth wasting time on."

"What else should I waste time on while I'm waiting?"

"Waiting for what?"

"Something we're all waiting for."

"Something good, I hope."

He shrugged.

I said: "It may be very trite and old-fashioned of me, but what
I'm waiting for is the end of the war — victory and peace — all
that."

"Oh, sure."

"Don't you think we'll get them?"

"We'll get victory."

"But not peace?"

"Depends. We shall see."

"I wish I knew what you think we shall see."

He said glumly: "Maybe a bad word written in the sky."

I sat down next to him; he was in swimming trunks and had
been in the pool, because the towel near him was damp. His body
(which I had never seen so near nude before) was slim and muscu-
lar, though he could well have taken on a few more pounds. The
desert air had browned him, the mountain air was now adding a
clear gloss. He looked fine, except for his eyes, which offered a mi-
nority report on his general recovery.

I asked what the lie was he had told Framm.

He replied: "Call it twice two are five."

"If you say things like that I shall bring out a mathematics textbook and ask you to give me lessons."

That made him laugh. I didn't like the laugh either. And I didn't
like the thought that Newby had been around. I suddenly felt a

deep urgency in what was beginning to dominate me — I must find out what was on his mind quickly . . . before it was too late. The idea of no time to be wasted came to me unarguably, yet with frightening sureness.

He began to talk about the work he and Framm had been busy on in Berlin until the outbreak of the war. It was concerned with the mathematics of nuclear structure; the construction of a field theory to account for certain phenomena already noted experimentally; but also, if the theory were correct, to point the way to phenomena *that had not yet been observed,* because adequate experimental technique lagged behind. The theoretical work had been in progress for months, with Framm giving it all the time he could spare, and Brad with him as an equal, except that he saved Framm's time by doing all the laborious computations. There was nothing remarkable in the apparent slowness of the procedure, but to some of the high-up Nazis it was hard to explain or defend. They lacked sympathy with anything so unproductive; visionary stuff was not truly Germanic; Hitler was planning for a short war, and a single new weapon in the blueprint stage was worth a whole territory of long-range speculation.

Then events moved fast on all sides. The Danzig crisis boiled up into the actual imminence of war, which meant that the intrigues of Framm's rivals to have his department reorganized under a more "practical" head rose to an equal climax. And also . . . something stirred inside the private world of experiment and visionary analysis, so that Hugo Framm and his assistant began to discuss, like conspirators, the chance that they were on the edge of something big — something that would not only widen the scope of theoretical knowledge, but could in due course affect the practical character of life on earth. As scientists they were intensely skeptical of all such dreaming, yet as humans they could not forbear to tiptoe a few paces into the unguessable, just far enough to send them back to work with rueful anxiety. For the thing was not even yet at a beginning — it was only at the beginning of a beginning. In those talks with Brad, Framm revealed the curious division of his soul. Part of him, perhaps the deeper part, was the pure researcher, impatient of other people's impatience, willing to devote years to an inch's extension of the mind's territory, willing even for that inch itself to be unknown to all save the few initiates. Never had Brad heard him trounce more scathingly the "practical" scientists who had grown to high favor with the regime by setting teams of underling scientists to work on some immediate problem of industry. *Engineers,* he sneered. "One of these days you and I will write all we have discovered on the back of an old envelope and send it to them. In a few years they will begin to learn what it is all about. Then after a few more years Siemens will be interested in the patent rights. And meanwhile you and I will still be fighting those who would close down this laboratory and turn it into a gymnasium for teaching storm troopers how to crack skulls."

That repeated "you and I" gave Brad a feeling that was not a qualm, but a nudge of reminder inside himself. "So we must continue our work," Framm went on. "One of these days the world will wake up to what we have done."

Brad did not care for this sort of magniloquence. "The world won't do anything of the sort," he said. "A few scientists in other countries will read about it in the technical journals and you'll probably be asked to deliver some lectures."

"You are forgetting there will be no communication with foreign scientists during the war."

"Oh, they'll manage to exchange ideas through Sweden or Switzerland somehow or other."

"Not this time." Framm was emphatic. "There is already the rule of secrecy in operation."

"But surely that doesn't apply to mathematics."

"Perhaps it doesn't, but perhaps also it should and must."

"If it did, then don't forget I'm foreign myself."

Framm put on the roguish smile that was the sign of an approaching display of charm, but which Brad had learned to recognize as less charming in what it often concealed or preluded.

"Perhaps we shall have to make a German citizen of you then. . . . Or perhaps since you are American it does not matter. Americans have no ambition to conquer."

"What's that got to do with it? Why should they? Why should anybody?"

"I think I must prepare a number of answers to your question, Bradley. But the argument should be at Berchtesgaden, not here. It would be interesting to demonstrate that by a proper application of quantum mathematics Germany can become the first master of the world."

"That sort of thing ought to appeal — at Berchtesgaden," Brad said dryly.

"Ah, but only if it could be done in six months. That man is obsessed with *Blitzkrieg*. You have no idea how impossible it is to talk to him of serious matters. Planck could not. Haushofer could not. Anything that he cannot understand is no use, and he can understand so little. He has pushed his luck too far. Bradley, there are times when the second-rate mind is criminal. And there are things that history will not forgive unless they are done once only to achieve world conquest. The end can only justify the means if the end is large enough."

"You see world conquest as a real possibility?"

"Provided other countries are not already ahead of us in these matters. And provided our *Quatschkopf* can be persuaded to look further than the end of one of his long howitzers."

"What makes you think the world would gain by being under German domination?"

"Bradley, I think there must be a world order if there is to be any world worth living in. I can see no possibility of world order unless it is imposed on those who would be too selfish or too stupid to submit voluntarily. I can think of no country with both the power and the will to perform this task but Germany. . . . And Germany is now at the mercy of a crystal-gazer!"

He seemed after that to regret having been so outspoken, and there was a barrier between them, as if he could sense in Brad's attitude some new dimension of hostility.

*　　*　　*

Dan brought us cocktails and Brad said: "Dan, these are always so good. Where did you learn to make them like this?"

"In San Francisco," Dan replied. "I used to mix drinks at the Seacomber bar there."

"Ever been in Houston?"

"No, sir. You wouldn't get a drink like this in any bar in Texas. They don't sell hard liquor."

After he had gone, Brad said: "I keep on thinking I've seen Dan somewhere before. . . . Maybe not. . . . Where was I?"

I said: "You were telling me what Framm said about Germany."

"Oh yes . . . Well, I decided then there was no more time to waste. The truth was, I'd been postponing things because I'd been so damned interested in the work we'd been doing."

He sipped at the drink and looked at me over the rim of the glass. "Would you want any more proof?"

"Of what?"

"Of the state of my mind. How I hated that man and loved the work I did with him. I hated him more than I'd ever hated anybody — more than I'd ever loved Pauli, for that matter."

"How can you compare love and hate?"

"Hell, I don't know, but you can." He went on: "He was away, out of Berlin, wrangling as usual with the big shots. So I didn't get any chances. . . . I think I told you before that we often worked all night, when the building was practically empty — only janitors and guards who knew us well and never came near. . . . But he was *away*. . . . You see how it was?"

I caught the rising excitement in his eyes; I said quietly: "Yes, I see."

"Actually, he did go to Berchtesgaden, though I didn't learn that till later. Everything was racing to a climax. The British were threatening war if Poland were attacked. Framm's personal enemies were closing in on him — he was in the doghouse, the way it looked. Mostly his own fault — too many tricks and treacheries had caught up with him. But it was also the war emergency that put him in a real spot — because the mounting hue and cry was for less theory, more practice — for results certain and immediate, not distant and problematical. That gave his enemies just the weapon they needed, so that his last chance became his only chance — to sell some enormous novelty in the very highest market, and entirely on trust. If he could pull it off it would be a master stroke, but from the point of view of sober science, it was all far too premature. Some of our earlier checks had been encouraging, but there was a crucial one still to come. I was working on that while Framm was at Berchtesgaden, or perhaps I should rather say on *those* because it included a statistical analysis of all the checks. Nothing absolutely accurate was either expected or conceivable, but 95 per cent would be encouraging, 80 per cent would leave us still in doubt, and less than 70 would put us back where we'd been before we started. It was an especially delicate part of our calculations that was involved — something speculative and — if you can imagine that in mathematics — a bit *inspired*. I've been trying to think of a rather wild parallel — not to the thing itself — but to the kind of wild-goose chase it was. Suppose that by sheer chance in reading a certain chapter of the Bible you discovered that the forty-ninth word from the beginning was "Shake" and the forty-ninth word from the end was "spear." Suppose some mad genius told you that this wasn't a coincidence, but a secret clue to the meaning of the universe provided you could find other poets' names embedded similarly in other books. Suppose you were crazy enough to try, by picking up books and counting words at random in a public library. Then suppose some even madder genius offered a formula for taking you directly to a certain page of a certain book on a certain shelf. So you tried it, and there, counting up and down, you found the words 'bitter' and 'nut.' But you'd never heard of a poet called Bitternut — his name wasn't in any of the encyclopedias — maybe he was only a very minor poet indeed. . . . Does all that sound *too* fantastic?"

"Probably less so than the mathematics would."

"Well, anyhow, it was the sort of question I'd got as far as — How much of a poet was Mr. Bitternut? Was he even a poet at all? All night I tried to find out, alternating between the laboratory and my office desk, assembling the results and fitting them into place. I was very tired — I'd been on the job, more or less, for two days and two nights. I hadn't even gone back to my rooms in Wilmersdorf, but had snatched a few intermittent hours of sleep on the couch in Framm's office. And meanwhile, if I looked through the window, I could see ominous signs of events — armored cars rattling by, men in field-gray scampering along the pavements. The radio, whenever I turned it on, gave fresh news of the crisis, instructions for mobilization, rationing, air-raid precautions. It was all cold and efficient, with no jubilant crowds, cheers, or flag waving. Never, it seemed to me, had a country moved to war with less enthusiasm — yet the lack of it had its own peculiarly frightening quality. During the evening the sirens shrieked and a few minutes later a rather agitated janitor rushed into the room to order me to the air-raid shelter in the basement. I told the old man I'd rather stay where I was, I was very busy

— which wasn't bravery, by the way, but just my own guess that it could only be either a false alarm or a practice drill. The janitor finally compromised by saying I could stay there provided I put out all the electric lights. I said all right, I could work by candlelight. So I did, and when he'd gone, with the city blacking out all round me, I ate a sandwich and drank some cold coffee. Then I got down to the job again. Within an hour, I reckoned, I should have pushed the results to a point where success or failure could be tentatively applied to the work of many months. The calculations were not only fairly difficult, but extremely laborious. Towards four o'clock (I had been too optimistic in my forecasting) I came to the last calculation. It was one in which two sets of figures, neither of them predictable, should — according to the theory — bear an algebraic relationship; the final process was the plotting of positions on a graph. As the minutes passed and I got closer to what I knew must be the finish, I couldn't have imagined anything in the world more dramatic than my own solitary behavior in that lonely room, working by candlelight in the middle of the night at the outbreak of a world war — and yet I suppose most people would have reckoned it, compared with events outside, a very dull business. Even by technical standards it didn't look much of a climax. There were no color changes on litmus paper, no test tubes held up to the light, no retorts bubbling over Bunsen burners, none of the rigmarole of magazine-ad science . . . even the X-ray machine, which usually made noises, had been switched off into silence. All I had to do was to sit at a desk and put a few pencil points on paper. I did so, then joined them up to make a curve. The curve bulged to a position that gave a reading, by a prefigured scale, of three-point-five-seven-five-five; the predictable reading, based on theory alone, had been three-point-five-five-nine-three. It was near enough. Mr. Bitternut was a poet."

He drank the rest of his cocktail at a gulp, but waved away any more. Presently he continued: "When I realized what this amounted to, the word success did come, but it had a strange sound, almost like a sound without meaning. What I chiefly felt was an overwhelming weariness, both of mind and body. I gave myself a shot of Framm's brandy and lay down on his couch. I must have slept instantly, for when I woke there was dawn at the edge of the window blinds. I had not heard the 'all clear' sirens even if there had been any. I crossed the room to look down at the street; there was a line of trucks and armored cars parked outside the building and knots of men were gathered about. I turned on the radio; the voices of announcers, full of their ghastly tired eagerness, were repeating old news, but it was new to me: that the German Army was already far across the Polish frontier; war had begun.

"I suppose that was a turning point of my life — a moment of complete flux, when I might have done almost anything if one of a number of impulses had been a mite stronger — perhaps if I had had a few drops more brandy, or even a few drops less. If Framm had returned exactly then I think I should have killed him somehow or other — and been promptly caught, tried, sentenced, and hanged. An American spy, they'd probably have said — not a real scientist at all. I thought of that as I stared down at the street, and then the thought came to me — supposing that was what I had been, all along, would Framm have suspected it? But of course America doesn't have spies — or didn't have then. We were so God-damned innocent in those days. We'd debunked the First World War so thoroughly that it was hard to believe in another — much easier to sell scrap to Japan and at the same time blame the munition makers. . . . I won't try to tell you all the thoughts that ran riot in my mind, while every now and then the announcer on the radio would say 'Achtung' and give out an emergency instruction about something or other . . . that word echoed inside me like a bell tolling . . . Achtung . . . Achtung. . . .

"Perhaps I was only five or ten minutes in that condition, but it seemed a long while, and then all at once it came to me that there was only one thing I could do, in Framm's absence, and now indeed *because* of Framm's absence. It was something very quiet, involving no one else, and it was also something no one else could do. But it would take time, perhaps not less than several hours, and whether I should have that much time I could not forecast. So there was the need to begin immediately and not stop till it was either finished or interrupted."

"And forget about killing him?"

He nodded. "Private revenge would only have got in the way of what I intended to do. Don't you see, he *trusted* me — and that was more essential to what I now planned than his death could ever have been. I wanted him to *live* — and to go on trusting me for a while longer. Viewed against that, my original desire to kill him seemed almost like a sort of self-indulgence — like putting my own affairs first. The enemy I really hated wasn't to be countered by any personal vendetta, and the hate I had wasn't sharp and emotional, but glum and also rather limitless. That was the mood I was in as I set to work. First I assembled all the results on the desk before me. They were roughly penciled with many erasures already; this helped rather than hindered. Framm had never looked them over; he had had (and it was ironic now to think of it) implicit confidence in my ability to do the job, and there was also a certain basic laziness in him that made it tempting to hand work to others. He had never checked where another type of man might have been concerned to do so, and he had been far too busy lately, fighting his battles with the authorities, to acquaint himself with even a minimum of detail. All this made it less difficult to do what I set out to do. It took me just over two hours. By the time the sun was hot on that early September morning there was a collection of rough notes, computations, and graphs, in perfect shape for him to examine. But the end-result now was a reading of two-point-one-three-four-eight. Not near enough any more.

"When I had written it down I was not only utterly exhausted but also — and this is a confession — I had a deep depression of spirit. It was so different from anything I had ever felt before that I tried to analyze it in my mind; it could not be remorse, because I had accomplished my purpose, and I was tremendously relieved at having been lucky enough to have the chance. And yet I felt worse, not better, for having done something I did not regret. It was as if I had committed the sin I always puzzled over when I was a small boy at Sunday School — I puzzled over it because I didn't know what it was, and for that reason I suspected that, like most sins, it must be something pleasant to do even if one were wicked for doing it. But now it occurred to me as something exactly the opposite — it was *horrible* to do, even if, in this particular instance, it was justifiable. It was the sin against the Holy Ghost, if one believed in science as I did, and as Framm did too, with one part of his damned schizophrenic soul."

The dinner bell sounded from the house. "Don't bother," I said. "My father isn't coming down, so it can wait as long as we like."

"Why isn't he?"

"He's not too well. I suppose when you've had a stroke you never really get completely better."

"Sometimes you do."

"Not at his age."

"Yes, he's old, isn't he? . . . Much older, I remember, than your mother was."

"Yes."

He was moody for a moment, then said: "Let's have dinner, though. I've talked enough."

"I'd like to know what happened when Framm came back. I suppose he did?"

241

"Yes. I'll tell you afterwards — if we can come out here again."

"We'll have coffee here. It'll still be warm. You could even bathe again if you wanted to."

* * *

He went off to change, and we dined alone, talking little while Dan was around. Not that there was anything special that mustn't be overheard, or so it seemed to me; but I had noticed before that suspicion was deep-sunk in his general attitude towards people and circumstances — doubtless part of the snarl of phobias and complexes that made up what was wrong with him. And in the dining room, so full of shadows and dark perspectives, his unease was very noticeable. It lifted a little afterwards, when we sat by the pool again. The air was still warm — even warmer than sometimes during the day, for the breeze came from the long valley, full of earth scents. A small moon curved over a hill and lit the edge of it.

* * *

Brad went on:

. . . I was asleep when Framm arrived, about ten o'clock on that September morning, but the commotion he made woke me. He had the radio on at full force so that he could hear it as he moved from room to room. As soon as I saw him I knew he was in a mood that would make it easier for me. The war news, or else the trip to Berchtesgaden, had brought out the *Junker* stuff in him — he was Prussian-born though he had lived most of his life in Vienna. And his mood had a peculiar way of showing this in his movements; when the *Junker* superseded the scientist, he seemed to stiffen to a height of a few extra inches and his walk became quick and military. At other times he would stoop and amble; it was an extraordinary phenomenon of change — as if he felt a need to dramatize something that went on inside him.

He did not tell me whether he had seen the man whom he some-times called "our *Quatschkopf*." But he radiated an impression that his mission had been well worth while, that he had done much of what he wanted to do, and had prepared the way for more. That also — his air of mystery and secrecy — was part of the transforma-tion; he did not confide at such times, but snapped out minimum facts like communiqués. So now I got only part of a story. I didn't care. It was better for me not to have him put his arm on my shoul-der and say: "Well, how goes it, Bradley? Have we yet found out what makes the universe tick, or only the philosopher's stone?" But now he just said: "Been working? Not finished yet? We've got to hurry."

I said: "It's finished. The results are on your desk."

He picked up the papers, briskly but without apparent excite-ment, merely muttering: "I think they will show that I am right." For a moment then the sick depression came over me afresh. His whole attitude was a mixture of something superb and something arrogant, and at the last moment of all, with a touch of the incon-sequent that so often intrudes, he couldn't find his glasses — he won-dered if he had left them on the plane, or if he had a spare pair at his house. "Well, tell me, tell me," he said irritably. "I can't read without them. . . ."

So I told him. "It doesn't work out," I said. "The bulge is in the wrong place."

He glared at me, and for an incredible second I wondered if he could read in my eyes what I had done; but I knew that without his glasses he couldn't even see me properly. The sudden fierceness was just the Prussianism, the age-old barbarian reaction to the bearer of bad news. He banged his fist on the desk. "So it is in the wrong place, eh? And it could not have happened at a worse time! No — not in a century!"

Behind him on the blackboard were a number of equations connected with the general plan of the work we had been doing. He swung round to give them a stare that lasted several moments, then in an access of rage seized the duster and wiped the rows of chalked symbols into a smudge. "Very well . . . since these are our mistakes, the truth must lie elsewhere." It was clear that any idea of doubting the accuracy of my calculations had not even remotely entered his mind — which was in a way dreadful, and yet exactly what I had hoped. "But I shall find it," he muttered angrily, as if even the truth were capable of yielding to threats.

That gave me my chance to say: "I'm afraid I shan't be able to help you in it, Dr. Framm. The war makes it necessary for me to return to America."

He seemed hardly interested. "Oh it does, does it? When do you want to go?"

"Immediately."

"Very well."

I left his office a few minutes later. At the doorway as we shook hands he turned on the charm for a few seconds, but it was tired and semiautomatic; I could see his mind was elsewhere. "Of course you are deserting me," he said, but that too was automatic, just one of his numerous attitudes, posing as a martyr when he was in no position to play the tyrant. I had seen it work so often, but now there was nothing for it to work on . . . and it was hardly a wasted effort because it was not even an effort.

I gathered up the few personal things that were in my own laboratory and then went down the slow elevator for the last time. And I never saw Framm again.

But an odd thing happened that same afternoon as I was leaving the American Express office. I ran into a biochemist named Muller, whom I had sometimes chatted with in the corridors of the Institut — a quiet decent fellow who disliked Framm and had often expressed surprise that I apparently got on so well with him. I told him I was leaving Germany and he said: "I'm very glad — for your sake. It will save you a good deal of trouble." He then told me that the war crisis had generated a good deal of feeling against foreigners working on scientific projects, and Framm, he added, had recently thrown out hints that he considered me not altogether "reliable," and that he had been "watching" me for some time.

This threw me into a mood of near-panic, coming when it did; and for a moment it seemed to me an example of special villainy on Framm's part, until I reminded myself that my own behavior and intentions, if he had suspected them, would have amply justified him. Actually, however, though I did not decide this till long after I had left Germany, I don't think Framm suspected me at all, ever, or of anything. I think he *trusted* me — personally as well as professionally. I think he found me a willing and occasionally able slave, and was ready to use me as long as possible, but he was also preparing an alibi for himself, in case the antiforeign feeling should increase. All this would have been exactly like him, for I had seen him do the same sort of thing to others far more innocent than I was. . . .

* * *

"So it was a good thing you didn't kill him," I said.

"Well, I wouldn't have had much chance to get away with it if what Muller said was true."

"I think you got away with quite enough, if it prevented his success in whatever it was he was trying to do."

"Don't exaggerate. In itself it was a very minor piece of sabotage. What, if anything, it prevented or delayed, nobody can ever say exactly. Perhaps very little. The Germans were often so stupid that no outside assistance could have made them blunder more than they did." He added, as if eager to leave the issue: "There's an ironic little anticlimax to file away with the rest. Just before I left Berlin I went to the bank to close my account. My weekly salary had come that morning and though I couldn't take money out of Germany I thought it might buy something on the train trip. But when I tried to cash it I found it had already been stopped. . . . Now that's what I call attention to detail. It must have been one of the first things he did after I left . . . perhaps the *very* first. I couldn't help laughing, right there at the bank counter. To think that after the wrong figures I'd given Framm the wrong one he gave me was only on a check!"

* * *

That was the night, after the talk, when I was wakened by hearing a scream; I sat up in bed to listen and it came again. It didn't sound like Brad, but immediately I thought of him, and when I got outside his door he screamed again, so I knew. But it still didn't sound much like him. I went in and shook him; he was in a state of complete nervous terror; I had never seen anything quite like it. When he was properly awake he mastered himself and began to apologize, but the sweat still gathered in beads on his face. I told him it didn't matter, nobody else had been disturbed, and only I because I was a light sleeper.

He kept on saying he was sorry.

"Brad, *will* you forget it? . . . I don't mind a bit. Is there anything you'd like? Some coffee? . . . I could go down and make it . . . Or would you like me to get a book and read here till you go to sleep again?"

He said if I would just stay for a little while without a book or bothering with coffee . . . "I'll be all right. It's happened before. It's not important provided nobody else thinks it's important. . . . Did I *say* anything?"

"*Say* anything?"

"Was I talking . . . when you came in?"

246

"No."

He eyed me sharply. "But you'd say that even if I had been, wouldn't you?"

He saw me wondering if I would have; that made him laugh a little.

"Never mind," he went on. "It's just one of the things I'm up against. The feeling that everybody's watching me all the time, listening to me when I'm asleep . . . hoping I'll have a nightmare and spill something."

"Was it a nightmare, Brad?"

"Sort of."

"About flying?"

"No."

"What then? Or don't you want to tell me?"

"I'd tell you if I could. Maybe it was too much of that wonderful fish chowder at dinner."

"Or too much Framm after dinner."

He smiled nervously. "We're through with him now, anyway. . . . So he was killed at Peenemünde."

"You said you knew."

"We . . . I . . . yes, I had that information. But one couldn't be sure. I suppose they got proof after Germany collapsed."

"Maybe."

He was silent for a moment; then he said thoughtfully: "I wonder if the bastard was brave . . . at the end. Probably. But physical bravery's a swindle. The worst people can have it — yet you like them for it . . . more than you like screamers in the middle of the night."

"You know what you're asking for when you say that."

"What?"

"An argument, Brad. If bravery's the opposite of screaming in the night, then *what is it you're afraid of?*"

247

He answered moodily: "I'm not afraid *of* anything. I'm afraid *for* something. I'm afraid for the whole bloody world."

I waited for him to add to that, but he shook his head in what I took to be an advance refusal of any of the possible questions I hadn't yet asked. I said at length, cheerfully: "Anyhow, it wasn't about flying."

"No, not this time. And I've an idea about that — or rather it was your idea. Maybe I *should* go up again?"

"You would? Oh, that would be fine — when would you like to? There ought to be a place where we could rent something."

"Not so easy these days."

"We'll find out."

"You mean you'd go up with me?"

"Why not if you can fly? You said you could."

He hugged me as much as he could in the positions we were in; he was leaning up in bed, I was sitting on the edge of it. "You'd trust me as much as that?"

"That isn't so much."

"Oh, but surely . . ."

"No," I answered. "I'd hate you to think me *too* trusting. I fly a bit myself. I think I could land a dual-control if you got scared."

"Of course that spoils it all." But he was smiling again.

"Oh no, it just makes it sensible. I'm quite serious about it if you are."

There was a book on his bedside table that had a map of California; we measured a rough line a hundred and fifty miles inland, for the seaward side of that was forbidden to private flying in wartime. We figured it could not be more than fifty or sixty miles from where we were to the nearest likely flying ground we could use; that would be in the desert somewhere. "Or the mountains," he said, studying the map.

"Except that it wouldn't be too safe over mountains. Those small planes don't go higher than eight or nine thousand. And there are downdrafts."

"You've done some real flying, then?"

"A few hours solo — in the East."

He began to talk technicalities, and if anyone had been listening at the door it must have sounded a rather teen-age conversation. I left him after about half an hour; we were both sleepy by then.

*   *   *

The days that followed had a degree of eventfulness that made them timeless. I suppose there are only a few weeks in every century when the accumulated stresses of years break through to absolute flash point. July of 1945 was like that. The Okinawa battle was over; the great fire raids on Japanese cities had begun. A total end of the war looked near, and then nearer.

In my own life the pattern of California sun and sky slipped over the days. They were not without happenings. My father had another slight stroke — not more serious than the first, but cumulative in its effect. He did not now leave his room, and there were nurses in attendance; he regained part of the lost ground but it was clear he would never recover completely. I did what I could to cheer him up, but it was little enough. He spoke with a slur, like someone at pains to conceal the effects of drink; and he was sad about himself, with moods of reminiscence that took him back to old times and places. He pondered a great deal about his will, in which (he said) I was the chief legatee. There were relatives of my mother's in England (he also said) to whom he had left less than he had once intended, because now he didn't want much of his money to go out of America. (Could this be patriotism?) But surely, I argued, with

249

lend-lease at the rate of millions a day what difference could it make? But no, it wasn't that; it was the new English Labour government. He didn't like them. He remembered once meeting Attlee — he hadn't thought much of him. And as for that fellow Strachey whom they had made Food Minister — a most peculiar person, he had met him also once, and there was a portrait of him in the Tate Gallery with a beard and very long legs lolling in a wicker chair. Fancy a man like that being given a ministry!

"You're thinking of *Lytton* Strachey," I said. "He's dead. The Food Minister's another Strachey. . . ." I had to convince him of that.

"Well, anyhow," he said, "England's changing. They wouldn't like me there any more. I remember poor old Neville Chamberlain saying the last time I saw him, that was in January 1939 . . ."

He was always poor old Neville Chamberlain to my father, perhaps because he too had been disappointed. . . .

*　*　*

Mr. Small telephoned once. What was happening? Anything? Was it worth while yet for us to have another meeting? How *was* he? Had I anything special I wanted to convey?

I said no; he was all right; we were taking walks; there was no need for a meeting yet.

"You think you're getting anything out of him?"

"Well, I don't know quite what you're expecting. . . ."

"Get all you can, whether it's what we expect or not."

I didn't like the way he said that, or maybe it was the telephone voice that sounded more strident than it really was. Yet I couldn't think of any sufficiently challenging reply, so I just waited in silence till he exclaimed: "Hello . . . hello . . . what's the matter? Are you there?"

"Yes," I answered. "I'm still here."

I was childish enough to think that would confuse him but seem-ingly it didn't. He merely said: "Well, I'm not going to bother you, but do remember he's not simply on holiday. Taking long walks and climbing mountains is all right, but . . . oh well, never mind. We'll give you a bit more time, but if nothing happens we'll have to have him back."

"*Back?*"

"Sure. He's not well yet by any means. Newby wanted a lot of convincing before he'd agree to the experiment, and if it doesn't work — "

I interrupted: "I think it will work. Give me another week. I'll call you then."

"No, I'll call you. Or else one of us will come up and see him. . . . Okay, then. Good-by."

As I hung up the receiver one decision was already made in my mind. Brad must get discharged from that hospital. I hadn't an idea how I could expedite this, but there were doubtless things I could do or help him do for himself.

As I walked away from the library table something else occurred to me, quite icily. I didn't think I had ever said anything at all to Mr. Small about mountain climbing. Or had I? And if I hadn't, how had he known? And had his slip, if it were one, been acci-dental, or deliberately to intimidate?

I told myself that the spy business was catching, that the imagined eye and ear at every keyhole was the most diabolical softener-up of everything gutlike in one's brain and personality; all the more rea-son, then, why Brad should free himself.

* * *

And I lunched again with Paul Chandos. This time it was I who noticed that *he* was preoccupied. I asked if he were worrying about the picture.

He said no.

"That's good. I hate to ask you, because you never mention it — but of course I'm a bit interested in how it's coming along."

"Fine. I'm halfway through."

"*What?*"

"The writing, I mean. I'm what they call a writer-producer."

"But — but — you mean — you've already got a story?"

"A sort of one, though I may change it. The main thing is, I've got a character."

"Who?"

"You."

He went on hastily: "I didn't intend to tell you yet, but I don't suppose it matters. I think you're a rather remarkable person. Your whole book is really about you — not egotistically, that's what's so good — but because you're real. You're real in the book. And now that I know you actually, I know that you're *really* real."

"I don't quite get it. You mean that these meetings we've been having have been just to study me, as it were . . . like sittings for a portrait painter?"

"At first I thought they were, but I've enjoyed them so much that . . ." And he suddenly leaned forward across the table. "I don't know how you feel — I don't know if you even like me, though I know we look at things the same way . . . so many things. . . . Incidentally, are you — by any chance — engaged — or tied up to anyone?"

"No," I said, doubtfully. And because I wanted to spare him whatever he might be risking, I added: "I like you very much — perhaps as much as any man I've ever met, with one exception."

"Ah," he replied. And then, quite briskly after a pause: "You know, Jane, you *are* the part. What a pity you can't act!"

"How do you know I can't? I can when I'm nervous enough. I'm acting a bit now. . . . Shall we break a rule and have a drink before lunch? I feel like it. . . ."

"Sure, but it's no rule. I hate rules, anyway." He summoned the waiter and ordered two martinis. "How's your scientist getting on? Recovering?"

"I hope so. It's mental more than physical. He's staying with us — with my father and me. I'm trying to set him right. He's the man in my book — on page 117 — the man in the Burggarten in Vienna."

"The one who thought the Binomial Theorem would survive along with Beethoven?"

I nodded. The sweetest compliment he could have paid me was to know that so instantly.

He said: "Now I *would* like to meet him. When can you arrange it?"

"Soon. You might be able to help him too — by talking and arguing. I think he's your kind of person. Perhaps we both are."

*　　*　　*

And one morning I drove eastward towards the desert. Dan had found there was an airfield at a place called Lost Water, used by the C.A.P. since the war, but owned by a certain Mr. Murdoch who sometimes rented out a plane if he knew who you were. Because of the gas shortage you weren't supposed to fly for pleasure, so it was all very chancy; I should just have to go there and see what it was like, or perhaps let Mr. Murdoch see what I was like. The distance was over eighty miles, but the last thirty were arrow-straight, so that far ahead one saw where Lost Water must be. It had an elevation of twenty-two hundred and lay in a shallow saucer with gritty hills rimming it on all sides. A plume of smoke on the horizon indicated a small town that from the map was half a dozen miles further on.

The "airfield" turned out to be nothing but a T-shaped patch cleared of scrub, but not of stones, sand, and weeds. A tumble-down hut surmounted by a windsock was the only likely sign of habitation; a few rough sheds housed planes. When I drove up a grizzled dust-gray character came out of the hut to introduce himself as Murdoch. He looked like an old-style sheriff who had somehow switched from the horse to the air age without anything in between. He scratched his head and stroked his chin when I asked if there was any chance of going up. He wasn't supposed to do it, he answered; he would get into trouble; there were so many government regulations nowadays. But even as he said all this I could see he was the kind of man who resents government regulations enough to break them now and again out of sheer nostalgia for pioneer freedom. All he asked after we had talked for a while was which plane I preferred; I chose the newer-looking red-painted Porterfield. Quite efficiently then he checked the oil and gas, warmed up the machine, and climbed inside. "Now show me what you can do," he said. I removed the chocks, got inside with him and took off. After about ten minutes in the air he told me to land, which I did. He made no comment, except to warn me of prohibited military areas near by, so I flew on my own for an hour or so, made several near-landings, then came in finally because of approaching dust storms. The warm air and the ground altitude were conditions new in my experience and I was glad to have had some practice with them.

When I paid Mr. Murdoch I asked if he had any suggestions for a full day's excursion somewhere. You couldn't do it, he answered promptly, because of wartime restrictions and gas shortage and one darned thing and another. But presently he said that the real trouble was too few landing grounds near enough; except for one at Giant's Pass there wasn't any that a civilian could use.

I told him I wasn't asking on my own account, but for an Air Force friend who had crashed and wanted to get rid of a fear-neurosis about flying. But he wasn't impressed by that either. *"What's* he got? We didn't have it when *I* started flying — that was in nineteen-oh-four. Not much good then if we'd been scared of a few crashes. . . . I've crashed a heap of times — never got hurt, though — not to speak of."

He was still a pioneer, but now of a new species — the ancient airman, yarning of old times.

I listened, and I could see him enjoying an audience; soon he was enumerating all the interesting spots one could fly over on the way to Giant's Pass. There were rocks where the bandit Valdez had hidden for months from the state guard back in the eighties, and a cave where a German spy in World War One was supposed to have operated a secret wireless station, and another place where legend said were long-lost gold mines. All this seemed to cover such a wide territory of popular fiction that I thought Hollywood might have done far better to engage Mr. Murdoch's services than mine. I liked him, though, and I had him in the end promising to telephone me some very early morning when the weather looked suitable for a trip.

Then I drove back and told Brad. I said the call would come on the right sort of day, and if he really wanted to fly, that was fine, but if he didn't we needn't go, and even if we did go and he changed his mind, that would be all right too. I described the place and the plane and Mr. Murdoch, and with the map spread out on the library floor I tried to remember the spots he had said were worth flying over. We decided also to take sandwiches and coffee and make a picnic of it, provided it didn't look like a picnic.

"Not that I've any conscience," I said. "You made one flight that wasn't a picnic — you can use a little gas now for your own pleasure."

Physically, now, I would have called him almost well, but though there had been no more nightmares he was still moody and nervous. The look in his eyes, a haunted look, was sometimes as if it must tear through them; and during meals, when Dan was around, conversation was always difficult. At other times, after he had suspiciously made sure we were alone, he talked at random about his past, though only up to the time of his leaving Germany. I asked him once if he thought the false results he had given Framm would be repudiated by later investigation; and he said yes, he hoped so.

"You *hope* so?"

"Sure, if it hasn't been done already."

"You think it may have been?"

"On the whole I'd guess it hasn't. Not because it couldn't easily be, if anyone took the trouble, but because nobody was likely to waste time in a direction that Framm would appear to have given up as unpromising. Even with all the secrecy it would leak out that he'd taken a wrong turning. That's what research is for — not only to find the truth, but to rope off the blind alleys. And you tend to take people's word that they *are* blind, just as you take on trust the logarithm tables." He smiled grimly and then ceased to smile. "After all, why not? If scientists can't trust each other, whom can they trust? Nobody, perhaps, these days . . . and for that reason the world can't even trust science."

"Maybe it can still trust God."

He said whimsically: "But He moves in such a mysterious way."

"I don't know why anyone should mind that. It may make him hard to track down, but then, so was your Mr. Bitternut."

He looked puzzled till he remembered the name. I went on to tell him that recently I had got hold of a book about quantum mathematics. "From what I could gather, the universe is governed by statistical probability rather than logic. But that still makes it wonderful. If life is like throwing a six a hundred times in succession, we know that isn't likely to happen oftener than once in so many centuries, but we also know it could happen in this room tonight without upsetting the cosmic applecart. That's reassuring."

He said thoughtfully: "Is it? . . . What made you want to read about mathematics?"

"*You.* . . . Of course it was only one of those popular books — the romantic smattering, as you once called it. I'm not arrogant enough to think I could ever climb into your mind."

"Be damned glad you can't. And don't say *climb*."

Our talks so often ended in this kind of bitter barrier that I said: "I don't even want to. It's what's *on* your mind that still bothers me."

When he didn't answer I thought I might as well be hanged for a sheep as a lamb, so I asked him outright: "What happened after you came back to America?"

He replied, far too casually: "I just bummed around for a time."

"Various jobs?"

"Er . . . yes."

"How did you manage about the draft?"

"Oh, I was . . . er . . . deferred."

"War work?"

"More or less. . . ." He added, as if jumping with relief to firmer ground: "And then I got fed up and joined the Air Force."

"You mean you quit the war work voluntarily?"

"Yes."

"You said just now you got fed up. What were you fed up with?"

He answered, rather testily: "With not being in uniform . . . let's settle for that."

I said okay, I'd settle for it, but he was already on his way out of the room. I followed after a moment and overtook him by the pool. "Oh Brad," I said, "don't be in a huff. I promise not to ask you anything else. Whatever secret you have and want to keep, I'll try not to be curious about it. It's only that . . . if you weren't being bothered by *my* questions . . . you'd be having to put up with Newby's nonsense . . . or worse. . . ."

"Or *worse?* What do you mean?" His voice was angry, but he had seized on the one word that had slipped out. I answered vaguely: "I didn't mean anything special . . . Newby's a fool, but there *might* be worse people put on you . . . that's all I meant."

"No, you meant more than that. I want to know. What are they going to do to me? You know more than you'll say!"

I took his arm. "Honestly, I don't. But that's an odd remark, coming from you. Don't *you* know more than you'll say?"

He let me walk him through the gardens till he was calmer. "They won't leave me alone," he kept saying. "They never did let me alone — even in the service. Mysterious teletypes all the time. 'Bradley, I've had an inquiry about you from Washington. . . .' They wouldn't send me overseas . . . you know that? They kept saying I'd be in the next outfit, and then somehow or other I wasn't. And they tailed me when I was on leave in New York — I knew it — you can feel when you're being watched. Even here sometimes . . . what do you know about the servants? What about Dan? . . . I suppose you just think I'm crazy for asking that. . . ."

It was on my tongue to say something, but at that moment Dan appeared, hurrying along the path from the house. The timing looked sinister, but could hardly have been anything but accidental, for he came to tell me I was wanted on the telephone.

"I'll stay here," Brad said, so I walked back with Dan. I asked who it was and he said Mr. Small.

When I saw the receiver lying on the blotter on the library table top I had an almost physical reluctance to touch it. I waited a moment before picking it up.

A voice said rather curtly: "Miss Waring? . . . This is Small. I'd like to come up to your place tomorrow morning, if you don't mind, for a discussion. I'm not satisfied with the situation as it is. . . . Don't tell Bradley. . . . No, we can't talk over the phone. . . . Tomorrow, then, about ten. Good-by."

I walked slowly back to Brad. It was after early dinner; dusk was falling; the beauty of the scene assembled itself almost excessively. Beauty to me is like that; up to a point it has the freshness of daffodils, but beyond that there can be too much, a tropical surfeit, foliage too rich and groves too dark, a place for fears to stalk. Or perhaps all this was only in my mind as I saw things then. I was relieved when Brad said he was tired and would go to bed.

* * *

I slept badly, thinking of Mr. Small and what reason he might have for not being satisfied. There had been something in his voice that worried me; or perhaps something in me was now prepared to worry. Already it seemed years, not merely days, since I had come to Vista Grande. I suddenly wished my mother were alive, because she had always known so easily how to deal with men. She, I felt sure, could have found out what was on Brad's mind; and she could handle Mr. Small, whatever mood he was in tomorrow. She would sweep them both into some realm of inconsequence and reign over it like an absent-minded queen.

The telephone woke me. I saw by the clock it was 4 A.M. I didn't recognize the voice at first and was too sleepy to ask. Somebody talking about the weather . . . perhaps a wrong number. . . . Then I caught Murdoch's drawl. "Dawn looks fine from here. Might be a good day if you don't mind it a bit hot. Sorry to waken you but that's what you asked."

I was just about to tell him it was too bad I had an engagement that morning when an idea came that held me still listening. Presently I said: "Well, thanks, we'll probably be along. . . . Oh, as soon as we can make it. . . ."

Then I went to Brad's room and woke him. He yawned, looked indifferent, and replied, as if he were doing me a favor: "Okay. Give me ten minutes to dress."

I took less time than that. Afterwards I made coffee and sand-
wiches downstairs, and left a note for Dan. I told him to give Mr.
Small my apologies and say we had gone away "for a few days."
I thought that would stop him from waiting around for our return.

So we were on the road by four-thirty.

*　　*　　*

"Feel like going up?" I said. "You don't have to. It's a nice drive,
anyhow."

He answered: "I'll probably try. But alone — first of all."

"Oh no."

"So you think I need an instructor?"

"Of course not, but just in case . . ."

"Just in case. I like that. I'd have you know I had five hundred
hours to my credit before the Air Force decided I was only fit for
map reading."

So it still rankled. But I liked the mood he was working himself
into. "All right. But in that case why bother to try it yourself first?"

"Because I want to show off in front of you."

I doubted that. I think his real reason was twofold: he thought
he might be scared, once he was in the air; and if he were, he didn't
want me to see it, and perhaps also he didn't trust me to take over
in such an event. I had noticed before his deep reluctance to discover
me able to do anything but write.

When I quit the argument he seemed almost disappointed.
Throughout the drive he was alternately jaunty and fretful, peeved
at the car radio because at that distance it wouldn't yield the morning news bulletin. "We can get a paper somewhere," I said, but he
shrugged indifferently. The sun rose, showing first in saffron tints
on the peaks of mountains. Soon I could point out the plume of
smoke that was just a few miles beyond the airfield. "Desert towns,"
he said, rememberingly. "You can spot them sometimes a hundred

miles away — even if they don't have any factory smoke. They show up like a kid's breath on a windowpane . . . someone said."

"Who said? I like that."

"A friend . . . the only fellow I really got to know in the army. His name was Bill Manson. He said it once flying east from El Paso. Those little Texas towns, stuck in the middle of nothing. . . . Bill was a fine pilot, a cowboy before the war. Not well educated, but he thought things out and he saw things clear."

"What happened to him?"

"Died in a hospital, after a crash at sea. He was ten days drifting about. One of those raft stories. There were five on it, three died before they were picked up. Bill died after being brought home. A shark had mauled him. He was unconscious most of the time. The papers made a thing of it — about how the two survivors had prayed all night for rescue and then a ship had seen them at dawn. As the fifth man was the only one who could tell me what had really happened I got leave to see him. He told me. Before I left I asked if it was true they had prayed. He said — 'Well, I didn't, but I guess Bill did, if you could call it a prayer. He kept calling out "For Christ's sake, God, what are you trying to do to us?" Of course that was after the shark got him.'"

Brad stirred uncomfortably. "I suppose that's what some folks would call blasphemous, but to my mind it's in the same key with other things Bill said, and I don't call it a bad prayer . . . if you're on a raft. And we're all on a raft these days, if we only knew."

"Knew what?"

"Knew we were on a raft . . . drifting."

I had purposely slowed down for him to say as much as he would, but I couldn't spin it out any more; we were already at Lost Water and Mr. Murdoch was waving from one of the planes. There were three now; I wondered if business were looking up, but he said when he came over to us: "I got a better one for you this time, miss."

I had thought he would have respect for Brad as an Air Force man, but he didn't show any. "Don't let him get up to any tricks," he warned me. "None of that acrobatics stuff." I was tickled that he assumed I was to be in command. In point of fact I had no right to be; I hadn't yet got my certificate and taking up a passenger was forbidden. But Murdoch had never asked about that. "He wants to go up alone first," I told him.

Murdoch looked even dubious, and I was beginning to reassure him when I noticed Brad's face, moody and rather pale as he stood a little way off. "I don't have to," he interjected, coming over. And then rather superiorly: "No thrill to me." I recognized that as an act put on for a stranger. Fine, if it helped him.

While Murdoch was checking the gas I asked again: "Brad, are you sure you want to go up at all?"

"Let's get into the damn thing and see," he snapped. "*You* take off. . . ."

A few minutes later we were high above the desert and Mr. Murdoch's hut looked like a nutshell on a yellow carpet. The seats were back and front; Brad was behind me. I could feel the pressure of his hand on the dual stick and rudders; he was letting me fly, but doing so, I thought, with an effort. I turned to look at him once, but his face was clenched; I thought he was nervous. Then suddenly I felt no pressure from him at all; he had given up the back-seat driving. I looked round again; he was staring out of the side window. "All right?" I shouted.

"Sure," he shouted back.

The plane was too noisy for conversation. I climbed to five thousand, then headed for Giant's Pass. It was about a hundred and fifty miles, almost due north, and against a head wind. The air was bumpy over the scrubby hills. I watched the instruments, checked on the map, looked out for emergency landings — the routine I had learned. There were pans of dried-up lakes here and there. Soon I went off course to pass over the rocks where Valdez, whoever he was, had hidden. I pointed them out to Brad, but he seemed unconcerned, and so was I — they were just like any other rocks. But a mood of exaltation came over me as we flew on; I shouted back to him — "Like to take over?" I half let go of the controls and in a few seconds he was flying. Of course anyone could have, even a pupil having a first lesson; yet as I sat there, my hands and feet idle, I felt I was accomplishing something in what he was accomplishing. I unpacked the sandwiches and he took one, but the air was too bumpy for coffee. I thought that now he had settled down he would probably find the rest of the trip dull.

Abruptly he swung the plane in a complete right-about turn, then throttled down. In the sudden near-silence the wind through the struts was like a fingernail on piano wires.

"What's the idea?" I asked.

"Just to talk. I hate shouting."

"How do you like it?"

"Fine."

"I guessed you wouldn't be scared."

"I thought I would, but I'm not. Perhaps you give me confidence. You're not bad. Maybe you'll really know how to fly one of these days."

"Well thanks." It was as much of a compliment as I could have hoped for. "Another sandwich?"

"Not yet." He began to sing "Auld Lang Syne" at the top of his voice, and I remembered the last time I had heard that was at the Hampstead house years before. "Sorry," he said, after a few bars. "I guess that's like wanting to skywrite."

"Go on," I said. "Sing all you want."

"No — we'd best get back to the right direction. I'm turning, then she's all yours again."

"Don't you want to keep on?"

"No, I'm lazy. You do the work."

"Okay."

He throttled up, made the turn, and I took the controls. We flew for an hour and Giant's Pass was still some thirty or forty miles ahead. The wind blew now in gusts and flurries; sometimes the plane seemed to stand still in the air, like a bird hovering. Once I watched the shadow of the wing as it passed a certain rock; I didn't know how large the rock was, but I was sure that a car could have quickly overtaken us on the ground if there had been a road. I checked as well as I could from the map and confirmed this. Not that it mattered; we had all day. But suddenly Brad leaned over and shared the same misgiving — how were we for gas? I said, not wanting to alarm him: "Getting a bit low, but I think we'll make it."

A few minutes later he shouted back: "We won't. Better look out for a place to land."

I had already thought of that too.

We covered a few more miles. This would be my first emergency landing, though I had often pointed out to instructors where I would make one if I had to, and had come down to within a hundred feet of some likely field. But that was not quite the same as actually doing the thing, and in any case, fields were different from the desert in a high wind.

Brad touched my shoulder and pointed far ahead to a white patch gleaming in the sun. "Try for that," he shouted. I changed course, and the white patch approached so slowly that the ground as well as the air seemed in battle for every inch. Even descending did not give much extra speed, because at the lower levels the wind was a hurricane. I had never flown, much less landed, against such odds, and had there been gas I would have turned back to Lost Water rather than try it. I glanced at Brad and saw his face a little set; I wanted to beg him to make the landing himself; but I couldn't ask, because he had said he had confidence in me and if he were nervous that was all he was depending on. I flew down to a thousand feet and at one moment had trouble in keeping the plane right side up; I wondered what would happen if it did capsize; there were things you could do if you thought of them quickly enough. I tried to re- member them. The white patch rose like a wall as the downdraft increased; I pulled back the stick and then felt a forward pressure as Brad checked the movement. I realized a few seconds later he had probably saved us from a stall. "Try again," he shouted over my shoulder. "But with power this time."

I had never done that before either. I flew round again and re- made the approach. A terrific gust dropped the plane five hundred feet in a single swirl, but with power on I managed to level up till the white patch lay beneath. It proved to be the dried bed of a lake, smoother than any airfield runway; except for the wind a landing would be easy. I waited for lulls between gusts, then came down in a hurry. After we had touched ground the next gust almost blew us over. "Don't stop," Brad shouted. "Taxi over there. . . ." He pointed in a direction where the lake bed elbowed into surrounding upland. We covered half a mile, tacking like a yacht whenever the big gusts came. Presently in the lee of a hill the wind lessened. We stopped and clambered out.

"Well!" I said.

"Well?" he answered, and slapped me on the back. Then he put stones against the wheels and climbed up to unscrew the cap of the gas tank. "Down to the last drop," he reported.

"We were lucky."

"The motor's fouled up too — didn't you notice the engine miss- ing?"

"I didn't notice anything. . . ."

"Bad gas. Or else worn rings. Or loose bolts on a cylinder head. . . . You made a pretty good landing. I'd half a mind to do it for you, at the end, but then I thought you'd like the practice."

"Practice! Do you know I've never done a thing like that before?"

"I thought you hadn't. That's why I said you did pretty well."

"And . . . and weren't you scared of letting me?"

"No. For one thing, I was a bit confident you'd make it."

"Any other reason?"

He was already pouring coffee from the thermos. "I don't want to sound melodramatic, but I suddenly realized while we were flying that I don't give a damn about certain things any more . . . and one of them's my life."

"Another must be *my* life, in that case."

"Sure. . . . Sit down. Coffee's only warm — altitude always loosens corks. You should squeeze them tight again after you climb."

We sat in the shade of a yellow rock and I had a queer feeling that nobody else since the earth began had been exactly where we were. Which was quite possible, for we were a mile from the roughest road, and twenty from the nearest town. "We've got to get gas," I said, searching the map.

"*You* have. My job's on the motor. I didn't quite like the way she behaved those last few miles."

"No? What's wrong?"

"Just that I wouldn't want to fly her anywhere else without a checkup. I'm a good mechanic — did you know that? Take me about a couple of hours — time for you to hitchhike to the nearest gas station. . . . But no hurry. Eat your sandwiches and have a cigarette. . . . I like it here. For the first time in God knows how long I'm reasonably sure I'm not being spied on." And suddenly he drew me down to him on the desert sand and kissed me. It was different from that time in the car. Perhaps the relief after tension made us both responsive to something no longer within bounds.

He said later, beginning quietly: "You think I'm still out of my mind, don't you? All this stuff about being watched everywhere. . . . Neurosis . . . psychosis . . . one of those jargon words. You're calm about it, that's one thing. You're always calm. I like that. It's my favorite cure. When I saw your head in front of me while we were flying I was calm too. And I didn't care what happened. That was part of the calmness. I kept thinking of Bill — probably because we'd talked about him in the car. When we were in those gusts I thought 'For Christ's sake, God, what are you trying to do to us?' — but I wasn't mad about it, as Bill was, I was calm. It seemed a good question. Something worth a bit of research, if anyone had time for it these days and wasn't being watched. There I go again — the neurosis. Just for the moment I even suspected Murdoch — because they put the unlikeliest people on to jobs like that — just as they did in the army . . . in New York . . . Washington . . . and . . . other places. . . . Of course it sounds incredible. I sometimes dream it's still just algebra — with a flaw in it somewhere. A big dud. That's what I hoped — that's what they knew I hoped. So they watched me afterwards. Maybe in case I suddenly wrote the truth in the sky. The mysterious way in which God moves, specially prepared for those over two-thirty-five, and when you read God backwards it spells Dog. In another moment I will give you my prediction for the end of the world, but first, a message from your announcer. . . ."

"Stop talking like that," I cried. "Whatever it means, stop it — stop it!"

"I'm sorry. Perhaps I *am* out of my mind. Maybe they don't watch me half as much as I imagine. Or maybe I'm not watched at all and it just proves I'm out of my mind for thinking so."

"No, no, don't worry about that. You're not out of your mind."

"But if I think I'm being watched when I'm not . ... because *you* don't believe it, do you?"

I saw the look in his eyes and knew there was no longer any alternative. I said simply: "Darling, yes. I believe it."

"*What?*"

"I believe it. I believe *you.*"

"Hey, let's get this straight. So I *am* being watched? It's true, then?"

"Yes, yes, I believe you — "

"But what evidence have you? You know more than you'll say, don't you?"

"Brad, please — please don't — "

"Listen, I want to know what *you* know. What makes you agree with me that I'm being watched all the time? Who's on the job now? Is it Dan? Why do you think *anyone's* watching me?"

I pulled his head against mine and held it there while I whispered: "Because *I* am, Brad."

"*You?*"

"Yes, darling."

"What do you mean?"

I told him then about Mr. Small. I told him how I had gone to a downtown office in New York to be interrogated, how Mr. Small had followed me to California for further questioning, and how Brad's visit to Vista Grande had been arranged so that I could keep an eye on him, size him up, try to get him to talk — but precisely about what, they wouldn't tell me. It was the vaguest assignment. "So I said I'd try, but I didn't try — except for what I wanted myself, and that was to get to know you again after all these years."

After the first shock he was calmer than I had expected, and he wasn't angry with me at all, as I thought he might have been. "So *you've* been watching me," he said reflectively, as if he must make it fit in with other things in his mind.

"Yes — but not for him. For myself."

"And what are you going to tell him?"

"Either everything or nothing, darling, but not half and half."

"Why do you say that?"

"Because it's the mistake I've already made and perhaps you have too."

He said with a sigh: "You're uncanny sometimes. . . . And you've helped me tremendously. D'you know, I'm *relieved* at what you've said — about you watching me. I began to think I was going out of my mind — I wasn't sure . . . sometimes I wondered if it were all my imagination. Now I *know* it isn't. . . . Fine. . . . And I can fly too — that's something else you've shown me." He took my hand and held it rather solemnly. "Just like you, Jane. Remember that time in Vienna when I said you'd always be on my side?"

That wasn't quite what he had said, but I liked the misquotation.

"What do they suspect me of?" he asked quietly.

"I don't know, Brad. Maybe the fact that you worked with Framm started them off. But after what you did in the army I don't see why you shouldn't be able to make them trust you. . . . That is, unless there are other angles I don't know about."

"There are."

"What?"

"I can't tell you — now. I wish I could and it's perhaps absurd that I can't, but — "

"All right. Don't bother."

"What's so wonderful is that *you* trust me. It doesn't occur to you that I might have done anything bad, does it?"

"Have you?"

He shook his head. "But I love the way you ask. You remind me of the priest who heard a confession of murder and merely asked very calmly 'How many murders, my son?' Not that the parallel fits me, but I think it does you."

"It might. Or maybe I'm just remembering Daniel Webster's remark that there's nothing so strange as truth. I can always imagine you getting into the most complicated trouble from the highest possible motives. I'm capable of doing that myself, that's why it doesn't shock me so much."

He laughed and then asked seriously: "When do you see this man again?"

"I don't know, exactly. He was coming today, to the house, but we've missed him by making this trip. I did that deliberately."

"Good for you."

"But he'll come again. You can't keep him off."

"What sort of man is he?"

"That kind. The kind you can't keep off. Otherwise not so bad. Fairly fair. Nothing Gestapo-ish. He told me they don't know anything against you. I guess they just can't let you alone — any more than I can, but not in the same way."

"Did he want to see me today?"

"No, only me. To find out what I'd found out — or if I'd found out anything. He seems to think I have an inside track on you."

"And you have." All his nerves, and mine too, came to rest in the way he said it.

"That makes me very happy."

"Me too." He leaned up on one elbow. "I wish we could stay here longer, or come again, but perhaps that's impossible. . . . I'm glad we had this day, anyhow. A lovely time. . . . When you see him again, will you tell him something?"

"Yes, of course."

"Tell him . . ." He hesitated and half smiled. "I'm sorry it sounds so mysterious, but I can't help it. . . . Just tell him I've kept my word so far. Will you tell him that?"

"Yes. You've kept your word — so far."

"But don't make the 'so far' sound like a threat. It's a fact. I can't be blamed if . . . well, never mind. . . . That's all." He began to get up. "And now, if you're ready . . ."

"Sure . . . the gas."

"And the motor. We've both got to get busy."

*   *   *

The road was round the corner of the hill, according to the map, but I had no idea what chance there would be of a lift. It's an experience to start off alone across the desert land; you set a course, as when flying or sailing, but distances have a fabulous unreality; the place you keep your eye on may be one or five or ten miles away. I aimed just for the outer edge of the lake bed; caked hard, it made good walking, and soon the little plane was beyond sight against the background of hills. Presently I came to a jutting rock round which the road should be; but then came the hot wind, laden with dust and tumbleweed. I fought my way and struck the road almost before seeing it. A dirt road, not very encouraging, though there were fairly recent tire marks in the ruts. I began to wonder what I could do if no car overtook me. Just nothing, I supposed, except keep on walking. Twenty miles to Giant's Pass — say six hours. I should be scorched and thirsty and dead-beat, but probably I could do it.

A car came along after a quarter of an hour — an aged Ford, driven by a Mexican. He spoke little English, and grinned when I used my Spanish on him. I don't think he understood much of what I explained, but he cheerfully made room for me amongst crates of eggs and bundles of alfalfa. We bumped along for four or five miles, then joined a paved highway for the rest of the journey.

Giant's Pass was a small place, with not more than one of anything except wooden shacks. It looked like a ghost town either reviving or not quite dead. But for its altitude it would have been impossibly hot. Dogs lay sprawled in the shade; their barks and the occasional bang of a screen door were the only sounds. At a single gas pump in the midst of a litter of weather-worn auto cabins a boy of about fifteen listened curiously to my tale of a forced plane landing in the desert. It occurred to me later he probably thought it a trick to buy gas without coupons. Even when I had convinced him of the story there was another problem; he said he couldn't leave his place to drive me anywhere, nor did he know anyone who could. I tried to talk him into a change of mind till suddenly I saw the Mexican repassing; I yelled out to ask if he were on his way back. He answered with the same cheerful grin. So I handed up the cans and found the eggs and alfalfa replaced by enough groceries to keep a large family for a month. Perhaps that was what they were for. At the last minute, as we were leaving Giant's Pass, I remembered the newspaper and dashed back to the general store for one.

It's curious to recollect where you were when you learned of big events. I was having a music lesson in the New York house when John came in to tell us excitedly that Lindbergh had landed in Paris; I was with a group of friends in Boise, Idaho, arguing after a long late Sunday breakfast when news came over the radio that the Japs had attacked Pearl Harbor; I was walking in Central Park when I saw all kinds of people struck by some strange dumbfoundedness and presently a girl's voice, overheard as I passed by, told me with sobs that Roosevelt was dead.

And I was riding with a Mexican through the California desert when I picked up the paper and first saw the name Hiroshima.

*   *   *

The Mexican, with a beaming disregard of his tires and springs, had insisted on driving right through the scrub to the plane. He helped fill the tank, accepted a reward with genial dignity, and drove off in a second cloud of dust. Brad said he had fixed and checked everything. It hadn't taken either of us as long as he had expected, so we could now relax again before leaving. "Sit down and smoke. It's an easy take-off and whatever wind there still is will help us back, though it'll probably slacken by evening."

"It's begun to slacken already," I said.

He lit a cigarette and lay outstretched on the sand. "I still say I like this place. I don't want to leave it somehow." I handed him the paper; he let it fall on his lap. "Oh, so you got one? Any news?"

"Yes," I said.

Then he picked it up, glanced at the headlines, and I saw the glance become a stare.

He made no comment at first, and I watched him covertly while I packed the picnic things. I stowed them away in the plane, still to give him more time; then I came over.

"Read about this new bomb?" he asked.

"Yes."

"Extraordinary thing."

"Yes."

"I reckon a good many people are finding it pretty hard to believe."

"Probably."

"Looks like they can only split atoms out of rare stuff like uranium — so far. And at terrific cost. One of these days, though, they'll find out how to do it cheaper out of common material — hydrogen, say. Nothing impossible about that — in theory."

"Isn't there?"

"Sure no. All it needs is the short cut. Somebody'll find it sooner or later."

All this casualness had been so absurdly overdone that I simply looked at him, wondering how best to convey not so much what was in my mind as the fact that he would have to act much better if he wished to conceal what was in his.

Presently he said: "What's the idea, staring like that? Anything wrong?"

I lay beside him. "You've kept your word long enough, Brad."

"What do you mean?"

"Seems to me you're free to talk — after these headlines."

He made smoke rings through an uneasy silence. Then he said: "I guess that's so — to some extent. But I see they don't go into the science of it much."

"Oh, to hell with *that*. Tell me what happened to *you*. That's what I'm interested in."

"It oughtn't to be."

"I know . . . the world . . . the future . . . science . . . all that's more important. But with me, last things come first."

"What last things?"

"The last things we'd have if we lost everything else. Human relationships."

"I suppose that must be what they call the woman's angle."

*   *   *

PART ~~~~~~~~~~~~~~~~~~~~~~~~~~~~~~
~~~~~~~~~~~~~~~~~~~~~~~~~~~~~~ FIVE

HE TOLD ME, during the several hours that followed, more or less what had happened. The story was often disjointed in the way he gave it, and I had to probe to get certain parts clear; but in the end it assembled itself.

He had intended, he said, to return to America at once, in September 1939; but after his year in Berlin he found that crossing the frontier into a free country gave him a part-fascinated, part-frantic interest in the world drama that was developing. With the release of his mind from technical work he turned with something of the same intensity to a grandstand scrutiny of chaos. Perhaps oddly, he said, he hated the Nazis more and not less when he saw them in this perspective; it was as if Berlin had been too much the center of the whirlpool, just as America would be too far beyond the outer edge. At any rate, he lived in France, the nearer distance, throughout the so-called phony war and most of the invasion. In June, just before that country's fall, he crossed to England and was in London during the worst of the blitz.

I asked him what he was trying to get out of all this and he answered: "Experience. You yourself once said that scientists lived in an ivory tower. I'd lived in one so long I couldn't even wait to come down the stairs — I had to jump out of the window."

"How did you make a living?"

"I didn't. For the first time in my life I idled — idled while Rome was burning. I pottered about France and then I pottered about England."

"During the blitz?"

"Well . . . I took my turn at fire-watching, air-raid work and so on. I wanted to see what was happening."

"And you saw?"

"Yes, I saw plenty. I guess you did too. Only I hadn't the excuse of a book to write — it was just for my own private education."

"What did you use for money while you were idling as you call it?"

He laughed. "Those twenty A.T. and T.'s that my uncle had left me. I sold 'em without a qualm."

He went on to say that he lived quite happily — yes, that was a true word, however strange it might sound — throughout 1941. Once he tried to enlist in the R.A.F. (he had always wanted to learn to fly), but there were difficulties about his citizenship. They didn't worry about that in air raids, though. He liked the English very much, he said — much more than he had during his earlier period in London. But of course after Pearl Harbor he wanted to return to America. He reached New York in January 1942, an out-of-work and practically penniless mathematician, than which there is normally no more maladjusted person on earth. But for him, just then, his own country seemed a wonderful place. He tried again to enlist, and again in the Air Force, but to his surprise they found something wrong with his blood count — it was the first time in his life he had ever had to think of his body in a way that less fortunate people do all the time. The doctor heard where he had lived during recent years and suggested that he take things easy for a while, fatten up on sunshine, fresh air, and plenty of good food. But he had no money to idle any more, besides which, he wasn't in any mood to idle in America. The only thing he could think of was to go back "home," and home was North Dakota, where members of his family still lived. To his surprise he got quite a warm reception, which was just as well, because almost immediately his health broke down, the accumulated strains and stresses of many years exacting a sudden price.

He said: "I don't know what I'd have done if it hadn't been a farm. When you're ill on a farm people don't bother much about you, they don't fuss, they have their own work that can't be neglected, and their contact with animals and animal ailments makes them very considerate yet also very practical. And then when you get better you can always find some little job that really helps them yet doesn't tax you too much."

"What really was the trouble — your trouble?"

"I suppose you'd call it a nervous breakdown. If I'd taken much notice of it I'd probably be having it still."

"I'm not sure that you aren't having it still."

He retorted harshly: "Oh, nonsense. There's nothing the matter with me now except . . . well, anyhow, let's get on with the story. I improved. I worked on the farm. I learned to fly — got my license — did quite a bit of local flying. That took me up to pretty near the end of 1943. Then one day I went on some farm business to Chicago. On the train I ran into an old school friend who had since gone into teaching and was science professor at a college in Iowa. He knew roughly what my own field was because he was interested in it too, and he told me of some important research being done in Chicago that was altogether in my line. 'It's war work,' he said, rather mysteriously, 'and I daresay they could use you.' So while I was in Chicago I called at the place. They were cordial if also a bit mysterious; they said it was quite likely they could give me a job. But they had to pass me on to someone else who made all the appointments, and after more questions and form-filling I was told they would let me know. I went back to the farm and didn't really expect to hear from them again. But after a few weeks I did — they wanted me in Chicago for another interview. This was a different kind — very thorough, not quite hostile but *almost* — a bit like a cross-examination in court. I found they knew much more about my association with Framm than I had told anybody. Anyhow, in due course they sent me to this place in Tennessee — I see one can mention its name now. They gave me a job there. Perhaps I'd better not say what, though it couldn't be much of a disclosure, because it was the sort of thing any sixteen-year-old physics student at college could have learned in half an hour."

"Why didn't you ask for something more suitable?"

"I did, and nothing came of it. Then I figured that after all, my name was unknown and my credentials weren't of surpassing weight. But the real reason was probably in me — I'm not personally ambitious, never have been, and if that was the way they wanted me to help win the war, it was perfectly okay. They had some fine mathematicians already working for them — I wasn't boastful enough to think I had anything unique to contribute."

"Not even your knowledge of the kind of thing Framm had been doing?"

"I'd told them about that. It wasn't exactly on the same lines as their work. I'm sorry I can't explain more fully."

"I probably wouldn't understand it if you did. So you settled down at this elementary job and what happened?"

"Nothing much. There's really no eventfulness in this part of my story. After Vienna and Berlin it's quite without drama. I'm afraid you're going to be disappointed."

"No, I'm not. I'm glad. You've had enough drama for one lifetime. Or don't you think so?"

"Yes, I think so too."

"What was it like to live at this place? Tell me all the unscientific things about it."

He answered grimly: "That would certainly get to the root of the matter."

"What do you mean?"

"Never mind. . . . I know what *you* mean. The everyday details. Well, that's fairly easy. The place grew to have a population of sixty or seventy thousand — mostly laborers on the actual construction of buildings. They had to be housed, with their families, so there were shops, banks, schools — just like any other town. But you couldn't drive in and look round. You had to have some business there before they'd give you a permit, and even then you couldn't get in the plant without another permit. And inside the plant you had to have extra permits to go from one part to another. One got used to it after a time."

"Where did you live?"

"In a sort of two-by-four apartment — just a room and bath — or rather, it was a stall shower which I shared with three other men. I shared the room with one other. Rather primitive, but that couldn't be helped — the place was impossibly crowded, you were lucky to have a roof over your head. The rent was low — the government fixed it that way; and we also got our meals at government cafeterias — cheap and fairly good. And there were movies and dances and tennis courts and everything else you could wish for in the way of normal recreation. I've no complaints against the physical conditions of living — they were as good as could be expected in the circumstances. My roommate was a nice boy out of Harvard. Presently he was drafted into the army, put through basic training, then sent back to the Project on army pay — that was done with a good many of the younger men. Some of them resented it, but compared with the boys who were doing the fighting overseas I couldn't myself see what they had to kick against, except, of course, that munition workers and longshoremen weren't treated that way — only scientists. I half expected the authorities would do the same to me, because I was sure I was quite fit again, and I wouldn't have minded at all, but I was thirty-one and I guess that put me over an age limit they must have had. I got quite friendly with this Harvard boy —

he had the same keen and almost emotional interest in science that I had had at his age, and so he was less able than I to accept our common fate — which was routine work far beneath our capacities. An even harder thing for him was that there were no facilities to continue study — no classes to attend that would have given him the feeling of not entirely wasting his time. There was a library in the place, but it contained no books of any advanced character in his field — in fact I was told that all such books were quietly withdrawn from every public library throughout the country. Anyhow, I taught him some tensor analysis in the evenings, and I think it was a relief to both of us while it lasted. When he came back from the army he was put on another job — not better, just different — and I didn't see much of him then. It wasn't easy to make or keep friends except by the coincidence of working or rooming with them — times and places were hard to arrange, unless you were just satisfied to see a movie or watch a football game. Personally I'd been somewhat schooled to an isolated life by working with Framm, though there had been the compensation in that of doing a job that taxed me fully. And of course there were certain things that never did bother me at all anywhere — the regimen of work and sleep, plain meals, little social life, long walks in the country — it was all the kind of thing I'd been used to, and I was far happier with it than some of the others were. One thing it did — it gave me a chance to read, and I filled up some deplorable gaps in my general education — history, economics, literature, political science. You'll find me not quite so stupid as I used to be."

"I'd already noticed it," I said dryly. "And I've also noticed that you're a bit on the defensive about this place. You didn't really like it, did you?"

He demurred; it wasn't quite so simple as that. It was true there was an atmosphere there that weighed irksomely at times — an atmosphere hard to describe except by the negative word "unscientific"

— which, of course, for a scientist was a very bad word indeed. All the paraphernalia of secrecy and counterespionage — possibly quite necessary — got on one's nerves after a while — and especially on a scientist's nerves. Maybe it didn't get so much on a soldier's nerves or a lawyer's.

"Why a lawyer's?" I asked.

He said there were a good many bright young lawyers working on counterespionage — the type that would have been forging ahead in district attorneys' offices but for the war. "I expect your Mr. Small is one of them."

"And you didn't like them?"

"I rarely met them. You may be right, though — their presence didn't make life any smoother. And yet, when I come to think of it, the only two lawyers I've ever known personally — Julian Spee and Hans Bauer — were men I liked very much."

"Tell me some more about the place."

"There's not much more. As I said, nothing exciting happened — nothing in the personal sense. Plenty, of course, in every other sense, though I wasn't high enough up to be told anything."

"But you knew what was being done?"

"More or less. I knew what it was a race for between us and the Germans."

"And you stayed on the job because of that?"

"Well, partly. It wasn't hard to hope that we should win. And yet . . ."

"Yes?"

"I can't quite put into words the feeling I had — and which others may have had, though I never discussed it with them. We didn't want the Germans to get the thing first — that was firm enough in our minds to build a cathedral on. But, assuming that the Germans didn't get it, did we want to get it ourselves? *Did* we? . . . Perhaps some of us did — I don't really know. I can only confess that a sort of cynicism grew in me as I saw the whole place getting bigger and bigger and costing more and more — I'd have guessed the truth from that, even if I hadn't known it from any other source. I'd have been sure that no government on earth could afford so much for anything except destruction. And I half wanted the thing to turn out to be a gigantic dud — not from mere technical mistakes, but because of some basic factor that would rule out the whole thing forever as an impossibility. There wasn't much hope of that, I already knew, but I clung to it, and if in the end the damned thing hadn't gone off and all the billions had been proved wasted I think I should have joined quite a few of my co-workers in the thankfulest horselaugh that ever was heard on government property."

He got up then and stretched himself. "Wind's dropped," he said, staring into space. But the still air was hotter. He walked a few paces, then came back to lie against my side.

"Oh well," he went on, "we've practically won the war and that's quite a thing. If I were on a Pacific island or an aircraft carrier I'd help myself to some strength through joy tonight."

"So will thousands at home who have boys out there."

"Sure. Looks like there'll be a surrender in a day or two. Must be — if we have a few more things like this up our sleeve. You're a sap, Mr. Jap. I guess we've proved it."

"But as a scientist you feel that isn't quite everything?"

"Oh, forget the scientist. As a draftee I feel it's a hell of a lot."

"I know. And it is. And yet . . ."

"And yet what, for God's sake?"

"You were saying 'and yet' just now. Can't I?"

He didn't answer. He lay back again, face to the sky. He looked old-young, like so many men these days; premature age and retained youth neatly packaged and telescoped into the standardized product, the sort of man you would like to be seen with, the sort that smiles at you in cigarette ads, or wisecracks from the screen in the zany comedies. All that on the surface. Beneath it there's something you have to discover for yourself, if it exists — the freakishness or the frailty, occasionally the sainthood.

I said: "Go on telling me what happened even if nothing happened."

He pondered. Then he said that one day he had grown mildly excited at a development in his work that seemed to offer scope for a promising though quite minor piece of research. It was mainly theoretical and required no special equipment, only time and patience, of which he had both to spare. So he began to work late, after most of the men in the same building had packed up for the day; and this went on for some time till he realized that his behavior was attracting notice.

"You mean you were being watched?"

He said they were all watched, but that in his case there seemed something a bit extra about it. Anyhow, he'd made no secret of what he'd been doing, so he went to the head of his department and explained the whole thing fully. Then he received a graphic demonstration of the size and character of what was going on, for this head of a department, quite a big shot in his way, proved to be only a somewhat larger cog in the complicated machine — he revolved with just as much precision and with a conditioned distaste for extraorbital behavior. All he said was — "H'm, very interesting." And a few days later he called Brad to his office and asked if he would please discontinue the research.

"He sounded rather embarrassed," Brad said, "especially when he gave me some reason about keeping the guards on duty after hours, which I knew was nonsense, since guards were on duty everywhere at all times. However, I said that naturally I'd give it up if those were his instructions, and he didn't like the hint that he'd been instructed, and because he didn't like it I knew he *had* been instructed. That was the way one was apt to get to know many things, and it didn't add to one's mental or spiritual comfort. But of course the Project wasn't designed for our mental and spiritual comfort. One had to remember that."

"And did you — always?"

"I think most of us managed to, though there were moments when you felt you'd raise a little hell when the war was over."

"Which is practically now."

"Let's hope so."

He was silent and I tried to bring him back to the subject. "Well, so you were asked to stop the research and you did. Then what happened?"

"Nothing. That's the end of the incident. There were a few others — not similar, but equally unimportant. And nothing dramatic, as I warned you. No Central European high jinks. I just went on with the job."

"Getting more and more bored and cynical all the time."

"Not even that. *At* times, not *all* the time."

"Anyhow, you gave the job up and joined the army. What finally drove you to it?"

"There again it's hard to point to any specific cause. Perhaps meeting Sanstrom had as much to do with it as anything else. . . ."

"*Sanstrom?*" The name struck an echo in my mind; I tried to remember where I had heard it before; then suddenly I knew. It was Mr. Small who had asked me, during our first interview, if I had ever met one of Brad's London friends named Sanstrom.

Brad caught my look. "What's the matter? Heard of him?"

"Yes." And I told him when.

He said grimly: "I see."

He relapsed into another silence and I had found there was no better way to start him again than by simple pestering. "Go on," I said. "Tell me about this meeting with him."

He called his thoughts to order. "Yes, Frank Sanstrom. I hardly recognized him at first. A man suddenly rushed up and began pumping my hand one day as I was walking to the cafeteria for lunch. As I say, I hardly recognized him — he'd changed a good deal in ten years. We'd been friends at University College, partly because we were both Americans and studying physics, but chiefly because you couldn't help being friendly with Frank. I think he left college the same year you came — that would be 1936. He had the lab next to mine before Mathews took over with those stinking animals. . . . We hadn't kept in touch, but I'd followed his career sketchily — I'd read a few papers of his in scientific journals, so I knew he was doing advanced work and establishing a reputation. And here he was, full of the same warmth and geniality, though about thirty pounds heavier than he ought to have been. We said the usual things one does on such occasions — how good it was to see each other again, and what were we doing there, and how had life been treating us — all the questions that aren't intended to be answered at the time they're asked. 'I'm just on a visit,' he said, beaming. 'The Cook's Tour . . . and these gentlemen are the cooks.' He had to say something, I suppose, because two army officers had by this time come up; I realized afterwards that they had been escorting him and he had broken away from them on seeing me. They didn't look too pleased at his little joke. He seemed to think they'd know me, and when they didn't he made the necessary introductions — explaining that I was an old friend of his London University days. I can't remember their names or even their rank. They didn't find his affability infectious, so he ended the conversation by shaking hands again and telling me to look him up if I happened to be in Washington during the next few weeks — he'd be at the Carlton Hotel. . . .

"I don't know quite why, because I'm not usually sensitive to the glad-hand kind of reunion, but meeting Frank Sanstrom like that had a big effect on me. Of course the warmth of our early friendship came back, and I was pleased to have been so well remembered; but I think also it was the contrasting iciness of the military gents and the way they looked at me — the officer-private look plus something else that wasn't any more palatable. Anyhow, I had vacation time due me and I made up my mind to take Frank at his word and call on him in Washington.

"Which I did — without notifying him ahead, because I didn't want to make the visit seem more than casual. I just went to Washington, found my way to the Carlton, and called him up on the house telephone. If he'd changed his plans by that time and gone, or if he weren't in, it didn't matter. I'd never been to Washington before and I could enjoy some sightseeing. But he *was* in. And I caught a note of surprise in his voice when he heard mine — well, perhaps surprise was natural, even in spite of his invitation — but there was another note which I could almost diagnose as dismay. I had time to think things out in the elevator going up to his room; I said to myself — Something's happened but he probably won't say what. I was used to that sort of thing — we all were. It was part of the technique of secrecy — do what has to be done, don't talk, don't explain, don't accuse, don't confirm or deny. When the Harvard boy was drafted, for instance, I couldn't help wondering whether it had been partly my own fault — but I knew I should never find out, and that he wouldn't either."

"I thought you said they did that to be able to put people on army pay?"

"Often it was the only reason one could think of. But they didn't treat everyone like that . . . and I knew it had been noted that I'd been working out mathematics problems with the boy in the evenings — nothing was said about it to either of us, but I had a suspicion — quite unprovable — that my wastebasket had been examined. . . . On the other hand, that might have been just routine. Watching was also routine. It carried no stigma."

He was on the defensive again. He said that I mustn't get him wrong; he wasn't complaining about the system. "When pure science becomes a war weapon, you're bound to have secrecy, espionage, counterespionage, and all the tricks. If a scientist feels less happy in the atmosphere of an Oppenheim novel than a college lecture room, it's just too bad, isn't it? And there *are* secrets, no doubt, that it's in the national interest to safeguard — and therefore the system can be held justifiable. I don't know whether it kept the spies in the dark, but it certainly kept the outside public — you, for instance — and to a large extent the unimportant insiders, such as me."

"And you didn't like it," I said, as I had said once before.

"Hell, no . . . how could I?" he replied, less cautiously. "When you've been brought up to an idea of scientific truth as something that transcends frontiers — something that can't be bought or sold or patented or hidden — when you've been used to wandering about from one laboratory to another and asking questions about another man's work — or submitting a problem to someone in another country to see if either of you can save the other's time . . . it's a bit hard to get the viewpoint that you're working for Macy's or Gimbel's but not for both. . . . Mind you, I'd had a part training for that sort of idea in Berlin. Only somehow there it was Nazi stuff — easy to hate and therefore easier to discount. Over here it was harder to hate because you knew it might be necessary, but being harder to hate didn't make it much easier to forget. . . . Is that too complicated? . . . Anyhow, where was I before I began all this? . . . Oh yes, on my way to see Frank Sanstrom at the Carlton. He had a small suite on one of the middle floors — elegant and impersonal till he'd littered it up, just as he'd always littered up his rooms in London. He was that sort of man. As soon as he greeted me I knew again that something was wrong. He offered me a drink and mixed one for himself. I had a feeling he wanted time to make a decision. Then he began to talk about the weather and Washington and the war news in a way I simply couldn't stand. I'm afraid I . . . I rather lost my head. I realized then the effects of the strain that I'd perhaps not entirely recovered from, and that the plant life — h'm, I didn't mean that, but it'll do — the plant life hadn't helped. I realized also how much I'd been looking forward to an utterly free conversation with someone in my own field. I flew off the handle a bit — I said he couldn't deceive me, I knew something was the matter, and I challenged him to tell me what it was, to forget for one moment the never-confirm, never-deny technique that filled the air at times so that one couldn't breathe. . . . He looked at me for rather a long time, then suddenly motioned me into the bedroom. 'We'd better talk in here,' he said. The bedroom was on an outside corner; the inside walls were against the bathroom and the sitting room. I knew what he meant, but the fact that he should be so cautious magnified the concession he was making in treating me like a human being, an old friend, and a fellow scientist. It moved me almost to tears. He sat on the bed while he told me what he knew. He said that after our chance meeting at the plant he had been questioned about his early knowledge of me in London, and he had gathered that for some reason I was under a cloud. They didn't say why — of course they wouldn't. He then asked me what my particular job was, and I saw no reason not to tell him. 'Good God,' he commented. I asked if it surprised him, and he answered: 'No. I guessed something of the sort — that's why I asked. It's probably their idea of how to keep an eye on you with least trouble and risk.'

" 'You mean it's *deliberate?* They know the sort of thing I'm qualified for, yet they prefer to waste . . .'

" 'It isn't a question of waste. They probably don't want you to know too much about what's going on.'

" 'But why?'

" 'Perhaps because they think you know too much already. Ever hear the old Russian proverb — "Those who know enough are my friends; those who know too much are my enemies"? . . . Tell me about your association with Framm.'

"So I told him."

*　　*　　*

"*Everything?*" I asked.

"Pretty well," he answered. "He'd heard about Pauli already — but of course from a rather different angle."

"So you put him right?"

"Yes. I explained the arrangements about the trial and my suspicions when she died, and the way I went a bit out of my mind afterwards."

"Did you tell him you planned to kill Framm?"

"Yes, and that the war started before I got a chance — "

"And that you gave him false results instead?"

His face clouded. "No, I didn't tell him that. I've never told anyone that except you."

I wanted to ask why, but another question seemed more urgent. "What did he say? I'm curious to know how it would strike another person."

What I really meant was that I wondered how far his not quite complete story would seem plausible to anyone who, unlike me, had no personal verification of any part of it.

Brad answered: "He said he thought it explained why the authorities weren't so sure about me."

"I'm surprised he was even sure of you himself."

He laughed. "Oh, I'd be sure of Frank, so I guess he'd be sure of me. We were really friends, you know, in London. Besides, he'd met Framm once — at a scientific congress somewhere. He hadn't

liked him — he'd got the impression that the man was just a shyster.
Of course I told him he was far more than that in both directions —
a crook, and also a very great scientist."

"So once again you found yourself defending Framm?"

"*Defending* him? . . . Heavens, no — but I knew Frank hadn't
sized the man up properly. After all, I'd *worked* with him."

I was a little moved by that, because it seemed to give me, in a
flash, some central vision of Brad's personality as well as the clue to
what had often made trouble for him, and doubtless would again.
I suppose if you concentrate on getting one thing into clear focus, as
he did, everything else gets a little bit out of focus; and the sort of
thing that comes naturally to you, as a mere instinct of fairness or
logic, carries an air of eccentricity or even untrustworthiness elsewhere.

"All right," I said. "Go on."

*   *   *

He went on:

. . . I asked Sanstrom what he thought the authorities suspected
me of, and he answered: "Nothing — which is probably the worst
thing to be suspected of if you're suspected at all. Because it means
there's nothing you can do about it. They're not accusing you, so
you've nothing to refute or disprove. You're like the coin that
the automatic machine refuses — not necessarily bad, maybe only
bent."

"Except that they didn't refuse me, Frank."

"That's so. For bent ones they have another automatic machine
that combines the most effective methods of Henry Ford and Sherlock Holmes. . . . Of course you can always quit if it gets on your
nerves, and with a good conscience, I'd say. Matter of fact if I were
you I *would* quit. Why don't you? You might be doing far more

useful work somewhere else — teaching, for instance — I seem to recollect you had a real aptitude for that. I could fix you with a job if you like."

He then told me he had been "loaned" to the government for liaison work between the educational world and the Project; in other words, to steer into it young scientists fresh out of college. "Sometimes," he said, "I feel like the Judas animal they use in the stockyards to lead the other animals to the slaughter — except that I'm saving some of them from another kind of slaughter, there's always that consolation. I only hope we'll get a good many of them back in the colleges when the war's over. Assembly lines aren't educational, even when you staff them with Ph.D.'s."

And then, with extraordinary freshness and freedom, he began to argue the whole issue. Perhaps it wasn't really so extraordinary, but after the atmosphere I'd lived in it seemed so. One hardly ever discussed what we were doing in the place where we were doing it. There had been a sort of social taboo. Some moment must have come when even the least intelligent guesser had an idea what was shaping up, but the chances are he wouldn't share his guess with anyone else, or if he did, the other fellow would neither confirm nor deny. . . . So now, in this hotel bedroom with Sanstrom, I felt that something like a miracle was taking place. He assumed I knew plenty, and of course I did; but for him to take a chance of telling me something I mightn't know was a return to sanity that made me gasp with relief. He even discussed some of the details, scoffing at the idea that any secrets should exist between one accredited scientist and another. "In any case," he said, "most of this secrecy concept has been built up by nonscientists. It tickles their vanity. Some of them enjoy stamping 'restricted' on stuff that might as well be sold for junk for all the harm it could do. Every time they show a badge or whisper a password it gives them a kid thrill straight back from their boyhood. Their private opinion of scientists is that we're a bunch of irresponsible long-hairs with queerly subversive and international ideas who're at last being made to toe the line and behave. Secrecy makes a good excuse to put us in separate cages where we can do what we're told like good little boys and leave the grand strategy to the short-hairs. . . ." I began to laugh at that, because it was in Frank's old familiar vein of exaggeration, and he laughed too, recognizing what had always been my own impulse to check his wilder extravagances. We had been good foils for each other that way. "Don't mind me," he continued, "I'm in a mood to let off some steam — just as you were too just now. Because — my God — don't they realize that about 90 per cent of the whole thing's no more secret than yesterday's weather? Einstein's equation dates from 1905, the spectograph's nearly as old, so is the principle of gaseous diffusion, even chain reaction goes back to 1939 — yet from the way some of them behave you'd think it was Lydia Pinkham's formula for a magic dandruff remover!"

I said soberly that there was a good deal of difference between knowing how a thing was done and knowing how to do it, and that the real secrets were probably in the field of engineering and production methods.

He waved that aside; oddly like Framm, he had the purist's disregard for the nontheoretical. "The real secret," he said, "is what's going to be done if and when we've made the thing. Is it to be *delenda est* Berlin or Tokyo, or will there be a trade show on some uninhabited place? That's the sort of secret that keeps a sane man awake at nights. Because it seems to me that if we *do* use the thing ruthlessly, then we can never again call anything in warfare an atrocity, and the fact that we finish the war with it and so save life numerically is merely the end-justifying-the-means argument that Hitler used when he machine-gunned refugees on the roads during blitzkriegs. Of course you can say that our war's righteous and his isn't, which is true enough comparatively, but it's an argument that won't make it easy to outlaw the total use of the thing when the war's over and other allegedly righteous nations want to use it for *their* wars. So frankly I hope we don't use it. Which means I devoutly hope the war ends before we can."

There was always something about the way Frank Sanstrom presented an idea that made you want to dispute it, if only as a devil's advocate. I replied that, the way I saw things, all countries in war adopted an end-justifies-the-means policy, because the use of physical force implied that. The real problem wasn't the technics of war but war itself.

"True in theory," he answered, "but in practice the use of atomic energy for destruction makes such a difference in degree that it constitutes a real difference in kind. For the first time in human history it becomes possible to destroy whole cities and populations in an instant."

I said that the slow death of thousands by economic blockade didn't seem to me more merciful than the quick death of thousands by bombs.

"It isn't a question of mercy. The humanitarian approach was always wrong — "

"That's why I say, Frank, the real problem is war itself. And the scientist should tackle that not only as a scientist but as a citizen. What I dislike about the present setup is not so much that the powers-that-be want us to make bombs, but that they don't seem to want us to do anything else. They never invite us to use the scientific method plus unlimited funds on the general problems of world affairs or the organization of society."

"You're darned right they don't — and why should they? We'd throw most of them out on their ears as quick as we'd scrap a leaky vacuum pump."

"To correct the simile, Frank, we wouldn't scrap a leaky vacuum pump — we'd repair it. And some of the people who run things aren't bad — they just need an educational repair job. . . ."

"Try and do one on them. Suggest an educational qualification for political office. You'd run straight into the right divine of a democracy to elect all the shysters and nitwits it wants."

"An educational qualification wouldn't keep out the shysters."

"Then let's have one for voters. That might do something."

"Yes, it would give the shysters the best chance they've ever had of fixing elections."

"Not if it was done properly."

"It wouldn't be. The one-man-one-vote idea may have its absurdities, but in practice it keeps the fixers at bay. And the fools cancel each other out on either side."

"That's the most cynical argument in favor of a two-party system I ever heard. But what if somebody starts a party that doesn't have any fools?"

"In the circumstances, Frank, only a fool would do that."

He laughed enormously, enjoying the argument as much as I did. I wish I could remember more of it; it lasted several hours, and though I didn't agree with him altogether, and he tended to overstress and overload his points, much that he said was somehow a crystallization of my own drifting misgivings. I particularly recall one of his remarks — that if the development of atomic energy was, as might be claimed, the biggest landmark in human knowledge since the discovery of fire, then the decision whether or not to use it for destruction was the biggest ethical question mark since the one that faced Pilate.

"And the odd thing is," he added, "that even in a democracy this decision has been or will be made without the mass of the people having the ghost of an idea of what's afoot. Is that bad? Or is it inevitable? Or both? . . . Mind you, I'm not suggesting you can hold an election or a referendum about it in the middle of a war. But if the ethical question should crop up any time in the future, would it be a valid excuse for an average citizen to plead that he didn't know what was going on in his own country? Because that's the excuse we'll get from a lot of Germans when we blame them for the concentration camps."

"But in their case it won't be true."

"Oh, I don't know. Middle-class respectable folks are so damned innocent — what does my Aunt Lavinia know about the brothels that exist only a few blocks from her house? . . . But the time's coming when ignorance *won't* be an excuse, it *mustn't* be, it ought to be the last of all the excuses one can ever accept. Which, incidentally, is why I'm all for free speech and free education. *Mehr Licht,* Goethe called it."

I asked what he thought an individual could do, and he answered: "Little enough, till the war's ended, except think things out and occasionally talk them over with a kindred spirit — as we're doing now. Matter of fact, I'm very loyally co-operating with the authorities — you noticed how carefully I brought you into this bedroom before we began to talk? I insist that when I discuss science with a fellow scientist no bellhop shall be listening at the keyhole."

He went on to talk of the future and the possibilities of infinite disaster to the world. Once or twice what he said reminded me of that old argument with Julian Spee at your house years ago — it was frightening to realize how much that had then been purely speculative and philosophical had since become sober prophecy. And it was frightening also to realize that such a phrase as "the collapse of civilization" struck an almost stale note — the sort of subject you'd set for a schoolboy's essay or a college debating forum. We'd all been warned so much and so often, the average man was bored rather than scared. "Yet you can't exaggerate the mess we're in — a technological crisis bringing to a head the moral crisis that we've all shirked for centuries. It's infinitely beyond any question of how much can be kept secret by one nation for a few more years at most. I tell you frankly I *am* scared, and when I talk with people who aren't I get more scared than ever. Mind you, don't think I'm in favor of handing over secrets, such as they are, to all and sundry as an act of faith. If any country's got to get ahead, even in a rat race, let it be ours. But there's the whole pity of it. Atomic energy's such a big thing it's the curse of Cain that we should be thinking first of bombs. It could make heaven on earth if only we'd let it — if only we'd use it for peace with a tenth of the energy we've worked on it for war. And that's where research comes in — open research inside a framework of free science. So far as I'm concerned, Free Science is the Fifth Freedom, and if we don't get it back and hang onto it, then count me out of science altogether — I'd rather go fishing for the little time that's left — rather anything than be a hired witch doctor muttering top-secret spells behind barbed-wire fences. Might come to that in the end — or just before the end. Might come to a point when you and I stage our sit-down strike — what you might call an all-war-short-of-aid policy — while our harnessed and muzzled colleagues carry on till the bombs start falling and they finish up, like everyone else on that doomsday, Men of Extinction. . . ."

I said I didn't think a sit-down strike would work, and in any case it was defeatist; and then suddenly something flared up inside me so that I remember saying: "By God, Frank, the future's not a club you can resign from! It's part of the whole world's problem, and as you say, we've shirked it for centuries. But now we've got to stop shirking it, and in that fight *count me in* — both as a scientist and also, if you'll pardon the expression, as a good American!"

Sanstrom laughed and patted my arm. We were both good Americans, for that matter, and therefore a bit shy of striking the patriotic note. The telephone rang while we were still arguing; it was a girl Sanstrom was having to dinner; he asked me to stay and make a third, he thought I might find her interesting. I did; she was English, working for British Information — rather good-looking and vivacious and well-schooled in that phony understatement about her country that impresses so many outside it. She dropped most of the phonyness when she learned I'd been in the blitz; she was really quite a sincere person. And she didn't know anything about the Project, which was a relief; so we chattered on general topics over cocktails and then went out to a restaurant where they served New Orleans food. The conversation sank in importance as it rose in agreeableness — I guess that's one way of describing the rest of the evening. We returned to the hotel for more drinks and took her to the British Embassy, where she was staying; after which Sanstrom and I strolled back along Massachusetts Avenue in the chill evening air and calmed ourselves down. But we were still a bit exalted. Finally, as we shook hands at the hotel entrance, he said: "It's been good seeing you. Don't let things get you down. Look at me — I worry all the time but I don't lose weight."

He was a big man, Sanstrom, not unlike Emil Jannings, if you remember those old films. Everything was rather oversize about him — arms and head and mouth and arguments and gestures — it had been hard for him to lower his voice in the hotel bedroom, and when I had told him what Framm had said about the Buck Rogers strip — "Science is the opiate of the people" — any cruising bellhop could have heard his laugh as far off as the elevators.

*   *   *

I asked Brad if he had talked to Sanstrom again, and he said no; he knew he was a busy man and he didn't want to trade on an old friendship. As a matter of fact, he wandered about Washington on his own the next day, seeing the sights; and in the evening, because he found he could get a seat on a plane to Knoxville, he made the return trip with a day to spare before he was expected back to work. So he set out for a walk in the surrounding country. The air was cold and the northern slopes of the hills ribbed with snow — the kind of weather he liked best. He walked a long way — much further than usual. He felt that the talk with Sanstrom had staged some sort of revolution in his mind; not that he had entirely agreed with him, but the unaccustomed freedom of speech and exchange of ideas had shaken loose some of his own; and he tried to chart out this new mood of his, as accurately and as scientifically as he would have done any other observed but puzzling phenomena. Soon he came to one of the road blocks; a soldier stopped him, he showed his identification papers and chatted for a while, but the interruption made him ready to walk back. When at last he came to the hill from which the enormous size of the plant was spectacular, he stopped to stare as if he had never seen it before. He lit a cigarette and sat on a fence near an abandoned farm. A phrase came that seemed to fit his predicament — his own and Sanstrom's and the world's — a predicament symbolized by the identification papers he had to carry and by the soldier guarding the exit to the vast enclave. *A conspiracy of silence*. He must have seen that phrase unnumbered times — a cliché if ever there was one. But then, because he was physically and mentally tired, his mind glided easily into another phrase, not such a cliché. . . . *Conspiracy of science . . . silence . . . science . . . silent science* but not exactly *holy* science . . . and at that he thought he had better pull himself together and stop the output of what the psychiatrists call echolalia.

He slept badly that night and by morning was certain of at least one thing — that he was headed for another breakdown if he didn't get a change. He realized now that even in spite of the routine character of his job he had been overworking, or perhaps overworrying; he knew, at any rate, that he had reached some climax of misgiving hardly to be put into words.

He went to the head of his department that day and offered his resignation. It caused a small stir.

What was his reason?

He hesitated — he hadn't really thought out an adequate reason.

Ill-health?

Well no, not exactly.

Overwork?

Partly.

Or perhaps some personal reason?

Well yes, in a sort of way — a personal reason.

The head of the department passed him on to a doctor, who examined him thoroughly without offering any comment, but said afterwards that he would gladly certify him in need of a rest. They were very careful (it occurred to him) in a considerate way, or else very considerate in a careful way. No need to talk of resigning — how about a leave of absence? All right. To go where? Oh, anywhere. New York, maybe. For how long? A month? Yes, that would be fine. He was by that time simply anxious to get away.

He went to New York. Before leaving he was reminded of the penalties under the Espionage Act for any disclosure of official secrets; he said that of course he understood all that.

In New York he rested by seeing plays, movies, and walking the streets. One day in the circular bar of a hotel on Lexington he thought he saw the same man whom he had seen a few days before walking along upper Broadway. It might have been, of course.

Then suddenly he made up another part of his mind. He called on his draft board (he had been registered in New York on his return from Europe). They listened to what he had to say and promised to get in touch with him at the address he gave, a hotel on West Forty-fourth, very convenient for the Algonquin.

A few days later a man came to see him at the hotel. He had the wrong kind of personality, and the interview ended with Brad exclaiming sharply: "I guess this is still a free country — a man can choose whether he offers his brains or his life for it, especially when they don't want his brains. . . ."

That, he realized as soon as he had said it, was absurdly melodramatic and by no means fair.

But he insisted, and rather to his surprise they let him have his way. He got his calling-up notice, he took his physical (and was relieved to find himself passed as medically fit); he was inducted, given his choice of the Air Force, and in due course found he was too old to be a pilot. But he made a good navigator, passed all his tests in fine style and waited to be shipped overseas. That was about October of 1944. But they didn't send him. In fact he was somehow unaccountably omitted from one overseas outfit after another. He began to feel sure that this was deliberate. And about this time also he began to have an additional feeling that he was watched. Additional, that was, to any earlier kind of feeling. Once in a New Orleans restaurant, for instance, when he was talking to some civilians, he thought he recognized a man he had seen before in a movie house in Montgomery. But of course it might not have been, because when you begin looking round for faces you have seen before *and seeing them,* a certain danger point has been reached. From then, doubtless, his special neurosis dated.

And then came the crash in Texas.

*   *   *

We lay back in the warm air, and the story somehow petered out in random afterthoughts prompted by my own questions, but presently both question and answer followed at longer intervals till there was at last a silence; and it was then, without any words between us, that I knew he loved me. It wasn't entirely love-making that had made me sure of that, because love-making isn't so very unique, but there was something quieter and rarer that showed in the way he looked at me — the deep unspoken assumption that all was well between us, no matter what was ill with the rest of the world.

The sun dipped behind the ridge and it was time we were beginning to return. We walked to the plane, still without speaking; he climbed in and gave me the signals; I swung the prop and got in the seat behind, willing for him to do the flying if he wanted, though there had been no arrangement about it. He taxied across the lake bed into what wind was left; it was almost a glassy calm by now; the mountains looked like stage scenery. He made a sharp take-off, the professional kind, and set an immediate course for Lost Water, climbing till the sun was visible, then higher than necessary till the far ranges came in sight, pink-tipped with snow. Nothing moving caught the eye except the long shadows of the wings, crawling over rock and sand; and all the time I was thinking over what he had said, till suddenly the effort of thought broke through a barrier and I wasn't thinking at all, but just living the moments through with him, whether he knew it or not.

About six thousand feet he closed the throttle.

"Well?" he shouted, over his shoulder.

"Fine," I answered.

In case he wanted to talk I chose one of the many topics, but not the most abstruse. "I like what you told me about Sanstrom," I said. "I wish I'd been in time to know him in London."

"Yes, he's a good fellow. A bit technicolored for a scientist, if you know what I mean, but perhaps that's not always a fault. Some of us are too black-and-white."

"You ought to keep in touch with him. Where is he now?"

"I think in the Galápagos Islands."

"*What?*"

"They're about a thousand miles off the coast of Ecuador — "

"Yes, I know, but what on earth made him go there?"

"He was sent. They suddenly put him in the army — he was only thirty and unmarried, so I suppose there was reason enough. . . . And the Galápagos Islands are quite interesting scientifically. Anyhow, he'll be back when the war ends. I'll see him then."

"Are you hinting that because he met and talked to you — "

"I'm hinting nothing. I don't know. Maybe. Maybe not. We were watched, I suppose."

"Watched in the hotel?"

"Probably. After all, why not? If they distrusted me they'd want to keep an eye on whom I contacted. Just as they took a look at you after I wrote you the postcard."

He throttled up and made a steep left bank till we were facing the distant snow line. We climbed again to make up for lost height, crossing the valley over ridges of nearer hills. It would be dusk soon and I was puzzled by his change of direction. I shouted once to ask the reason for it, but either he didn't hear or chose not to reply. I didn't ask again, because what he had said about Sanstrom had made me feel icily indifferent to whatever happened so long as I was with him. The thought even came that he might have some strange idea in mind, and if he had I believed I could make terms with it without rebellion. As the sky grew darker and the last glow left the snowpeaks I felt easier, almost cozier, than I had ever felt on earth. He looked round once, as if expecting me to say something, but I didn't. Then abruptly he made the turn.

We almost had trouble at Lost Water, it was so dark. But Mr. Murdoch had turned on the headlights of several cars, so that we made a rough but satisfactory landing. He cursed us, threatened to report us, and finally asked us to remember that when the war was over he could put us in the way of good bargains in used planes.

Brad drove the car — another symbol, I hoped, of his own self-conquest. We were several miles along the straight stretch before either of us spoke. Then I told him very simply that I wanted to go on helping him.

"Okay," he answered, matter-of-factly. "But you might wish you hadn't taken on the job."

"I'm not scared. They can't send *me* to any islands."

"Now listen," he said, embarrassedly. "Maybe I shouldn't have told you that about Sanstrom. I've no proof — and besides, if they really suspected me I can see their problem. I wouldn't have minded being sent there myself — might have been a good place to think things out. I'm an odd creature — you ought to be warned about it. I don't seem to have the knack of being most likely to succeed, and some people won't ever be sure I'm not in the pay of the enemy, whoever the enemy is, but I guess there'll always be an enemy."

"Then you'll always have me to sort things out and put things straight. Even with Mr. Small."

"You think you could? And with Newby too?"

"Sure . . . but why him particularly?"

"It's a good deal up to him when I get let out of the hospital."

I was glad he had brought up a matter which had been heavily on my mind; I had been chary of broaching it myself lest the question of getting a discharge might begin to worry him. I didn't myself know yet whether he would find it hard or not.

I said guardedly: "Does the idea of going back to the hospital bother you?"

"Not especially, but I've a feeling I don't want to waste any more time."

I thought that was the best kind of answer he could have given, so I promised as much as I dared. "You won't have to. I think you can count on that. So far as I can see, you're cured."

We drove on another mile or so, and I wondered whether what I had said was true. Perhaps true enough. We're none of us cured, in any strict sense. And if he still had a complex, of guilt or persecution, or whatever it was, hadn't we all . . . or if we hadn't, shouldn't we have?

I said presently: "We've talked each other nearly hoarse, but there's one other thing that's been a puzzle ever since you mentioned it. You said you never told anyone else about the way you faked the results for Framm. I know that makes it a great compliment to me — "

"No — not really — "

"No? Well, never mind. But it does seem to me that if you *had* told others — when they questioned you — it might have been better. . . . Or were you afraid they wouldn't believe you?"

"They mightn't have, that's true. But I was more afraid that they might."

"I don't understand — "

"They might have thought well of me."

"Exactly. And wouldn't that — "

He interrupted: "No, no — I'd hate to be thought well of for something that's on my conscience."

"But you still don't regret what you did?"

"I'd probably do it again in the same circumstances."

"Then why should you have it on your conscience?"

"Don't ask me. It's irrational, no doubt. I told you I was an odd creature."

"You also told me it was a sin against the scientist's holy ghost, but I thought that was just the way you felt immediately after you did it."

He smiled. "Perhaps the ghost still haunts. . . . You know, Jane, choosing between God and Mammon gets all the publicity, but it's easy compared with some of the other choices. . . ."

He looked at me as if he thought I wouldn't catch that, and as if he wouldn't mind if I didn't.

"Don't you worry about me," he went on. "I'll never be any different — I mean, about certain things."

"I don't want you to be. Just tell me about them. As you have been doing. That wasn't so hard, was it?"

His mind was still on the one thing, for after a considerable pause he answered: "It was certainly easier than telling a fellow like Sanstrom. The idea of deliberately falsifying results, no matter what the reason, would seem a bit unprofessional to a scientist. At least I hope it would."

"In other words, you told me because you didn't care what *I* thought of you?"

He was thoughtful for another moment. Then he said: "D'you know, in a sort of way that's true. And yet, in another way . . ."

"Yes?"

He laughed. "Damned if I can explain exactly how I do feel about you."

"Can't you? I can explain how I feel about you. It's simple. I love you."

I had often wondered what he would say if I told him, but since afternoon I had found out enough not to be apprehensive — only a little more curious.

He said nothing for a while, then he slowed down and put his arm round me. "That's nice," he said quietly.

I wasn't sure whether he meant what I had said or what he was doing till he added: "Because I love you, too."

"I'm glad you mentioned it," I said, half laughing because I found it impossible from then on to speak in a level voice.

"Well, you knew, didn't you, Jane?"

"Yes, but — it's — it's made me so — so very happy to be told."

We drove on another mile or so before he said: "There was always something between us."

And till now there had always been *somebody* between us, I thought, but did not say.

307

He went on musingly: "The right mixture of caring and not caring — I suppose that's what love is."

Oh well, if he wanted to diagnose, analyze, dissect, interpret — all that was all right with me. His mind might be up there, but his arm wasn't; and we had actually said, once and in those words, that we loved each other. But words were my field, just as analysis was his, so we were both putting happiness to the test we valued most; perhaps even in mathematical terms I could be somewhere in his mind, just as he would be somehow in my next book, whatever it was.

Oh God, I was happy as we drove on. It was like coming home after a winter walk, expecting a fire in a warm house, yet not realizing how warm and bright it could be . . . and how dark the night outside.

*   *   *

When we left the desert and climbed into the hills there was a mist that covered everything but the section of road ahead and the white line down the middle of it. Brad drove slowly and the miles crept by as if we should never get to Vista Grande at all. I couldn't help recalling Mr. Chandos and his story of the road that went nowhere, and my own suggestion of the voice on the radio reading the psalm that began — "Teach me, O Lord, the way of thy statutes"; and this, I suppose, made me switch on the car radio there and then. It was very faint — a news bulletin from somewhere — I could only catch the phrase: "This morning, on the Japanese city of Hiroshima . . ."